The COURTING of BRISTOL KEATS

The
COURTING
of
BRISTOL
KEATS

MARY E. PEARSON

BRAMBLE

First published in the US 2024 by Flatiron Books

First published in the UK 2024 by Tor Bramble
an imprint of Pan Macmillan
The Smithson, 6 Briset Street, London EC1M 5NR
EU representative: Macmillan Publishers Ireland Ltd, 1st Floor,
The Liffey Trust Centre, 117–126 Sheriff Street Upper,
Dublin 1, D01 YC43
Associated companies throughout the world
www.panmacmillan.com

ISBN 978-1-0350-5401-5 HB
ISBN 978-1-0350-5402-2 TPB

Copyright © Mary E. Pearson 2024

1 3 5 7 9 8 6 4 2

A CIP catalogue record for this book is available from the British Library.

Printed and bound by CPI Group (UK) Ltd, Croydon, CR0 4YY

Visit **www.panmacmillan.com** to read more about all our books
and to buy them. You will also find features, author interviews and
news of any author events, and you can sign up for e-newsletters
so that you're always first to hear about our new releases.

For the man who invited me on a little walk,

and turned it into a magical journey

TATTERSKY

RESTLESS DEAD

QUEEN'S CLIFF

MIRTHLESS SEA

POMORIA

MISTRIVEN

BALOR PASS

THE WHELKY LANDS

BLEAKWOOD FOREST

BLEAKWOOD

STONE OF DESTINY

ELD

GREYMARCH

GILDAWEY

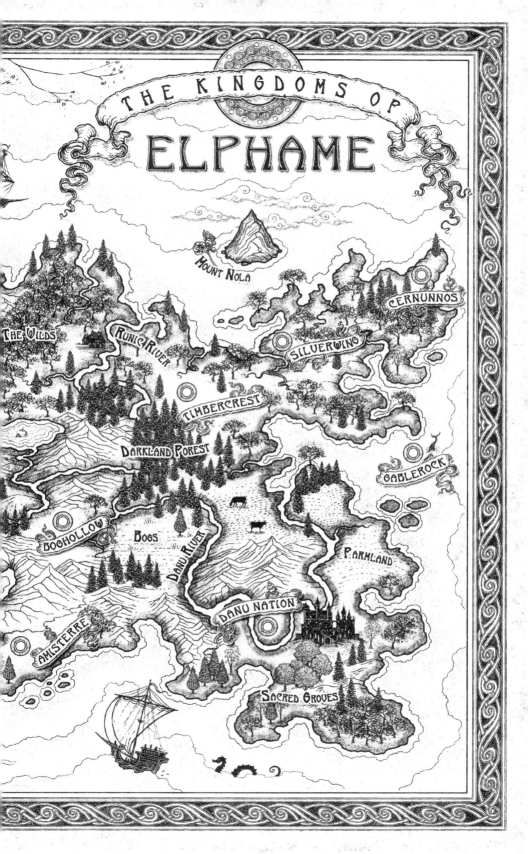

The universe opened a door for me,
and who was I to look away?

—ANASTASIA WIGGINS

The COURTING of BRISTOL KEATS

CHAPTER 1

At the end of Oak Leaf Lane, dawn arrived fifteen minutes early. Most folks didn't notice, as they rarely did about such things, but eagerness circled the air like a hungry buzzard, watching and waiting. Wild grass shivered; droplets of dew danced to the ground. The earth trembled as low whispers tumbled over hummocks, making geese startle into the sky. *Something was about to happen.*

But Bristol Keats slept soundly, oblivious to the long-fingered light prying its way through her drapes at such an early hour. Nothing could wrestle her from her bed but a good night's rest. Drool dampened her pillow, and her arm hung limply over the side of the bed. She had worked late. Her tips lay in a satisfied heap on her nightstand, a ruffled monument to her determination.

Finally, midmorning, she stirred, groaning, then rose from her rumpled bed and shook herself into her jeans. As busy as Friday nights were, festival days were busier, which was a good thing for Bristol. The late notices were stacking up. At the top of the pile lay the electric bill—forty days past due, and shutoff was imminent. Bristol's tips that day, combined with those from the past week, would take care of that one and leave a little extra for groceries.

With sleep still in her eyes, she sniffed her hair for the oily scent of the parlor, then swiped it into a quick messy ponytail, unaware that the

day would be anything but ordinary. It wasn't something you could
see, but as she splashed her face with water, then brushed her teeth,
her head turned slightly to the side, a strange velvety warmth filling
the air, though it was only a vague sense that she couldn't name. She
didn't even realize she leaned into it, like a cat arching its back against
a doorway.

A doorway. Yes. That is what she leaned into.

But she didn't know it yet.

Bristol whisked back her drapes and shielded her eyes from a sun that
already glared over the trees, too eager to remind her of the day. It had
been one year since she returned home. For her, it seemed far longer. A
lifetime was packed into the past weeks and months. The year bulged
like an overstuffed suitcase that couldn't be shut.

Home. Even now, it was a hesitant word on her lips, foreign and
new, a word she toyed with in fits and starts. A word she was afraid to
love. *Run. Move on.* Those were the words ingrained in her like dirt
beneath her nails.

She turned from the window and riffled through a basket of clean
laundry on the floor, pulling out a black tank top, then slipped it on.
Her figure smoothed out the wrinkles.

"Bri!"

Harper's voice bellowed up the narrow stairway like she was a six-
foot bouncer instead of a skinny fourteen-year-old still waiting for a
growth spurt. What Bristol's little sister lacked in stature, she made up
for in volume.

"I'm up," Bristol called back, getting down on her belly to search
for a missing shoe under her bed. She was certain she'd kicked them
both off beside the bedpost last night, but it was late, and she had been
exhausted.

"Bri!"

She paused from her shoe search. That wasn't her sister's usual
wake-up call. Maybe a spider in the kitchen sink? Besides paying the

bills and mowing the front yard weeds when she had time, Bristol was the designated spider retriever. Or maybe, worse than a rogue spider, another pipe had busted? *Damned old house.* Bristol rested her forehead on her fist for a moment, willing it not to be that. The balance in her head tipped and swayed, waiting for disaster to fall. They couldn't afford another plumbing bill.

Rushed footsteps pounded up the stairs and Bristol stood, bracing herself as her bedroom door flew open. Harper's cheeks glowed with a deep rosy hue, and her glasses hung crooked on her nose. Bristol's stomach squeezed at how young she seemed, how urgent everything was to her. There were seven years between them, but they may as well have been a century.

Harper held a letter in her hand. "We got another one!"

Bristol pulled Harper into her room and closed the door. "Is Cat gone?"

Harper nodded and Bristol eased out a sigh. At least something was going right. She didn't want Cat going into another tailspin over a simple letter. Technically, Cat was older than Bristol by ten months, but strangers usually guessed Bristol was the older of the two. Something about her reserved demeanor. Bristol was admittedly more calculating, weighing options before revealing her moves, while Cat was reactive. She felt everything passionately and didn't hold back. Bristol loved that about her sister, her passion, except it also made her rants long and passionate, and she had no time for a high-pitched tirade today. Cat's last rant came with tears when Bristol said she planned to drop her classes and search for a full-time job. Cat went on for a full hour. *Are you crazy? Daddy paid good hard cash for those classes. He'd want you to see it through.* Cat always knew the buttons to push, and their father was one of those buttons.

Bristol took the envelope from Harper, shrugging to prove her disinterest, and casually flipped it back and forth like it was junk mail. She did a lot of things for Harper's sake these days. When it was too obvious, Harper's jaw would jut out and she'd say, *You're not my mother.* And then Bristol would snort, and they'd both laugh at the absurdity of it all, laughter its own strange release from their reality.

At least Harper had brought the letter to Bristol instead of Cat, who thought the letters were worse than junk mail and had squeaked like an injured mouse at the previous two. She proclaimed them a scam and ordered them burned. Bristol suggested the garbage would suffice.

"Aren't you going to open it?" Harper asked.

Bristol rubbed her thumb over the smooth vellum envelope. It was the same expensive stationery as before and, again, no return address, but the handwriting was different from the previous two letters. This time it was heavy and bold, as if to say, *Pay attention!* It had the same red wax seal as the others—another pay-attention gimmick. In her years traveling the fair circuit, witnessing spinning wheels and last-chance deals, Bristol had seen them all. Still, she opened it, the wax cracking and falling to the floor. She rolled her eyes as she pulled the letter free, additional proof for Harper that it was only a transparent scheme that wasn't fooling her at all, but inside, her heart sped up. *A third letter. They aren't giving up.*

Her parents' instinct to run that had governed her entire life kicked against her ribs like a last warning from them. Harper pressed close, reading the letter too.

Dearest Bristol Keats,

Your great-aunt Jasmine is sorry you were unable to accept her previous offer to meet for tea. She offers another invitation, but this time at a location closer to you, the Willoughby Inn on Skycrest Lane just outside of Bowskeep. Please come and meet with her at 4 o'clock today in the tearoom. She has many warm memories of your father she wishes to share with you, as well as a gift—a rare piece of art that might help you and your sisters, similar to the art your father acquired not long ago. Please come alone. Your aunt's health is fragile, and she shuns crowds.

Sincerely,
Eris Dukinnon, Counselor DN

Whoever wrote the letter was certainly trying harder. *Dearest?* They knew nothing about her father either. He didn't have an aunt. He didn't have so much as a scrap of a relative anywhere on the planet. He was abandoned as a toddler and grew up in foster care, bouncing from one home to another. A social worker gave him his name. Logan. There were no "warm" memories for any fictitious aunt to share.

But the offer of rare art was a new angle, one that hit closer to home. A chill tickled Bristol's spine. They were digging, finding things out about the Keats family.

Harper nudged closer. "Do you think it's possible—"

"*No,*" Bristol said, too harshly, and hoped Harper didn't notice. A single sharp word from her could instill all kinds of worry in Harper. "No," she said again, this time with practiced boredom, reluctant to meet her sister's gaze. A disappointed breath hissed through Harper's teeth. She was the brainiest of the sisters, her nose always in a book, but she was also the most softhearted and hopeful of the three. She still believed in happy endings, and, some days, that terrified Bristol. It wasn't something Bristol could deliver. Harper took after their father in almost every way, from his warm brown skin to his straight black hair. She also had his big dark eyes rimmed with thick lashes that could disarm anyone. Their mother had been fond of saying that his eyes cast a spell over her from the day they met. Harper's eyes had a different kind of power over Bristol—they made her wish she could set everything right for her, that she could undo all the wounds of the last year.

Secretly she shared Harper's curiosity. Didn't everyone wonder about who and where they came from? It was a question that never went away. Their father's origins were a mystery. Ever since Bristol could remember, she and her sisters had ventured every possible guess. But his answer had always been the same: *I don't know*. Her mother's past was just as enigmatic, but unlike Bristol's father, she simply refused to talk about her family other than to say they were rotten. If pressed about what *rotten* meant, she left the room. Something about it was too painful for her to discuss, and their father would shake his head, silently signaling the sisters to drop it.

But dropping the subject didn't make the questions vanish. Even now, when she passed someone with warm brown skin and beautiful dark eyes like her father's, she wondered, could they be a cousin or uncle? Likewise, when she passed someone with pale skin and shimmering copper hair like her mother's, she wondered, could they be one of those rotten relatives?

Cat took after their mother, with the same green eyes and hair the color of a summer poppy—and then there was Bristol. With medium brown hair and height, she didn't look like either of her parents.

Maybe that was why the ancestry question still poked at her. Even her eyes were a color somewhere between the two of them—hazel—a catchall name for a color that couldn't decide what it was. Greenish? Brownish? Goldish? It was as annoyingly noncommittal as her parents were about their pasts.

Instead of fading away as memories should, her parents' origins pricked her thoughts more often these days. Maybe it was the psych course she was taking at Bowskeep Community. Something her professor said burrowed into her head, and she couldn't shake it out again: *Our past is a shadow that follows us. For better or worse, it shapes us, and sometimes it controls us.*

That was what it was like. A shadow tracing her footsteps. Just when she pushed the past out of her mind, a shitty letter like the one in her hands would arrive, stirring up old questions again. Who were the faceless monsters that had made her parents run? Did she look like any of them?

"Bri?" Harper waited for her decision.

Bristol crumpled the letter into a ball and threw it onto her already overflowing trash can. It tumbled to the floor, and Angus, their ferret, scurried over to sniff and investigate. He loved to shred paper, and snuck out the door with it.

"It's only a scam, just like the others," she said, but Harper's eyes still drilled into her, dark clouds heavy with questions. Bristol grabbed her hoodie from her bedpost. "Gotta run, Harp. Today's going to be crazy. Sal will kill me if I'm late." She rushed out the bedroom door.

"But they're not asking for something," Harper argued from the landing as Bristol hurried down the stairs. "They only want to *give* us something."

"Something that comes with a catch," Bristol called back.

A catch they couldn't afford.

People who lied about who they really were always had an angle, something they were working that, in the end, would cost you more than you could afford. And the Keats sisters had already lost too much.

CHAPTER 2

A gust of air blistered across the floor, a thousand stinging nettles warming Eris's skin. The counselor's long silver hair billowed behind him, caught in the tempest. Seconds later, heavy boots echoed off mirror-smooth black floors.

Tyghan was back. He rounded the corner and met the counselor's gaze.

The young man's face was laced with a fine spray of blood and his black wind-tangled hair was caked with mud.

"It didn't go well," Eris ventured.

"Glad your observational skills remain sharp." Tyghan continued down the hallway. "My suite."

"After you're cleaned up, we can—"

"*Now.*"

Eris followed without comment. He understood the stress the young man was under. He hadn't seen him rest in months.

Once in his suite, Tyghan stripped, flinging his clothes to the floor, then walked into the shower basin. He cupped his hands, catching water streaming from the golden spout, and splashed his face but flinched when the water hit his back.

Eris eyed the swollen slashes across Tyghan's shoulder. Blood trickled in rivulets down his muscled back and thighs. "Shall I summon a physician?"

Tyghan didn't respond, only focused on removing the blood that spattered his face. "Two of ours are dead," he finally said. "Or worse. We couldn't retrieve the bodies." He was methodical as he described the encounter that turned into an ambush. "Three months. That's all we have left—"

"Three months is still—"

"*Not* enough." Tyghan's reply cut the air like a cleaver. "I've spent fourteen years in training. So have my officers. The rest of our ranks, at least five. Three months is laughable."

Eris answered quietly. "It's all we have. We'll make it enough."

Tyghan went back to scrubbing. "Any more responses to your inquiries?"

"A few. I've expanded my search. I have someone coming in from Paris, and another from Lon—"

"*Paris?* Dammit, Eris! There must be someone closer!"

"The meager skills we need have become distant and rare, through every fault of our own." Eris knew it was not what Tyghan wanted to hear, but it was true.

Tyghan shoved his face back into the stream of steaming water. The marble basin swirled with dirt and blood. "Not rare enough, unfortunately."

Unfortunately. It was an understatement of epic proportions. Eris understood his frustration, but it was more than today's loss that seethed through him. Betrayal was a bitter wound that still held Tyghan captive, a wound Eris feared he would never recover from. He weighed his next words, unsure if it would be welcome news or not. "I'm meeting with another potential candidate today—if she shows up. She ignored my previous two letters, although I provided ample incentive."

"If she's too stupid to take advantage of a valuable gift, she's useless to us. Search elsewhere."

"Or it could be she is too clever."

Tyghan turned. He wrapped a towel around his waist and dried his face with another, his hair still dripping onto his shoulders. "How so? You haven't even met her."

Eris swallowed, taking his time to answer, trying to word his reply in the most artful terms he could muster. "Our inquisitors have been watching her and reporting back to me. We can't be certain, but we think she may have what we're after." The rest wasn't going to go well, but it had to be said sooner or later. "She is Kierus's daughter. And Maire's."

Tyghan froze, molding his features to stone. "You found Kierus?"

"Dead. An accident."

The color drained from Tyghan's face. Eris had known the news would shake him.

"You're sure?" he asked.

"He was going by another name, but very sure. A car hit him. I heard the gruesome details."

The muscles in Tyghan's neck rose in tight cords.

Eris wasn't sure if he was angry because he'd been cheated out of killing Kierus himself, or because there would never again be words between them. *Answers.* Their pasts together would remain forever unresolved. It was impossible to move forward when part of you was trapped in the past.

"They had a child so soon?" he whispered.

"It's been over twenty years. She's not a child. She's a grown woman."

Tyghan shook his head. Eris understood his disbelief. He'd been struck too at how much time had passed, but time was always a capricious thing, speeding fast or slow at will. It was the one thing not even Tyghan could control.

"How long have you known about her?"

"A few weeks."

Tyghan gaze shot up. "And you didn't think to tell me before now?"

"Because I knew you would respond like this. These matters are delicate. You can't—"

"I want her here by tonight. Do you understand? *Tonight.*"

"She has to choose, or it's all for naught. The giving of a gift is a tricky thing. And we don't even know for sure if she'll be of use. You know how these matches are."

"No, I *don't* know how they are! This match was never supposed to happen. Where is she? I'll—"

"No! These matters require finesse, a courting if you will. Let me handle this."

"Are you saying I'm tactless?"

Eris replied with silence.

Tyghan walked to his bed, shrugging on the robe that lay across it. He looked at the white fur rug beneath his bare feet. Quiet seconds ticked by. Eris knew Tyghan was as shrewd as he was explosive and would weigh his choices carefully. He glanced up at Eris. "You can handle it. She won't even know I'm there. I'll remain hidden."

"But I will know."

Tyghan's bright eyes darkened. "All right," he conceded. "I'll stay out of it, but squeeze her. Make her choose, or I will."

CHAPTER 3

The empty stretch of road was as serene as any Monet landscape, bright with poppies and golden yarrow sprouting among wild field grasses. It should have spawned dreamy thoughts of lazy spring days and picnics. But Bristol wasn't thinking about poppies or picnics. Instead, she wondered what it was like to die at the side of the road.

She wondered about the pain. Was it unbearable? What was it like to lie there broken and bleeding, not knowing if anyone would find you before death did? What were those minutes filled with? Disbelief? Bargaining with an unknown god? Whispering hasty messages of love to your family and hoping that, by some miracle, they would hear them? Or was it filled with wondering about the person who hit you? Was it deliberate because they were settling an old debt?

They were morbid thoughts, Bristol knew, but they crept into her mind every time she passed the makeshift memorial on the side of the road. It marked the place where Logan Keats died five months ago. Who had made the memorial, she didn't know—townsfolk he had become friendly with? Everyone had taken to him in Bowskeep. He was a hard man not to like. But she had already knocked the memorial down twice, scattering the rocks with her foot and throwing the tattered silk flowers over the barbed wire into the neighboring field. Within days the memorial reappeared.

The sheriff's report said there were no brake marks, that the person who hit Logan may not have known it in those early morning hours. There was a light fog that day. The driver might have mistaken the thump for a rabbit. They were thick along that stretch of road. Sheriff Orley had hit several himself. One of them badly dented his right fender.

Logan Keats was six-foot-four, a large, broad-shouldered man, more suited to wielding a javelin than an artist's brush.

He'd had his heavy duffle of art supplies slung over his back.

The thump he made would have been loud and hard and damaging.

Logan Keats was not mistaken for a rabbit.

There was no question in Bristol's mind, it was a hit-and-run. Only one question lingered. Was it an accident—or calculated?

She paused at the rebuilt memorial, her feet straddling her bike, peering down the road one way and then the other, revisiting the question that never had answers. The shoulder was wide, the road straight and flat, but it might have been a distracted driver looking at their phone.

Heat flushed her temples. The driver hadn't even stopped to see if he had a pulse. No one knew how long he suffered at the side of the road before the sheriff found him, mangled and still, his art supplies scattered along the highway. Sheriff Orley spared Bristol and her sisters the task of identifying him. *You don't want to see. You don't want to remember him that way.*

She swung her foot out, kicking the top stones off the memorial, the sun-bleached flowers tumbling with them. *I don't want to remember him this way either.*

Bristol only wanted to remember the man who was kind and tender, the man who painted with thoughtful strokes, because there was more to being an artist than forcing paint onto a canvas. It was a way of seeing and listening, and he did both in equal measure. He was a man who adored his daughters as much as he had his wife. Whenever one of them got lost, he always came for them, his large hand wrapping around theirs. That was the man she wanted to remember, not the one who was broken long before he died.

She resumed her trek into town but at a slower pace. She had lied to Harper. She wasn't going to be late. Probably early. And Sal wouldn't kill her even if she was late. Sal was mostly chill. Her job was a bright spot in her life, and she was grateful for it. Sal took a chance on her when no one else would. But Harper's eyes, when they struggled not to be sad, wrenched something so tightly inside her, Bristol couldn't breathe. All she saw was her father. All six-foot-four of him, trying to carry on, trying to smile. It was worse than watching him sob.

He had died sad, never getting over his wife's death.

His easy smile, his laughter, the brightness that had always been in his eyes, it was doused and gone forever.

For that, Bristol would never forgive her mother for leaving him, for sneaking out of their lives and dying so carelessly.

At her funeral, Cat had sobbed.

Harper had sobbed.

Bristol sat dry-eyed in the front pew staring at the urn of ashes that had once been their mother, silently wondering, *Why?*

It was Cat who had called her—a year ago, today.

Come home.

And then more earnestly, *Come home. We need you. Mother is missing.*

Bristol went, of course. She had no choice. Cat's voice broke her. Still, she had hesitated, afraid if she returned, she would never leave again—even if she wasn't leaving much behind.

For over a year, she had drifted aimlessly, maybe because it was the only life she knew, picking up odd jobs that paid her under the table, working booths at swap meets, staying in cheap motels, running and rootless, afraid to get attached and then lose it all again—embracing the shadows she thought she was running from. When she finally lucked into a plum housesitting job, she forced herself to dig in. For two months she worked to pull together the loose threads of her life, doing things normal people did, like getting a birth certificate—even if it was fake—the only kind she could get. Her parents had never bothered with paperwork. She began to entertain dreams. Big ones that included universities, and art, and travel of a different kind.

A week after she returned home, Leanna Keats's body was found.

Then Bristol couldn't leave. Her father was lost without her mother. She had been the sun rising in his mornings and the moon whispering him to sleep at night. He couldn't move forward. His paintings remained unfinished.

She thought a lot about forward movement these days—and standing still. Sometimes, even if you were pedaling for all you were worth down the road, it was hard to tell if you were getting anywhere. But every day she told herself she was making this work. She *would* make this work. For Harper, for Cat, and even for herself. She kept her dreams small, so they were reachable. Today she would pay the electric bill.

She was only a short distance down the highway, the whir of wheels and wind humming in her ears, when rock by rock, the memorial was restored to its former height and the silk flowers were returned to their position on top of the pile. They waved in the breeze at Bristol's back, like a hand beckoning her to return.

CHAPTER 4

The Willoughby Inn had been abandoned for years. Structurally, it wasn't sound, and weeds wove their way through the clapboards like fingers working to tear it down. Do Not Enter signs were posted at every entrance, but those were the first things to go. The shabby furniture left behind was quickly spruced up, the curling, stained wallpaper returned to its former glory, and a sparkling gleam was added to the wooden floors.

"Flowers," Esmee chirped, surveying the parlor. "There should be flowers. I'll take care of it." She picked some wild weeds crowding the front porch and worked her magic to transform them into stunning arrangements.

Olivia blew pinches of dandelion and lavender powder toward the four corners of the room to sweep away the mustiness and create an alluring atmosphere of trust.

Freda brought books from the library and arranged them on a shelf, saying they, too, would help create tranquility.

The inn was indeed transformed.

Still, Eris was uneasy. What if—

"Don't worry," Ivy said as she adjusted drapes across a window. "If this one doesn't work out, Cully says the recruit from Longforest is showing promise, and the others are coming along."

Eris heard a low rumble from Melizan across the room. *Coming along* was not nearly good enough. He eyed Tyghan's sister. She was a powerful woman with plenty of duties of her own. Why was she here helping to put spit and shine to a broken inn?

"Did Tyghan send you?" Eris asked. *To spy on me* was left hanging in the air, but she understood the implied question.

She nodded stiffly. "Tygh spies on us all."

"But he's not coming, correct?"

"That's why I'm here," she growled.

Melizan's method of dealing with problems tended to be swift and deadly. Her frustration was not unlike her brother's at having her hands tied. Neither one liked having to go through the proper steps. Neither did Eris, but he didn't make the laws of the world. As counselor, his job was to find the best way to use them—or find ways around them—which took time and patience. And this young woman was different. She wasn't just any potential recruit, not with her family history. They needed her. At least he hoped they did. He was running out of options.

Eris laid out the artwork on the large dining room table. His inquisitors had learned she was well schooled in art history; in fact, it was the only history she was ever taught, which didn't surprise him. The rest of her education was just as uneven, qualifying her for university credit in several subjects—French, Spanish, English literature, and world history—an exceptional student in many respects, but she had to take remedial courses in other subjects. Apparently Kierus and Maire hadn't bowed to all the laws of their new lives. When he searched through her file, her academic advisor found her to be a paradox and wasn't quite sure what to do with her.

But Eris knew what to do. He was counting on her knowledge of art to close the deal for them that day. He had brought half a dozen sketches for her to choose from—similar to the one stolen from the Epona Conservatory. Priceless art. And she would know it. It reeked of age and wonder and rare magnificence.

In her circumstances, she'd be a fool not to take it.

A gift, a bargain, an agreement. Her willing compliance. That was all they needed for this to work. But it was all for naught if she didn't show.

Squeeze her.

This was his last-ditch effort. Eris left the inn for town.

Nothing could be left to the capricious whims of the world—or the fleeting fancies of this young woman.

CHAPTER 5

Bowskeep was a town in search of an identity. Maybe that was what Bristol liked most about it. She understood its casting about, trying to find its best self—an identity hard to nail down. With a population just over four thousand, it wasn't exactly a small town, nor a large one either. Something in between, like her. But artists, farmers, clerks, students, and shopkeepers were slowly growing the town together into something. Into what? She wasn't sure even they knew, which she found oddly reassuring.

But living anywhere for more than two months was a miracle for the Keats family, and Bristol became intrigued with seeing mere ideas grow and come to fruition. Seeing trees, landscapes, even people transform with the seasons, flourish, watching them become one thing, something else, and then turn back again. It was a strange circling rhythm most people took for granted, a continuity that was slightly sobering. Life wasn't always about change but sometimes about sameness. And sometimes sameness made you look beneath the surface, look at the bones that held it all together—and the flaws that could be its undoing. Change was a distraction. Sameness demanded reflection. Bristol wondered if it was the sameness that drove her mother away. That it made her see things she didn't want to see.

The town lay in the distant shadow of Kestrel Cove, the much larger

and flashier resort town eight miles west on the coast. That was where
Cat worked as a barista because jobs were more plentiful there. Until
a decade ago, Bowskeep was mostly just a potty and gas stop for tourists heading to the seaside. But it was "coming into its own," as Mayor
Georgie Topz liked to say. She was a Little Person with inventive
ideas, and Bowskeep was eager to follow her lead. Bristol admired
that about the mayor, that she was a smart businesswoman who made
fresh starts seem possible. One of her first moves as mayor was to pro-
pose three new stop signs on the main highway so Bowskeep wasn't
just a blur for tourists passing through. She also orchestrated a facelift
for Main Street with colorful paint and flower boxes. The pièce de
résistance of her marketing campaign was her chickens—Rhode
Island Reds, Silkies, Faverolles, Orpingtons—the mayor's pride and
joy, which roamed freely on the sidewalks. It wasn't just tourists who
loved them. The merchants on Main Street gave them names. Fern
was Bristol's favorite, a leghorn who had more attitude than a Mack
truck.

Another creation of the mayor's was the Menagerium—a monthly
street fair that filled the wide center parkway. That was how the Keats
family came to be there. Merchants of every kind came to the Menagerium to sell their goods, from painters to potters to local farmers. The
sheer variety at the Menagerium gave it an energy no other festival
had—and Bristol had worked more than she could remember.

With Main Street blocked at either end on festival days, it meant
more deliveries for Bristol. Sal paid her a wage of course, but tips made
all the difference, and festival days were rife with them.

It took some convincing for Sal to hire her. He wasn't keen on the
idea at first. He needed a part-time assistant manager who could also
drive and make deliveries, but Bristol didn't have a driver's license.
Their run-down house was free and clear, thanks to a rare art piece her
father lucked into at a swap meet—but paying the rest of the bills was
no small feat. Utilities, groceries, endless repairs, taxes, Harper's new
glasses—they ate up most of their paychecks and there was no extra
money for another car, much less a driver's license and insurance. Cat

was already driving without either of those things, and if she was ever pulled over, they were screwed.

Bristol had always gotten along fine with a bus and a bike and explained to Sal she'd been in plenty of towns where people delivered close to everything on bikes. In desperation she boldly claimed she could get pizzas to his customers faster on her bike than in his delivery car. It turned out that most of the time, that was true—especially on busy tourist weekends.

When she wasn't delivering pizzas, Bristol worked the counter and closed the shop three nights a week. Her first night managing the cooks and counter still made her smile. Sal had hovered. And hovered.

"I've got this, Sal, you can go."

"But the menu—"

"Memorized."

"All three pages?"

His worry was almost an insult. "Four," she corrected. "I can recite them in French and Spanish too, if you'd like?"

His brows had pulled down like he didn't think anyone could replace him for a few hours, which she understood. His shop was his baby, but his heart doctor insisted he cut back on his hours. He nodded toward a loud group at a corner table. "But it's Friday night, and—"

"I can handle an unruly patron, Sal. Trust me."

And then, as if on cue, one of the loudmouths stumbled up to the counter, slapped his card down, and ordered another pitcher of beer. He had already finished off the last pitcher almost single-handedly.

Bristol slid his card back to him. "How about a soda on the house?"

He slid his card back. "You heard me, honey. Don't give me any shit about a soda."

Bristol tucked her smile away. "First of all, I am not your honey. And second of all, if you don't go sit your ass down right now with the soda I'm about to give you, you're going to find out what real shit is." And then she pulled out her calm but withering stare.

Their stare-down lasted for only a few seconds before he caved.

"I'll have a Coke."

Sal smiled and left for the night.

He called her his no-nonsense problem solver after that because it wasn't the last time she juggled a room full of demanding people, or defused tempers with a few careful words.

Over the last few months, her proficiency working at the tiny pizza parlor made Bristol muse about what it would be like to have a shop of her own. That was a definite commitment to stay—which both intrigued and frightened her—but it was only an amusing diversion to occupy her mind on longer deliveries, like filling a dollhouse with furniture that would never really be used. Her shop would be a mini-Menagerium and would have the best of everything she had ever tasted or seen in all the cities she had visited, some cities that no longer had names in her memory, blending in with all the others. But certain sights and tastes remained sharp, her only keepsakes from a fractured life that required traveling light.

In her imaginary shop, she would sell beautiful gourmet dough-nuts, specialty coffees served in unique handcrafted mugs, and local art like her father's would hang on the walls. Cat would come on Fri-day nights and sing, and customers would swoon and get misty-eyed with the magic of her voice. Bristol would have regular customers too, ones who would ask after her health and other details of her future life that she didn't know yet, but that future would have continuity, something she could count on like the seasons. She would be a savvy businesswoman, and a curator of sorts, like in a museum—and every table would have a mason jar of wildflowers she picked from her own garden and . . . It was a dollhouse that was never quite completely furnished. Something was always missing. Maybe that was what kept it interesting.

As she pedaled, Bristol's mind drifted back to the letter. She pulled out her phone to remind Harper not to answer the door for anyone suspicious, but couldn't get a signal. She held it in the air, moving it one way and then the other, like she was trying to divine water out of the sky. Nothing. *Crappy phone.*

She shoved it back in her pocket, turning her thoughts again to the letter, and entertained the idea of an aunt. A real one. And a rich one. It was an enticing thought. Was it possible her father had lied? He had gotten that rare piece of art from somewhere. What if it wasn't a chance find at a swap meet? But why would he deny he had an aunt? Unless she was awful. Or *aunt* was a code name for "hit man." She didn't consider the possibility entirely as a joke. Her parents' secrets provided fertile ground for speculation.

She was only five the first time she noticed them looking over their shoulders. *What are you looking for?* she had asked. The answer that day and ever after was always the same. *Nothing.* But it didn't keep Bristol or her sisters from noting their quick glances backward, or their slow, stealthy scans of a crowd, nudging each other to attention. Or the quick packing up at a swap meet when the day was only half over and eager customers still circled around her mother's beautiful handwoven scarves, and her father still had plenty of paintings to sell. If her parents had been cats, they would have arched their backs and bared their teeth. Sometimes Bristol did hear the hiss under their breaths. Their survival patterns became her own. *Pack up. Ease out. Don't cause a stir.* Their fear made something grip tight in her gut, and she could only breathe again once they were on the road.

Their constant moving from town to town was confirmation that they were running from something—something that was relentless. Before coming to Bowskeep, they had never lived anywhere for more than one or two months. They moved from swap meet to flea market to street fair, living out of their van at highway rest stops, or tiny motel rooms, or under the stars when weather permitted. Bristol and her sisters were schooled in the same way—on the road and under starry skies, reciting the plays of Shakespeare from memory, learning about art movements and the histories that fueled them, formulating math puzzles, or learning stick fighting when their childish energy needed an outlet. Their parents were both suspiciously well educated, even if they wouldn't discuss how that came to be. The girls knew their lives were not like anyone else's. Her parents claimed it was the artist's life.

Then Bowskeep happened. Their family had been crammed into

a garage loft for two months. A small, hole-in-the-wall gallery just off Main Street bought two of Logan's paintings—and sold them for an astonishing price—five times what he got at fairs. The gallery owner asked for more art, but shortly after, Leanna Keats announced it was time to move on.

Bristol and Cat had known it was coming. They'd seen the usual signs in their mother—her pacing, the dark circles under her eyes, biting her nails until her fingers bled, incessantly simmering herbs until the loft smelled like a potpourri shop—but Harper had already made some fast connections in the town. The library became her second home, and she was on a first-name basis with Freda, the librarian. At her mother's announcement, Harper burst into tears and blurted out, "Were you two part of organized crime?" Her voice was loud with accusation. "Is *that* why we have to go?"

Bristol had glanced guiltily over Harper's head at Cat. The night before, they'd been huddled on the loft porch, sharing a beer, musing that their parents were witness protection program dropouts. They hadn't thought Harper was listening or would confront them. Bristol and Cat had always known their parents were lying to them about something, because maybe, the truth was too dangerous for them to know. The oddness of their lives was the elephant in the room they were conditioned to walk around, and after so many years, they were good at it. At least Bristol thought they were, but lies could rub subtly, like a dull blade against fabric until, eventually, threads began popping.

That night, Bristol and Cat anxiously waited, right along with Harper, for their answer.

Their mother's eyes went wide.

Their father's eyes narrowed. "Where'd you get such a wild notion?" he finally answered.

His answer came too late. They had already seen his gaze meet their mother's as they exchanged some silent question. Later that night, her parents argued bitterly in the bathroom, the only place where they had any privacy. Their voices stayed in hushed, tight tones. The only distinguishable thing she heard was her father saying, "There is always a way to accomplish something."

A few days later, Logan Keats announced he had sold a valuable sketch he had stumbled on at a swap meet—a lucky find, he called it—and they used the money to buy a house on the outskirts of Bowskeep. They were staying. Harper cried and hugged their father. Her mother smiled. It seemed genuine, and she hummed as she worked at her loom that night. The tune was cheerful, like it marked a new beginning for the Keats family.

But Bristol remained cautious. She had learned from a young age not to become attached to people and places she would just have to leave behind. It seemed too late for second chances, too late to become something they had never been before—a family with roots. She was afraid to love Bowskeep the way Harper did. Bristol had made that painful mistake too many times in the past. She was certain the rumblings and restlessness would take hold again. They always did. Two days after they moved into the new house, Bristol packed her duffle and left.

Maybe that was when the undoing of the Keats family began.

CHAPTER 6

link.

    Clink.

    Tyghan lay on his stomach, staring at the floor. More digging. He winced. "Are you almost done?"

Madame Chastain dropped another stony claw into the copper bowl. "They're poisonous, you know? They'll leach into your blood. Shall I leave the last few in? Or take my time and get them all?"

Tyghan knew exactly what the claws would do if left under the skin. Madame Chastain knew that he knew. She just wanted to drive home the point that he was once her student, and that, in some matters, she was more knowledgeable. He offered a noncommittal grunt. Madame Chastain returned it with one of her own.

    Clink.

She pressed on the wound, feeling for more claws. Sweat ran down Tyghan's face, dripping from his nose. A low rumble ran through his chest. He heard the shuffle of boots on stone. The heavy tap of hooves. A dark brown hand clutching leather gloves flashed past his vision. Quin. The other officers trailed in behind him.

Two in the squad they led—Nisa and Liam—didn't make it back. They had volunteered for the mission and their commander had recommended them, but Tyghan barely knew them. He prayed they weren't embedded with claws, too.

"There. That's all of them. Seven," Madame Chastain said, swirling the claws in the copper bowl. "Must have been a big one that got you."

It was.

Tyghan pushed up awkwardly with his left arm, trying to suppress a moan. His officers lounged in chairs across from him. Cully's lips twisted with amusement. Tyghan leveled a cool stare at the youngest member of the company, and his lips returned to a vacant repose.

Madame Chastain lowered her gaze to Tyghan's. "Avoid those claws next time, why don't you? It would certainly save me a lot of trouble."

Tyghan pasted on a stiff grin. "Now, why didn't I think of that?"

She swabbed the wound with a healing ointment and dressed it with a clean bandage. "Leave that on for an hour. It should be healed by then. You're young and healthy. For now."

She gathered her supplies and left, still swirling the claws in her bowl, trying not to look too pleased. Tyghan knew she'd put the claws to good use in other ways, her mind probably already plump with possibilities.

He gingerly tugged his shirt on, his right shoulder tender. Madame Chastain never bothered with anything to numb the pain. *Better that you remember the pain*, she'd say, *so you'll be smarter about it the next time.* Tyghan didn't want any more next times, but he knew they'd come.

Quin offered him a goblet of some unknown liquid. "Maybe this will help."

Tyghan took a healthy swig, then coughed violently.

Quin smiled. "I didn't say it wouldn't burn. Takes your mind off your other troubles, though, doesn't it?"

Kasta rubbed her bandaged head. She'd been hit, too. "Sad state we're in, isn't it? When one pathetic little skill can't be had in a whole nation."

Glennis frowned and sat back on her haunches. "Not so pathetic now that we need it."

"The recruits are improving," Cully offered, whittling the tip of a thin ash branch, unmindful of the leavings that spilled to the floor.

Dalagorn rumbled. "Not enough." He leaned on the window ledge, staring out at the city. Liam came from his ancestral village. Dalagorn had recruited him.

Tyghan took a more careful sip from his goblet, his stomach warming with the bitter brew. "Eris is meeting with one today that he says has potential."

Kasta rolled her eyes. "That's what he said about the others."

"Meeting?" Quin scoffed. "All this courting. Why doesn't he just haul her back by her toenails?"

"The counselor's too preoccupied with his books and laws," Cully answered.

"And we're running out of time," Dalagorn said, shaking his head. "Let's go get dinner." Food was usually his solution to unpleasant situations or conversations he wanted to avoid. "I could eat a whole goat."

"But not this one," Glennis replied, slapping him on the back of the head as they headed for the dining veranda.

Tyghan stayed behind, saying he'd be along later, but he still heard Quin's comment floating on the air when they were far down the hallway. "Two skins says Eris comes back empty-handed. . . ."

Not this time, Tyghan thought. This was Kierus and Maire's daughter. If she wasn't useful one way, he'd make sure she was useful in another.

CHAPTER 7

Miriam at the Nail Emporium waved Bristol down like she was hailing a taxi and asked her to wait while she ran back inside to get the lunch order from the manicurists. It was a semiregular thing, especially on festival days. Bristol didn't mind waiting at the curb. The manicurists tipped well, and Sal appreciated their advance orders. Bristol always threw in extra garlic knots for them.

While she waited for Miriam, she spotted Willow shuffling down the sidewalk, her battered hat pulled over her head, her face in shadows as usual. She wasn't exactly homeless—but you'd never know it by the way she always prowled the roads and streets, even at night.

"Hey, Willow," Bristol called as she passed.

Willow nodded shyly in return but kept walking, continuing her low singsong humming.

Bristol often left canceled pizzas on her stoop, just to make sure she had something to eat. Willow was as thin as the light poles that lined Main Street. No one in town really knew much about her other than she regularly left gifts of wildflowers tied with twine hanging from doorknobs and she went to every memorial service at the mortuary and cried in the back pew.

A jarring rattle made Bristol turn. It was Pippa Hawkins at Best Threads wheeling a sales rack out onto the sidewalk to encourage shoppers to come inside. A tacky red sign on either end blared 60 Percent Off. They were long, shimmery dresses. The Founder's Dance was three months ago, and these were the dresses no one wanted. Almost no one.

Wedged between them all, Bristol spotted the mossy-green gown she'd tried on and imagined wearing to the much-talked-about affair. Bristol had never been to any kind of organized dance, much less a fancy one. She remembered the way the dress made her feel. How smooth and snug it was against her skin. Like it was filling up all her empty spaces. Maybe she only loved it because for those few minutes it made her feel like someone else, someone who wasn't always eyeing the road and the exits, someone who wasn't aching inside—someone who was staying. That was a lot of love and hope to pin on one overpriced dress.

But with everyone else constantly talking about the dance, including Miriam and Mayor Topz, and with Mick suddenly swooping into her life, hot, charming, and attentive, she'd toyed with the idea. She'd thought maybe they were a *thing*. Whatever that was. She had never stayed in one place long enough to find out. But Mick had intrigued her. He had a compelling magnetism that had caught her unawares.

His pickup line had been *Nice bike*. Bristol rolled her eyes at that now, but at the time she was vulnerable to his flirtations. He was a cyclist who gave pricey bike tours along the coast to rich tourists. It was obvious her secondhand bike was on its last legs, but he'd stormed into her life at a weak moment, just a few weeks after her father died, and she was scared witless, unsure how she would keep it all together for Cat and Harper. Mick had asked questions like he cared, and she soaked up his attention and touch like it might heal everything that hurt so badly inside her. Sal's storage room after closing time became their meeting place. Unfortunately, Mick's intense interest only lasted two weeks. After several steamy encounters, he disappeared without so much as a *see ya later*. Maybe he had to leave on a sudden tour, but everyone in her life seemed to leave without saying goodbye.

"Here's our order," Miriam called as she hurried out, waving a piece of paper.

"Order?" Pippa said, turning away from the rack of clothes she was primping. "Sal didn't call you?"

"My phone's not working," Bristol answered. "Why would he call?"

"He's closed for the day. Electricity is out."

The tiny interior of Sal's Pizza was dark, and the Closed sign was still displayed in the window. There was no scent of baking crusts or simmering sauces. Outside, Sal was in a heated conversation with three hardhats from the power company. Mayor Topz shifted from foot to foot nearby and, when she spotted Bristol, told her what happened. "Apparently, a strange power surge fried the power to his shop."

"A strange power surge? What does that even mean? Why aren't they fixing it? How long—"

"Hold on, Bri," Georgie said, "I can only answer one question at a time."

But Bristol wanted them all answered at once. All she saw was the prime lunch hour evaporating, her tips disappearing, and the next power outage happening at her house. Between a water line leak and a blown tire on their old van two weeks ago, their small budget was decimated. "But how can—"

"They're working on it, dear. They said maybe in a few hours—"

Bristol looked up at the sky. *Shit.*

Sal approached, curbing his cursing when the mayor cleared her throat. Bristol knew the mayor could swear the paint off a wall—but not when the streets were crowded with tourists, especially not on festival days. "Sorry, Bri," Sal said, his round cheeks slick with perspiration. "Shop's closed for now. They guessed they might have it fixed by tonight if we're lucky." He rubbed the back of his neck. "I don't need luck. I need fucking power."

The mayor cleared her throat again.

"What caused the surge?" Bristol asked.

"They don't know yet. They think the transformer's fine. It's still powering ten other shops. Only mine was fried. Even they said it makes no sense." He huffed out a resigned grumble. "You can go home. I'll call if they get it working before the dinner crowd hits, but it's not likely."

Home? She couldn't go home.

Bristol left, aimlessly riding her bike down Main Street, dodging the crowds. There had to be work somewhere, something she could do. Maybe Miriam—

The letter.

It was a cool whisper, tickling her ear. *Remember the offer.*

She braked, skidding into a turn, and headed for Second Street.

She wasn't going home without money for the bills. All the bills.

The bell on the gallery door tinkled, barely breaking the silence. Bristol closed the door gently behind her. The empty gallery was a stark contrast to the bustle of the festival streets. The first thing Bristol saw was her father's painting hanging on the back wall like it was center stage in a play. *Tempest. Tempest #44* to be exact. This one was by far the largest and darkest, painted in blacks, ultramarines, and tiny smears of crimson riding the crests of thickly applied paint, the heavy swaths creating their own dark shadows. *Tempest at Midnight*, Bristol called it, but her father only numbered the many versions of the painting he sold more frequently than any other. There was something compelling about every single one. *All artists have their obsessions*, her mother used to say. *This is his.* Bristol thought it was her mother's obsession, too, the way she studied the swirling canvas like she was part of her husband's strange, dark world. Each painting revealed something slightly different, this one the bare hint of a haunting figure emerging from a swirl of shadow. An apparition that was and wasn't there.

"It hasn't sold yet."

Bristol turned to see Sonja emerge from her office, her long salt-and-pepper hair wound into a crown atop her head. She walked behind the counter and set down an armful of catalogs. "*Yet* is the key word," she added, raising her brows. "I have faith it will sell, just like the others. And for more. Don't worry." Sonja's voice was always a sip of cool water. She understood artists, their obsessions, their poverty, and maybe their daughters, too.

"I'm not here about my father's painting. I wanted to ask how much you would give me today if I brought you a rare piece of art."

She smiled. "I guess that would depend on the art and how rare it is. I'm only a small—"

"A sketch by Leonardo da Vinci."

Sonja laughed.

Bristol didn't waver. "I'm serious, Sonja." A small da Vinci sketch no bigger than her palm was what her father sold to a dealer several big cities away. The money given to him was a fraction of its worth—but it was enough to buy their house, and the dealer offered anonymity. Her father didn't want a wave of questions or attention. Sometimes when her parents spoke behind closed doors, they didn't speak quietly enough.

A curious line formed between Sonja's brows. "That's impossible."

"Maybe," Bristol answered. "But if I did bring something to you—"

Sonja's gray eyes shone bright against her soft brown lids. "What have you gotten yourself into, Bristol Keats? It's quite illegal to peddle forgeries, much less stolen art. Besides—"

"I don't know if it's stolen. But someone wants to give it to me."

"Give it to you?" She laughed again. "Undoubtedly fake. They're preying on your—"

"If I bring it here, what can you give me *today*? There are recovery fees for stolen art. I'll split them with you."

Sonja shook her head. "But—"

"How much?"

"You can't just—"

"*How much?*"

Sonja sighed. She stared at the ceiling, wrestling with her common sense and the mad pleadings of a determined young woman she liked very much. "Bring it to me. *If* it's safe for you to do so. And if it seems reasonably authentic, I will advance you a thousand dollars while we have it checked out by experts—which might take a while. If this 'rare art' doesn't check out, I will take the advance out of the proceeds of your father's painting when it sells."

"I'll be back in an hour," Bristol said, heading for the door. "Go to the bank. Get cash."

CHAPTER 8

Tyghan studied the loose pieces of art lying on the table, a certain casual desperation in their display, considering their value. They were all preliminary sketches for various works. Famous works. They came from Jasmine's personal collection archived at the conservatory. He knew how she loved her art. Why would she be willing to give any of it away? Why had Jasmine been brought into this at all? Considering her connection to Kierus, he couldn't trust her—and there had been words between them—accusations that still smoldered. Besides, there were other valuable enticements that could be offered. That *had* been offered. Was this girl even worth it?

She ignored my previous incentives.

Art.

It made Tyghan wonder, made him remember things he preferred to forget.

"The counselor's back," Ivy said as warning.

Tyghan had told Eris he would stay out of it. He would, to a point.

He nodded to Ivy and stepped out of sight. But Quin's suggestion to haul her back by her toenails was beginning to appeal to him more. It could certainly be arranged.

CHAPTER 9

I t was only noon—hours too early. Bristol's pulse raced as she headed out of town. Normally, she loved riding the open highway, but this time her destination robbed her of all pleasure. This was desperate business—and possibly dangerous. She only had a vague recollection of where Skycrest Lane was, but there weren't many roads that intersected the highway outside Bowskeep.

Her frustration grew as she pedaled. First her worthless phone, then Sal's fried power. She was tired. Tired of struggling for every damn thing in her life. Maybe this art would change that. Getting there early was a good thing. High noon. Lunch hour. Witnesses. Coming early, she would catch them off guard.

Them.

Who were they? Somehow, they knew about the art her father had acquired, and they had promised her more of it. She would call them on that promise or expose them for the frauds they were. The sheriff was only a phone call away. If her phone worked.

The wind hissed past her ears, and seconds later, a faded street sign humbly offered up Skycrest Lane. Bristol paused at the leaf-littered street. A mouse skittered across the disused road, frightened by her sudden presence. She pressed down on her pedal before she could change her mind, and headed down the narrow, winding lane.

Around a bend in the road, a two-story inn appeared, large and very blue, as if it had just received a fresh coat of paint. The window trim was white, and cheery red geraniums filled window boxes. Only a few cars were parked outside—fewer than Bristol would have liked. The chandeliers inside the inn burned brightly through lace-draped windows.

She balanced her bike against an oak tree near the entrance, then combed stray wisps of hair back into her ponytail. *This is it.* She squared her shoulders, but as she headed for the steps, all she could think of was how infuriated Cat would be by what she was doing, how her pale cheeks would glow with fire and her eyes would glisten with tears as she yelled how careless Bristol was being—as reckless as their mother was the night she drove across a rain-swollen creek and was swept away in the current.

Bristol hesitated halfway up the stairs. Their mother's battered body was found a week later for her father to identify. He was never the same after that. What was so important to her mother on the other side of that creek? What was more important to her than her family? Was Bristol being reckless now, just like her?

She glanced at the front door and the welcome mat laid at the entrance. This was not the same as crossing a rain-swollen creek in the middle of a stormy night far from home. Bristol was doing this for her sisters. It was a once-in-a-lifetime chance to make things better for them. She smelled something sweet and glorious baking—and then the earthy whiff of lavender. Her nerves settled, and she walked through the front door.

Bristol was greeted in the entrance hall by a highly polished table that held an enormous vase overflowing with fresh flowers. She was also greeted by deep silence, as if she had entered a museum that was closed for the day. As if she had walked into an empty inn. No voices, no vacuums, so dishes clattering.

She took a few hesitant steps. "Hello?"

There was a crash, then hushed mumbling. A door at the back of the parlor swung open, and a young woman stumbled through it carrying a tray of tiny colorful cakes. She was dressed in a crisp blue blouse and skirt that matched the fresh paint on the outside of the inn. *Willoughby Inn* was embroidered over the pocket. She stopped a few feet away, wide-eyed, like no one had come through that door in decades.

"I'm here to meet with a guest of yours?"

"Oh, yes! The Lu—I mean, Miss Jasmine! Of course! They told me you were coming! My name's—" She hesitated, like she had forgotten her name. "Ivy! But that's not important." Her features were angelic, but then they pinched with worry, and she searched for somewhere to set the tray, missing the table that was right beside her.

Bristol took the tray from her and set it down. "First day on the job?"

She nodded, her blond hair shimmering in soft waves over her shoulders. "Yes, that's it. My first day. Please sit down. I'll let her know you're here."

Ivy's feet didn't make a sound as she dashed up the stairs. The inn was strangely mute again, not even a creak or groan. Apparently, every floorboard was sworn to silence.

Bristol sat on the burgundy settee in the parlor, running her fingers over the luxurious nap, surveying the outdated wallpaper and ornate chandeliers that had an odd yellow glow about them. She listened for any noise at all—a sense that someone was coming. The upstairs remained quiet, but then—

A prickle.

Heat. All the way down her spine.

Her fingertips burned.

No, don't turn around. Don't. But the feeling she was being watched bore down on her.

She jumped up and spun, her gaze shooting from corner to corner. Nothing.

But the oppressive feeling was still there, like someone stood within inches, their heat radiating onto her. She swallowed, taking a step backward.

Get out, Bristol. Get out now.

But then out of the corner of her eye, she spotted a brightly lit room at the end of a long hallway. The tall double doors were open, and in the center of the room was a table with several pieces of paper on it. *The art.*

She eyed the hallways and stairs, and there was no sign of anyone coming. She took a few hesitant steps, then a few more, until she was inside the room.

Bristol circled the table, staring at the yellowed paper. *Sanguine chalk.* Leonardo da Vinci's preferred choice for sketching. Not a surprising choice for a forgery, but her pulse still raced. If these were forgeries, they were good ones. Excellent forgeries. This was what she had come for, but now the reality was stealing her resolve. Who were these people? These pieces were going to lead to trouble. Big trouble. They should not be there. Da Vincis, all of them. Or very good fakes, but the burn deep in her gut said they were real. Her parents had dragged her to every gallery and museum across the country.

She picked up a sketch of a dragon and a lion, knowing she should have gloves on in case it wasn't fake. She tested the small piece of paper between her fingers, careful not to touch the chalk. The paper was rag linen like none she had ever handled before, though not as brittle as she had anticipated, and there was no visible foxing, which would be expected on paper so old.

Still. There was something convincing about it. Was it a preliminary sketch for the reproduction she'd seen in countless galleries? Or the final? This sketch alone could be worth millions if it was the real thing.

The hallway was still empty. She could take it and be gone before anyone returned. A thousand dollars in her pocket within the hour, with much more to come. It wasn't really stealing since they already offered it to her. She unzipped her hoodie. She had a large interior pocket—

"Miss Keats? Are you Bristol Keats?"

Bristol whirled, sucking in a startled breath. She set the art back on the table like she'd been caught in the middle of a heist.

A tall middle-aged man filled the doorway, his brows raised in expectation.

"Yes," she answered as she sized him up. Was he the mastermind behind this meeting? What did he want in return?

He smiled, his face not unpleasant, a certain ease about it. His long white hair was combed back into a ponytail, and he wore a sharply tailored black suit and a white silk tie. He smacked of polish and money. She wondered what he could possibly want from someone like her.

"Forgive me," he said. "I didn't mean to startle you."

"Startle? Not at all. I heard you coming," Bristol replied, trying to regain her footing, even though she hadn't heard him and wondered if everyone in this inn had the footsteps of a damn cat.

He held his hand out. "Eris Dukinnon. I sent you the letter."

"Multiple letters," Bristol corrected, as she shook his hand. "Letters you wrote for my *aunt*. Where is she?"

"I'm afraid we weren't expecting you so early. She's napping, but her nurse is trying to rouse her now, so she can come down. It may take a few minutes for her to get dressed. I think I explained her health is fragile, and this was a difficult trip for her. I hope you don't mind waiting?"

A nurse? The concern on his face rang true. Was she making a frail old woman jump through her hoops? "I'm sorry. I shouldn't have come early. I had a break from work—"

"It's not a problem. While we're waiting, why don't you peruse the art? You can choose before your aunt comes down."

"I already looked them over. These are reproductions?"

"Oh no. All originals."

"Original *Leonardo da Vinci*?" she said, not trying to hide her skepticism.

"That's right," he answered, his tone and demeanor remaining buttery smooth.

"Stolen?" she prodded.

He laughed. "Dear heavens, no. Your aunt has had them in her private collection for a very long time. Go ahead, choose one."

She eyed the drawings. People didn't just give away da Vincis. "What's the catch?"

"No catch. Just a gift from your aunt to you. Take your time."

Just a gift. There was a catch, all right—even if she didn't know what it was yet.

Mr. Dukinnon's attention was drawn away to notes he held in his hand. "I have information on each piece. Here, let me find . . ."

While he ruffled through his notes, Bristol circled the table, pretending she was looking at the art. The overbearing heat pressed down on her again, touching her skin, her throat, sliding down her arm to her fingers, like every move she made was being evaluated. Her fingertip grazed the ragged edge of the dragon sketch. She already knew this was the one she wanted.

Ivy rushed into the dining room, and Bristol pulled her hand away.

"Your aunt will be down presently," Ivy announced. "She wants you to go ahead and choose the art while you wait."

Again, the eagerness. Like they were trying to close a deal. Something about it wasn't right. Bristol leaned over, pretending she was studying one of the sketches, pursing her lips studiously, but she could barely focus. This all had to be illegal in some grand way. *What have you gotten yourself into, Bristol Keats?*

"Hmm, I see the resemblance."

She turned to see a woman standing in the doorway. Her gaze rested on Bristol like she was the prize at the end of a long quest. The woman was tall, slender, with a long gray braid trailing over her shoulder, all the way to her knees. Her face was an intricate map of elegant wrinkles, each one carefully drawn, a face rich with story. Her skin was as white as a flower petal, her nose straight and sharp, her eyes deep set and shimmering with the color of a pale summer sky.

Bristol couldn't look away. It was a face that belonged in a painting, a museum, a face that had history, depth, something intangible that Bristol couldn't name. She was quite possibly the most beautiful woman Bristol had ever seen—but the one thing she didn't see in this woman was any family resemblance. She looked absolutely nothing like her father. And if this woman had ever seen her father, she would know that Bristol didn't resemble him, either. This was not her father's aunt.

"I really don't look much like my father," Bristol ventured in a gentle challenge.

The woman's head angled to the side, taking a closer look. "You're like him more than you may know."

Bristol had to hand it to her—it was a good evasive reply. But she said it with perplexing sincerity. "You're my father's Aunt Jasmine?"

The woman nodded, then eased herself onto a chair set against the wall. "Let me get my breath for a minute and then we'll talk. But please, while you wait, choose the piece you prefer."

They all stared at Bristol, waiting.

She swiped at the moisture sprouting at her hairline. They were too eager. "I need to think it over for a few minutes. Maybe in the lobby? It's so warm in here."

"Of course," Mr. Dukinnon replied. He started to follow Bristol, but she waved him off, saying she needed to be alone to think. Bristol didn't know if she needed to think or to run, maybe both. But could she really walk away from a da Vinci—even a stolen one—when it could change everything for herself and her sisters? She sensed Mr. Dukinnon's eyes glued to her back as she walked down the hallway, and it wasn't until she sat on the settee that she heard the *click* of the dining room doors closing.

Low murmurs rolled from the room, and her shoulder muscles relaxed a bit. At least the inn was no longer deadly quiet. None of these people seemed dangerous, but of course, appearances could be deceiving.

She took a tiny pink cake from the tray Ivy had brought in and popped it whole into her mouth—and then another. They melted on her tongue like little pieces of heaven, and she was certain they were the best cakes she had ever eaten. She popped a third. It helped settle her stomach. *Just take the art, Bristol. Take it and get out of here. It's not that big of a deal. You're making too much of it.*

She stood, surprised at the turnabout in her confidence. It was obvious now. Take it and go.

She headed back to the dining room, her decision made, but as she did, the low murmurs inside grew louder. There were more than a few voices now. She didn't remember another door leading into the dining room. So where did the others come from? She paused, listening just outside the door. She was certain they were arguing, but she couldn't understand what they were saying. They were speaking another language. She leaned forward and pressed her eye to the narrow crack. It took her a moment to focus, and then—

She blinked, pulled away, and looked again. She squinted to be sure. Her blood drained to her feet.

What was she seeing? *How?*

It wasn't just a room of people anymore.

Creatures were inside. No, worse, they were *monsters*. A grotesque menagerie of them. Some had wings, some had fur like they were part animal, others had features molded from a nightmare. One had tusks protruding over its upper lip like a wild boar and yet it stood upright and wore clothes. In the corner a hulking creature hovering over them all had on a policeman's uniform, and when he moved, she got a clear view of a badge pinned to his chest: *Sheriff Tom Orley*. Her stomach lurched.

Was it the cakes she had eaten? Costumes? There had to be a reasonable explanation.

She rubbed her eyes, but her gaping stare became obsessive. She desperately wanted to run away but at the same time, she was too horrified to leave. She was frozen to the crack in the door like she was witnessing a train wreck.

Standing beside the sheriff was a woman with the face of Freda the librarian, but small horns jutted from her forehead. Eris and the few humans who stood among the beasts didn't seem disturbed by their presence. Ivy was there, too, but now veined black wings drooped from her back to the floor and iridescent scales covered part of her face. It wasn't makeup.

In the middle of it all was a tall man with midnight hair who held their attention. He was human as far as she could tell—an angry human. He leaned across the table, still speaking low to Eris. A black cloak that matched his hair waved from his wide shoulders as if wind swept through the room. His bright blue eyes were an icy shade of winter, and a blizzard stormed in them. His words stung the air.

But then, midsentence, he went still and stopped speaking, his head turning slightly. His attention jumped to the crack in the door, his eyes now fixed on Bristol, like there was no door between them at all. She couldn't breathe. Couldn't move. Terror pounded in her chest. *Run! Get away!* It was a chilling scream in her head, but before she could make her body obey, the doors flew open, and she stumbled forward.

The room instantly quieted. She was surrounded by beasts and their hideous eyes were on her.

How are you going to play this one, Bristol? Fear shot through her, then giddiness. Like she might start laughing hysterically. Why not? She was going to die. She was certain. What did she have to lose? But she began backing up an inch at a time, her survival instinct kicking in, preparing to flee.

"Choose," the man with midnight hair ordered, now in a tongue she understood. His gaze held every inch of her like cold iron.

Choose? They were still fixated on the art? What was the matter with them? Were they all mad? Or was she?

"Don't push, Tyghan," Eris whispered to the man. "The choice must be hers."

She glanced back at the art, only an arm's reach away. Her hand trembled, and she snatched the dragon drawing from the table.

The one called Tyghan nodded. "Good. Now you're in service to the king."

Bristol lifted her chin, battling a line between terror and restraint. She had to gain control of this situation—fast. Act like the creatures didn't rattle her. As if she saw rooms full of strange beasts every day. She eyed the mouthy one like he was a disruptive patron at Sal's, staring him down, hoping to pin him in place.

"A gift is a gift, in case you haven't heard," she told him. "I'm not in service to anyone—especially not some *king* I've never met."

The beasts surrounding her sucked in furious breaths. Rumbled. Smoke came from one of the creatures' nostrils. The blood pooling in her feet turned to ice. Yes, she was going to die. She tucked the art into her hoodie and took another step backward.

Tyghan moved around the table toward her, like an animal closing in on prey. "A gift is not just a gift in my world. It's an obligation."

His world?

She met his searing stare. "Then too bad you're in Bowskeep." Her voice didn't sound half as tough as she intended, so she doubled down. "*My world, my rules.*"

The room was instantly hot, her skin on fire, like a furnace door had been opened, but then Eris stepped between them, pressing his hand to Tyghan's chest as he spoke to her. "Please, let me explain. In return for the gift, we only want your services for a short period, a few months at most. Something you—"

She shook her head, her lip curling with disgust. "I do not provide *services.*"

"No, no, you misunderstand. Not anything untoward or illegal. You have some skills. That's all. We've noticed your ability to maneuver through town on your bike. You appear to have special instincts. We'd like to utilize them if possible."

She gaped at him, stunned for a moment. *I deliver pizzas, you bone-head. It's not rocket science.* What kind of scam were they running? But as she edged backward, she said more gently, "Delivering pizzas doesn't take skill."

"It's your directional instincts that we're interested in. We only want to recruit you for a small task." Eris motioned to the art. "This gift to-day, and another when your task is completed."

"What's the task?"

"Finding a door for us. That's all. We assure you, we'll make it worth your time."

That's all? Not likely.

"Sorry," she said, "not interested."

She turned and ran.

A commotion exploded behind her. The quiet inn was instantly deafening. *The door. Just make it to the door.*

Everything slammed around her, doors, windows, all moving on their own, like the inn was a living thing trying to stop her. Paintings flew from walls, crashing to the floor, tables slid in front of her, forcing her to change her path, jump, look for a clean way out. What sort of madhouse was she in? She kept moving, dodging obstacles that flew of their own accord. When the front door wouldn't open, she turned down another hallway, still ducking from flying objects, until she came to a side door. She flung it open, stumbled down the steps, and sprinted toward her bike. Branches and leaves batted her like they were flocks of furious birds swooping through the sky—it was impossible to dodge them.

This was the catch, but it was only a fleeting thought, because all she could concentrate on was getting away. She grabbed her bike and raced down the driveway, struggling to see the path through the whirl of dust, moving forward on trust and memory. Her eyes stung, and the barrage continued to hit her, shingles from the roof flying past, something hitting her face. Her lip exploded with pain, but she kept going. She made it to the main road, leaving the roaring pandemonium behind, but her pedaling didn't slow. She rode like monsters still snapped at her back.

Tyghan's elbows rested on the front porch rail. The old wooden porch creaked under the weight of so many crowding outside to watch their prospect run away, analyzing her, wondering if she held potential. Behind him Eris sighed with deliberate drama.

"You have something to say?" Tyghan asked.

"You promised me you wouldn't come."

"I don't recall promising," Tyghan answered. "I said I'd let you handle it. And I did, for the most part. If I'm practiced at twisting the letter of the law, I learned it from you."

Eris's lips smacked like he was sucking a lemon. "Well?" he asked. "Impressed?"

Tyghan stared after the young woman racing down the drive, maneuvering her bike like it was a weapon. Mortals made deliveries on such flimsy contraptions? But Eris was right, she wasn't a child by any means. He hadn't been prepared to actually see her, to look directly into her eyes. Her gaze unsettled him. She was astonishingly like Kierus— and Maire. Not in her features, but in other ways. Her mannerisms. The way her lips pressed together in a tight line like Kierus's when she was thinking, and the dangerous glint in her eyes when she was angry. Kierus had always been slow to anger, preferring a smile or turn of phrase to control a situation, but when that spark flared in his eyes, everyone knew to step wide.

And her voice. He had only heard Maire speak once, but the smooth lilt, the cadence, it was there.

"So she maneuvered past a few objects," Tyghan finally answered. "I'd hardly call that a reason to celebrate."

"But she found the only open door. What else do we have?"

Nothing. But Tyghan wouldn't admit it.

"And surely you noticed that her eyes are hazel," Eris added.

Tyghan noticed. He shrugged. "Which usually means nothing."

"But *sometimes* it means a lot. They have a greater potential for change."

"Should we go after her?" Quin asked.

"No," Eris said, waving him back. "She'll return of her own accord by tonight."

Melizan grumbled. "She has the art. Why would she come back?"

"Your brother told me to squeeze her," Eris answered. "I'm far from done."

CHAPTER 10

Trees, the town, honking cars, they all raced past Bristol in a horrible gray blur. She barely saw the road. Her throbbing lip was the only proof she hadn't imagined the room full of creatures, because it was all too impossible. Who—*what*—were they? And what were they doing here, in Bowskeep? Some of them had scowled at her with blood in their eyes. The sketch was safely tucked in her hoodie pocket, but she didn't stop at Sonja's gallery. She'd get the money later.

She was in the last stretch before home, the world finally quieting. Knee-high grass alongside the road rustled in the breeze, but then up ahead, she spotted the roadside memorial. Rebuilt. And someone stood beside it.

Her heart went back into overdrive. As she drew near, she recognized the familiar battered hat. Willow. She watched Bristol approach like she was waiting for her. Was Willow the one who kept rebuilding the memorial?

Even though she knew Willow, Bristol was suddenly wary. She stopped several yards away. "Willow, what are you doing way out here?"

Willow pulled off her hat, and long hair tangled with grass and leaves tumbled out past her ankles to the ground, more hair than Bristol thought could fit beneath one hat.

"I saw your father with trows just before he disappeared," she answered.

Bristol swallowed. "Trows?"

Willow took a few steps closer. "Mountain trows, vicious little creatures they are. Most of them no bigger than yay high." She brushed her fingers across the middle of her thigh. "But size? That don't mean nothing. They're dangerous little devils. Teeth like knives."

Bristol wondered at the dark circles under Willow's eyes, how gaunt she had become, and the strange raspy tone of her voice. "My father didn't disappear, Willow. He's dead."

"Hmm . . . that so?" Her bloodshot eyes widened. "You ever see a body?"

Bristol's stomach rolled over, woozy. The question churned up memories she was trying to forget. No, she didn't see the body, but the sheriff—

The sheriff saw him. The sheriff who was also a monster.

She eyed Willow with new dread.

Willow laughed. "Ah, the sheriff." Her head bobbed like she knew what he really was. "But those trows, they're a wily bunch. They can trick just about anyone. Even a sheriff. Can't trust anything about them." She began walking away.

"Willow! Wait!" Bristol called. "What are you trying to tell me?"

But then she was gone. Gone, like she was never there. She became a fading bit of light that twinkled out of existence.

Bristol struggled to breathe, still staring at the spot where Willow had vanished. Her eyes stung, hot and dry.

And then she heard a trailing whisper: "The trows got him."

CHAPTER 11

Angus scurried up the couch, nosing the curtain aside to look out the window. Harper joined him, but saw it was only Cat pulling into the driveway. What was she doing home so early? Cat slammed the van door and marched through the high weeds that were once a lawn.

When she burst through the door, her eyes were red and swollen.

"What's wrong?" Harper asked.

Cat's nose wrinkled. She shook her head and tried to push past Harper. "Nothing. It will be all right."

"*Cat*," Harper said, grabbing her sister's arm.

Cat's lip trembled, and then it burst out of her. "I was fired. No notice, no severance. They might press charges. Money was missing from the safe, and I was the only one working last night who knew the combination. I didn't take it, Harper! I would never steal from them."

She began ripping off her uniform right there in the living room, throwing it piece by piece in whatever direction she was facing at the time until she was down to her bra and panties. "Burn them while I'm gone, will you?" She stomped upstairs, saying she was going to change and go look for a new job, but halfway up, she spun. "It makes no sense. Even the security cameras couldn't help me. A power surge fried them."

CHAPTER 12

*T*rows. What were they? What did Willow mean? *Got him.* That trows killed him? Or they *took* him? Was it possible her father was still alive?

In a matter of minutes, Bowskeep had turned inside out into a place Bristol didn't recognize, a coat with seams and dark hidden pockets she didn't know existed. First Freda and the sheriff—and now Willow. Was anyone in this town who they claimed to be?

You ever see a body?

Her stomach twisted again, and the cakes she had eaten bobbed in her throat. No, she hadn't seen the body. Did that mean the sheriff was in on it? Or had he been tricked the way Willow implied? Could Bristol even believe Willow? *What was Willow?*

Bristol's bike was still moving when she jumped off, letting it clatter to the ground. She ran up the front steps and slammed the front door behind her, her chest burning from her crazed ride home. Her mind was a blur of images—Willow, the room full of monsters, the man ordering her to choose. Eris called him *Tie-gun*. What kind of name was that? Not a name from around there. *His world?* What was that world?

Harper rushed out of the kitchen. "What happened to your lip?"

"I—There—" Bristol's mind still raced, one thought colliding with another. "I went to the Willoughby Inn."

"*You what?*"

Bristol touched her swollen lip. The metallic taste of blood swam in her mouth. "A shingle hit me. I think. There was no real aunt there, but there were—"

"What? Who was there?"

She couldn't say it out loud. It was impossible. But she was still too stunned to offer something more plausible. Her careful filters were shredded.

"Monsters," she answered, and once she said it, her words poured out in a continuous stream. "A whole menagerie of monsters, ones with horns and wings and hideous faces, and some had hooves like deer, and Freda was there. She was one of them. And so was the sheriff, but they didn't look like themselves anymore. They were creatures. Willow is one, too. She vanished into thin air right in front of me. Even the ones who looked human—there was something different about them. They were big and powerful and wore strange clothes and weapons, and one had eyes that seemed to glow when he was angry and then—"

Harper's brows pulled down. "*Bri?* You okay? Have you been drinking?"

"And some others have Daddy. Willow told me. They took him."

"You're talking crazy, Bri." Harper cautiously stepped closer, sniffing the air near her sister. "Who took Daddy?"

"Vicious creatures. That's what Willow said. She saw him with them just before he disappeared. She said trows got him."

Harper blinked. "Trows?" she repeated.

Hearing Harper say the word like it was familiar made the chaos in Bristol's head vanish in a swift gust. "You've heard of them?"

"You're sure she said trows?"

Bristol nodded. "What is it? Tell me."

Harper eased down on the end of the coffee table. She took off her glasses and rubbed her eyes, staring at the floor like she was trying to see something through her blurred vision. "I heard Daddy making fun of Mother just after we moved in. They were out in his studio, and I was about to go in to ask a question, but I heard them arguing—at least

Mother was—saying trows were animals that couldn't be trusted. But Daddy was laughing, telling her to relax. He told her we were safe—and then they started kissing, and it seemed like it was all a big joke. I never asked them what trows were. Even once I found out, I still thought it was only a joke."

"You know what they are?"

"I read it in a book I got from the library last month. They're fae. Willow and all those creatures you described?" She put her glasses back on. "I think they might be fae, too."

"Fae?"

"Another name for fairies. Do you think—"

Bristol shook her head. "No, Harper. What I saw were strange beings. Grotesque monsters. Not cute little things with wings—"

"But there's all kinds of fae, Bri. Some are good, some are bad. Trows are wicked."

"Fairies aren't real, Harper. They're imaginary."

"Then what you saw wasn't real?"

Bristol touched her throbbing lip. Real. The creatures she saw, real. Willow, vanishing before her eyes, real. But *fairies*?

She crossed the room and sat on the couch, wedging her hands between her thighs to keep them from shaking. Harper plopped down beside her. "Tell me exactly what you saw."

Bristol hesitated, but it was too late to dismiss it now. She described the creatures in detail, from their claws to their horns and wings, as well as she could remember. It all happened so fast. And then how they insisted she take art from the table, but they wanted something in return.

Harper's eyes went wide. "You didn't take the gift, did you?"

"The art they promised was valuable—"

"No! *No, no, no!*" Harper jumped up and ran from the room. In seconds she returned with an old worn book, a crossed-out library label on the spine. Bristol recognized it as one of the many books Harper brought home from the twenty-five-cent bin at the library. She called them the weeded books, and she had a whole shelf full of them because Harper couldn't resist any book, especially one that was a bargain. The title of this one was *Anastasia Wiggins's Encyclopedia of Faerieland.* She sat at the kitchen counter and splayed it wide, its pages mottled and musty.

"How old is that thing?"

"First edition, 1940," she replied. "Fae have rules, Bri. Lots of them. Strange secret codes they live by."

Bristol's brows rose. Strange secret codes? That was something she understood. They had always been a family of nods, short smiles, plain clothes, blending in with crowds, a family passing through, unconnected, meant to go unnoticed. Even at swap meets, there was a certain invisibility about them, no phone number, no address, no website. Her parents took a perceived weakness and made it work for them. Buy now because there was no later.

Harper ran her fingers down the pages of the book, expertly flipping them, searching for information. "Here's her top twelve *don't*s in Faerie," she said, pointing to a passage. "Anastasia says accepting a gift from anyone in Faerie puts you in their debt. You can't get out of that debt."

Bristol stared at the words on the yellowed page.

*8. Never accept a gift from fae because then you owe
one in return—and faeries never forget debts.*

It was only a myth from an old book with torn pages that even the library had tossed out.

Impossible. This couldn't be happening.

Was that why they wanted her to take the art so badly? *In my world, a gift is an obligation.* He said that like it was written in blood. The room floated around her like she wasn't fully anchored to the kitchen floor. Were they really discussing fairies? A dangerous hidden world?

Harper's gaze met Bristol's. A grim knowing settled over them both. The insanity of fairies suddenly made the madness of their lives make sense—all the years of running and secrets. *Faeries never forget debts.* Had her parents accepted a gift from a trow and then run from their

debt? Was that who had been stalking them all these years? Not organized crime, but creatures called trows? Would the fae at the inn know
these trows?

She fingered the sketch in her interior pocket. A debt. "Just because
a book says—"

"Anastasia Wiggins was the foremost authority on Faerieland,"
Harper said.

Bristol went to the kitchen sink and splashed her face with water,
hoping it would wake her from this enormously bad dream.

Instead, the dots kept connecting.

Trows got him. And Willow wanted her to know. It didn't mean he
was alive, but why would she tell her that if he was dead? There was a
chance that her father was alive.

Her mind raced. She touched the art in her pocket again. *An obligation.*

"You didn't answer me. Did you take the gift?"

Bristol nodded and pulled the art from her pocket.

Harper groaned, her eyes bright with panic. "Give it back! You have
to—"

"Wait. Let me think. *Let me think!*" Bristol pressed her palms against
her temples, her head exploding with this new reality. She circled the
kitchen twice and then her gaze landed back on Harper's pinched face.
Time stood still, blurring and focusing at the same moment, and then
it wasn't Harper she was staring at anymore, but herself, ten, twelve,
fifteen years ago—that familiar fear gripping her gut. Bristol, ready
to run. Always ready to run. "*No,*" she whispered to herself, "*No.*"
Something inside her splintered, shadow and flesh tearing in two. She
couldn't stop it any more than her next breath.

"I'm going back," she said. "I'm going back to the inn." Words she
hadn't even formed in her head yet didn't surprise her when they tumbled off her tongue. The balance had just tipped. Finally tipped. She
needed answers. They all did. They had to know with certainty if their
father was alive or dead. *Trows got him.* Wherever these creatures lived,
Bristol had to find it. Find them. Find her father. Make all of this stop.

This.

The insanity of their lives.

It wasn't just Cat who was reactive. They all were. It was all they had ever known. React. Hide. Run from a monster they couldn't even see. No more.

Obligations worked two ways. She could set ground rules, too. She could negotiate for more. Eris said it had to be her decision. Nothing was a done deal yet.

Harper's face pinched, but before she could protest, Bristol tried to sound logical. "These fae want something from me. And now I want something from them. Help finding Daddy. It's a smart business trans-action. That's all."

Said aloud, the thought grew in her: *I want something from them.* It became a hot coal glowing in her gut. Something bold and strong. A piece of power. And she wanted more.

She went to the freezer, plucked out an ice cube, and held it to her lip.

"Wh-*What?*" Harper sputtered. "You can't go back there. Look what they did to you. They'll do worse. We should pack up and run while we can. That's what Mother and Daddy would want us to do."

Bristol's hand trembled, the ice melting between her fingers. Trows had made them fearful to even build a life, to stand up for anything. The years of packing up, rushing out in the middle of the night—she wasn't going back to that—living like prey. The unanswered questions they'd been trained to ignore burned inside her.

"Please, Bri," Harper pleaded.

Bristol whirled and threw the ice in the sink. "Run for what, Harper? So we can spend the rest of our lives running? Over and over again? The way Mother and Father did? What kind of life is that? When does it end?"

She grabbed her backpack from the hook on the wall and threw it on the counter. "I'm done running, Harper. This is going to stop, and it's stopping now. For all of us. I can't—" Her throat swelled. "We can't live this way anymore. We always thought the truth was too dangerous to know. The doubt is worse. It's ruining us. We can't keep looking over our shoulders for the rest of our lives. This Aunt Jasmine said she knew Daddy. I have to find out what she knows about him. About us. I *need* to know if he's alive. This is our chance. Maybe our only chance."

After twenty years of running, a brief stint in their world was nothing—a small price to pay for answers they desperately needed. Before Harper could try to talk her out of it, Bristol pulled out the junk drawer in the corner of the kitchen and rummaged through it for a small four-inch switchblade her father used to keep in the glove box of the van.

"I need to go now," she told Harper. "Hopefully they're still at the inn and haven't disappeared like Willow did." Her fingers found the carved ebony handle of the knife at the back of the drawer, and she threw it into her backpack. It wasn't likely to impress the creatures she saw, but she knew how to use it, and it was at least something if things went south.

"I'll go with you—"

"No! You will *stay* here!" Bristol ordered. "Do you understand? They want my services, not yours."

Harper's chin dimpled with defiance for only a moment before she began skimming the pages of Anastasia's encyclopedia again. Books were her default for comfort and answers, and Bristol was glad she was occupied while she packed.

"Okay," she said, still searching the pages, "if you won't change your mind, there are more things about fae you should know before you go. They have a lot of rules."

"Then it better be a crash course," Bristol answered as she grabbed a flashlight out of the drawer and checked to see if the batteries worked. Miracle of miracles, they did.

"Iron!" Harper's finger pointed to a sentence in the book. "It says here that iron will protect you."

"So will my knife."

"It's stainless."

"Close enough."

Harper pried a nail from the wall anyway, throwing the calendar it held onto the kitchen table. She slid the nail into Bristol's back pocket. "It also says you shouldn't eat any food in Faerie, or you'll become bewitched and never be able to leave."

"No food? How am I supposed to manage that?"

Harper went to the cupboard and began pulling out whatever she could find—six granola bars, four packets of instant oatmeal, dry soup mix, two cans of sardines, a box of raisins, and a bag of chips. "The book doesn't say anything about water. You can probably drink all of that you want." She winced, having second thoughts. "Maybe boil it first." She filled the largest water bottle they had anyway, then ran to the bathroom and returned with Bristol's blister packs of pills, a box of tampons, aspirin, and a toothbrush.

She sighed. "Are you going to pack my pajamas next? I can't take everything."

Harper's brow rose as she contemplated the pajamas. "All right. But when this is all gone, you have to come home. Deal?" Harper stuffed it all in, determined, barely getting the zipper closed. Maybe it was her way of letting Bristol go at all, believing everything would be all right, as long as she was prepared. Was she really packing to go to a hidden world? This morning she didn't believe in such things, and now—she remembered the iridescent scales that framed Ivy's face and her heavy black-veined wings—now it was all real.

"Deal," Bristol answered.

Harper nodded, her chin dimpling again. She returned to her book.

"Wishes," she mumbled as she read a sentence. "It says right here, *Be careful what you wish for, because in Faerie, a wish can be a trick and not go the way you intended.*"

"All I'm wishing for is answers." But it made Bristol wonder. Myths and legends always came from somewhere, from some kernel of truth.

"It also says fae can't lie. That's a helpful thing to remember. And find out if they're from the Seelie or Unseelie court before you go with them. Unseelie are very bad. Seelie are kind and agreeable. And they're big on manners. Don't piss them off whatever you do. They like respect. And—"

Harper was only making Bristol more nervous by reminding her of everything she didn't know about this world. "I don't have time for you to read the whole book," she said, and ripped out a handful of pages and shoved them in her back pocket.

Harper's eyes were shocked moons. "That was a library book."

"I have to go, Harper," Bristol said. "If I'm not back by tonight, it means I made a deal with them. I might be gone for a while. Take the art to Sonja. She's expecting it. She has a thousand dollars waiting for you. A lot more money will be coming your way soon. Pay the bills— and get new phones that work." She drew Harper into her arms and held her tight so she wouldn't have to look into her eyes. "Stop worrying, all right? You know me. I always manage."

"What will I tell Cat?" Harper whispered into Bristol's chest.

"The truth. No more secrets. Tell her I've left to find Daddy, and I'm bringing him back with me." She hoped. Willow called the trows vicious. There was no guarantee he was still alive.

"But your birthday is next week. Cat and I—"

"It can wait. We'll celebrate later," Bristol whispered.

"But the last time you left—"

"No, Harper. This time I'm leaving so we can *stay*. I'll be back. I promise."

She kissed the top of her little sister's head and swallowed. A promise was not crossed fingers or a fleeting hope. A promise was a certainty, and nothing about this felt certain—except that she had to go.

CHAPTER 13

The chandeliers no longer glowed through the Willoughby Inn's windows, and most of the panes were jagged teeth of broken glass. No cars remained in the littered parking lot. Weeds had swallowed up the front stairs. It was once again the abandoned inn it had been for years.

The neglect didn't keep Bristol from walking up the steps. The front door was ajar, and its rusty hinges groaned as she pushed it open. The interior was dark and in shambles. The silky settee she had sat upon just hours earlier now had gaping holes, and the stuffing and springs flowed out of it like the entrails of a gutted animal.

Bristol surveyed the transformation, smelled the musty abandonment hanging in the air. Somehow it didn't surprise her that it had all been an elaborate charade.

And now they were gone. She was too late.

Something inside her slipped, a fist beneath her ribs losing its grip on a rope. The hope she held of finding her father alive plummeted. The power that had surged inside her cooled. *She missed her chance.* And suddenly that chance seemed like the only thing that had kept her standing. She stepped into the lobby anyway, compulsion pulling her forward. The inn creaked with age as its darkness slid around her.

But then a dim glow caught her eye. It was small and golden, barely floating down the long hallway. A candle burned in the dining room. Did they forget to put it out?

Bristol's pulse thumped as she walked toward the flame. Loose floorboards creaked beneath her steps, ghosts announcing her presence. When she reached the dining room, she cautiously stepped inside. The small candle flickering in the center of the table did little to light the interior. She squinted into the dark corners. They were empty, too. She was utterly alone. A small click sounded behind her and she spun—the dining room doors had closed.

"You're back."

She spun back around, muffling a scream behind her hand.

It was him. The one Eris called Tyghan. He leaned back in a chair on the opposite side of the table, cocky, sure of himself. The candle cast a warm glow on his face, but his eyes remained as cold as winter.

"You asshole! Are you trying to scare the shit out of me?" she yelled. Her heart hammered against her chest. She whirled, searching the corners of the room again. "Are there others hiding too?"

"Only me. I wasn't sure you'd come back."

She cleared her throat, trying to compose herself. "Where's Mr. Dukinnon? I want to speak with him."

"Eris isn't here. You'll have to talk to me."

She hesitated. She had been counting on dealing with Eris—or her reputed aunt. Anyone but this one called Tyghan. He unnerved her more than the others. And now he sat there like an unmovable mountain, like he owned the universe.

"When will he be back?"

"Never."

She considered this, shooting a desperate glance into the corners of the room again for a sign of someone hiding. Anyone. But no one else was there. She had no other choice. She turned back to him, scrutinizing as much of him as was visible. He didn't have any unusual parts, no horns or claws, at least none that were visible. What was beneath his clothes? She could only guess those were formidable muscles filling out the sleeves of his shirt.

"I can take it off if you like?"

Oh my god, Bristol thought. *He thinks I'm checking him out.*

Which she was, but not in that way.

"*Not* interested," she said. "I only came back to negotiate a deal."

"There is no negotiating. You took the drawing. The deal is made."

"Not until I agree. You think I didn't hear what Eris said? It has to be my decision."

His right eye flinched, like he was restraining a full-blown tirade.

There. She liked seeing him thrown off-balance for a change, but it didn't last.

"You took the art," he said. "Did you think we would just let you steal it? We know where you live."

Fear clamped around Bristol's throat, but fury exploded right behind it. She leaned forward, planting her palms on the table. "Is that a threat? Are you threatening my family? Because if you are—"

"No. I'm simply stating the obvious. We know where to retrieve the art. But it can be a threat if you prefer."

"It was a gift!"

"A gift with an obligation."

It was an argument they'd had before, and Bristol guessed she couldn't win it. These were strange beings she didn't understand, ones who could appear and disappear at will, ones who could steal six-foot-four men from the side of the road and make it look like an accident.

Tyghan remained unruffled, steady and certain about what he was going to do. Before he did it, she needed to set ground rules. *Respect, they're big on manners, don't piss them off.* He was pissed at her from the moment he laid eyes on her. Why was he so angry? He didn't even know her. And didn't he want something from her? This was not the way to get it. At least not in her world. But now she was stepping into his world. She had to learn some new rules—or bring him around to hers.

There are only two people in this room, Bristol. Do what you do. Manage it.

She sat down in the chair opposite him and spun her voice into smooth silk. "I only want to ask you a few simple questions. Is that too much to ask?"

He eyed her coolly, not buying her change in demeanor, but he finally nodded, granting her permission to proceed like he was a god.

Bristol bit back a sharp reply and worked to maintain a friendly air. "First, what are these services you mentioned? A door?"

"We want you to find it for us."

"Something illegal inside?"

"No."

"Will finding it be dangerous?"

He offered a bored shrug. "Probably not any more dangerous than crossing a busy street on that bike of yours."

"Why can't you find it yourself?"

"That's for others to explain."

What was he? Second string? Was that why they left him behind? Or because he argued with Mr. Dukinnon?

"All right. What if I can't find it either?"

"You'll be sent back home a very rich woman, both pieces of art yours to keep."

"Those are real da Vincis?"

"Yes."

"How did you come by them?"

"The artist spent time in our world. A sabbatical, he called it. He left the sketches and numerous paintings behind."

Leonardo da Vinci in their world? It was impossibly far-fetched, and yet . . . here she was in a dilapidated inn that only a short time ago had sparkled with fresh paint and polish, and now she was talking to a—

A what, exactly?

She eyed the man sitting across from her. She didn't care how he interpreted her scrutiny. She wasn't going to be pushed into a quick decision. He was tall, broad-shouldered, the kind of figure that could do damage, and he knew it. There was a commanding presence about him, like he was used to getting his way—yet he was left behind like he was the grunt of the pack. He appeared to be human, though so had the sheriff. She couldn't count on appearances. This man could be a beast, too. He certainly had the temperament of one.

She felt foolish even saying it, because she hadn't gotten used to this whole new reality yet, but it had to be asked. "My sister thinks you're fairies. Are you?"

He didn't flinch or laugh. "Me personally? I'm Tuatha de of the Danu Nation, which is one of the twelve ruling kingdoms of Elphame, so yes, that also makes me fae."

Tuatha what? Harper made no mention of a Danu Nation or twelve kingdoms, only Faerieland. This was getting more complicated already.

"And this Aunt Jasmine of mine, she's fae too?"

He dipped his chin in a single nod.

"And I'm told that you cannot lie. Is this true?"

"Where did you hear that?"

"My sister read it in a book."

The corner of his mouth twisted, almost in a grin. Or was it a sneer? Bristol wasn't sure. She prided herself on being able to size people up, to determine their archetypes like they were walk-ons in a play. The eccentric. The career criminal. The pushover. A quick estimation came in handy at crowded fairs. She had grown up being the second eyes and ears for her parents, and perfected her sixth sense during the time she was on her own. She *knew* people—but everything about Tyghan was veiled.

"That's right," he answered. "We can't lie."

"Then this presents a problem, because you see, this so-called Aunt Jasmine looks nothing like my father, nor is my father one of your kind. It seems I've caught you in a lie already. How can I trust anything that—"

An angry tic pulsed at his temple. "Are you calling me a *liar?*"

Heat radiated off him, and Bristol sat back, drawing a shallow breath. Harper had warned her not to piss them off. "I'm just trying to understand what I'm getting myself into," she explained calmly, though her heart pounded in her chest. "This is all strange and new to me."

His gaze dissected her for long, uncomfortable seconds, like he was planning her demise. "It's true, your father was mortalborn," he finally answered, "but he grew up in our world. Jasmine was one of his four guardians. She fostered and helped raise him. Where we're from, that's considered an aunt. And if you know what's good for you, you'll never call her a so-called aunt to her face. She nurtured him like he was her own."

Fostered.

The word punched her with its truth. *I was raised in foster care*, was the only thing he ever said about his childhood. Was that why he wouldn't talk about it? Because it was a bizarre sort of foster care they wouldn't believe anyway?

"You knew my father?"

He raked his hand through his hair in a slow, controlled movement. "I only know what Jasmine told me. Anything else?"

"Are there trows in your nation?"

"A few are probably holed up in the dark corners of the city. But none are at court. They're not the most sociable creatures. They usually stick to the Wilds." He explained that the Wilds were the untamed lands in his world—mostly forests, swamps, and mountains. "As the name implies, it's not a place for a picnic."

"So your nation has no connection to trows?"

"No. We steer clear of them. They're not trustworthy."

"How so?" she asked.

"They'll slit your throat if you turn your back on them. Just for sport."

Bristol blinked, trying not to look alarmed. "Always?"

"Not if they want something from you."

Tyghan started to rise like their discussion was over.

"I'm not done with my questions, and I still haven't made my final decision."

He eased back into his chair, and a low grumble rolled from his throat.

"I need to know if you're a Seelie or Unseelie fairy."

He was silent for a long while. "And just what do you think Seelie means?" he finally asked.

"I'm told it means kind and agreeable."

An amused spark lit his frosty eyes. "Then you tell me. . . . Do I look kind and agreeable to you?"

Bristol swallowed. He was quite readable now.

"Perceptive," he replied as if she had answered aloud. "But it's all a matter of degree. Like your kind, fae come in all types, and we tend to mix and congregate in the same way. We're not rocks that you can classify. Try to remember that."

Beneath the table, Bristol's fingers curled into fists. "Very well. I'll do my best to remember that, for the most part, you're not a common rock. And now I need to know about your sheriff. . . . Was he in on it?"

"My sheriff?" he repeated. "What—You mean, Orley? He's not my sheriff. I barely know the man. He's an outlier. He's lived in your world for years. Eris only brought him in for questioning." He leaned forward. "Is he in on *what*?"

But Bristol's mind had already moved on, spinning back to that morning Sheriff Orley knocked on their front door to notify them about their father. The true sadness etched in his face. His voice had even wobbled, and he needed to clear his throat twice to tell them the news. She guessed it was as Willow said—the trows had tricked him, too. The sheriff was an outlier, not really one of them at all.

Her attention returned to Tyghan as she formed a reckless proposal in her head with unknown costs, but she didn't care. If she parsed out the price tag of every detail, she'd talk herself out of it and she'd never go. "My final and most important question: If I agree to go to your world and help you, will you help me find my father in return?"

His brow furrowed. For the first time, he seemed at a loss for words. "Your father? I was told he was . . . dead."

"I just learned he may be alive, that he was taken by trows into your world. I intend to find him and bring him home."

CHAPTER 14

Tyghan betrayed no expression, but inside he was nodding. So that was how Eris did it. He made her think her father could still be alive, and in Elphame, no less. That was a low blow, but Eris did promise he'd pressure her, and with only three months until the cauldron was passed on, there was no time to waste. The counselor had played it cleverly. Tyghan couldn't blame him for that. She was here by her own choice. Some magics—especially this one—might be prodded along by twisted measures, but they couldn't be forced. That was assuming she possessed any magical abilities at all, and he hadn't detected any earlier, when he'd stood within inches of her, so close he felt the rush of blood in her veins and tasted the salty fear on her skin.

Even now, he sensed no magic from her. It was rare that such unions produced purely mortal children, but even so, fae blood could be recessive and of little use. Millions of mortals had vestigial traces of fae blood in them, but it only offered them minor instincts and no true magical skills. It was possible that was all she had—and they needed far more than a few small instincts.

"Well?" she asked, still waiting for an answer about her father.

The anticipation on her face made him shift uncomfortably in his seat. He turned his focus to his fingers, weaving them together in front of him. Promise to find a dead man? Could an impossible promise be made? Could he be held to it? This was one of those moments he could use the counselor's advice. Eris should have told him about this ahead of time.

He glanced from his fingers to her face. Her skin was warm in the candlelight, like the soft sands of Amisterre, and her long, dark lashes cast a shadow over her eyes. A loose strand of chestnut hair fell in a wave over her cheekbone. She was disheveled, but it suited her. She owned her space without apology. In some ways, she seemed like she could be any mortal woman, one close to his own age, except she loved a man whom he despised. It was only the hope of finding that man that had made her come, not the art. That was the deal—what she really wanted. *She was Kierus's daughter.* It was still sinking in. For over twenty years, Kierus had been in the mortal world. He had lived a lifetime— *with Maire*—while Tyghan's own life was brought to a jolting halt.

She continued to stare at him, unblinking, waiting, her hazel eyes changing color, the brown flecks growing darker, troubled. As composed as she tried to be, her emotions showed in her eyes. Anger, fear, determination, they bobbed in her gaze like an oarless boat on a rough sea, struggling to stay afloat. This mattered so much to her that she couldn't conceal it.

That trait was not like either of her parents. Kierus and Maire were good at hiding things—hiding nearly everything. She wasn't. She truly believed her father was alive, not *might be* as she had said. She wanted to rescue him.

He wasn't sure if the thought enraged or sickened him. He thought once that he could rescue Kierus, too. He had risked everything to save him. He'd been a fool.

She edged forward in her seat, her lips slightly parted, impatient for his answer. Her tongue slid along the edge of her top teeth, his focus caught up in the motion of it. He needed to say something. "Tell me about your father. What was he like?"

"Why? What difference does it make?"

"If I'm going to spend time searching for a man at my own risk, I want to make sure he's worth it."

Maybe Tyghan was stalling, maybe he simply wanted to know what had transpired during all those years. What had her father been to her, and how much did she actually know? She knew nothing about Kierus's prior life if she was asking Tyghan for help, the last person who would ever want to help him. It was plain, Kierus had lied, even to his own daughter.

"His name is Logan Keats, and—"

Keats. The name didn't come as a surprise. Kierus always liked the poet. They had all been friends.

"Was he an honest man?"

She sat for a long moment, thinking it over. "Sometimes he had to do creative things to provide for our family, but—"

"Like what?"

"Various things," she answered more firmly. "But for the most part, he was a very good man."

Good? The word smoldered beneath Tyghan's skin. The Butcher of Celwyth was called many things, but never good.

"What did he do in your world? For a living?"

"He was an artist, and a somewhat successful one. But we moved around a lot. It was hard to establish a reputation on the road. My mother was an artist, too."

Tyghan's jaw clenched. Discussing Maire was like trying to swallow broken glass. "Was?"

"My mother's dead. She passed away a year ago."

"Did you love her?"

Her eyes turned molten. "That's none of your business. Do fae always ask such personal questions?"

She loved her mother. Beneath her blistering stare, he saw the anguish in her eyes, the longing.

Disgust twisted through Tyghan. It was a knife stabbing his gut all over again. He stood. He'd heard enough. "It's time to go."

CHAPTER 15

Bristol jumped to her feet, her palms raised, determined to stop him from leaving. "Wait! I need your answer. Will you help me find my father?"

He remained still, silent. It wasn't a hard question. Why was it so hard for him to answer? He finally cleared his throat like something was caught in it. "I will help you *search* for him."

"You swear?"

"You have my word. I'll help you search. I can't promise more than that."

"Fair enough," she agreed. The deal was made.

He grabbed a wide leather belt that hung over the back of his chair and lifted it over his head, then adjusted the enormous sheathed sword it held between his shoulder blades. He fastened another strap across his chest. Bristol's lips parted in wonder. He was overly comfortable with a sword hanging from his back, like he was simply shrugging on a jacket. What kind of fae lived in this Danu Nation? Why did he need a sword? She thought about the iron nail Harper had stuffed in her back pocket and almost laughed at its uselessness. A nail was not going to bring this one to his knees.

This is it, she thought. She was going to this strange Faerieworld, or whatever that word was he called it. Elflan? Was it going to hurt? It hadn't occurred to her before. She knew almost nothing about this place except that it had trows, and trows took her father. A nervous tremor shivered down her arms. She forced a smile and asked, "So, how do we do this? Do we click our heels together three times?"

His expression darkened. Did he ever smile?

"It's a joke," she explained.

He snatched his cloak from the chair and whirled it over his shoulders. "I'd advise you to curb your *wit* when you reach court. The fae there will not find your quips so clever. There could be unpleasant consequences."

Her nerves were already raw, but the slight roll of his eyes was the match that set them afire. Even the rudest patron at Sal's could only expect so much diplomacy and he had used up the last of hers. Her trepidation blew out in a string of sharp words. "You condescending ass! I think I already told you that this is all new to me, so let's just get this straight right now, Mr. High and Mighty Who Never Smiles. When I'm nervous I might try to lighten the mood with a joke or two or maybe even act like a smart-ass, and I'm a little nervous right now, so if you stop acting like Lord of the Monsters, maybe I won't have to curb my witty tongue."

He finally smiled, but it wasn't a lovely smile. The danger in it reached all the way up to his eyes that were now piercing her. "Well," he said, huffing out a generous half chuckle, "I guess it's good to know you're only acting like something you're not. I, on the other hand, am exactly who you think I am, Lord of the Monsters."

Bristol looked down, struggling to compose herself. Even with a deal struck, he was still her means to an end until she could speak to Jasmine or Eris, or someone else in charge.

"Listen," she said, glancing back up. "I think we've gotten off to a rocky start, and we're going to be working together, right? Can we start over?" She held out her hand. "I'm Bristol Keats, but my friends call me Bri."

He viewed her hand without taking it. "I'll call you Keats."

She silently stewed as she dropped her untouched hand back to her side. "And you are?" she prompted.

"Tyghan Trénallis of the Danu Nation. My friends call me Tygh. But you . . . you may call me Mr. High and Mighty."

He took something out of his pocket and flipped it to her. A coin. She caught it in her palm. "Don't lose it," he said. "It's your ticket back to this world."

And with that, in a blink, he was gone, and the room was filled with a band of armed people and creatures who took her away.

CHAPTER 16

It was a world of ogres and trolls, demons and dragons, kings and queens, sprites and jesters—and the gods who walked among them. And it was a world that went on forever.

That was all Bristol thought when she scanned the horizon of this land known as Elphame. *Forever.*

She didn't know all the secrets this world held yet, nor the creatures, their schemes, or hungers—that part would come later. No, it was the vastness alone that bore down on her now. She stared across the land from a high rocky crag. *They live beneath little hills* were the last words Harper had called out to her, still reading from her book as Bristol rode away on her bike.

"No, Harper," Bristol whispered to herself now. They lived on majestic mountaintops and in sweeping valleys, in jewel-green forests and moorlands, beside twisting rivers that disappeared behind rocky peaks, in cities with spires that reached into purple-painted clouds, and they lived in the nearby woods that slithered with unknown shadows.

And somewhere in all this vastness was her father. Faerieland was not just one destination, but many. How would she ever find him?

Danu knights on enormous white steeds surrounded her. They were preparing their weapons. She rode with the one named Kasta. She said the easy part of their journey, the one that had already taken hours, was behind them—the part that left the world whirling past them in a breakneck blur, colors like flames spiraling beside them, at times their horses leaving the ground, taking flight though they had no wings, passing through Bowskeep, then over deep canyons and deeper oceans. Bristol's eyes had watered from the wind, and her hips ached from the horse pounding ground and air beneath her. Sometimes it was hard to even breathe. She hadn't been able to ask the knights any questions, the whir, the pounding making it impossible to think, much less talk. She held on to the horse's mane until her knuckles were stiff and white.

And now the hard part was about to begin? They still needed to travel through the Wilds. Kasta's dark eyes darted across the landscape, contemplating the moving shadows. Her pale fingers raked through her short black hair. "That way, I think," she said, then nodded.

Quin, another of the knights, studied the vista below and concurred. He was short and stocky, and built like a muscled wall. He wore a sleeveless tunic and his brawny biceps shone in the sun like burnished bronze. Bristol wondered if it was flesh beneath his skin, or pure iron.

Kasta placed a cloak over Bristol's shoulders. "This will keep you out of sight, if we're lucky. Our enchantments won't work on them all. Stay low on our horse. We'll do our best to protect you."

Their *best*?

Kasta drew her massive sword, its hilt encrusted with precious gems. Cully drew a long, lethal arrow from his quiver, and Quin and Glennis lifted glistening golden spears that could stop a train. What kinds of beasts lived in these Wilds? The creature, Dalagorn, who Kasta said was an ogre, rode forward, a small bow and quiver of tiny silver arrows strapped to his sprawling back. It was a humble and benign weapon compared to everyone else's. Glennis sat high in her saddle, her hands rubbing her furred haunches, and her hooves pressed into the stirrups, eager to go. Kasta didn't say what kind of creature Glennis was, and Bristol wasn't sure if it was polite to ask, but based on the large white horns curling around her head, Bristol thought she might be part goat. But her face was entirely human—and beautiful. Thick white hair cascaded around her shoulders. And she was kind, at least Bristol thought she might be. She often glanced at Bristol with a reassuring smile or nod.

"She ready to go?" Cully called to Kasta. Tips of pointed ears peeked through his sleek copper hair.

"What do you think?" Kasta asked Bristol. "Feeling better?"

Surprisingly, other than being overwhelmed by the view that greeted her, Bristol felt mostly fine now. Her back still ached, but just minutes ago, she had fainted when they had passed through the portal that led to Elphame. Never before, in her entire life, had she fainted. The last thing she saw in the mortal world was the Eiffel Tower in the distance. When they leapt through a portal that looked like a massive tree, she was instantly gripped with unbearable pain, like a giant hand was trying to break her in half.

When she came to, she was slumped in Kasta's arms and a thin line of blood trickled from her nose. Bristol asked if it was always so painful to pass through a portal.

Never, Kasta had answered, eyeing Bristol with confusion. Because of her fainting episode, they decided, as a precaution, to proceed by land at a slower pace.

"Well?" Kasta prompted, waiting for an answer.

Was she better? Bristol wasn't sure. Her mind still reeled at a world that was steadily growing bigger. *The Wilds. As the name implies, it's not a place for a picnic.* She pulled the cloak that Kasta placed on her shoulders closer, wishing it were made of armor instead of cloth, and answered, "Ready."

CHAPTER 17

On the far side of Elphame, high atop a rocky cliff, a door opened.

From a distance, the swirling flutter in the sky might have been taken for a flock of starlings, their undulating swarm mesmerizing. On closer inspection, one might think the pointed wings belonged to bats.

The monster watched them swirl, intoxicated with the power of bringing them forth, the riders on their backs stirred into a frenzy at the shout of their liberator's voice.

Power surged though the monster, invincibility thrumming in her veins, hot and heady.

But a memory still lingered, persistent, tugging, trying to break through the rising crescendo of flapping wings, to remind the monster.

A promise.

The monster paused.

The swirling flutter paused.

The promise, delicate and quiet, tried to rise.

The monster turned her head to the side, curious. Longing pulled at her breastbone—but then the dark flutter in the sky screamed, the riders raising fists, their howls surging, and the monster breathed deeply and smiled, the tug of the promise buried beneath the luscious rush of power.

CHAPTER 18

A rosy hue bled over the palace grounds as the sun descended and the landscape glowed with soft pink light, a luminescence that centuries of artists had sought to capture on canvas. The sculpted balustrade of animals lining either side of the grand staircase appeared to come to life in the shifting light—the lion ready to leap onto Sun Court, the dragon ready to soar above it.

Twilight and evening were the favored times of day for most fae, but Tyghan was only focused on the business of finding his sister. He spotted her at Sky Pavilion, leaning on the banister, framed by a panoramic view of the city, but he noted her focus was fixed elsewhere—on a circle of her knights congregating on the plaza below them. He was sure it was only one who held her attention. The knights were oblivious to her gaze. Their attention was fixed on the next plaza just below them where a dozen fae were beginning to pluck harps while others danced to their music.

"I heard they're finally back," Melizan said, without turning her head. "But you didn't bring her back yourself, I see. Bad form, Tygh."

"Almost back. They're still in the city. But they'll be here soon," Tyghan replied, ignoring her jab. "They made it through the Wilds without incident, but I'm told the girl fainted when they passed through the portal."

Melizan laughed, her long silver tresses shimmering in the twilight. "Well, isn't she a precious flower? Not very flashy, though. And those clothes." Melizan wrinkled her nose. "Practically rags. Her trousers were shredded. But she's pleasant enough on the eyes—like her mother."

"The girl doesn't look anything like Maire."

"I didn't say she did." She turned to face him. "And you do know she's not a girl. Every inch of her is fully a woman. Surely you noticed. Everyone else standing on the porch as she scampered off certainly noticed."

He noticed, but he wasn't about to admit it. "Semantics," he answered.

Melizan snorted. "Semantics with curves. Either way, you'll have to start calling her by her name eventually."

Tyghan shook his head. "What kind of name is Bristol? I've never heard of it. Her sisters have equally strange names."

"So Kierus and Maire fully embraced the absurdities of the other side. Somehow, I'm not surprised. The other sisters weren't useful?"

"According to Eris, no. Outliers concurred. Some Tuathan traits, a musician and a scholar, but they couldn't find a treasure on their own bed without a map."

His sister pursed her lips at this bit of news. "The steward of Elphame grows increasingly nervous and annoying," she said, like it was Tyghan's job to soothe the steward.

He was fed up with the frequent missives, too. He didn't need any more reminders that the Choosing Ceremony was only three months away. And now there was a barrage of desperate missives from him reminding them about Beltane Eve too—as if Tyghan wasn't aware. The annual gathering of kingdoms was his last chance to garner kingdom support before the Choosing Ceremony. The timeframe pressed Tyghan on all sides every day. It meant every decision he made had to be the right one. The steward's nervous ramblings had arrived with regularity ever since the queen of Elphame died one year short of fulfilling her hundred-year reign. Her steward had been forced to take over her duties until the next Choosing Ceremony, and he wasn't handling it well. As the ceremony drew closer, it was one duty in particular that was causing him distress—passing the Cauldron of Plenty on to the successor. Everyone feared it would be King Kormick. With his newly acquired army, he was unbeatable—and Fomorians weren't known for their benevolent governance.

"He shouldn't have taken on the position of steward," Tyghan answered.

"But he did. Let's hope your newest recruit can end his whining. The novices we have so far are tragically weak, and the days are quickly passing."

"That's what I wanted to talk to you about. I want you to take Keats on with your recruits. The throne room is full of petitioners, and I'm busy with—"

Melizan belted out another laugh, drawing the attention of the knights below. Cosette's eyes swept upward, landing on both of them. She ran her fingers through her emerald hair in a seductive gesture and began making her way up the winding stairs.

"Not a chance, dear brother," Melizan answered. "I already have twice as many recruits as you, in case you haven't noticed, and that one is trouble. Resign your position as Knight Commander if you're too busy. Or maybe you're simply afraid of her? It's understandable, considering who she is."

"Don't twist this around. I'm not afraid of her. I'm exactly what I said, *busy*. I need you to take her on, Melizan."

"Is this a direct order?" Her aqua eyes locked on his, waiting. Tyghan could make it an order, but he knew if he did, his sister could make life difficult for him in other ways.

She chuckled. "I didn't think so. Really, Tygh, don't be such a wounded dog. It's tiresome. You never dance anymore. You just nurse your whiskey in dark corners with your dreadful friends. You need to get out more. When was the last time you had a good f—"

"What I do in my private time is none of your business, Melizan."

She shook her head with mock pity. "That long, huh?"

"It's not the solution to everything."

"Ho! Who are you? You used to work hard *and* play hard. Oh, unless—" Her brows arched as she glanced at his crotch. "Maybe you aren't capable anymore because of your injury?"

He only replied with a frigid stare.

She shrugged. "I guess I'll just have to play twice as hard for both of us."

Cosette reached the top of the steps and walked toward them, a confident swagger in her steps that Tyghan interpreted in a dozen different ways. Melizan smiled. Cosette sidled close, laying a long, leisurely kiss on Melizan's mouth, her thinly webbed fingers brushing his sister's cheek with familiarity.

"Oh! Your Greatness, I'm so sorry," Cosette said when she finally stepped back and gave Tyghan a token glance. "I didn't notice you there." She dutifully offered a minimal bow of her head and turned back to Melizan. "I'll see you back in our—your chambers."

She strolled away, Melizan's eyes following her.

When she was out of earshot, Tyghan hissed through his teeth.

"Come now, brother, she's an exceptional knight."

"You could have any woman in court," Tyghan grumbled. "Why does it have to be *her*?"

"Correction, I could have any woman or man in this entire kingdom. But I fancy her."

"She's merkind. I don't trust her. She's dangerous."

"So am I. Besides, being dangerous is what makes her valuable."

"We have traitors in this city, Melizan, and she slinks down to the river every night. We don't know who is in that water."

"Her family." Melizan groaned. "She goes to see her family. That is all."

Tyghan shook his head. His sister was impossible to corral. "That better be all. She's your knight, and it's your job to keep an eye on her. Make sure you do."

"The way you kept an eye on Kierus?"

Tyghan was silent, feeling the hard punch of her words. Melizan never held back a fist that could be put to good use.

"We can't always know what's in someone's heart," he finally answered.

"My point exactly, dear brother," she said, and kissed his cheek. "I suppose that means eventually we all have to take a chance on someone. I'm taking my chance on Cosette. And now I am going to my chambers to keep my eye on her just as you commanded—and I will enjoy every minute of it."

CHAPTER 19

Seven stone bridges spanned the sleepy river that curled through the city. Each bridge was named for a god, and they were all cities in their own right, cornucopias of bustle and abundance, and the opposite of everything Bristol thought she knew. Her logic battled with the implausible. For the hundredth time, her nails dug into her palms to make sure she was awake, not drugged by the cakes she had eaten, or sleeping off a rough bout of food poisoning. *It's real*, she reminded herself. But from that moment in the kitchen with Harper, her gut already knew it was true. A lifetime of question marks had hooked together in a chain and dragged her to this reality.

"What are they saying? Should I worry?" Bristol asked when groups of fae stepped close and erupted into animated chatter she couldn't understand.

"Not as long as we're with you," Kasta answered, then solved Bristol's communication problem with astonishing ease. She whispered words against her index finger, then pressed her finger to the side of Bristol's forehead and drew it across. "*Tugache rai*," she said. "That should take care of it. Now fae and other tongues will be your own."

And just like that, the city was alive with words Bristol understood.

She and the knights continued their trek over the largest span, Lugh Bridge. It was a riot of colors and shapes. Shops, homes, gardens, and grand towers were jammed together on either side of the bridge in smug anarchy, teetering and defying gravity. Fae filled the center pathway, weaving through crowds to unknown destinations, while others shopped leisurely. Still others lounged on gold filigree balconies that overlooked the street below. From their perches they sipped mysterious smoky drinks, plucked out tunes on fiddles, preened their feathered arms, or simply observed those passing beneath them with mild interest.

Some fae were hooved like Glennis; others were more human in appearance but with small telling features like pointed ears, clawed hands, or, most unnerving, yellow eyes with long narrow slits for pupils. But many appeared to be fully human like Kasta, Quin, and Tyghan—though Bristol wondered what might be hidden beneath their clothing. Nothing could be taken at face value, but one thing was readily apparent—her father would not stand out in a place like this.

And yet, *she had*. From the moment they crossed the bridge, heads turned.

"They smell you," Quin said, noting a small group of fae wearing bloodred caps drawing closer to get a better look. "The other world clings to your skin. A bath and new clothes will take care of that."

Smell? She *smelled*? She hadn't showered that day, but Bristol resisted the urge to sniff her armpits.

When they reached the end of the bridge, an even more astounding city greeted them. Winding streets churned with activity, and in the surrounding terraced hillsides, great manors began to glow with lights as evening descended.

Lavish carriages rolled past them, drawn by dappled horses of surprising colors. The carriages stopped in front of a large building with beautiful, scrolled pillars, and passengers emerged dressed in elegant flowing gowns and long suitcoats trimmed with velvet, satin, and sapphires. Some of the partygoers boasted gossamer wings that glimmered in the streetlights that were beginning to twinkle on. On the next avenue, the opulence gave way to tidy streets with humble shoe shops, pubs, and other establishments offering hats, belts, and boots. One crowded storefront was packed with potions in colorful bottles.

As Bristol took it all in, little orbs of light darted past her face and buzzed in her ears. She startled, waving them away.

"They won't harm you," Glennis said. "They're only curious river sprites."

They hovered nearby, and Bristol wondered if she might have swatted one. She didn't want to make enemies here—not even with a river sprite no bigger than a firefly.

As she and the knights waited for several carriages to pass, a stout woman with a wrinkled-apple face and pointed furred ears approached them. "And who is this?" she scolded Kasta, waving a crooked finger at Bristol. "Does she know the rules?"

From her high position on Kasta's horse, Bristol eyed the woman's sharp teeth looming close to her foot. No doubt this woman's fangs could snap right through her flimsy sneaker and take off all five toes. She wished she was wearing those sturdy leather boots from the shop they had just passed.

"She just arrived, Street Mother," Kasta said. "We'll tell her everything."

"See that you do," she said, shoving her hands onto her round hips. "I keep a clean street."

Bristol's resolve rose as the woman began to stomp away. She sat tall in the saddle and called after the woman. "Pardon me, Street Mother?"

The woman whipped around.

"Shh," Glennis warned Bristol.

But Bristol was already committed. "This is your street?"

"Every inch of it," the woman confirmed.

"Then you would know if there were any trows on it?"

The woman took a step closer, her bulging eyes narrowing to slits. Her thick upper lip twisted, exposing the full length of one menacing fang. "What kind of question is *that*?"

Bristol swallowed, wondering if even the mention of trows was an insult here. She met the woman's glare and told herself the street mother wasn't any more intimidating than Sal had been when she went begging for a job. Except Sal didn't have sharp teeth that could open a can of tomatoes with a single bite. "An honest question," she answered firmly. "As Kasta said, I'm new here, and it's a question I need answered by someone who understands this world down to its last inch, and you are clearly that person."

The sharp slits of the woman's eyes softened, and her lips relaxed, the fang safely tucked away once again. She nodded approvingly. "You're a fast learner. That's a good thing. You'll need that around here. Your best bet for finding trows is out in the Wilds. There aren't any on my street, but over in the East quarter, you might find a nest of mountain trows at the end of Mugwort Street. But don't tell them I told you."

Bristol nodded. "I won't. Thank you. One more question, if I may? Have you heard of a man named Logan Keats?"

The woman's face grew more wrinkled in thought, and Bristol's hope rose. The street mother finally shook her head. "But I'll ask around for you. Check back with me in a few days."

Bristol thanked her again, and Kasta urged their horse forward.

"What was that all about?" Cully asked when they were out of earshot.

Quin drew close. "Who is Logan Keats?"

"My father. I was told that trows stole him away and brought him here. Your friend Tyghan promised to help me find him. It was our bargain. Can we go to Mugwort Street now?"

Glennis's furry white brows shot up. "Tyghan promised you?"

"Promised to help you find your *father*?" Quin clarified. "Are you certain about that?"

"I know Mr. High and Mighty is disagreeable, but yes, he agreed."

A grin curled Cully's mouth. "Did he, now?" The knights exchanged peculiar glances that made Bristol uneasy. Did they doubt her? She had no proof of his promise, nothing in writing like a contract. She doubted he would have given her one anyway, considering his temperament. But he did swear, and that part had seemed genuine.

Kasta shook her head. "No, it's getting late, and Mugwort Street is in the opposite direction of where we're going. Besides, Tyghan's promise, Tyghan's duty to take you there."

Glennis chuckled and mumbled, "Mr. High and Mighty."

"And where would I find Tyghan?" Bristol asked.

"There," Quin answered, pointing to a spot behind Bristol. She twisted in the saddle and drew a startled breath. With the enormous boulevard trees no longer blocking her view, she gazed up at a sprawling manor high atop a hill. Its massive walls glowed, not just from the setting sun but from within, like it burned with an inner light. It dwarfed every other structure of the city, spreading out over the terraced hillside on several levels. The spires on the top level disappeared into the clouds.

They were what she had spotted in the distance when she first came through the portal.

"What is that place?" she asked.

"The royal palace," Kasta replied.

"Tyghan lives there?"

"Of course. He's king of the Danu Nation."

CHAPTER 20

Decadent ambience rolled across the palace grounds as fae of every persuasion emerged from forest, pond, and palace. Sorcerers strolled through the merriment with watchful eyes, ready to quell any magic fights that might erupt between well-oiled fae who couldn't hold their brews.

It was the same every night, the carousing lasting until dawn— except for the knights. Their days began at sunup, so they needed a measure of sleep, but most, like Tyghan, didn't require more than a few hours. New recruits from the mortal world, accustomed to long hours in their beds, didn't fare so well.

"Look over there," Glennis said when she spotted Tyghan working his way through a crowd of dancers, scanning the terraces. "Who do you think Mr. High and Mighty is searching for?"

Cully laughed at Tyghan's newly acquired title. "There were a lot of sparks flying between those two at the inn."

"Bad ones," Dalagorn replied.

"I'm not so sure." Glennis's head angled slyly. "There was definitely *something* flying between them."

Kasta sighed. "It's like he doesn't want to lose sight of a poisonous serpent, but wants to keep a safe distance too."

"With good reason." Dalagorn downed the last of his ale, foam clinging to his thick upper lip. "Maybe she is a serpent—or worse."

"That weak little thing?" Glennis shook her head. "Not a trace of magic in that girl. I feel sorry for her. She won't last long here."

"And yet," Kasta mused, "besides gaining valuable art, she managed to wheedle a promise from Tyghan, too. That's no small feat. I would have loved to watch that negotiation."

"Looks like she may have her father's persuasive powers," Cully agreed.

"Let's hope she has more than just that," Kasta said, still weighing the pros, cons, and inherent risks of bringing her to Danu at all. She hoped Eris hadn't made a colossal mistake. Tyghan had already been bitten by one serpent. He couldn't afford another. She was Kierus's daughter after all. And worse, Maire's.

Tyghan spotted his officers and headed over. Kasta answered his first question before he could ask it. "She's settled in her room. She refused to come."

He bit back a curse, remembering Melizan's comment, *That one is trouble*. He hated when his sister was right. "She's not going to eat?"

"She brought food," Kasta replied. "She's quite resourceful."

"Her own food?" Tyghan recalled the small bag she carried over her shoulder. Did she think they wouldn't feed her?

"Yes, and she's already hatching a plan to find her *dead* father," Glennis remarked. Her eyes sparked with reproach.

"What do you mean?" Tyghan asked.

Kasta swirled her glass of whiskey. "It would appear she's a lot like Kierus. In a few heartfelt words, she charmed Mae into a purring kitten. Mae is going to ask around to see if anyone has seen a Logan Keats. She told Keats to check back in a few days."

Tyghan worked to show no surprise. Mae never did anything unless a bit of gold warmed her palm first. It was hard to believe Keats possessed any charm at all when she'd only showered him with surly demands.

Glennis scowled. "Why did you tell her that her father was still alive?"

"I didn't. It was Eris. It was his way of getting her here by her own choice. Eris did what he had to do."

"It's still rotten," she replied.

Tyghan's blue eyes turned a shade colder. "A lot about our lives is rotten right now, in case you hadn't noticed. Get used to the stench."

"And if she finds out he's really dead?" Cully asked.

"She won't, will she?" Tyghan said to Kasta. "You'll make certain of that, won't you?"

Kasta nodded. "I'll speak to the others."

"And her parentage must be kept—"

"Eris already told us," Cully answered.

Glennis frowned. "But it won't be easy to keep that under wraps. If someone goes poking around Bowskeep—"

"You're officers of Danu," Tyghan said. "You didn't sign up for *easy*." He turned and walked away.

Not easy.

It was a truth Kasta lived with on a daily basis. Knighthood didn't allow for errors—not if you wanted to live. Kierus had learned that lesson. And Tyghan nearly had, too. But even perfection was no guarantee of survival. Kasta made a mental note to send a squad back to Bowskeep that night to quell any loose tongues.

"Not wasting any time, is he?" Cully mused as Tyghan headed for the grand staircase. They all knew where he was going. Recruits always joined the festivities, usually quite eagerly. It was part of their orientation. If they didn't care about those they worked with and for, they could hardly care about the outcome. They needed her to care.

But Kasta knew it was more than that, too. For Tyghan, this

particular recruit was different from any other. She held part of his past in her eyes, in her voice, in her very existence that was never supposed to be. She was a reminder of how everything had gone wrong. Even Kasta struggled to grasp that Bristol was here at all. If she had done her job even halfway to perfection, Kierus's daughter wouldn't exist. She carried the shame of it with her every day.

CHAPTER 21

Bristol skimmed her hand across the green silk coverlet on her bed. It was as bright and soft as a spring leaf. Every aspect of her room was lavish and large, but she felt lost within it, like a sitting duck on an open plain.

Cobalt-blue drapes covering tall windows flowed from fluted golden rods like waterfalls into graceful puddles. Their folds settled across a woven carpet that resembled a forest floor. She stared at a butterfly in the design, its tiger-striped wings opening and closing. She reached down to touch it, and it flew away, as butterflies do, but it was only woven of fibers within the confines of the rug, like it was part of a living painting.

She scanned the details of the rug with dark fascination as she rationed sips from the bottle of water she brought from home. Between sips, she nibbled crumbs from a crushed granola bar and read another page ripped from Anastasia Wiggins's book.

9. *Do not eat fairy food, or you will be trapped in their world forever.*

10. *A fairy will honor a promise or oath to the death.*

11. *Never join a fairy dance. You'll be unable to stop and will die of exhaustion.*

How could anyone know these things?

Unless Anastasia had been there herself—like Bristol's own father. She wished she had the rest of the book. The few pages she ripped out were only a small lifeline to this world.

Her room was whisper quiet. No clattering of dishes, no thump of the washer out of balance, no squeaking of Angus rummaging through trash, no pounding of footsteps up and down the stairs. But there *was* singing. Sporadic. Faint. It sounded like Cat singing scales. At home, she was annoyed by her sister's repetitive singing exercises, but now she found the sound calming. Distance gave her a new perspective on petty nuisances—a new perspective on a lot of things. Including lying.

When Tyghan had asked what her father was like, she didn't mention the times her parents skipped out in the middle of the night to avoid paying at a motel, lifting the girls out through windows, or the times they slipped groceries beneath their coats. *We'll pay double next time*, they'd say, but next time never came.

But there were the times her father invited strangers to join them at their campsite, sharing what food and drink they had because he knew the travelers were in need of both. Calling him a good man felt right. Her mother would have been grateful for Bristol's careful wording. Despite how things ended, she knew her mother had loved him. Bristol would never understand why she left. Leanna Keats was sometimes awkward at being a mother, like she had never witnessed mothering skills in her own life, but she was never awkward as a wife. It was no secret that Logan Keats was the love of her life.

When she talked about how they met, he working one stall at a fair, she as a competitor at another, noticing each other from afar, and the electricity they felt—the memory always made her mother smile, like it was a magical moment. Bristol had loved seeing that spark in her eyes. Just the mention of her father's name brought her mother to life. *I saw a once-in-a-lifetime chance*, her mother would say as she cupped her hand to his cheek, *and I didn't let it slip past me*.

But then, during the time Bristol was living on her own, something went terribly wrong. Cat told her about their violent argument the morning before her mother left. By that afternoon, Leanna Keats said she was going to the next town for supplies, that her wool stock was running low, and then there was a strange moment when she kissed Cat and Harper on their foreheads. It was only later that they realized it was no ordinary goodbye. Her mother planned to leave them, and was so determined that she drove through a flooded creek two states away. Guilt bit at Bristol. She always wondered if things might have gone a different way if only she had stayed, a small difference, like the fluttering of a butterfly wing that turns the direction of a storm.

A fern on the carpet stirred in a breeze that wasn't really there, catching Bristol by surprise again. It wasn't going to be easy to navigate this world, but she held on to the glimmer of power still inside her. *That* was real. She would be the hunter for a change. Caution be damned. Waiting for trouble to pounce was an impossible fear to wrestle. You never knew when it might grab you by the throat—like it had her father.

A sideways thought crept in, a thought she couldn't quite look straight in the eyes. Her father might truly be dead. She stood, trying to shake off dark thoughts, and went to the other side of the room where a lush berry-colored sofa faced an impressive hearth. She plopped down, letting it swallow her up with its luxury, and propped her feet up on the low table like she owned the place. A bottle of red wine sat on the table, already uncorked, like an invitation to drink up. Tempting after the day she'd had, but Anastasia's warning dug into her. She sipped her water instead.

A sudden rap on the door made her startle, and her feet dropped from the table. The granola crumbs in her hand spilled to the floor and a beautifully rendered fox raced across the carpet, gobbled up the feast, then disappeared back into a burrow in the carpet that she hadn't noticed before. Its golden eyes peered out at her.

Another rap. "Keats?"

She'd recognize that voice anywhere. At least he knew how to knock. That much was reassuring. "Come in," Bristol called as she stood.

Tyghan entered, and there was a prolonged silent moment between them as he gazed at her and she gazed back. His lips pursed in obvious disappointment.

Bristol's brows rose. The king? Had she heard Kasta correctly?

Even though he created a presence in the room that couldn't be ignored, he appeared much less intimidating this time. His black hair was no longer wind tossed like he was the spawn of a raging storm, and his menacing black cloak was gone. A simple white shirt graced his broad shoulders. His dark trousers were plain but superbly tailored. Or maybe he just wore them well.

He didn't dress like a king, though the only kings Bristol had ever seen were in Renaissance paintings of stout men sporting heavy jowls, extravagant robes, and shiny tights.

She liked Tyghan's attire better.

His scowl was gone too, and there was no longer a sword strapped to his back. He could almost pass for an ordinary citizen in Bowskeep. She tweaked her head to the side.

Well, no. Not really, Bristol thought as she assessed him again, feeling a warm twinge in her belly.

Not at all.

She had to admit, there wasn't anything ordinary about him.

He scrutinized her, too, still in her sneakers and torn jeans, her hair tangled from the long wild ride, and she guessed he was far less impressed with what he saw. "You haven't changed yet? Recruits are expected to attend festivities."

Bristol sighed. "One, I don't even know what *recruit* means. It sounds like far more than finding a door. And two, I haven't changed because I was nervous about undressing." She looked at him pointedly. "Not knowing *who* might be standing unseen right next to me. Like at the inn earlier today."

His steel eyes rested in hers, unrepentant. He wasn't denying it. "You were going to take the art, weren't you? Steal it before Eris walked in."

"I guess you'll never know," she answered. "Not to mention, you're changing the subject. You were the one spying on me. I know it was you."

"The inn was different. Trust me, the last thing I want to see is you naked. And secondly, I would never enter your personal chambers without an invitation, as you just witnessed. Thirdly, you'll have orientation in the morning. Everything will be explained in detail then, as I know Kasta already informed you. Now get dressed."

The last thing he wants is to see me naked? She was glad for it, but it still seemed like an insult. Besides being smelly, was her mortal body repulsive to look at, too?

"Thank you," she answered, "but I'm not going. As you can see, I've eaten."

He gave the granola wrapper lying on the sofa a cursory glance, then smiled. "My world, my rules. Sound familiar?"

"I'm not hungry."

He stared at her, cold and steady, like it would change her mind, until it became apparent it wouldn't. "Suit yourself," he said, and headed for the door, then stopped and offered one last bit of advice. "There's more than food at the nightly festivities. Staying in your room by yourself is not going to earn you friends—and you might find that friends are the most useful thing you'll acquire here."

She didn't budge, but then with the worst possible timing, her stomach roared like a ravenous lion. He glanced at her belly, his face all smugness, but she wasn't about to admit that she didn't trust his food. She didn't know how many things Anastasia Wiggins had gotten right or wrong, but Harper claimed she was an authority on Faerieland.

Tyghan left, but as soon as he did, Bristol knew he was right. She needed as many eyes and ears as she could get—accomplices, if not friends. This was a bigger world than she had bargained for, and so far, no one she had met had ever heard of a Logan Keats. She was only one person who didn't know her way around yet, and time was ticking. She would simply avoid food at the festivities for now.

She opened the door to call after him and caught her breath. He was already standing there like he knew she would change her mind.

"Hurry up and change. I'll wait here," he said. "And it's only the pixie food you have to avoid. The rest is fine."

Her eyes narrowed.

He grinned. "You think you're the first mortal who ever stumbled in here afraid to eat the food?"

She slammed the door in his face and went to change.

CHAPTER 22

T yghan tried to concentrate on the distant laughter and the pluck of a faraway harp—but all he heard was the mad beat of Keats's dress flapping against her legs and the anger in her steps as she worked to match his long strides.

She had bathed and changed amazingly fast, and he was surprised when she emerged so soon from her room. He tried not to stare, but it was strange to see her in Danu clothing. He was fairly certain her dress was on backward, the laces in front that were meant to go in the back, but it wasn't an unpleasant look. *Semantics with curves.* He hated the way Melizan's words stuck in his head. He hoped Keats didn't notice his gaze had lingered on her restrained breasts, the laces dipping low and tight. Or the cinch of the dress at her waist, revealing more curves. He was far from dead as Melizan liked to imply.

Her hair was damp and unkempt over her shoulders, but somehow, it had a certain appeal. He took in other details he hadn't seen before, too. Her fingers were long and slender, but her nails were trimmed short and unpainted, their white half-moons distinct. A tiny freckle rested in the hollow of her throat, and a faint jagged scar disappeared into her hairline, just above her temple.

The bruise on her lower lip he had noticed earlier now seemed brighter, almost matching the deep blue of her dress. His eyes were drawn to it again, the swelling disturbing the perfect symmetry of her lips. A simple touch of his finger could heal it, but time would take care of it, too, without generating more questions from her. She already had too many.

She was silent for the length of one whole hallway, but as they rounded a corner, she finally spoke, not with a question but a demand. "I want the other piece of art now. Delivered to my sisters' house."

"That was not our agreement. When your task is finished—"

"This world is far bigger than I realized, and everything's become more complicated. I couldn't make an informed decision. If something happens to me, I want to be sure my sisters are well taken care of."

"Is that what you came here for? Safety? Then you came to the wrong place."

He looked sideways at her. Steam was practically rising from her head, and her mouth twitched like words were snarled on her tongue.

He sighed. "You're not going to die."

"Is that a promise?"

Bloody hell, he thought, *she's like the counselor, analyzing every word.*

But this was not something he could promise. There were a thousand ways to die in Elphame that had nothing to do with her task. She could insult a short-tempered wizard, be trampled by a spooked horse, or choke on a fish bone. "I'll think the art over," he answered.

"Think fast. I want it delivered by tomorrow."

Tyghan's jaw clenched. Or she could be strangled by a king pushed past his limits. Kasta called her *charming*? If she'd been this charming with Mae, she would have had her throat ripped out. "Being a poor sport about the pixie food?"

"You could have told me earlier if you already knew what I was thinking."

"But that wouldn't have been half as much fun."

She stopped and faced him, her chest swelling against the laces. "I'm glad you could have some fun at my expense, Mr. High and Mighty, while I'm fighting for my father's life!"

Tyghan's blood ran just as hot. *Welcome to my world*, he fumed silently. *I'm fighting for lives too.*

Their iron stares remained fixed, she as unwilling to back down as he was, but as they weighed their choices, the angry heat between them dissipated.

"Well?" Tyghan finally said. "Shall we go get some food, or will I be forced to listen to your stomach grumble all night long?"

He waited for her stomach to rumble on cue, but she nodded before it could betray her again, and they continued down the hallway at a slower pace.

"Mae told me there's a nest of trows on Mugwort Street, and she's checking around for news about my father. Can we go back to the city in the morning? Kasta told me it was your promise, so your duty to take me there."

"As it turns out, I'm busy with other matters tomorrow and you have orientation."

"But—"

"Mae said it would take time to check around. Trust me, you don't want to use up her trifling goodwill. I'll take you there in a few nights."

"Can we go see Jasmine, then?"

"Why?"

"Because according to you, she raised my father, and she might like to know he could be alive, and I have a lot of questions. My father was secretive about his childhood, and—"

"She isn't well. I'll have Eris check."

Tyghan braced himself for another argument, but she was silent. *Thank the gods.* There was no arguing that Jasmine was fragile. She'd witnessed that with her own eyes. Finally, in a softer tone, she said, "Thank you. I'd appreciate that."

The welcome silence continued for only a few more steps before she added, "In the meantime, maybe you can tell me how my father came to be here?"

Tyghan's pace slowed. The conversation was easier when she was angry. He had a hundred replies ready that could spike her fury again, and hopefully shut her questions down, but Eris had advised him to be civil and even charming, if possible. *We need her on our side.* "That would be a question for Jasmine," he answered.

"I thought you might know, since you were aware that she raised him."

He could tell her the story of how Kierus came to be in Elphame, but this might lead to other questions. For the time being, he needed to keep a safe distance from Kierus. Still, telling her a few early details was probably safe enough.

Tyghan was barely walking himself when Kierus arrived. "I'm told he was a toddler found wandering in a meadow, but the truth is, he was probably taken. The fairy who brought him to court was confused. She couldn't seem to remember where she got him. She wanted to give him as a gift to the queen."

"My father was *stolen*?"

"It would seem so, or he stumbled into Elphame on his own. It still happens from time to time."

"And no one tried to return him to his parents?"

"They tried, but by the time they found out who his parents were, they were dead."

"He had no other relatives?"

"All of them were dead."

"How could they all die? Was there an accident?"

"I—I'm not sure. I was—"

"Of course. It was a long time ago—you probably weren't even born yet." She peered sideways at him. "How old are you?"

"Twenty-six."

"Is that the same as human years? Or are you ancient?"

He suppressed a smile. "The same, more or less. Tuatha de age in a similar fashion to mortals until they reach maturity, which is around seventy years."

"Seventy? It takes that long for you to become mature?"

"You'd be surprised. And even though some of us do make it to a great age, we're not exactly immortal. We die from accidents or illness or by tiring of life. Royals tend to have shorter lives, because they have more enemies. The oldest fae I know of is more than two thousand years old, but most fae don't live beyond three or four centuries. Our lifelines are left to fate, bad choices, and the will of Danu."

"If you're only twenty-six, then I suppose you couldn't remember my father. He was in my world for at least twenty-four years. That's when he met my mother at a swap meet near Los Angeles. LA's a large city in—"

"I know where Los Angeles is."

"Really? You've been there?"

"No, but we have maps of your world."

Her brow rose, suspicious. "Had you ever been to Bowskeep before today?"

"No. I don't go to your world often. I find the smell disagreeable."

She frowned. "You fae have sensitive noses, and you, Mr. High and Mighty, have gone to the wrong places. Most of it smells beautiful—the seashore, laundromats, pizza parlors. Anyway, according to my father, when he and my mother met, it was love at first sight. They married a few months later."

Tyghan's pace picked up. Sun Court seemed miles away.

"My older sister, Catalina, was born a short time after that. They named her after a ferry ad they saw on a bus bench. It's an island. My parents weren't too inventive when it came to names. I was named for a flea market in a city they were passing through at the time, and they named my little sister, Harper, after a magazine at the supermarket checkout. But my father had pet names for us too—nonsense names, really—but it was the way he said them, it made us feel undeniably loved. He called my older sister—"

Tyghan didn't want to know more. He stopped abruptly, interrupting her before she could continue. "Why are you telling me all this?"

She glanced down, her dark lashes veiling her eyes. Her temples flushed with color. For all her bluster and demands, was she still nervous? Or maybe this was a ploy, and she was as devious as Kierus. But when her gaze rose to meet his, her pupils were earnest black moons. There was no guile in them. "You wondered if my father was worth the risk of finding him," she answered. "I want you to know, he is worth it."

Her eyes remained fixed on him, practically begging him to believe the way she did. He nodded like he understood, but he didn't. He could never understand.

All he knew was he needed a drink.

Music thrummed the air, intoxicating, leaving a golden sheen on skin, scale, and horn. A sensuous scent hung in the air, heavy, like blossoms drunk with spring. Beltane was approaching, and no one was immune to its pull. Not lords or knights, nor ladies, ogres, or pixies. Not even kings.

Heat and restlessness stirred inside Tyghan.

He leaned back in his chair, sipping his drink, the goblin whiskey burning his throat as he watched Bristol from a distant shadowed niche. His words to Melizan doubled back on him. *Keep an eye on her.* He would. The way he should have kept an eye on Kierus.

She was settled on a stone bench, eating from a silver tray. He had followed close behind her at the buffet tables, looking over her shoulder, guiding her in her choices to avoid the bewitchment she feared. Now she ate the food leisurely, sometimes closing her eyes with pleasure. Braised boar shanks. Sometimes her brows rose with surprise. Spiced kumquats. Sometimes a small smile curled the corner of her mouth after she licked her fingers. Pomegranate cream pastry.

Tyghan took note of the things she liked and the things she politely nudged aside. She was definitely hungry, and he wondered when she last ate any real food. Eris had told him she lived in a run-down house and her finances were strained. The art she took would change that. She didn't need to worry about her sisters—at least financially.

He watched her movements and where she gazed, trying to make sense of her. She obviously had Kierus's talent for charm. And as Melizan noted, she was easy enough on the eyes—like Maire—though her features were different. Her hair had dried, and in the warmth of the torchlight, her long chestnut locks glowed. Her eyes were a warm gold, rimmed with dark lashes, making her gaze penetrating.

It didn't take long for gentry of all stations to swarm around her, but they always did with newcomers. They were a novelty, at least for a short time. Just the same, he posted Cully to stay at her side so none would try to lure her away to a dark corner. It was only her first day, and while she appeared capable, her sharp tongue was no match for their magic.

Her foot occasionally tapped with the music, the tune difficult to resist, but then she crossed her feet and tucked them beneath the bench to avoid the temptation. She must have learned how music affected mortals—maybe from that book that mentioned pixie food. Most mortal books about fae were absurd, painting them all with the same brush, but they got some things right.

He had tried to get a sense again as they walked to Sun Court if she was fully mortal. It happened sometimes with these unions, and he still sensed no magic in her. Had Eris been fooled, or simply been too hopeful? Was she only someone who knew her way around a small town? Elphame was not small, and it was not tame. His expectations for training grew bleaker.

Several lords took turns showing off simple magics to her, mostly glamours that changed their appearance. She smiled, nodding her head, appearing to take Tyghan's advice about making friends, but as the lords laughed, trying to top one another, he noticed her look away and focus on a circle of dancing faun, bracing herself before she had to look back at some new grotesque glamour.

She would have to get used to it. This was Elphame. This was the world she would have to navigate—one way or another. It was what she agreed to. If she couldn't stand viewing the cackling boar head on Lord Csorba's shoulders, she would never withstand a shrieking sky full of beasts set on her destruction.

And if, in the end, she couldn't adjust or offer the valuable skill they sought, well, there was still the option of using her as a hostage.

This morning, with his knights' screams still ringing in his ears, their blood sprayed across his face and claws still buried in his back, it had been an easy thought, a strategic maneuver that anyone in his position would use. But now that he had struck a bargain to help her hunt for her father—a man he knew was already dead, a man she unmistakably loved—

He took another gulp of his goblin brew, his chest burning. He liked to think of himself as honorable, but knew he had stooped to far lower things. Honor was like glamour, useful only when it served a purpose; otherwise, it just got in the way of who you really were. Honor was for a time when the great gods still walked the earth and sat shoulder to shoulder around campfires celebrating their victories. These were not those times.

She shifted her position on the bench, pressing her hand to her spine. No doubt she ached. A mad gallop to Elphame was not the same as a bike ride around a small town, though he had never ridden a bike, so he couldn't say for sure. But *faint?* No recruit had been that fragile before.

His gaze traveled back to her bruised lip, studying it, the full curve of her mouth, and then he slid his thumb along the side of his finger as he focused on the bruise. He didn't need to actually touch such a small wound to heal it.

By the time his hand was lifting his whiskey again, her lip was healed. He owed her nothing, he told himself, not even this, and certainly not the art she demanded, but having her well fed and not distracted by a throbbing lip served his interests, too.

Her head tweaked to the side as if she was confused, and she lifted her knuckle to her lip, gently testing the flesh. She glanced his way. He was certain she couldn't see him sitting in the dark, but somehow, she seemed to know he was there.

His skin burned again. He didn't have time for this.

He gulped back the last of his brew and began to rise, but was intercepted.

"There you are," Eris said, taking a seat opposite him. Even in the dark alcove, Tyghan noted the flush of Eris's cheeks. No doubt his evening began with a visit to Madame Chastain's private chambers. Eris readjusted his robe, like it was thrown on in haste. "What's this about you promising to search for Miss Keats's father?"

"I had no choice. After you told her that he was alive—"

"I didn't tell her that."

"Then whoever you tasked with the job—it worked. She agreed to come here on the condition I help her find Logan Keats."

"I didn't task anyone with telling her such an outlandish thing. Why would I?"

"But you said you were going to squeeze her. When she came back to the inn claiming her father was alive, I assumed—"

"I did apply pressure. Her family was in dire financial straits, so I extinguished their last source of income—her older sister's job."

They both went silent, caught up in their thoughts, retracing words and events.

"Maybe it was Olivia or Esmee who told—"

"No," Eris said. "They had already left the inn by the time she showed up."

Tyghan lowered his voice. "Who would have told her, then?"

"I—" Eris shook his head. "I don't know."

Why? Tyghan thought. *Why would someone tell her that?*

Unless—

He leaned forward, and his next words were as quiet as a sharp blade. "How do you know he's dead, Eris?"

"He's dead! The sheriff told me. He saw the body with his own eyes. He told me the gruesome details, including watching as the body was scraped off the road. He didn't even know who Logan Keats was at the time other than a local artist. He only found out when we showed up a few weeks ago. He'd have no reason to lie."

"What other outliers are there in Bowskeep?"

Eris told him those he knew about, including Freda the librarian, a local farmer, and a shop owner on Main Street. "There's surely a few more I don't know about. You know how they are. That's why they're called outliers. They keep to themselves. What did Miss Keats say? Who told her he was alive?"

"She didn't say."

But Tyghan was already standing and on his way to find out.

Trows took her father. He had an uneasy feeling about this.

Was it just a miscommunication?

An easy explanation?

No, his gut told him. Nothing was easy when Kierus was involved.

CHAPTER 23

The Butcher of Celwyth sat hunched over the coals, warming his hands. He'd forgotten how cold the high country could be, especially tucked back in a damp trow cave. He was stuck here, at least for the time being, but it gave him time to retrace his steps in months and years. He should have listened to Maire. She was right when she said it was time to go. Complacency was a sword in your chest, instead of someone else's. How had he forgotten that rule?

He'd only been navigating the Wilds for a few days now, but how much time had passed back home in the mortal world? The question nagged at him. He'd probably been gone for much longer—far too long. He regretted that, but with no timemark, there wasn't anything he could do. His daughters would manage.

He couldn't let it cloud his thinking. Regret was a sword in the back. Another rule he needed to remember. There were as many ways to die in Elphame as there were ways to kill. All the rules he'd abandoned, the rules he used to live by, were flooding back to him now, sharp and honed, ready to stab, swing, and bludgeon, the rules that had made him the wonder of Danu.

"You can never grow tired of running ever again," he whispered to himself. He saw that now. Running was his destiny. The tithe for his choices. When you're sent by the gods to seduce and kill your enemy but fail in your task, when you become the seduced instead of the seducer, few options were left to you and only one involved staying alive: run. Run away with the enemy and hope you both run faster than the gods.

If only they'd kept running.

He wouldn't allow himself to think that it was too late to save her. It could never be too late.

He twisted the head from the salmon he was roasting and sucked on its hot juices, his tongue burning, praying the spotted salmon would bless him with the wisdom of Danu.

As he settled into sleep, knowing the trows would be back soon, the only wisdom he heard was, *Run and keep running, until the gods die—or you do.*

CHAPTER 24

T he sun rose behind the spire with perfect precision, lighting its golden pinnacle like a torch. Bristol knew it was not a chance of design. It filled her with awe.

Orientation was about to begin. It appeared she was going back to college after all—at an impressive university, no less. Buried dreams stirred inside her. Studying art at the greatest universities and museums in the world had always been out of Bristol's reach, a star in the sky that twinkled and taunted. A lofty goal reserved for others, not her. Bristol's love of art was different from her father's. Her passion was not in the creation of art but in studying its history. Its twists, turns, genius, and resilience; its continuity, and the way it kept reinventing itself over and over again on the shoulders of what came before. It was like following a treasure map that revealed the minds, aspirations, and machinations of millennia.

Of course, she knew she wouldn't be studying art there. This was more like auditing a single class than being an enrolled student, and whatever she learned would probably be of no real use in her world.

Still, a thrill ran through her as she beheld the ancient fae institution. Ceridwen University was an architectural marvel. It magically melded the styles of the ages, utilizing Gothic spires, sculpted facades, floating staircases, towering columns, whimsical stonework, and intricate leaded windows that winked against a cerulean sky. It left her breathless. Where were these design ideas born? In her world? Or theirs?

"It looks like a magical marriage of the Sagrada Familia and Notre Dame," Bristol said.

"You're a student of architecture?" Ivy asked as she walked beside Bristol down the center path that led to the entrance.

"Not exactly," Bristol answered. But she was a student of art, and architecture was art as much as paintings, sculpture, books, or anything else. It was the product of history, fashion, politics, dreams, and imagination. It revealed people, both living and dead. Purpose and pleasure were its mortar. "But anyone can see it's remarkable."

"I'm glad you appreciate it. We're quite proud of it here. The university draws fae from kingdoms all over Elphame." Ivy guided Bristol through a soaring arched entrance.

The inside was just as striking. They walked down a wide open-air cloister that looked out onto beautiful gardens. Mosaic marble floors with intricate floral inlays decorated their path like grand carpets. They only passed a few students in the quiet halls, most presumably in classes.

Her stomach fluttered. It was still hard to believe she was there. *For services that were neither illegal nor untoward?* She smiled at Mr. Dukinnon's awkward phrase. She would have given him a fucking kidney for that art. Anyone would have. It was going to change her sisters' lives. And asking her to locate a door and sit through a few lectures was little enough to require in return for Tyghan helping to find her father. She'd made a good deal.

As they walked down one hall, and then another, Ivy shared the history of the university and its namesake, the goddess of inspiration. Ivy reminded Bristol of a museum docent, poised and confident, not at all like the jumpy young woman carrying the tray of cakes at the inn. Here, her role was palace guide, ambassador, and greeter of guests. Her boxy blue inn uniform was replaced with a pale green gown so delicate and fine, it seemed it was painted on her. Her black wings flowed down her back like a graceful lace cape, occasionally fluttering to life as she spoke. Bristol was surprised at how quickly she adjusted to these oddities—things like wings and the beautiful iridescent scales framing Ivy's face. Or maybe her initial shock had fried the surprise out of her, and last night's festivities finished the job.

"It's that door at the end," Ivy said as they turned down another long hallway. "The others are already there."

"Others?"

"The other recruits. Five of them. They just arrived in Elphame, too."

Ivy went on to explain that the initial orientation and instruction only lasted two weeks. You either showed potential and went on to the next level of training—or were sent home. Bristol's chest tightened, remembering her promise to Harper. What if she hadn't found her father by then? Could they still send her home? She needed to make herself valuable, fast.

"Here we are," Ivy said, leading her into a room and motioning for her to take a seat. There were at least three hundred of them—available seats, that is. Only five in the first row were occupied. Bristol's footsteps echoed in the expanse. She took a seat beside the others.

The room wasn't at all like the cramped, creaking portables at Bowskeep Community College that had water-stained ceilings you could reach up and touch. Here, the six recruits were specks in a cavernous hall. There was no touching ceilings here unless you could fly. She discreetly eyed her fellow recruits and wondered if that was a possibility.

Looming above them on either side were four floors filled with shelves of books. Leaded clerestory windows flooded the interior with soft shafts of light, and in the highest reaches, dust motes danced in their beams. Bristol squinted. Or perhaps they were sprites like the ones she swatted at the bridge? Holy shit, she hoped not.

"Your instructor will be along soon," Ivy said, "but first let me introduce you to one another." She motioned to the recruit at the end of the row. "This is Julia, a renowned professor recently retired from the University of Paris."

Bristol eyed the chic woman with streaked gray hair swept into a

French twist. She had a regal, assured air, like none of this was new to her. Ivy went down the line, introducing Rose next, a sixteen-year-old concert pianist from London. *At sixteen?* Bristol thought. *Did she begin playing as a toddler?*

Next came Avery, a grad student from Iowa working on her master's in agriculture. Beside her was Sashka, a twenty-year-old Olympic gymnast from Germany, and finally Hollis, a high school English teacher from Seattle with long, pink, curly hair, the shade of cotton candy.

Bristol tried not to cringe when she was introduced, though Ivy was positive about Bristol's attributes, praising her management and delivery skills at Sal's Pizza, which only made her squirm more. Their accomplishments vastly exceeded hers.

"And that's it," Ivy said cheerfully. "Welcome. Your instructor will be right along. Feel free to chat with one another until then."

When she excused herself to attend to other palace duties, the group exchanged a few polite hellos. Everyone was reserved except for Sashka, who was elated by the stunning breakfast tray that had arrived at her room that morning. "The raspberry cream tarts were swoonworthy. I ate three!" She held her hand over her heart and rolled her eyes with dramatic flair as she discussed every item. "And then there was my bath chamber! It had—"

She was cut off when a tall, elegant woman walked in, her heels clicking on the polished floor. Bristol guessed the woman was somewhere in her fifties. Her silky silver hair flowed into multiple loose chignons wound around her head, a few tendrils artfully hanging loose. As she made her way to the lectern at the front of the room, the woman's gaze rested on each of them for a few seconds. Bristol offered a small smile when their eyes met, but the woman only returned it with a short nod. Her expression was decidedly noncommittal, Bristol thought, like a proctor at state exams knowing some of them would fail.

"Good morning," she said. "I'm Madame Dahlia Chastain." Her voice was cool and matter-of-fact. "I'm lead member of the Danu Council, the appointed High Witch of this nation, and the final word when it comes to spells, incantations, and cures. I'll set aside other niceties and welcomes, because, frankly, we don't have the time. Let's just get down to why you are here. Elphame is under attack."

She already had everyone's attention, but her last statement was a stiff wind in a sail, and everyone's focus snapped tight. She explained that a door had been opened by a monster using a talent that was at one time nearly as common as dust. "Now, unfortunately, it's an extremely scarce talent here," she continued, "which is why we recruited you from the mortal world. A lack of need long ago allowed it to fall out of fashion, so to speak, but now the need is great. We're hoping one or all of you have this undeveloped ability buried within you, which will enable us to shut this door again. It is that simple, really."

Of course, it wasn't that simple. And she explained that, too. To close the door, it first had to be found—that was the difficult part.

Bristol struggled to understand how her pizza deliveries were connected to this. Delivering pizzas to someone's door was easy, but yes, first you had to know where to take them. She'd been given plenty of butchered addresses before, numbers transposed or written down wrong entirely. She'd call Sal's or the customer's number to get the address again. That was it.

"We haven't been able to locate the door so far," Madame Chastain continued, "because the door, of course, is invisible, as most portals are."

Bristol's back pressed tighter against the chair slats.

Invisible? *Like the one she leapt through to come here?* Bristol didn't *do* invisible.

The other recruits were nodding.

Their unique features now took on new meaning for her—the nubs of horns sprouting from Sashka's black curls; her silky butterfly blue skin; Julia's vertical pupils; Avery's crown of twigs and moss that grew from her wheat-colored hair. Even the two recruits who had no telling fae features—Rose, the pianist, and Hollis, the teacher—nodded with the others. They all shared an understanding of who they were and what this world was.

Bristol's toes curled in her shoes. Of course they were nodding. They belonged here. They didn't balk at every mention of things like hidden talents and invisible doors.

She wished she had taken a seat at the back of the hall. She wasn't a gymnast, a scholar, or a champion. When she wasn't taking orders behind a counter, mopping up spilled beer, or settling the occasional bar fight, she delivered pizza on a bike in a small town, her life on perpetual hold, halfway between dreams and reality as she tried to keep her sisters afloat. Her connection to the fae world was loose at best—a father who had tumbled in as a toddler and hadn't belonged there, either.

She hadn't even been able to make it through the first portal into Elphame without fainting. Embarrassment clutched her. What wild notion ever made Eris, Tyghan, or even Madame Chastain think Bristol could find and close an invisible door that even they couldn't find? And maybe most important—

Hollis, the teacher from Seattle, voiced the question forming in Bristol's head. It reassured her that, maybe, these recruits were novices in this world, too. "What's so terrible about this door that you need it closed? And why would we be able to do it?"

The High Witch stepped out from behind the lectern. "I'm glad you asked. First, we must go back to the beginning."

And then the lesson began in earnest.

Her hand swept outward in a circular motion and, in the same instant, a cold churning mist crawled across the floor, swallowing up table legs, the recruits, and even most of Madame Chastain. It rolled up the walls and across the distant ceiling as she continued to speak. Bristol stilled, mesmerized as figures emerged from the mist. Gods, Madame Chastain called them, and as she spoke, they continued to fill the room, walking past Bristol and the others, their ancient story playing out around them.

"When the creator Danu sent her children into the world to gather knowledge, she first sent them to the four mystical islands of Fálias, Gorias, Murias, and Findias to be trained by the most brilliant poets, philosophers, crafters, and sorcerers. These mages schooled Danu's children in the sciences, arts, magics, and the powerful wisdoms of the earth and stars."

Bristol watched as a young god transformed another into a swan, and another god made a plain river rock in her palm explode with light, each spark becoming a star in the heavens.

"When Danu's children were equal to their teachers, they were sent off with treasures to help them in their new lives. From Falias came the Stone of Destiny, to declare new queens and kings to govern their realm. From Gorias came the Spear of Lugh, which made the bearer prevail in battle. From Findias came the Sword of Light, which delivered only mortal blows. And from Murias came the Cauldron of Plenty, so Danu's children would never go hungry.

"But there was a fifth treasure, created by the mother goddess herself, the only talisman of creation, the Eye of Danu, a golden needle Danu gave to her beloved daughter, Brigid, so she could thread a path from one world into another. A portal."

Bristol watched the goddess lead the others through a gray mist to a rocky shore, where they set to work, plowing, gathering herbs, and building their new lives.

"But the world was also inhabited by sea gods, and war came. Battles were won, blood was shed, again and again, until the gods grew weary of fighting."

Bristol watched, riveted as the gods gathered around a campfire, warming their hands. She felt the fire's heat on her cheeks.

More come, Brigid said. *Mortals, this time. I hear their oars strumming the water. They will be here soon.*

We are ready, Dagda answered. He nodded at Brigid, for they had already set a plan.

I am weary of spilling blood, Nuada said.

We must fight this one last time, Dagda told him, *or they will not think it an honorable victory and will hound us into the next world. Let the mortals' eyes be veiled with victory this time, so they will not see our deception.*

Bristol sat, fascinated, as she watched it unfold. *A trick, a con.*

"The battle went as planned," Madame Chastain continued, "the mortals claiming victory, along with the land above the earth—then sentenced the gods to live beneath it. But the gods were not to be banished to rabbit holes. Brigid used the Eye of Danu to divide the worlds, the first reserved for them and other magical beings, and a portal to a second world for the mortals to dwell in. Peace would be found at last.

"The gods' world grew in strength, beauty, and knowledge, no longer marred by the tides of war. Later, when they were called home to the Land of Promise by Danu, Brigid pricked her finger with Danu's needle and held a drop of blood to the lips of three babies in the village. *These daughters and their daughters to come will have the power as I do, to navigate between worlds, to create portals, and to close them. The power granted to me by my mother, Danu, I pass to them and to no others.*

"When they departed, the gods only left behind the Cauldron of Plenty and the Stone of Destiny. Over the centuries, those bloodmarked by Brigid multiplied and spread throughout Elphame, creating portals for anyone who requested one, until finally, portals were so plentiful that mortals stumbled into the fae world as often as if it were their own. Troubles began anew. To solve the problem, the twelve kingdoms of Elphame gathered and agreed that all but one hundred portals should be closed, and no new ones opened for the well-being of all. Thus it remained for generations. There was no use for Brigid's bloodmarked anymore, and their gift faded away."

The mist receded. The walls, the floors, all as they were.

"So there are no bloodmarked left?" Sashka asked.

"There is definitely one," Madame Chastain replied. "The Darkland monster is the last known bloodmarked, and though King Kormick denies it, he uses the monster to terrorize Elphame into submission, in anticipation of the upcoming Choosing Ceremony."

She explained that once every century, the Stone of Destiny chooses a new king or queen to oversee all twelve kingdoms of Elphame. The next ceremony was less than three months away, and Kormick was covertly using the monster's power to open a deadly portal that Brigid had closed long ago. "It leads to an inexhaustible army that, coincidentally, attacks any kingdom that defies him, burning villages and killing anything and anyone in their path. As a result, eight kingdoms have already acquiesced to his demands, and the rest are on the brink. None dare challenge him at the next Choosing Ceremony."

"Except for the Danu Nation?" Bristol said.

"Correct. Though it's not a battle even we can continue to wage for long, especially now that he's captured Tyghan's older brother—King Cael. That's why Tyghan is now acting king. Kormick claimed the abduction was in retaliation for Danu's interference in his affairs and promised to return Cael after the Choosing Ceremony—as long as Danu does not defy him. If Danu resists, Cael will lose his head."

Bristol absorbed this new information, seeing Tyghan's anger in a new light. His impatience made more sense now. His brother was hostage to a ruthless tyrant.

"Why would Kormick deny that he's responsible for opening the portal?" Hollis asked.

"Because it's horrific. Why does any despotic ruler deny their vile methods of conquest? They want to project a public image of virtue, but privately they revel in their cruel genius, because absolute power is their ultimate prize."

Julia frowned. "But would the Stone of Destiny choose a ruler like Kormick?"

"In the absence of a good leader stepping forward, someone else is always destined to lead."

"What sort of army is inexhaustible?" Rose asked.

"The restless dead," Madame Chastain answered. "A host of demons that plagued this world before Brigid banished them to the Abyss. They are the worst of fae, mortals, and monsters throughout millennia, their long-dead spirits still eager to create mayhem. They craft bodies in their dark world as tools to wreak their havoc, then ride their winged beasts through the skies. We can, of course, destroy these bodies in battle—and we do—but the demons only return with reanimated corpses, leaving more terror in their wake."

Bristol sat back in her chair. Spirit demons from hell that couldn't be killed?

A knowing silence fell over the room.

That was the door they needed shut.

Fine print, Bristol thought. *Always read the fine print.*

CHAPTER 25

Lir Rotunda was dim, lit only by a single flickering torch. Dalagorn and Quin guarded the entrance while Olivia and Esmee watched for unwelcome shadows.

"Who is Willow?"

The sheriff was still huffing and puffing from his ride. Years of driving a sedan had left him unaccustomed to the rigors of riding a beast. Quin and Cully had ridden during the night to retrieve him. Tyghan leaned close, asking him again. "Who is Willow?"

The sheriff nervously rubbed his thick, knotted hands over his belly. He hadn't been back to Faerie in years, and never to court before, much less been interrogated by royalty. Even as an ogre twice Tyghan's size, it unnerved him. He coughed, hoping someone would offer him a sip of the drink he spied on the table. He did remember the sweet pixie wine as divine.

Kasta poured him a glass and shoved it into his gnarled hand.

He took a quick sip. "Willow? I never exactly asked her. She's a banshee, I suspect. Tearful sort. Always wandering the valley. But she doesn't cause any trouble. Leaves wildflowers on doorsteps. Most folks in town like her, so—"

"Willow told Bristol Keats that her father was still alive. That she saw trows take him."

"No. No. Impossible." The sheriff tapped his head. "Willow's not all there sometimes. Only ones who took Bristol's father were the cleanup crew. Hauled him off to the morgue."

"Did you touch the body?" Eris asked.

"Touch it? You mean check for a pulse? I didn't need to. It was in bad shape."

Tyghan leaned closer. "Are you certain it *was* a body? His body?"

The sheriff knew about glamour. He used it himself to fit in. He saw right through it when other fae passed through town. If he made the effort, that is. Most days there wasn't a point. Fae or mortal, he didn't care, as long as they behaved themselves in Bowskeep. But if some other type of spell was used . . .

His eyes glazed over as he recalled the accident scene, how bright the blood was, something about it not quite right, but he had thought it was only the sun in his eyes . . . and then there were the drivers from the county morgue who were new to him. Strange fellows. But he had been shaken. He liked Logan Keats, and those poor girls had just lost their mother. He was mostly thinking about how he was going to break it to them, not about touching a dead body. . . . *But* . . . He remembered watching the morgue truck drive away, how quiet it was, how quickly it disappeared around the bend, and then there was the autopsy report that never came. He had meant to follow up on that.

He gulped the last of his wine, knowing he had fallen for a trick. *Trows.* He never had liked them, but who did?

The king's eyes burned into him. He'd heard what the demigods were capable of, the things they could turn you into with a mere thought. He didn't want to leave there as a fly. "About that body . . . I could have been mistaken."

The oldest trow stunt in the book, Tyghan seethed as the sheriff was ushered out. Faking injured bodies at the side of the road was their standard ambush tactic.

Once the sheriff was gone and the door secure, he turned back to the others seated at the table. "He's here. Somewhere in Elphame, Kierus is here. Alive and well."

There was a long silence as everyone weighed what that meant, as they recalled Kierus's skill at navigating the terrain, the favors he could call in. As they remembered just what he was capable of, and all the ways they had helped train him.

"He knows the Wilds as well as any of us," Cully lamented. "And with trows helping him, we'll never track him down."

Quin cursed. "Those filthy trows. He had them eating out of his hand like trained rats."

"Which we found useful at one time," Eris reminded them. "And they revered his title—as did his fellow knights when they gave the title to him."

"You promised Keats you'd help find her father," Glennis said. "Now what?"

Everyone waited to see what Tyghan would do. This changed everything.

"My promise holds," he said. "I will help her find her father, but I never promised what I would do once I found him."

The knights nodded approvingly, glad for the vengeance they saw in his eyes. Kierus's broken oath burned in all of them.

Kasta tapped her lips with a knuckle. "But why would he risk it? Why come back?"

Another long silence.

"Because she's back," Tyghan answered. "We've had four reported sightings and the door to the Abyss has been reopened. He came back for Maire."

※

Orders were given. Every trow's den outside the city was to be found. Every trow in the city to be hunted down and questioned. "Mugwort Street. Go there first. Mae told Keats there was a nest of them there. Kill them if you don't like what they tell you. Let it be a lesson to the others. We want answers."

When the knights were dispatched, Eris grabbed Tyghan by the arm, his voice cutting with a rare edge. "Wait, you're going to let that order stand?"

"What choice do I have? He's here, and the trows are malicious murderers colluding with him."

"You don't know that with certainty," Eris said. "Don't let the darkness decide who and what you will be."

"The darkness has always been the one to decide."

"You're one of the gods."

"A descendant, Eris. That's all. I'm only their distant shadow."

Eris hissed and threw his hands in the air. "The shadow of a thousand gods. You've become numb to your powers, Tyghan. You control the sun and the rain, the earth and the wind. You're more powerful than your brother, and wiser too. You should have been king from the start. Everyone knows that."

"Regardless of what you *think* everyone knows, the Fomorian king has all the same powers I do. And he has a formidable monster in his ranks. While I have a finite number of soldiers, his army is now uncountable, which means his power is greater than mine by far."

"There's more to greatness than power alone. The greatness lies in how you use it."

"Really, Eris? A clock is ticking, and there's an ax hovering over all our necks. Look at my options. I don't have time for greatness."

CHAPTER 26

Avery was the first to speak up and ask Madame Chastain the obvious. "Will it be dangerous for us to close the Abyss door?"

"That's what training is for. You'll have the very best team protecting you, but you'll still need basic skills of your own. We don't want knights dying because of foolish mistakes."

And recruits too? Bristol thought. She hoped their *very best team* was good enough.

The High Witch moved on, still in a hurry. "Let's see what abilities you already have. I understand some of you are shape-shifters?"

Julia motioned with her hand. "A cat." Bristol quickly learned it was an understatement. At first, she changed into an ordinary house-cat, small, white, and sleek, her meow cute and harmless. But then she continued to grow, her white fur growing thicker, her paws becoming enormous and clawed, until she was a large and lethal lioness. The wooden floors creaked under her weight as she gracefully circled the lectern, her tail twitching in the air. She stopped midway in her pacing, offering a bone-chilling roar, and displayed her sharp, deadly canines, then returned to her seat and her former self.

"A hawk here," Rose said, and gave a brief demonstration, too. Her arms stretched out and changed to feathered wings, as her legs shrank, and she transformed into a red hawk with fierce yellow eyes. She flew to a rail on an upper floor, comfortably perching there before Madame Chastain waved her down again.

"A mouse," Hollis said, warily eyeing Rose and Julia, opting not to demonstrate.

Sashka eagerly shared her speed and leaping abilities.

"I can glamour just about anything," Avery said.

"Glamour can be a helpful distraction, though temporary. Most fae, with a little effort, will see through it. What about elemental spells?"

Avery brushed a wilting vine from her forehead. "A few."

The rest nodded in agreement, discussing what they knew, which to Bristol seemed considerable. But the High Witch appeared unimpressed, her lips pursing into what looked like boredom. She glanced briefly at Bristol, waiting for her to share, but when Bristol remained silent, she only shook her head and moved on.

From there, lessons became dry and to the point.

Madame Chastain dove into facts.

Bristol learned there were five kinds of magic. The High Witch listed them in beautiful scrolled writing on a smoky veil that hung in the air.

> *Innate magic—the kind you are born with.*
> *Learned magic that must be practiced.*
> *Magic that is gifted, mostly in the form of amulets.*
> *Magic that is unanchored—wild, unpredictable, but,*
> *   luckily, rare.*
> *Dark magic that feeds on the user, the most dangerous kind*
> *   to practice.*

She swept away the last three in a gust of wind. "For our purposes, we'll concentrate on the first two, developing your innate magic and teaching simple magics that will aid you and your team. In the mortal world, your experience with magic was limited, so let's review the possibilities."

She said many of the innate magics centered around the elements of earth, air, fire, and water. "Some fae have a natural kinship with one element or another, which is why, here in Danu, they are referred to as kinship magics. Kasta, for instance, has a kinship with water. She can summon mists, rouse rough seas, or even part rivers with little effort." She explained about other kinships too, like those with plants and animals, and how a few rare fae were graced with multiple kinships, which made them especially powerful, and she compared them to the old gods.

Other fae's strengths were in areas such as the spoken arts, allowing them to recite whole libraries of history from memory. And then there were the hobs, whose power lay in their unbridled enthusiasm for order and cleanliness and keeping kingdoms from falling into chaos on a daily basis. They kept the palace spotless, sometimes to the annoyance of other fae who preferred a certain degree of disorder. Still other fae had heightened senses. Elven in particular had sharper acuity than most, seeing and hearing from great distances. They perceived the smallest details that others missed.

Bristol understood now why Tyghan bristled at the notion of classifying fae like rocks.

Madame Chastain went on to discuss traits that surfaced randomly. "Shape-shifting, for instance," she said, "is a relatively uncommon trait. Only a small fraction of the fae population has the ability. I, for instance, do not. We're very fortunate to have three in our ranks here." She nodded at Julia, Rose, and Hollis. "Eris chose wisely."

But when she eyed the remaining three, her gaze remained on Bristol longer than the others and coincided with a long, slow blink. Bristol was certain the timing wasn't an accident. "Now let's see what abilities we can find and develop within the rest of you."

With a few words, she called books from the upper libraries, and they swooped down to her lectern like eager birds called to a feeding dish, their pages fluttering like wings. "The Danu Grimoires," she called them with reverent inflection, "the ancient spells, potions, and secrets the gods brought from the Mystical Isles, and the magics created by generations of practitioners since." Her hand casually swept the air and the pages obediently turned until she commanded them to stop. With a flick of her fingers, she shooed the books off one at a time to lie before the impressed recruits.

This is why she's called the High Witch of Danu, Bristol thought. Her magic came effortlessly. Oddly, other than when he disappeared at the inn, she hadn't seen Tyghan do any magic at all.

Avery raised her hand. "Is this talent held only by fae?"

"Yes, of course," Madame Chastain answered. "None of you would be here if fae blood didn't run in your veins, and Counselor Dukinnon believes you all have a strong potential for being bloodmarked, as well. But a deeply buried talent deemed useless for centuries will take coaxing to bring it to the surface."

A slow ripple ran beneath Bristol's ribs that felt something like panic.

She thinks I'm fae.

Madame Chastain's lips continued to move, but Bristol only heard a dull roar in her ears. How could the witch have made such a massive error? Tyghan knew her father was mortal, and her mother was born in a small town to a rotten family and could barely scramble an egg, much less cast a spell. It had to be Mr. Dukinnon who misled her. Maybe he was under the misguided notion that because her father grew up in Elphame, he was fae too?

Should she confess and point out their mistake? But the consequences—

We know where you live.

Would they take back the da Vinci sketch that was allowing her sisters to pay the bills? Or worse, send her home immediately without the chance to look for her father?

She weighed the costs. It was their mistake, not hers. She made a bargain in good faith and wouldn't let their mistake send her on her way before she even got started. She shook off the panic and settled in, listening like every word applied to her, like all the magic and history was familiar, nodding at the appropriate times. A simple con.

She could do this. At least until she found her father.

CHAPTER 27

Tyghan suited up to join his knights.

Kierus. Bristol's father. He's here.

It was still sinking in. He should have seen it coming after Kierus turned their plan and Elphame on its head to save Maire. Their *failed* plan.

He couldn't remember whose idea it was, if he or Kierus had come up with it. They'd both been as tight as corks in a jug, drunk on pixie wine trying to forget a miserable day and the dismembered dead they had to leave behind, not to mention the blistering tirade it unleashed in Cael. *Devil's hell, find a way to stop this monster! What good is an army of knights if they keep failing at their job?* It pushed Tyghan and Kierus to take solace at a pub in the city and discuss the rumors. She was a hideous monster. She was a matchless beauty, hair shimmering to her knees. But everyone agreed, she had a reputation and weakness for taking mortal lovers.

Look here, Kierus said, *I'm mortal and willing.*

Tyghan and Kierus both laughed, but neither thought it an empty offer. Besides being a mortal, Kierus was the darling of the Danu court—an extremely skilled and charming warrior who could disarm both friend and foe. Every fae in Danu called him to their deathbed to gift him blessings, talents, and rare amulets. It made him more powerful than any mortal, and even many fae. He had a reputation, too. No doubt the Darkland monster, as she was already being called in the lowlands, would see him as an enticing challenge. The risk, of course, was that most of her lovers ended up dead once she was finished with them.

Together, through heavy lids and slurred words, they hatched a plan, their fellow knights listening on from the next table. Finally, Kasta paid their bill, and Dalagorn, Glennis, Cully, and Quin scooped them up under their arms to take them home. By the sharp light of morning, even with throbbing heads, surprisingly, the plan still seemed feasible. It could work. Kierus would lure the Darkland monster to a secret meeting place. A fresh mortal to add to her conquests would be too great a temptation for her to resist. The rest, seducing and killing her, would be the easy part.

At least, that was what Tyghan had once believed.

He believed other things now. Things about duplicity. And that maybe there was no one you could truly trust.

CHAPTER 28

How long could she fake it? Bristol wondered.

As long as it takes.

She eyed the other recruits and mirrored their expressions so she'd fit in. She was relieved when other instructors took over afternoon lessons so she could escape Madame Chastain's exhausting scrutiny.

Olivia was a tall, slender sorceress with flawless dark brown skin, high cheekbones, and long hair braided with copper threads. Her voice was entrancing, deep and golden like amber honey, more soothing than Madame Chastain's, and her gaze far less searing.

Esmee, her colleague, was similarly more approachable. She was a short, curvy witch, with pale freckled cheeks, a quick smile, and her sandy brown locks were piled haphazardly on her head. Tiny birds no larger than a walnut flew in and out of it like it was a nest.

Both Olivia and Esmee were senior council members, physicians, and accomplished in Danu magics, especially incantations and potions.

"We hope none of you need our services as physicians," Olivia said, "but you're in the best of hands if you do."

"It's a fact," Esmee said in her melodic voice. "Not a boast."

Olivia was explaining a syllabus of sorts when the lecture hall door opened. "Here he is," she said. "Our fellow instructor."

Bristol felt his noxious vibes the moment he entered the room, and that didn't require any magic—only street sense.

"This is Master Reuben," Esmee informed them. "He'll be assisting us."

Master Reuben entered, carrying a large, boxy satchel in each hand. He made a ritual out of setting them on the floor beside him in a slow, precise manner. Bristol wasn't sure if he was a neat freak or if the satchels contained something explosive. When he straightened to face them, he didn't speak right away, giving them time to admire him. He was certainly something to behold, in a troubling sort of way. He was tall and quite lean, a scarecrow of sharp angles that his loose robe only partially disguised. His perfectly combed sleek black hair reached his waist, and multiple chains strung with beads hung from his neck. Bristol found his deep-set eyes the most unsettling. Hard and birdlike, the whites barely showed.

Bristol winced when he forced a stiff smile onto his sallow face. It only soured his appearance more.

"I'm here to assist in your instruction," he said. "You will refer to me as Master Reuben as I am the master alchemist of Danu. I'm accomplished at bonding spells to objects, and I specialize in amulets of protection." He motioned to the hundreds of silver, copper, and gold beads adorning his chest. "But none of you will receive any amulets until you've earned them. No exceptions." He waxed on for a good ten minutes about training and rules, but basically his message was no free rides until you learned to protect yourself. She noticed the other recruits fidgeting, and Julia all but rolled her eyes.

Thankfully, Olivia finally took over the lesson and said they'd work on levitation skills that day. "We'll begin with the simplest of spells that even mere mortals can learn."

"Just as a way to warm you up," Esmee chirped more cheerfully. "We know in the mortal world it's difficult to practice magic. Let's get those muscles working again."

Mere mortals?

Bristol prickled at the jab, but at the same time took her first deep breath since instruction began, grateful that even she, a mere mortal, could learn a spell. Maybe this would help cover her shortcomings until she found her father.

Olivia placed an apple on the table in front of each recruit, then went over the elocution of three different spells, because apparently even apples had their standards and responded to some words better than others.

"El. O. Cu. Tion," Reuben harped at Avery as she recited her first spell. "It is not an option like ribbon on a dress!"

Back off, asshole, Bristol thought, but she pasted on a smile and concentrated on the apple in front of her, praying she wouldn't send it hurtling into anyone's head—except for maybe Reuben's.

She said every phrase. Twice. She El—O—Cuted like her life depended on it.

She tried again in perfect French, and then in Spanish.

She wooed. She sang.

She even gave the apple her lethal stare.

It didn't so much as wobble.

Esmee frowned in a sympathetic way. "Having an off day?"

"Yes, that's it," Bristol readily agreed. A very off day.

When the recruits were dismissed, she grabbed the apple and ate it as revenge on her way back to her room. It still felt like the apple had won.

Apparently, she was the merest of all mere mortals.

CHAPTER 29

Bristol sniffed the air. Magic had a scent, she had learned. But in Elphame it was nearly impossible to detect individual scents because magic was everywhere, like being engulfed by the song of a full orchestra. Individual notes blended, but occasionally a few notes rose above the rest, sweet like ripe summer plums, or mysterious like alder smoke, or sensuous like autumn musk.

In the mortal world, magic was a single off-key note that didn't belong—a tangy knife cutting the air that was easy to detect. Fae could easily find other fae this way. The magic of everyday glamour was the exception, for even mortals used glamour in their own rudimentary way to be something they were not. Glamour was as dry and scentless as stale bread.

After three long, grueling days of intensive orientation and lessons, field drills were about to begin. Bristol leaned forward from the observatory deck, praying she would at least be more successful at this. She studied the winding course, certain she could smell the fear of the recruits below her, or maybe it was only her own fear she sensed. There was nothing magical about it.

The training grounds overlooked the distant Badbe Garrison in the valley just south of the palace. They had taken a tour the day before, meeting senior officers and viewing combat drills from afar. The garrison was where most recruits hoped to advance, snagging a coveted position in the ranks of Danu knights, apparently a prestigious appointment. Though it seemed she and her fellow novices were brought there for a very different purpose. *Bloodmarked.* The only mark she had on her was a large stamp on her forehead that said *Impostor.* Luckily, no one had seen it yet. She hoped.

When she and the other recruits had first taken seats on the deck, they saw a woman below wiping tears from her eyes as she was led away. Ivy said she was being sent home. She'd only been in training for a week. Bristol didn't know the woman, or why this was important to her, but she felt her loss, that familiar sense of losing something that was never in her grasp to begin with, all the towns Bristol had to let go of before they were even hers, the connections she never made, the people who didn't notice her absence once she was gone, or even remember her name.

Home. Maybe that was what the woman hoped to find here. Watching her walk away sent urgency beating through Bristol's rib cage. She learned from Esmee that the recruit numbers were quickly dwindling. It was down to their newly arrived six and only a few others. Danu meant business. Finding this door of theirs was as important to them as finding her father was to her. She had to perform better at field training than she had at spells. That morning she blushed with embarrassment when Olivia complimented her fine diction—pathetic pity-praise when there was nothing else to compliment. Throughout the morning every incantation she attempted was as limp and lifeless as overcooked pasta, the kind of pasta Sal would curse and throw out.

Even though the other recruits had grown up in the mortal world and their knowledge of fae history had plenty of missing pieces, they either already knew or quickly learned the basic spells for levitation or how to temporarily glamour simple objects, turning brooms into swords, or teacups into potatoes. This was like boot camp—the essentials a recruit needed to learn—and Bristol couldn't even get a lock of hair to rise in a strong wind.

When they left morning lessons for the training grounds earlier, Hollis slipped her arm through Bristol's, hugged her to her side, and said, "Don't worry about it. It's only been a few days." Julia fell in step on the other side of her. "I didn't master shape-shifting until I was forty. A late bloomer, I guess. You have time."

But Bristol didn't have time. She had already been in Elphame four days, and she wasn't any closer to finding her father. And then last night, Tyghan asked again about who told her trows had taken her father, like she had given him unreliable information. *Are you sure her name is Willow? Because we can't find her.* That didn't surprise Bristol. Willow was always the elusive sort. Bristol pondered his agitation, wondering if, with her lack of progress, he regretted his bargain and thought he was wasting his time. She had to convince him he wasn't.

She leaned forward on the deck rail as Sashka navigated the maze below, her blue skin glistening like a rare jewel in the sun. The maze was made up of tall hedges and twisting pathways like you might see on an old English estate. From her bird's-eye view, Bristol could see the endgame— the prize Sashka was meant to aim for—an opening in the hedges on the other side that led out of the maze, but the twisting pathway was confusing. Obstacles were sprinkled throughout the maze, and her assigned team of officers were making it even more challenging for her. Their distractions made it impossible to concentrate.

"That's Sloan," Avery said. "The one standing by the weapons rack. He used to be First Officer, but when Tyghan was named king, that position went to Kasta. I hear he's not too happy about it. He mostly trains second-year knights down at the garrison, but he's helping out with recruits now because it's more important—even though there's only a few of us left. Apparently they already sucked the nation dry looking for recruits."

Sloan appeared to be cut from the same cloth as Tyghan—an annoying wool that was hot and scratchy. He always had a single brow raised in disdain.

"How did you find all that out?" Bristol asked.

"Paying attention at the festivities. And that's the king's sister in the maze, Princess Melizan." Avery pointed at the silver-haired beauty who had just stepped out from a blind and casually tripped Sashka, sending her face-first to the ground. Sashka rebounded, scrambling back to her feet, then rolled to avoid a swinging pole. Her agility was stunning, and yet Bristol saw she was running in the wrong direction, caught in a mire of zigzags. She wasn't going to make it. A horn blew, its deep bellow vibrating across the observation deck. Her second round was over.

Avery exhaled a pitiful sigh. Julia offered a regretful *hmm*. Melizan walked back to the beginning of the course, agitation sparking in her steps. "I'm glad we're not on her team," Avery whispered.

So Tyghan has a sister, Bristol mused. *Melizan*. She was dressed to perfection. A creamy leather tunic hugged her curves as she strode through the maze clutching a silver riding crop.

Next up was Sashka, who, while petite, was made of pure muscle and grit. When she took her place at the starting position for her third and final attempt to beat the maze, she did a slow, fluid handstand before springing back to her feet. Whether it was for nerves or good luck, Bristol didn't know, but when the horn blew, Sashka leapt through the course like a determined gazelle, flipping and jumping over obstacles as they appeared. At one point it seemed she knew exactly where she was going. Bristol, Avery, and Julia all leaned forward, hoping—but then she took a drastic wrong turn, landing in a dead end, trapped as Melizan's team circled around her like a hungry pride of lions. Bristol guessed that was their version of saying, "You're dead."

Rose and Hollis didn't fare any better. Each of their three attempts ended in failure. Melizan shook her head when the final horn blew and walked away without words to any of them.

Left. Right. Second Right. Left. Third Right. Left. Follow the curve. Third exit in circle. Bristol closed her eyes, repeating the directions, memorizing the maze. All she needed to do was keep her wits about her. She was in her element maneuvering down tight, crowded streets, a sixth sense kicking in. She could do this.

"Get going. You're up."

Bristol's eyes shot open.

Tyghan stood at the end of the observation deck in his leather gear, his sword positioned between his shoulders, with a large knife sheathed at his side. His tunic was snug, his chest a wall of muscle. Behind him stood equally daunting warriors, Dalagorn, Glennis, and Quin, all dressed and armed in similar fashion. It was evident they took their practices seriously.

Tyghan's eyes met hers, a split-second lingering.

There it was again. Some message she couldn't decipher, like there was a history between them, a hidden language she was supposed to know. Like she had crossed him once. At night, he seemed to avoid her at festivities, only watching her from afar, but whenever their gazes met by chance, there were always words simmering behind his eyes.

She stood, eager to get her turn over with, taking a last look at the maze. She blinked. It was *changing*, new pathways forming, roots shifting, branches reaching into new places, becoming an entirely new maze. Her memorized directions dropped like useless keys in her stomach.

When she looked back at Tyghan, his cool eyes studied her again. He knew what she'd been doing. Memorizing a maze was *not* cheating. It was smart preparation. She hardened her stance and nodded toward him to show she was looking forward to his little field games.

Despite three tries each, neither Avery nor Julia made it to the end. Avery came out with a cut on her head that Olivia was tending. Bristol was last, and the long wait had tied her nerves in knots. She knew someone had to go last, but it felt deliberate, like they were setting her up for failure. Her neck ached, and her eyes were dry and hot. She reminded herself that even if she was not a champion gymnast or a stealthy cat, she was strong and fast. She had a chance. She forced calm back into her lungs, breathing deep as she anticipated the obstacles she faced and the team that was ready to deal her blows.

She toed the starting line and glanced up at the blazing sky. *Keep the sun on your left.* It was all she had to go on, assuming the exit was still on the opposite side of the entrance. But this time there were two entrances. Which should she choose?

The horn blew.

She hesitated, surveying the two entrances, and did a double take. *Shit.* Now there were *three* entrances. When did—

Her feet flew out from beneath her, and she slammed across the graveled ground, her right arm taking the brunt of the fall. It took her several seconds to understand what happened. Kasta had tackled her. The horn blew again. Her first try was already over, and she hadn't even taken a single step. Her humiliation stung more than her scraped arm. This was nothing like riding a bike across a busy street.

"You have to move, Keats!" Tyghan yelled from the entrance to the maze. "Stand there, and you're a target. Move! Get to your feet. Try again."

She glared his way. *Thanks for the remarkably obvious advice*, she thought, but pasted on a smile and nodded.

The horn blew before she was even fully standing. She ran, heading for the middle entrance. Blood trickled down her arm. A short way in, the path split. Left. No, right. A pole swung out, knocking her to the ground. She scrambled beneath it, getting up and running again. Forward, left, right, the sun back on her left, and then Dalagorn stepped out, blocking her path. She backtracked, but now the sun was on her right. *Wrong direction, Bristol.* She spun, trying to get reoriented, and then the sun was gone. Out of nowhere, heavy clouds blew in, darkening the sky. Her frustration grew. Tricks! She hated their tricks. She turned a corner to follow another route and ran straight into Quin's chest. He spun her, gripping her roughly against him, and whipped a very real knife to her throat. "Sorry," he said, "looks like you're dead again." Then he released her.

Her third and final attempt was the most terrifying of all. As she turned a corner, she met with a new obstacle that hadn't been in anyone's previous rounds—a sandpit. She leapt, her foot catching the edge, but the pit reached out, grabbing her like a hungry mouth and jerking her down. She fell hard on her stomach and tried to kick free, but its grip was more like steel than sand. Her leg burned as a thousand tiny sandy teeth tore through her trousers and bit into her calf. Her nails dragged across the ground as she was pulled deeper into the pit. She flailed desperately, grabbing for anything, and felt her hand grip something hard, the branch of a hedge, but even that wasn't enough, and her grasp slipped. "Help!" she finally cried out, terrified of being pulled all the way under the sand. "Help me!"

The pit released her, and she crawled out on her hands and knees, staring at the ground, her throat throbbing. Quin's boots loomed in her vision, and his sword swept a line in the dirt as a threatening reminder. "I know! I know! I'm dead," she snapped. Fury was the only thing that helped her get to her feet.

Tyghan stepped around a corner, shaking his head. He said nothing, though the scorn on his face was blistering.

What was his problem?

"Back to the starting line. A fourth round," Kasta said.

"But—" Bristol glanced back and forth between Tyghan and Kasta. She was tired, sore, and bleeding, and she'd already done three rounds. "But everyone else only had—"

"Don't question an officer's orders," Quin barked. "Back to the start."

But Bristol stepped past Kasta and yelled to Tyghan, who was already walking away. "So, you lay out all the tricks and traps, and I don't get any weapons. It's hardly fair that you have them all."

He turned. "I agree. Find the weapons. Take them. No one's going to do you any favors out in the Wilds."

"Including you, it appears. I thought it was my team's job to protect me."

"We might all be dead. Then what? You need to have the basic skills to save yourself."

Dead?

If there was any chance of them dying, what chance did she have? So much for crossing busy streets. This was more like being blindfolded on a rush-hour freeway. That was why he avoided promising her she wouldn't die. It was obvious now. She was glad she had demanded the second piece of art up front. Maybe she would demand a third, though what she really wanted at that moment was steel-tipped boots to kick his shins.

Quin led her out of the maze. *Find weapons.* Great advice that was. She didn't see any lying around. And wrestle a sword from Dalagorn? Or even Quin? Not likely. She wouldn't even know how to use one anyway. The only weapon she had ever used—

"Get to your starting position," Glennis ordered, though a shade kinder than the others.

Once there, Bristol didn't wait for the horn to blow. She ran fast, despite shouts calling her back. Her neck at stake—her rules. Through the middle entrance. Right. Left. This time when she leapt over a sand-pit, she cleared it. But at the next turn, a pole shot out from a hedge, jamming into her belly. She bent over, gasping for breath, a flash of pain burning under her ribs, but then managed to wrench the pole free from the shrubs, gripping it in both hands. She had some tricks, too. She continued to run, forgetting the sun and the sudden wind that was blowing leaves and dust into her eyes. Right. Left. Second exit in circle. She was gaining more ground this time, but then Tyghan stepped out of a blind. She thrust the pole into his side, catching him by surprise, then swung again, hitting his forearm and sending him reeling back into the bushes. But it was a short victory because he instantly emerged again, now with a stick in his hand, too.

They struck out at each other, the clash of sticks vibrating in the air, the fierce jolts stinging her bare hands and pulsing through her arms. His strikes were far stronger than Cat's, who she used to practice with, and he beat her backward step by step. His blows were relentless and methodical, like he was playing with her and letting her wear herself out—and she was. Her muscles burned, and her irritation surged. *Of course he's playing with me.* He towered over her, and all those muscles in his arms weren't there just for looks. He was twice her size, and he could probably send her sailing out of the maze with one strike if he wanted to.

But there were ways . . . if she could just get around him . . . disable him long enough to slip past. She wasn't above hitting him anywhere that would do the job. Winning was all that mattered, not how you got the win. She aimed low, jabbing her stick toward his crotch, but only managed to graze his thigh. He scowled, and his next strike came harder. She tried to adjust her grip so she would have a longer reach, but he was too close now, and his blows were coming faster. She spun, lunging backward as she freed the grip of one hand, then swung toward his head. She hoped to stun him, maybe even draw blood. It was a risky move, since now she had a weaker defense against his advances. She almost made contact with his skull, but she wasn't watching his feet—a stupid mistake—and one of his boots hooked around her knee, and she fell backward. The stick flew from her hand as she landed flat on her back with a loud *oomph*.

Tyghan pressed the end of his pole to her throat, firmly pinning her. The horn blew. Dead again. He stared down at her, his chest still heaving from the fight, mulling her fate, then said, "Your father taught you sticks." It was part question, part statement, and maybe part surprise.

She nodded gingerly.

He lifted the pole from her neck and tossed it aside. "Not well enough." He reached down to give her a hand up. A sheen of moisture glistened across his face, which gave her some satisfaction. His victory didn't come without at least a little sweat. She took his offered hand, his grip firm as he pulled her to her feet, but he didn't let go. He looked at her injuries, first the bloody scrape on her forearm and then her shredded trouser leg flecked with blood. His eyes met hers, that same uncertain question in them, like he knew something dreadful about her.

He released her hand. "Olivia will take care of your arm and leg," he said, and turned to leave.

"Or you could," she replied, still wondering if he was capable of any magic besides surly disappearances. Surely as ruler of a whole nation poised for war, he could do more than blink out of sight. She was almost certain he had healed her lip on her first night there.

He looked back over his shoulder and rolled past her question. "Be ready at dusk. I'll take you into the city to find your trows."

Your trows. Like she was wasting his time on a fool's errand.

"I can go on my own if it's too much trouble."

He snorted and kept walking.

CHAPTER 30

N*ot a pixie.*

The snake's tongue flicked to life.

Nor a sprite. Oh, but how he loved wood sprites. Ssso easy.

The golden serpent shivered free of the frame that held the hallway mirror, its carved wooden details transforming to scale and flesh. He slithered silently behind the intruder, his shimmering movement ghostly across the black marble floor. He eyed the large figure, disheartened that he'd been forbidden from eating creatures a long time ago. Still, the thought was something to hold on to. *Just one bite.* He missed the succulent juices in his mouth, the bulge in his belly.

He took note of the creature's path, where it gazed, what it touched, because it was the snake's task to report everything, even the inconsequential. The creature wandered aimlessly, its head cocked to the side, moving forward in starts and stops. *A confused rabbit*, the snake thought, his mouth aching with want.

And then the creature called out, "Cat?"

The serpent's tongue flicked out with hope.

Cat? Where?

Oh, how he'd love to caress a nice juicy cat.

But the creature had tricked him. There was no scent of cat, no matter how many times he tasted the air. The only thing he craved more in that moment, craved above all else, was a masked ferret. A very specific one that had long mocked him, always scampering out of his reach. Even if he couldn't eat him, one day he would catch the wily beast and embrace him so tightly, his little vermin eyes would pop out. That would be almost as satisfying as feeling him squirm in his belly. *Sssomeday.*

Bristol's heart skipped as the faint words rose and fell.

. . . the rose is full blown . . .

Searching for the source, she meandered down hallways that finally led to a closed door. It was Cat singing, she was almost certain, and it made her bolder.

. . . mosses and flowers to . . .

She knocked, and when there was no answer, she went in, her attention immediately drawn to a large mirror dominating the foyer. Its elaborately embellished frame teemed with flora, fauna, and a beautifully carved snake that wove in and out of its border.

Whose rooms were these? She stepped cautiously into the main hall, following the tune. As she moved through the suite of rooms, she didn't notice the snake wriggling free from its moorings. She was only focused on the whisper of a song that ebbed and rose like a fickle tide as she tried to find it.

The first room she encountered was a sitting room with an eclectic collection of furnishings that spanned the centuries, from Gothic to classical, but mostly they were unique pieces that couldn't be wedged into any art period she had ever studied. Elphame had its own unique style. Her attention was particularly captured by an enormous armoire with bronze doors containing detailed reliefs like something Lorenzo Ghiberti might have sculpted, though it told a very different history. It was a story of forests, stags, swords, and all manner of creatures engaged in deadly or amorous activities. In the center of the room were two plum sofas and a low table. Its base was carved to resemble multiple stalks of bundled barley. That was part of their lesson that day—the many things the Tuatha de took great pride in, foremost among them their horses, their art, their might, and of course, their plows and fields.

As she ventured farther down a hallway, she came to a bedroom more sparsely furnished than the previous room. Despite its expanse, it only held a large bed with a plain white blanket and a wardrobe. Tall Palladian windows at the far end of the room looked out to a stunning view of Danu. The sky was ribboned with violet seams, and the light spilling through the windows cast a lavender glow on the white fur rug at the end of the bed.

In the corner, almost lost in shadows, was a circular stone staircase. Bristol stilled, her head turned to the side, listening. Was the tune coming from there? She swiftly crossed the room, but the melody stopped abruptly. Before she could register disappointment, the tune was replaced with a nondescript hum that was steadily growing louder. An oddly familiar hum, but not human. *What was it?* She crept up the steps and faced a single door at the top of the landing. She pulled in a deep breath, hoping no one was inside, and warily pushed it open.

The room was empty, and she stepped into a large, messy study crowded with furnishings and odd collectibles. In the corner was a strange green globe with lands and seas and clouds flashing with lightning. A marble owl with burning yellow eyes stared at her from a shelf, looking like it could come alive at any moment. On the desk, at least a dozen misshapen stubs of melted candles leaned drunkenly atop tall brass candlesticks. Their wax had wept over the drip plates onto the desk and hardened into puddles.

Maps and etchings filled one entire wall in mismatched frames. Two frames lay shattered on the floor. Open books beside them appeared to be the missiles of their destruction. More books teetered in piles everywhere. Besides those stacked on the desk, books were piled on a nearby window ledge, and still more on an overstuffed ottoman—more books than could fit in the empty spots on the bookshelves lining the wall. The borrowed books of an avid reader? Frenzied research—or madness? She eyed the shattered frames on the floor and guessed the latter. Compared to the rest of the suite, the room seemed abandoned. Dust frosted the desk like a timestamp. But when she turned, the wall behind her was the most frightening of all. Tally marks. Hundreds of them. Some groups had only a few marks; others had a dozen or more. Some small, some large, some carved into the wall with a knife, and others made with dark liquid that dripped down the wall. Blood? Just below the marks was a green velvet chaise. A long gash ran its length, as if someone had mistaken it for a fish in need of gutting. Its stuffing oozed out like a layer of fat.

The musical scales started up again, clear as a starry night, and Bristol's heart jumped to her throat.

Cat.

Please don't let this be another trick.

Even though she knew it couldn't be her sister, it didn't keep her from frantically hunting for the source, if only to be closer. She searched behind the heavy drapes, a chair, and even peeked into a cabinet, but it held only ledgers and ink.

And then a bare breeze.

A cool tickle around her ankles.

And the scent of fresh laundry.

She dropped to her knees and peered beneath a side table piled with dirty goblets and plates.

All that greeted her was a gray stone wall. Still, she crept closer, reaching out to touch the stone, and her hand disappeared—into the wall. She gasped and jerked back, banging her head on the top of the table. Dishes rattled above her, but for a brief moment, a circle of bright light the size of a dinner plate spilled into the room, and the sound amplified. She moved forward on her knees again, pressing her hand to the same spot, and the blinding light returned, but as her eyes adjusted, she saw through to the other side.

Two beady eyes stared back at her.

It was Angus.

He sat alert on his haunches, balancing on the top of a washing machine, as shocked to see her as she was to see him.

Bristol blinked. Dug her nails into her palms to make sure she wasn't hallucinating.

A portal, she thought. *That's what this is. Some kind of portal.*

The knocking hum she'd heard was from the dryer in her mudroom.

Her sisters were doing laundry.

CHAPTER 31

Harper screamed. An arm shot out from the wall over the washing machine and waved madly. She dropped her basket of laundry and crashed back against the cabinet. Angus flew through the air like he had wings, to avoid the flailing arm—and then it disappeared back into the wall. Harper trembled, too afraid to move for fear the arm would appear again, but then a voice called out, "Harper, it's me! Bri!"

Harper remained frozen against the cabinet, certain it was a trap, but the voice called out again.

It sounded like Bri.

She cautiously stepped closer, peering into the dark hole in the wall. She saw two amber eyes looking back at her.

"My god, Bri! What happened?" Harper cried. "Are you . . . inside the wall? How did you—"

"I'm not in a wall. I'm here. In Elphame," Bristol whispered.

"What have they done to you?"

"Shhh," Bristol said, keeping her voice low. "Nothing. I'm fine. I promise. I think . . . I think this might be a portal."

She explained to Harper the deal she had made with the fae, what she had learned, and that one of them was taking her to question trows about their father in a short while.

"Faeries fostered Daddy?" Harper asked. "*That's* who raised him?"

"Yes."

"So there really is an Aunt Jasmine?"

"A foster aunt, yes, but I haven't had a chance to ask her questions yet. Did you take the art to Sonja like I told you?"

"Yes. She gave us a thousand dollars just like you said and sent the art off to experts. Yesterday more art was delivered and when we took it to her, she gave us another thousand dollars. What's going on, Bristol? Is this illegal?"

"No. It comes from this Aunt Jasmine's personal collection. At least that's what they told me."

Harper peered closer. "Where *are* you? Are you under a table?"

"Yes. I snuck into someone's room and found this portal. . . ." Bristol shook her head, not sure how to explain the strange passageway. It was nothing like the portal they had passed through to come here. That one had been enormous. "I have to hurry, Harper. Go get your book about this world. I need to know more. I don't even know which questions to ask. Hurry, go—"

"*Snuck?* I thought you said you were okay? I thought—"

"The book, Harper! Get the book! Now!"

Harper ran.

Bristol listened to the clanking hum of the dryer. Why was there a portal here that led to their mudroom? Even if the portal was small—so small it was impossible for anyone to get through. Was someone spying on her family? Or had her parents been spying on someone in this room?

She pushed against the edges of the portal, trying to enlarge it, but it didn't budge. Maybe it was one of those old portals Madame Chastain had mentioned, wiped from the records long ago but never fully closed. This one's small size made it useless. Maybe she should ask—*No, I better keep this one to myself so no one will find out I was snooping, and lock it away from me.* It was her only lifeline to her sisters.

Angus slinked back into the mudroom, sidling close to the broom. His shiny black eyes studied her. If a ferret could have a disapproving expression, his was condemning. Or maybe he was just leery of a human stuck inside a wall.

Harper rushed back in, at least Bristol thought it was Harper's footsteps until Cat's face loomed in front of her. Her eyes were swollen.

"What the hell do you think you're doing? I told you not to meet with anyone! I told you—"

"Cat, they took Daddy. Willow told me. It was trows that Mother and Father were running from all their lives. I had to—"

But Cat was already wound up for a long one and went on a lecturing tirade that ended in tears, ordering Bristol to return. "Come home. Now!" she cried.

Bristol reached through the portal and grabbed Cat's hand. "I can't. I'm committed to this." Her sister tried to pull away, but Bristol held on strong like when they were kids and they used to help each other up to a high tree branch. There was no letting go. They'd sooner tumble from the tree themselves than let the other fall. It was all or nothing. It didn't matter how old they were now; that bond was still there. It would be there forever. "Listen to me, Cat. Please. I made a bargain with the person in charge here, and I'm going to keep it. He's going to help me find Daddy. Once the art checks out, the money will be more than enough to—"

"We don't need any money, Bri," Cat pleaded. "The gallery called. Someone bought Daddy's painting for more money than Sonja was asking. All we need is *you*."

Bristol's heart twisted like it was being torn in two. She and her sister had a bargain, too. It was Cat who stood by her. Cat who understood her insecurities, Cat who was always there, not just sister, but best friend, too. After their mother died, Cat landed a full scholarship to the music institute. Bristol mourned for days after she left, but she was happy for her at the same time because Cat had a rare gift that deserved to be cultivated. Likewise, she grieved for Cat when she returned home, leaving a promising future behind. Cat came home when Bristol and Harper needed her. That was all Cat was asking for now. *Come home.* But what about their father? He needed her too.

"I can't leave Daddy behind if he's alive. He was always there for us. He came every time we got lost, every time we needed him," Bristol pleaded. "And we need answers. What if they come for us next? We can't run forever, Cat. Don't you want to stop running too?"

Cat leaned over the washer, like she had no strength left in her. She buried her face in her arms and silently sobbed.

Bristol's knees weakened. The worry Cat carried was breaking her. "It's going to be all right. I promise."

Cat looked up, shaking off tears that were long overdue. "It's my job to take care of you."

"And you've always watched out for me. Let me carry this load for a while."

Cat's eyes were glistening green pools, searching for another argument, not willing to let go, but then Harper rushed in, distracting them both.

"I've got it!" she proclaimed. She tried to shove the book through the portal, but it was too large to go through the small opening, no matter which way she turned it. Harper's brows pulled down as she contemplated the solution. She knew what she needed to do even though Bristol was certain it went against every book principle inside her. This would be far worse than creasing the corner of a page—it was practically book murder. Harper flipped back the covers, twisting and yanking at them like she was shucking a stubborn piece of corn, until they finally ripped free from the spine.

Doubt stabbed Bristol. Was she asking too much? Her sisters needed her. But Bristol needed something too, and it wasn't just her father's return. Something dark prowled inside her. There was a toll to be paid. Someone needed to pay for their years of moving on, for all the friendships she never got to make, for all the middle-of-the-night departures, for all the beds she could never call her own, for all the mercies her parents never received, for all the reasons that made them run.

Even if her sisters seemed reluctant, their silent acquiescence made Bristol believe they wanted those same things too. Bristol would collect the toll for them all.

Harper tossed aside the covers and rolled the remaining pages into a neat circle and passed them through the portal to Bristol.

"My apologies to Anastasia Wiggins," Bristol said.

An unsteady laugh jumped from Harper's throat. "I think she'd understand."

Be careful, little sister.

Be careful, big sister.

They didn't say the words aloud, but Bristol read it in their eyes as she said goodbye.

"Find him," Cat whispered, her throat thick with tears.

Bristol nodded. "I have to go. Another month. Max. I promise."

She cursed herself for saying it, knowing now how big this fairy world was. As she pulled her arm back to her side, her sisters disappeared from view, and the wall returned to stone. She remained crouched on the floor under the table, pressing the heels of her hands against her eyes until the stinging ebbed.

And then she heard something. The slamming of a door.

CHAPTER 32

Halfway down the curving staircase, Bristol stopped and pressed her back to the stone wall. There was noise coming from below. *Running water.* Her stomach somersaulted.

Someone had returned to the room.

Bathing? *Yes*, she decided, *they must be in the bath chamber.* Now was her only chance to sneak past them. She took off her shoes, not trusting the leather soles against the marble, and tiptoed down the remaining steps.

She was on the last step when the rush of water stopped. It was now or never. She was partway across the room, sneaking across the luxurious white fur rug at the foot of the bed, when a voice called out.

"Looking for something?"

She whirled.

It was Tyghan. A very wet Tyghan. He didn't seem to notice or care that his towel hung perilously low around his hips. Messy black strands of hair dripped over his brow onto his muscled and glistening chest. Hot needles stabbed her stomach. A trail of wet footsteps puddled on the dark floor behind him. *Look away, Bristol*, she told herself, but instead she stared, frozen, her thoughts reeling. Every inch of him was—

She swallowed. His shoulders, his chest, the tight ripples above his navel . . . He was like a statue chiseled from a single perfect piece of Carrara marble. Almost perfect. She thought about all the museum basements she had explored, looking at half-finished sculptures the masters had set aside because of some perceived flaw in the stone. Every inch of him was exquisite, except for one glaring flaw—a long, jagged scar on his left side. It looked like someone had tried to carve out his liver with a dull knife.

She forced her eyes away from Tyghan's abdomen and low-slung towel and met his gaze. Her temples blazed with heat, and she prayed he couldn't see it. "I'm sorry. I took a wrong turn. I didn't know this was your room."

He didn't answer, his cool eyes boring into her.

Her face grew hotter. "Really, I'm very sorry I interrupted your . . . bath. I—"

"It's not a problem. I suppose it could be easy to get lost in these halls. Though this room doesn't look anything like yours."

His tone was mocking. It was, indeed, a problem. A huge one.

"I realize that," she replied. "I just thought there might be another route through here and then I saw the stairs, and I—" *Stop, Bristol.* Her explanation was going from bad to pathetic. She was usually quite good at spinning half-truths, but not when speaking to a half-naked man in his own room she had just broken into. This was new territory for her, and her game was definitely lacking polish.

He eyed the shoes in her hand.

"They were pinching my feet," she explained.

"Really? Now, that's disappointing. I can probably take care of it, though. Sit down and put them on for me." He motioned behind her.

She glanced over her shoulder. *His bed?* Not a chance. "I don't want to trouble you. They just need breaking in. That's all."

He eyed her other hand and raised his brows. She had forgotten she was clutching the book Harper had given her.

"I brought it from home. Reading material."

"And you hate to be without a book, even when wandering the halls."

He was toying with her, she knew, letting her dig a deeper hole before he pushed her into it. It was time to stop playing his game and create her own. She knew something that might send his mind reeling in a new direction. "I'm sorry about your brother."

The amused glint in his eyes faded.

There, that's much better, Bristol thought, though she really was sorry about Cael. When it came to family, she didn't like playing games. Still, it was good to see him caught off-balance for a change. He looked at her like she had struck him, no reply forthcoming, but then his jaw tightened and his expression grew infinitely more dangerous.

"Madame Chastain told us about him and your predicament," she went on. "I'd be an angry pain in the ass, too, if—"

"Don't act like you know me. You don't."

"I completely agree. But I'm *trying* to know you, and the only thing you're giving me to work with is anger."

"I am *not* angry."

"Of course you are. You're always angry. You've just become comfortable with it and can't see it anymore. Don't get me wrong, though, I'm not blaming you. My sisters are my world, and I'd be full of rage, too, if anyone hurt them. I'd do anything to protect them, so I think I understand at least part of your anger."

She edged forward, her bare toes curling into the thick fur rug. "And today . . . I know I was less than impressive, but I'll do better tomorrow. I promise I'll do whatever I can to help you get your brother back safely." Bristol meant every word and waited for a reaction, hoping for a crack in his armor.

The air grew warmer between them, and he stared at her like he was trying to see inside her mind. His expression softened. "And just how much art will that little promise cost me?" he asked.

Her stomach clenched like she'd been punched. She spun, and walked to the door.

"It's almost dusk," he called after her. "Wait in the hallway while I get dressed."

Tyghan watched her leave, her bare feet padding across the floor, her shoes dangling from her hand. *I'll do better tomorrow. I promise.*

In just a few words, she turned the conversation from her being an intruder caught in the act, to being a sympathetic confidante trying to gain his trust, to painting him as the wrongdoer in his own room. His blood burned with her condescending air. He still wasn't sure what had happened. Her words tore through his head. *You're always angry.* So what? He had reason to be and didn't need to explain himself to her. Who did she think she was?

He stormed into the entry foyer where a large mirror dominated the wall.

"Wake," he ordered. "What was she doing in here?"

The snake stretched to life, its coils rippling, eyes opening, blinking. It seemed like it was already a century ago that the intruder had disturbed his peace. "The creature that was here? It was lost, like a rabbit, it was. It wandered aimlessly, touching nothing. It said it was searching for a cat."

"You spoke to her?"

"No. I heard the creature call out. But there was no cat. It lied. I followed it up the stairs to your study—"

"*My study?*" Sweat sprung across Tyghan's face.

"Yesss. And then the creature fell to the floor, talking to the air. Addlebrained, it was. Or possessed."

"What did she say?"

The snake's golden scales shimmered as it shifted its position on the frame. It was trying to buy time. It had become distracted by the strong scent of ferret and gone in search of it, not hearing every word the creature uttered. It was all nonsense anyway. "It rambled, my lord. It made little sense. Pleading and yelling, saying something about a bargain, wailing into the air for books. Bewitched, I think. Not to be trusted, that one. Choke the creature, I can. Choke it dead. Shall I kill it the next time it comes?"

The king was quiet, and the snake grew hopeful. Oh, it hadn't killed anything in ssssuch a long time. Not even a mouse.

"No. There won't be a next time. Sleep, Daiedes," Tyghan ordered.

The snake's stomach rumbled, and it rooted back into the frame, its dreams unsated for now.

Sometimes Tyghan thought the snake was useless. Daiedes was only two decades into his sentence, and had already forgotten he had once been a man. But the philanderer certainly hadn't forgotten his lesson. Never cheat on a witch. Especially not the High Witch of Danu.

Tyghan walked up the stairs to his study. He avoided the room and hadn't been back there in months. As soon as he stepped inside it again, he felt the room sway, like he had stepped back in time. Every corner was in shambles, ravaged by a madman who fell into a hole six months ago and was still trying to climb his way out. He couldn't remember most of the time he had spent in there. But he remembered enough, the shadows and the voices.

He stepped out again and closed the door behind him, steadying himself against the wall. What had Keats thought when she saw it? What did she think of him now?

The contents seemed untouched, the thick dust undisturbed. Was Daiedes right? She was only a lost rabbit? Delusional? He doubted that.

I'll do whatever I can to help.

Yes, she would. She couldn't even begin to know the ways she might ultimately be useful. But as he dressed to meet her, he couldn't shake her last expression of loathing. Her promise to do all in her power hadn't come with extra strings attached. He was the one who had put them there.

Always angry. She was right about that much. Maybe he was afraid not to be.

CHAPTER 33

Whispers traveled as softly as downy feathers on a current of air. *Knights are in the streets. Asking questions.*

Of course, the knights tried to be discreet, but they rarely rode into the city in the morning, and never in such a hurry. Their white steeds breathed curling steam into the crisp air. *They stopped to see Mae first*, a red cap told a hob. *And then they raced toward the east side.*

Mae jingled the gold in her pocket as she slipped back into her shop. The gold brought her less satisfaction than it usually did, but gold was gold, after all. Only a fool passed up such an auspicious deal. Of course, it would only go into her hidden chest, as one never knew when a fortune might be necessary, and Mae had been stockpiling her riches for centuries.

Still, she wondered about the simple request and how it could possibly be worth ten pieces of gold.

Easiest money she ever made. Knights were fools.

Across the city, in a windowless room on Finvarra Bridge, a trow pleaded for his life, swearing he hadn't spoken to the daughter, that he knew nothing about a Logan Keats. But the knight who broke into the tower room knew otherwise, knew this particular trow had been asking questions about Bristol, that he had a loose tongue and would give up his own mother for a piece of silver.

"Whether you do or you don't, this will ensure that you say nothing—and send a message to other trows of your ilk to hold their tongues as well."

"I promise—"

The trow leapt forward, knowing his pleas were futile, his teeth ready to sink into flesh. He recognized the knight as the one who was presumed dead. Surprise was all the trow had in his favor, but the jeweled sword slashed with skill, lightning fast and determined.

The trow's head toppled from his shoulders, hitting the ground with a solid thunk.

The nice thing about trows was, they were mostly bloodless. The knight cleaned the sword that delivered the fatal blow on the trow's own tattered coat until the steel gleamed once more, then shoved the blade back into its scabbard before slinking down the back stairwell unnoticed. But by then the knight had already shape-shifted into something else, a small four-footed creature skittering through the shadows.

By midday every known trow in the city was rooted out, questioned, dispatched, or had run on their own, but whispers still rippled, stretching past the city, into the Wilds. *Knights are on the hunt for trows—trows who knew the Butcher of Celwyth.*

And other rumors rippled lower and closer to chests, rumors passed trow to trow: *The get of Celwyth is here hunting, too.*

Tyghan ordered a carriage to take into the city. Keats had no experience with horses, not to mention a carriage was more discreet. Heads tended to turn when the king rode past, and he didn't want tongues wagging. Especially not about him and Keats.

She sat opposite him, her shoes now back on her feet, her hands kneading her thighs.

It was lost, like a rabbit.

Tyghan tugged on his sleeve. All his clothing was tight tonight, and the silent ride was intolerably long. He smelled the scent of lavender on her hair. Maybe a horse would have been better. He should have ordered a couple of dapples. Surely she could handle that much. He glanced at her, then back out the window, watching for their destination. Block after block plodded past. He finally banged on the roof, and the driver stopped.

Tyghan already knew what they would find at the end of Mugwort Street, but he went through the charade anyway.

They roamed the winding cobbled lane, and he let Bristol ask the questions. "Have you seen trows down this way?"

The milliner, who had already been paid handsomely earlier that day, stepped out of his shop and pointed to a door at the end of the street. Bristol knocked, but there was no answer. Tyghan pushed open the door, and light from the streetlamp flooded in to reveal a few bits of trash, a pile of rotting fish heads, and an overwhelming stench. Nothing else. Bristol covered her nose and stared at the emptiness.

"Looks like they've been gone for a while," Tyghan said.

Her attention shifted to other shops down the street. He saw the disappointment in her eyes, the creases around them as she peered from one side of street to the other, but she didn't give up. She questioned others on the lane about where the trows might have gone or where others might be found. No one knew anything. Tyghan knew there was not another trow left in the city, but he let her ask her questions, fulfilling his promise, including a return visit to speak with Mae.

"No," Mae answered soundly. "No one in the city has ever heard of a Logan Keats."

"But did you ask—"

"No one!"

Tyghan saw Bristol's lashes flutter briefly, caught off guard by Mae's harsh reply. It was clear she had been dismissed and the street mother was finished with questions. Bristol's expression went from eager to empty, her emotion smoothly reeled back like a finely crafted crossbow. She was no novice in managing situations—at least not once she knew what she was dealing with. She nodded slowly, not in agreement but in awareness that the street mother was not the ally she had hoped for. She generously thanked Mae anyway, perhaps hopeful favor might turn her way yet again, but as she stepped back inside the carriage, Mae shot Tyghan a larcenous nod, acknowledgment of a fair transaction. Mae would not be turning, not as long Tyghan's treasury remained full.

The ride back to the palace was silent except for the clip of hooves on cobble. Bristol stared out the window, not reacting to any of the sights they passed, her thoughts wrapped as tightly as a cocoon.

But Tyghan had a strong sense of the questions consuming her. *Where were the trows? What if her father really was dead? What if coming here was a terrible mistake? Why was the king such an ass?*

It was none of his concern, but her silence made him fidget. "I suppose you'll need to keep looking elsewhere," he finally said, hoping it would prompt her to speak.

She only nodded without breaking her gaze out the window.

When they arrived at the palace, she immediately reached for the carriage door, obviously eager to be rid of his company, but then paused, turning to face him. "I'm sure you thought I was stupid and naive to think it would be so easy to find my father, and you'd be absolutely right. I imagined I'd trip into your world, call his name, and that would be the end of it. For my entire life, my father was never farther than a call away. . . ." Her voice wavered.

Tyghan pushed back in his seat, deepening the darkness between them.

"But I want you to know," she continued more firmly, "you're very wrong about something else. My father did teach me well. If I'm not accomplished at sticks, it's through every fault of my own, and not my father's. You may think poorly of me, but please do not think poorly of him. My father is skilled and clever. Whatever he learned of sticks while he was here in your world, he learned it well."

She was still thinking about his comment from earlier that day? Tyghan searched for a reply, one that wasn't angry or sharp—an answer that would admit nothing that wasn't true. "I'm sure I would find your father to be a worthy opponent."

CHAPTER 34

The palace grounds were a labyrinth of walkways, courtyards, and dead ends. It had been built and rebuilt over millennia, magic and dreams always stirring in the artisans to create more. Architecture styles overlapped like a feast of favorite foods brought to a single table, somehow weaving together in harmony, a tribute to the artisans' craft and vision.

Cully knew every twist, turn, and playful trap. And some traps that weren't so playful. For decades his father had been one of those artisans, but when his father returned to his homeland of Eideris, Cully stayed behind. Danu was the only home he had ever known, and from an early age he had set his sights on becoming a knight.

When he was invited to join Tyghan's company, he couldn't believe his good fortune, so he didn't begrudge his current duty of nursemaid. Much. He had waited at the carriage portico for Bristol, to escort her back to her room as Tyghan had ordered—but this recruit made him uneasy. He saw her resemblance to her parents, even if no one else did, though elven always were better at details. The first thing he noticed was the underlying hint of red in her hair, which Maire was reputed to have. And then there was the arch of her left brow that was slightly higher than the right—like Kierus's. It was the weight of her steps he noted now, deliberate and unerring like she was navigating a fated path—another trait of her father's. But as he thought about it, he wondered if maybe it wasn't the similarities that made him uneasy, but the differences. He had never seen a worry cross Kierus's brow. He had admired that about him, a mortal navigating the fae world with so much confidence. This girl's brow betrayed her confident steps.

"You don't need to walk me back," she said. "I can find my way."

"I'm sure you can. But I am tasked with your safety."

"Are the palace grounds really so dangerous?"

Cully shrugged. "No, but they're large and confusing, and you are new."

The brow. He saw it again. The tug that said she was frustrated. He couldn't read her mind, but she wasn't quite her parents' daughter—which might prove a disappointment to Eris. Or maybe a relief? It could go either way. Cully understood about not being quite like a parent. His father never did grasp why he chose knighthood over a chisel and stone, but being a knight wasn't a choice for Cully. It was a calling. Were Tyghan and Eris expecting something from Keats that simply wasn't there? It was understandable. They were down to eleven recruits, and he was certain most of them didn't have what they needed.

Cully motioned for Bristol to turn. "Down this way. Judge's Walk. See? I do know a few shortcuts. You might learn something from me, after all."

Bristol barely noted the path as she walked beside Cully, still preoccupied with her lack of success and Mae's sudden dismissal. Had she pushed Mae too much? Making friends was not easy in this world, or maybe she was just gloriously bad at it. Growing up, she'd had dozens of could-have-been friends, other children her age she met at motels, splashing in pools with them, and others she met while sitting on laundromat benches playing string and guessing games before one of them had to leave. But as she got older, she stopped trying, maybe because she didn't like the wondering hole their brief encounters left in her. Where did they go? Would they remember her? It was easier not to bother. Even once she was on her own, she was too busy trying to survive to make the effort. Only recently had she been testing out the friendship waters with Sal and Mayor Topz.

But here there was a certain ruthless need for relationships. Be friendly in return for help. It was more of a cool business deal than a friendship, but maybe it was one way to grow a friendship, the deeper kind where intimacies were shared. *Intimacy.* It was sorely lacking in her life.

Cully, at least, smiled often, wide and generous. It seemed genuine, and the slight gap between his front teeth was endearing, making him look younger than his twenty years.

"I saw you last night whittling on an arrow. Is that a pastime, or are you required to make your own weapons?"

Cully laughed. "You don't know about elven arrows?"

Bristol shook her head. "No."

"They kill. Every time. When shot by an elven hand, that is. It's not a pastime. More of a survival strategy. But creating them is something I do enjoy. It's a repetitive activity that frees the mind. Knitting intrigues me too. One day I might take it up."

"So you can knit deadly sweaters?"

He grinned. "Now that's a worthy goal."

They walked down a short flight of stairs onto a wide, roofless colonnade. Tall columns that served no apparent purpose lined their path. They were only halfway down the walkway when a screech pierced the air. Bristol reeled backward as the marble of one column came alive, a monstrous head jutting toward her with teeth and scales and flared nostrils. She screamed as a marble dragon strained toward her, nearly pinning her against the opposite column.

Cully grabbed her arm and pulled her a safe distance away. "It's all right. All show, no bite. Sorry, that hasn't happened in years. He must have sniffed new blood passing by."

He stepped toward the writhing head of the beast, placing his palm on the creature's marble snout. "Lovely, isn't she, Pengary? We all think so, too. But you still have centuries to go. Back with you." Cully gave him a small shove and the creature keened with a pitiful whine before it retreated, and the column became smooth stone once again.

Bristol's chest pounded. "What was *that*? What is this place?" she asked, still staring at the now smooth column.

Cully smiled. "Judge's Walk. We sometimes have banquets down here to rouse them from their stupors. Looks like we only need you."

"Rouse *who*?"

"The worst of the worst. Malefactors who've committed crimes against the people of Elphame." He motioned for them to continue walking. As they did, he told her Pengary was a shape-shifter during the eighth epoch and a trusted counselor to Queen Breona, but organized a plot to kill her in order to take control of the throne. Criminals who perpetrated regicide were sentenced to something worse than beheading and death: a millennium of imprisonment to contemplate their treachery. Cully stopped and pressed his hand against the smooth side of one column, explaining that from their marble prisons they could see but never touch, smell but never taste, desire but never have. "Life passes them by on a daily basis, but they can't be part of it. By the time their sentence is over, they beg for death."

"Is he a dragon?"

"Of sorts. An avydra. A fair-enough-sized one too, but not like the giant wild ones of the north seas. His kind are far more cunning. Like I said, he's a shape-shifter, sometimes fully human, sometimes the beast you just saw. They've been banned from Danu and most of the kingdoms of Elphame for centuries. Their thirst for power is legendary. Luckily, their kind is dying out."

"Did Pengary do it? Murder her?"

Cully nodded. "Burned her to death, actually. Then ate her. And her three young heirs, to be sure the job was done."

Ate her?

Bristol gawked at the tall columns lining their path, her gaze trailing their entire length. "Do all these have prisoners?"

"Not yet," he answered. "Like I said, these are only for the worst of the worst. Those who need to suffer before they die."

Bristol's heart was finally settling back into a normal rhythm when she said goodbye to Cully. She shut her door and leaned against it, closing her eyes.

Tyghan loomed in the darkness behind her lids, his hair dripping onto his bare chest, the towel low around his waist—and his scar. He'd been furious that she saw him that way, like she had discovered a dark secret. His scar wasn't from a physician's knife. Someone had tried to kill him. *Who?* she wondered. Maybe the worst of the worst that Cully had mentioned. It was surprising he survived at all.

She eyed her bed longingly, but forced herself to walk to her wardrobe and fling open the doors. It was time to go make friends, to seek out whatever information she could find. Her new apparel ranged from practical to ridiculously extravagant. One side of the wardrobe was full of trousers, plain shirts, jackets, and sturdy boots, useful for classes and drills, and the other side held dresses and gowns that would ordinarily be far too fancy for Bristol to wear—but every night in Elphame was a grand celebration.

She rubbed the silky fabric of an aquamarine dress between her fingers. Whether plain or extravagant, every garment was exquisitely made, and on close inspection, she saw every tiny painstaking stitch. It must have taken an army of skilled hands to make them so quickly.

She'd worn the plainest dresses so far, still accustomed to not drawing attention, though she noticed at evening festivities, most fae reveled in flamboyant styles—long capes that shimmered like a hummingbird's throat, jeweled head coverings draped over hair, horn, and fur, flowing gowns made of thousands of small copper plates that rustled like wind chimes, each plate embossed with symbols that Bristol thought might be spells. She was careful not to brush up against those.

When she had remarked about the excessiveness of her wardrobe, Kasta explained that the tailors found great joy in their labor—Danu was well known for its fine fabrics and clothing—and if she never wore the clothing they made her, it would be an insult. They would think she wasn't pleased with their work.

After her disastrous encounter with Mae, Bristol definitely wanted them to think she was pleased. That she was kind and agreeable. A Seelie sort of mortal. Friendly. That she was someone who could be trusted with their secrets. Someone they *wanted* to help. She pulled out a beautiful rust-colored gown trimmed with gold on the bodice and hem, and held it up to herself, staring at her reflection in the long oval mirror.

The shimmering dress was breathtaking, and the color brought out elusive red highlights in her brown hair—as if the tailors had known it would. Highlights even she hadn't noticed before. Maybe it was only the lighting of the room, but it filled some holes inside her. It gave her a tiny connection to the gene train she always thought she had missed.

She put it on and smoothed her hands over the cool, silky bodice.

A worthy opponent. Tyghan's words about her father slipped into her head.

It was true. And what she had said was true, too—her father taught her well. By the time she was nine, she had graduated from practicing with Cat to sparring with her father. He had pulled her aside so Cat wouldn't hear and whispered, *You're the one with a fighter's spirit, Brije. One day it will be up to you to protect your sisters.* Except Bristol had never envisioned that day, and she had let those skills grow rusty.

No more.

She prayed that wherever her father was, he wasn't suffering, and that somehow he knew she was coming for him.

CHAPTER 35

The trow king kept the wine flowing, generous with his well-stocked cellar. His sprawling palace was carved deep into the mountain, the humble cave entrance deceptive.

"Our guest needs more wine!" King Motheuse bellowed to a servant, though Kierus's crystal goblet was still half-full. The king's heavy eyelids narrowed wickedly. "And maybe something to warm your feet, too?" he added.

Someone. Kierus knew what he meant. "I do need to get some sleep tonight, Your Majesty. I'm a mere mortal without the stamina of a trow king."

The king laughed, his pale gray skin as tough as thick leather, barely revealing any emotion. But Kierus knew he soaked in every word, from *Your Majesty* to *stamina*. Trows were accustomed to being the scourge of Elphame, and their reputations were well deserved. They were thieves and murderers. Respect and compliments from outsiders were nonexistent, but Kierus learned early on it was a currency they craved as much as gold and blood. Bring them a gift too, and you were their friend for life.

But Kierus had given them far more than compliments and gifts. He'd covered up more than one of their messy trails that would bring whole kingdoms hunting them in force, including a murderous trail perpetrated by the trow king's only son. King Motheuse owed him not just many favors, but large ones. Blood debts were among the few codes the trows lived up to.

Kierus had recognized the unlikely usefulness of trows from the time he was a boy and was just beginning to navigate the Wilds on his own. Their tunnels through the mountains were renowned, but impossible to navigate—unless you knew their secrets.

"If you change your mind, there's a whole court here eager to please you." The king nodded toward a pretty maid across the way—at least what trows considered pretty.

He had to be careful not to offend his host—the aid of trows offered his only chance at saving Maire—so Kierus acted like he was considering the maid. But coupling with a trow could be a dangerous proposition. They tended to use their sharp teeth indiscriminately. On their own leathery skin it wasn't a problem—on human flesh it definitely was, as he'd painfully learned firsthand long ago. It had taken two sorcerers to clean up the bloody mess his trow lover made of his shoulder. He nudged the king's thoughts in another direction instead, because no one but Maire would ever be in his sights again. She was all that mattered to him. This was all for her. He leaned back on a colorful pillow and praised the king's delicious spread, then admired the weapons he had gifted Kierus, a jeweled knight's sword prime among them. Three small rubies decorated the hilt, which meant it had belonged to a first-year knight. A *Danu* knight. *Who?* he wondered. *And how did they die?* Alone, if the sword had fallen into trow hands. Besides supplying him with weapons, the trows were also going to help him with passage through their tunnels so he could stay out of sight for most of his journey.

"More supplies are coming," the king said. "The cloak you requested may take a bit longer. There's been trouble in the city, so my messengers have gone to Amisterre instead."

Even as he spoke, Winkip, the king's doorward, limped in with a satchel of supplies that he dumped at Kierus's feet. The contents rattled with promise. "It's all there, except for the cloak. We hope to have that by tomorrow."

"The king spoke of trouble in the city?" Kierus said.

The perpetual lines furrowing Winkip's brow deepened, bits of his thick skin cracking and flaking loose. "Trows are being questioned. Or worse."

"Questioned for what?"

"It's your daughter. She's causing a fuss."

Kierus laughed. "My daughter? Impossible. None of my daughters are here. They're all—"

"A Bristol Keats?" Winkip interrupted. "She's claiming she's your daughter. The young woman is here searching for a Logan Keats, and the trows who helped you return here tell us that's the name you declared in the other world."

Kierus set his goblet down, stunned with disbelief. *Bristol, here?* His senses returned, hot and explosive, and he jumped to his feet in rage. "Kormick made a deal to leave our daughters alone! He promised—"

"It wasn't Kormick who brought her here," Winkip replied. "It was Counselor Dukinnon. But she evidently came of her own accord to search for you. Every trow has fled the city."

Kierus's blood blazed hotter. It wasn't the counselor behind this. That man had no taste for violence.

Tyghan. He was the one behind it. Which meant Tyghan knew he was here. *That* was why knight patrols were combing every inch of road and wild.

The back of his hand shot out, sweeping a bowl of fruit from the table. "Bristol didn't even know about Elphame! Maire and I made sure of that!"

"What can we do to help?" the king asked.

Kierus paced the room, thinking. *Of her own accord?* They had lied to her. They had filled her head with lies. Dread clutched his chest. His daughter was in Tyghan's hands. And now Tyghan was king.

"I need to meet with her," he told Winkip. "I need to get a message to her as soon as possible."

"That won't be easy," Winkip said. "Trows are banned from the city, not to mention she always has an escort at her side."

"Tyghan?" he asked.

Winkip nodded.

Kierus struggled to control his imagination. *What would his one-time best friend do to his daughter?*

"Find someone who can get a message to her," Kierus ordered. "There has to be a way. Find it."

CHAPTER 36

Bristol had intended to go straight to the festivities, but since the parties lasted late into the night, she wandered aimlessly instead. She needed a few minutes alone to process the day's flood of new information. *Everything will be explained*, Tyghan had promised on her first day there. And that was part of the problem. She'd been hit with so many new realities: spells, drills, *fucking dragons that ate people*. She rubbed her temple.

Even the minutiae of carefully choosing foods from the feast tables was overwhelming. The differences of this world and its people and creatures presented a steep learning curve. But the similarities between this world and hers astounded her, too. Like art and their love for it.

On her stroll she passed the Epona Museum and Conservatory that Olivia said they would tour tomorrow. It was a complex for the arts. *Besides Leonardo da Vinci, there are other famous artists you are likely to know as well.* Olivia dropped names like Cassatt, Kahlo, Donatello, and Hilma af Klint. Bristol was beginning to understand the strategy of orientation and lessons. They weren't just to coax sleeping traits to the surface or develop survival skills but to invest them in all the stakes—the survival of Elphame and a history that predated her own world. It was still sinking in. Bowskeep and everything she'd ever known was the *alternate* realm, an above-average forgery created by a god to keep mortals out of their original one. It was the ultimate bait and switch.

As she passed the conservatory, she spotted art students outside in the museum gardens painting by starlight. The conservatory's majesty rivaled the greatest museums she had ever visited, and she wondered why her father had left this world. What were the circumstances that made him leave?

Her rambling path led her to the sacred groves—the nine trees the fae revered. Regrettably, Bristol's father never told her that fact, at least not directly. Instead, in a lesson discussing wands, spears, and wisdom, it was Esmee who had told Bristol about the trees.

But her father had spent a lifetime telling her in other ways. She knew more about his upbringing than she'd thought. A part of this world that he loved was forever sewn into him and made him who he was as much as any DNA ever could. He might not have spoken openly about Elphame, but it surfaced in other, quieter ways. Ways that had become part of Bristol, too. His past was her past.

This ash, we'll keep it. Strong and straight, he said of several branches he had cut from a tree. *They'll make fine walking and fighting sticks.* He dried, smoothed, and sanded those branches until they shone like fine pieces of furniture, matching the lengths and weight to his three daughters, presenting each stick to them like they were scepters and his daughters were queens.

She scanned the ancient ash branches above her, seeing them through his eyes—a canvas to be painted. A canvas he *had* painted many times. Even his art made more sense now. Did he climb these trees as a child?

She ventured deeper into the sacred forest, and when she reached the last grove, she spotted a white marble bench perched near a cliff overlooking the back side of the palace. She sat, hoping it didn't hold live surprises for her the way the columns of Judge's Walk had.

An umbrella of hazel trees heavy with still-green nuts branched out over her head. Esmee said these trees were revered above all by the Tuatha de. Her father never told her the fae story of them either, like the salmon who gained the knowledge of the whole world by eating hazelnuts that fell into the river, or of the boy Fionn, who in turn gained wisdom by eating the salmon—that had been more of her history lesson that day. But her father had always had a tin full of hazelnuts in the van for eating on long drives, claiming they were brain food that would give his daughters wisdom.

She wished she had eaten more of them. If she had, would she have noticed her parents never told them fairy tales or stories about the gods? In their lessons, they even skipped the plays of Shakespeare that included fairies. Were they afraid that even speaking the names would summon the creatures that hunted them? How had she not seen all their artful layers of deception? But she'd only been a child immersed in what she knew.

A warm breeze teased at her hair and brought the distant croon of the plaza music closer. It was hard to resist dancing last night, especially once she recognized the steps. Her father had claimed it was a folk dance he picked up in Appalachia, but now she knew where he really learned it. She remembered dancing with her mother and sisters around their campfire, laughing, twirling, while her father played a tune on his harmonica, the buzz of cicadas in the meadow grass becoming part of the music, the scent of sweet roasted marshmallows in the air, and Harper's sticky toddler fingers lacing with her own.

Even with all the years of running, her parents managed to carve out a life for their family. Dancing and laughter had been part of it. Her foot tapped again, and longing gripped Bristol's chest, but Anastasia's warning about not dancing to fae music held her back. She couldn't take a chance on dying from exhaustion.

Leaves crunched behind her. *Footsteps.* She had spotted Cully following her back at the conservatory. "You can stop hiding and come out," she called over her shoulder. "You know by now that I don't bite, at least not fae that I like."

"Then I suppose I should be worried."

Her back stiffened. It wasn't Cully.

She stood and turned to face Tyghan.

He stepped closer. "Cully told me you didn't seem to be headed toward the festivities, so I brought you this." He pulled something from his pocket and tossed it to her. She caught the tiny projectile midair.

Tyghan shrugged. "I saw you tapping your foot last night, and I thought it might be the dancing that was keeping you away. The amulet will prevent you from being unable to stop."

Bristol examined the small silver cuff in her palm. "So, it's true what they say about the dancing?"

He nodded. "Mostly, though no one would actually let you die in the process. It's a rite of passage for most new recruits, at least those who have any mortal blood in them. Someone usually rescues them before they collapse."

She eyed Tyghan, wondering about this change in him. Had he pardoned her intrusion into his room earlier, or was he trying to prove that he wasn't always angry? Either way, she preferred this less irritable side of him. They were almost having a normal conversation that he had initiated. She held the amulet back out to him. "Reuben says we're not allowed to have amulets until we earn them."

"Keep it," he said. "I won't tell him if you don't."

She glanced at the cuff in her palm and then back at Tyghan. Awkward silence stretched between them. Was this a truce of sorts? Though she'd never been sure what war they were waging. Yes, she'd come on strong when they first met, but so had he. She'd been scared and in shock, and he made it worse. The fae world came out of nowhere and hit her head-on with no warning, like a speeding truck. But she had a better understanding of his anger now too. Maybe their collision had been inevitable. "Thank you," she said quietly.

"On a braid," he added, motioning to her hair. "That's how most fae wear them."

"I don't see any in your hair."

"I don't need amulets."

Was it hubris speaking or truth? She thought about the sizable scar on his side. It seemed he could have used a protective amulet at least once.

He shifted on his feet, lingering. "I also wanted to address something you said in the carriage. I want you to know that I never thought you were stupid for coming here. I wouldn't allow someone stupid in my ranks. Actually, I thought you were fairly brave to come to a world you knew nothing about."

She grinned. "Fairly? Now, that's a lukewarm compliment I will forever treasure. Actually, I was enormously brave."

His eyes sparked with something that wasn't anger. "Your modesty is astounding."

"So nice to see you're impressed at last."

His gaze fluttered downward for a moment. "Is that what you've been trying to do? Impress me?"

She thought for a moment. "Yes," she admitted. "I suppose I have. I want you on my side. Truly on my side. I'm on yours. I meant what I said about your brother, and I promise more artwork for my sisters had nothing to do with it. I'll do whatever I can to help you, no matter how things turn out for my father."

He raked his teeth over his lower lip. "I'm sorry for what I said about the art. It was a cheap shot."

Bristol smiled. "Cheap shot? Is that fairy slang, too?"

"I told you, I read. Even some of your modern works."

She studied him for a moment, then motioned to the bench beside her. "Would you like to sit?"

A crease instantly formed between his brows. "No. I need to go back. The king is expected at evening celebrations."

"As are recruits, right?"

"Yes," he answered. "But you can come along when you're ready."

No tricks or demands like the previous night? And had she just procured an apology? Before he could turn to leave, she asked, "Is this new for you, going to the nightly celebrations? How long have you been the acting king?"

"I . . . It doesn't really—" He exhaled a slow breath. "Six months," he said. "At least officially. I was crowned while I was mostly unconscious. There was an . . . incident, and I was injured. But even when I came to long enough to accept the crown—" He cleared his throat. "For another month, I was unable to rule properly. My recovery came with challenges."

"Did your long recovery have something to do with the scar on your side?" The scar she wasn't supposed to see. She immediately regretted her question.

Muscles in his neck tightened.

"I'm sorry. I shouldn't have asked—"

"Yes," he answered. "It had to do with the scar you saw. I was stabbed and nearly gutted. I guess that's evident by its size."

"But the scar?" she replied. "Today, Olivia healed the wound on my arm in minutes with a few words and salve. There's not even a scratch now. Can't they—"

"This scar can't be erased with salves or words. It's permanent. It was made by a blade of demon steel. No magic can undo it."

"A demon stabbed you?"

Her question burned in the silence between them, seconds ticking by. "A demon would be easier for me to accept," he finally answered. "Unfortunately, it was one of our own. A traitor. He acquired the rare blade from a Fomorian enemy."

She asked what made it rare, and he said it was forged for over a thousand years by a thousand different demons. "Every swing of their hammer seals in the demon's torment. The blade's cut leaves . . . a memorable mark."

Memorable in what way? Bristol wondered. She was certain he wasn't talking about the physical mark it left. "Being stabbed by one of your own must have made it even harder," she said. "Was he a knight?"

He looked away, studying the boughs of the hazel tree. Bristol was well acquainted with the art of turning away when hard things had to be said, the art of avoiding someone's eyes because they might see something inside you that you were desperately trying to hide.

He plucked a green hazelnut from an overhead bough and examined it like it was made of gold. "Yes, a knight," he said. "My best friend, actually. That's why I was caught off guard. I let my defenses down. He was the last person I ever expected—" He faced her again, his eyes now drilling into hers. "He stabbed me and left me on the forest floor to die. That's how I got the scar you saw. Other than the sorcerers who attended me, you're the only one who's seen it. That's why I'm telling you. I'd prefer it if you didn't share what you saw."

His expression was blank, tired, like the thought of what happened to him had wrung him dry. A heavy weight settled in Bristol's chest. *That* was the anger always simmering in him. He'd been stabbed by someone he loved. Someone he trusted.

"I'm sorry," she said. "Of course, I won't say anything. You're right. I don't know you. I can't begin to know what you've been through."

"You aren't expected to. What's done is done. It's in the past."

But it's not done, Bristol thought. It was poison still rushing in his veins. Was that another purpose of his anger—to keep everyone at a safe distance? Because if you couldn't trust your best friend, who could you trust?

"It's getting late. I should go. The king is expected at festivities," he repeated.

And yet he stood there, hesitating.

He wanted to stay. She was certain of it.

For a few seconds, he looked lost. Not a king or a powerful knight. Only a man caught in someone's crosshairs trying to figure out if he should run left or right—or maybe stand his ground.

The distant music whirled around them. She fingered the metal cuff in her hand. Even in the face of his horrific confession, did he feel the music's pull the same way she did? Would he—

But she waited too long to ask. Her chance vanished.

"I need to go. Guests are waiting." His tone turned cool, and he left before she could reply. Out of the crosshairs, back into the haven of distance. He walked away, but just before he was swallowed by the shadows of the grove, he paused and glanced back at her. He was too far away for her to see his eyes, but she imagined them softer.

And then he was gone.

Bristol looked at the silver cuff in her hand, wondering about the apprehension in Tyghan's eyes as he tossed it to her. It didn't fit with his personality. He had another side he was very good at hiding. She braided the cuff into her hair, pondering what he said. *My recovery came with challenges.* He picked through his words carefully like each one was a wasp, words he didn't want to touch.

It was surprising he took the risk to share with her at all, though she had probably caught him off guard with her direct question. Or maybe he just wanted to share with *someone?* An outsider. Bristol knew that feeling, the need to step outside her own suffocating circle into another one, the need for connection and a fresh perspective. That was what pushed her to enter into Mick's circle, even if it ended up being a huge mistake. Venturing into new territory carried unknown risks. It took a different kind of courage she was just beginning to understand.

She smiled again, remembering his backhanded compliment. Good to know she was *fairly* brave and not stupid. He definitely needed practice in that department. Maybe he would smile about it later too. Assuming he gave her a second thought.

When she was finished with the braid and the cuff was secure in her hair, she stood. Closed her eyes. Lifted her arms, swayed. And stepped outside her world.

She left the day behind her the way she did within the dark confines of her bedroom when she needed to shed who she was and be someone else, if only for a few minutes. Dancing was a different language she didn't need all the words for, something that wrapped her in its forgiving world of dips and twirls. There were no missteps.

Tonight she imagined she wasn't dancing alone in the dark but around a campfire, the way she did when life was simpler. At least, when she thought it was. Dancing with her sisters, with her parents, or with—*someone*. She turned, dipped, swayed, but the beat of distant drums hummed beneath her skin in a new way.

This music.

It made something primal pulse inside her, something hungry and addictive. The song knit into her bones, and damp beads sprung to her temples. She raised her palms over her head, and a current of air flowed up from the cliff against them. Her heart galloped. She stepped closer to the bluff's edge, seeking the cool breeze—but then suddenly the cool became searing warmth, her palms burning like another pair were pressed to hers, skin to skin, only a thin veil between them.

She opened her eyes, but only saw stars and forest around her. Still, heat burned against her palms, and as she turned, she felt the warmth of a back shadowing her own—and then the brush of hot fingertips dragging across her palm, igniting fire in her as they met again, and again.

What was happening? *The amulet isn't working*, she thought in a burst of panic, but in the next moment, she didn't care. She closed her eyes again, never wanting the feeling to stop. Maybe that was Tyghan's plan, trick her with a false amulet, seduce her with this world so she could never leave. But the thought vanished almost as quickly as it came. If she was enchanted, she wanted to stay enchanted forever.

The hazel trees faded, and the starry sky dipped low with its glittered magic and brushed her face. A thousand lights tingled over her skin. The music became more than sound, it was her breaths, her blood, all that she was and wanted to be. Sometimes her feet didn't seem to touch the ground at all, like she was lifted up, dancing on currents of air. The hands she couldn't see brushed closer, lingering, *needing*, the same as her, and then the drums paused, beat after beat held back in a fist, a taut keenness hanging in the air like a summer storm waiting to unleash.

She wanted it to unleash. Rivers of heat spread through her belly. *He* was there. Impossibly close. She was certain. A breath grazing her jaw. A muscled chest. The scent of leather and crisp cotton. The warmth was his. The hands were his. She wanted to whisper his name. *Tyghan.*

But she didn't dare speak, because she didn't want to break the spell.

She understood the safety of invisibility, the need for distance from the demons that stalk us. Sometimes invisibility was about survival—maybe it always was—and she didn't know what he was still trying to survive.

The dance continued until her back was damp and her lips parched, and the need in her so ripe she thought she might split open with the want, until finally, when the hour was late, she found she had danced her way to Sun Court, where there was food and more dancing, but then it was not with the sense of an invisible back against her own.

She danced with Julia, Avery, and the other recruits, Tyghan suddenly appearing and watching her from a distance, his face glistening in the moonlight, his brow damp like her own.

She continued to dance far too late and woke bleary-eyed in the morning to more magic lessons, and more field training, where Tyghan pushed her to her limits, showing no mercy or even recognition of their time together, and she wondered if the night before was only part of some needy delirium within her.

But then the next evening, and the next, when she was there once again, dancing beneath the hazel trees, the magic happened all over again, invisible hands mirroring her own, and she didn't care what it was—delirium or truth. She just didn't want it to end.

CHAPTER 37

"P ay the toll."

Bristol froze on the path, wondering if she should turn around, but it was the only way she knew of to get to Ceridwen Hall.

"There wasn't a toll yesterday," she said, feeling brave to challenge the creature at all. The eight-foot beast that vaguely resembled a man only repeated his demand and then grew even larger.

"Pay the toll," he demanded. His crooked teeth became bigger, his mouth wider, his nose knottier, and his enormous hands curled into fists.

Her spark of courage dimmed. There was a time to fight and a time to run.

"What are you doing over there?" a voice called from behind her.

Bristol spun and saw Tyghan. "Are you speaking to him or me?"

"You," he said as he walked closer. "Aren't you supposed to be at the lecture hall?"

"That was the goal. But this creature is blocking my path and shaking me down for money I don't have."

"Him?" Tyghan blinked long and slow, making his cynicism obvious.

Bristol's temper spiked. "Excuse me? It's been a while since I encountered an eight-foot troll in Bowskeep. Not too many of them order pizza."

Tyghan sighed. "Let her pass, Deek."

The creature frowned, stomped his foot in a childish gesture, then shrank to the size of a dragonfly, transforming into an impish being, his wings beating madly. He hovered in front of Bristol's face, holding his belly as he fell into fits of laughter.

"*You!*" she said. "You nasty little—"

He buzzed away before she could finish, his cadre of troublemakers following after him. Their laughter drowned out her curses.

"You've met?" Tyghan said.

"Yes!" Bristol snapped. "Yesterday, before class, your little neighborhood thugs descended into my hair and whirled it into a thousand tangles. Master Reuben reprimanded me for my disorderly appearance."

"Thugs?" Tyghan grinned like the word was infinitely amusing. "They're only harmless sprites."

"Not when they grow to eight-feet-tall trolls."

"That's only glamour, and they were just having a little fun. You should pay better attention to your lessons. Esmee covers palace creatures on the first day. Trolls aren't among them."

Pay better attention? "Well, thank you for that little gem of advice, Mr. Know-It-All."

His brows shot up. "What? I'm not Mr. High and Mighty anymore? I feel like I've been demoted."

"Trust me, I have a lot of names for you. I'm sure eventually you'll hear them all."

"You might just stick with Your Majesty."

She grunted and turned without reply, continuing down the path. *See you tonight, Your Majesty*, she wanted to say, a remark that would knock him off his secure pedestal. But she bit her tongue because she was afraid that it might make him stay away, and as annoying as he could be in the daytime—at night she wanted him to come. At night, there was a strange truce between them that she didn't quite understand, like for that tiny space of time, they had a safe secret place where they could both see what it felt like to be someone else.

"A sweet," he called after her. "That's the toll. Give them a sweet or a swatch of fine fabric, and those miscreants will be your friends for life."

That night she saved a cookie from the feast tables and cut a small length of red ribbon from one of her dresses and placed both on her windowsill.

The next morning, she found a perfect pink rose petal in their place. *Friends for life.*

She wished all the creatures in Elphame were so easy to please.

Especially ones who barked orders by day but were phantoms by night.

CHAPTER 38

ear your plainest clothes. A shirt and trousers.

Bristol turned one way and another, looking at her profile in the mirror, frustrated with herself. She didn't spend this much time worrying over her appearance when she dressed in her fancy gowns. Or ever. She tugged on her sleeves and smoothed back loose wisps of hair and left to meet Tyghan.

After days of training, disappointing twilight searches in the city, and secret nighttime encounters in the hazel grove, they were going out in the blazing light of day for a change. No dark carriage this time. They would be taking his horse. She'd barely slept last night, thinking about it.

We'll be traveling on narrow back trails.

They were trying a new angle in searching for leads on her father, and it sounded promising. She was growing impatient and wanted results, or at least some hope. She hurried down the palace steps, eager, but then slowed when she spotted Tyghan standing beside three gray dapples.

"One of these is yours?" she said. "I thought you'd have a larger horse like the other knights."

"I do, but the white steeds draw notice. We want to blend in. The dapples are easier to handle too. It takes years to master riding a hot-blooded destrier. You're not ready."

Tyghan noted the slight roll of Bristol's eyes.

They were venturing out to the more remote hamlets and winding paths of Danu where carriages couldn't go. It was a rare daytime excursion. There were only so many sectors of the city where Eris could plant leads that went nowhere. Every evening Bristol grew more discouraged, and he and Eris concocted a plan to give her distance from her daily disappointments, because ultimately, her searches would never produce the results she wanted. She'd brightened last night when he told her they were going to discreetly comb the eastern hamlets that day.

"Who is the third horse for?"

"Cully."

She stared at the horse like it had pissed on her boots. "We need a chaperone?"

"A third set of eyes and ears is always useful."

"Ready!" Cully said, coming up behind them, a toothy grin on his face, happy to be released from training that day to accompany them.

Tyghan wanted him along as a buffer to quell any growing gossip. During the bright of day, Tyghan was more likely to be seen, and there were already several lords and ladies ambling near the carriage portico ogling them. Departing alone with her would be a flame to tinder. They still blamed his brother's reckless excursions with his mistress on their current woes, and if they ever found out Bristol's parentage, there would be hell to pay. He'd been careful not to be seen with her beyond the boundaries of necessity. As far as they knew, she was only another recruit who came to this world in search of adventure—and a relative.

"We have a lot of miles to cover," he said. "Let's go."

Bristol lifted her foot, but struggled getting a firm foothold in the stirrup. She still had no training with horses. He looked at her back, her shirt neatly tucked into her snug trousers, the curve of her hips and her waist within easy reach. He averted his eyes and waved Cully forward. "Help her up."

Cully complied.

Once in the saddle, Bristol shot him a sharp glance. "Let's hope we don't run into more mistaken identities," she said. "There seem to be a lot of fae around here who don't know a mortal from a goat—or an insult from a compliment."

"He was a faun," Cully corrected. "Half goat." That was the last mistaken identity they'd encountered.

Tyghan mounted his horse. "I never said it would be easy."

A low hiss escaped through her teeth.

When they were out of the city, Tyghan veered them onto a narrow trail that led to a coastal hamlet, a place where he knew there would be no sign or word of Kierus. His knights had already scouted the area.

Along the way they made inquiries at farmhouses and the occasional inn.

"If you see someone who meets that description, let my associate in the city know—Mae at the textile house," Tyghan said at stop after stop. "He's come into some gold—I want to make sure he gets it."

"He's traveling with trows," Bristol added. "We want to make sure they get their reward too."

She received mixed reactions to her comment. No one traveled with trows.

Cully left Mae's contact information with them. That had cost Tyghan another heavy pouch from the treasury. But Mae's love of gold made her predictable and reliable.

When they were out of earshot of their last stop, Bristol asked, "Is it hard to kill a trow?"

Caution crept into Tyghan's thoughts. "Is that your goal? To kill them?"

"They have a lot to answer for. They hunted down my father."

Tyghan felt the stab of her assumption, and what she would like to do to her father's hunters. "Yes," he answered, intending to put her aspirations to an end. "It's hard to kill trows, because they're good at killing others first."

Her knuckles whitened on the reins. "My father is *alive*," she replied, like he had just implied otherwise.

"I didn't say he wasn't. Don't twist my words."

"I'm not twisting anything. But I'm not going to step around my words today, either. This is not the training grounds. You're on my time now—the other side of our agreement."

He stared at her for a long moment, his tongue sliding over his teeth. "*Your* time?" He didn't know what burr was in her saddle, but he was about to help her extract it.

Cully rode on the other side of her and shot Tyghan a warning shake of his head. *Back down.*

Tyghan never backed down, and he especially didn't take orders from a junior officer. But Cully's warning collided with Eris's last words to him. *Don't forget, we need her, and if all goes well today, she may leave the hunting to our knights. We don't want her nosing around too much. It carries risk.*

He gritted his teeth. "I'm sure your father's alive, too."

"Concur!" Cully quickly added.

Bristol nodded, like they had all come to an agreement. "Thank you," she said quietly. Her fingers relaxed on her reins, and she changed the topic. "Finish telling me about the other kingdoms until we reach our next stop."

Gladly, Tyghan thought. He wasn't sure what had caused her foul mood, but he wanted to move past it. Today was supposed to be about easing her tension, not increasing it.

In their nightly chats, he had been giving her lessons on Elphame. He knew her interest wasn't simple curiosity but also strategy, because she intended to navigate every inch of it until she found her father. Now he wondered if she was also out to kill every trow on her own. The look in her eyes a few minutes ago convinced him she was capable. She had the same expression Kierus sometimes got that said, *Step wide.*

As they rode he told her about the kingdoms, and in the deep Wilds, the caves of Stodderall that were actually the mouths of stone beasts. "Few who venture into them ever come out again. They become lunch."

"I took a quick look inside once," Cully said. "Bones are embedded in the sides of the caves." He grimaced. "Didn't stay long. I prefer my bones to stay inside my body."

Tyghan explained that they were created by a long-ago wizard. "Many have tried, but no one knows how to undo the magic. By chance, some magics last forever."

"Too bad," Bristol said. "If it was made in the mortal world, it would only come with a one-year guarantee."

Tyghan and Cully both looked at her uncertainly.

"It was a joke," she said.

He and Cully forced a small laugh like they got it.

At least she was joking again.

"Braised boar shanks for the lady, and I'll have your ribs," Tyghan told the barkeep. "And two ales." They had arrived at the coastal hamlet, and since it was midday, they decided to stop at a pub to eat before they nosed around. Cully wasn't hungry and skipped out before Tyghan could insist that he stay. The pub was busy, the tables full, but they managed to find a small one available in the middle of the bustling room.

"It's a beautiful little town," Bristol said. "It reminds me of where my sister works on the coast. Except for the ogres, fauns, and unicorns, of course."

"There are no unicorns here."

"Oh, well, it's just like Kestrel Cove, then. Thanks for the correction."

"What is the matter with you?"

She sighed. "Nothing. I'm out of sorts today, I guess. I'm sure the boar shanks will take care of that."

And maybe four ales.

Their food came, and they both dug in. It was easier to eat than to talk. Everything was so different from when they were together at night, alone in the sacred groves. He wished they were there now, instead of here, and had second thoughts about this escapade. She finished her ale and asked for another.

"Shanks good?" he asked.

She remained silent, sopping up the juices from the meat with a crusty slice of bread, but then her hand just hovered over her plate, the juices dripping. Her gaze shot up. "Why is my naked body the last thing you ever want to see? Is it only me, or do you find all of my kind repulsive? Or maybe it's just the bright of day that's the problem, when it's easy to see every ugly detail. You even made a point to step away and make Cully help me up on my horse."

The question punched Tyghan like a fist, and his mouth fell open.

A patron at the next table dropped his spoon into his stew bowl. "You don't want to see her naked? What's the matter with you, boy? I'd take an eyeful of that pretty thing."

Tyghan shot him a glare that was just short of piercing his skull. The man returned his attention to the stew.

Tyghan leaned forward, lowering his voice. "I said that to reassure you I would never spy on you in your private chambers. I don't find your naked body repulsive. At all. That is, if I had ever seen it." He cleared his throat and added, "Which I haven't."

The patron at the next table scooped another spoonful of stew into his mouth and, at the risk of his life, said, "If I were you, I'd fix that situation."

Before Tyghan could respond, Cully walked in and, seeing their plates empty, said, "Good timing. Ready to go?"

Tyghan paid the bill, and when he went outside, Bristol had one hand on the reins of her horse and her other hand poised on the seat of the saddle. Cully stepped forward to offer her help again.

Tyghan waved him away. "I'll handle this."

He stepped close behind her and placed his hands on her waist. A tremor shivered down her back, and he leaned closer, his chest brushing her shoulders. "I'm sorry I didn't help you before," he whispered. "There were nobles eyeing us from the carriage house. They watch every move the king makes, and what they see becomes fodder for their evening entertainment. I didn't want you to become part of that fodder."

"I see," she answered. "Is that why you sit in the shadows at Sun Court?"

"Once I've made my obligatory rounds, yes."

She nodded. "Maybe I overreacted. I've been self-conscious ever since my first day when Quin told me my smell was attracting attention."

"That was only the other world they smelled, not you."

"There are stares at Sun Court, too. A few of the gentry seem to single me out."

He was silent, his fingers tightening on her waist. He wanted to ask which ones, though she probably didn't know one flaming boar's head from another, but he'd seen a few of them studying her. He didn't know what lurid machinations played in their heads, but he might need to make more than a few obligatory rounds to instill some fear in their noble hearts.

"They stare at all newcomers," he said. "Not just you. Part curiosity, part lust. Just stay clear of them."

He turned to Cully, who waited patiently for their journey to resume. "You've been slacking in your duties, Officer. The new arrivals need lessons in horsemanship. Schedule some for tomorrow. Tell Kasta." He looked back at Bristol. "I forget sometimes that in your world, your main mode of transportation is clunky pieces of metal."

"We manage," she replied.

He gave her a first lesson in adjusting the stirrups, the proper placement of her hands to mount the horse, then gave her a gentle assist into the saddle, and they were off again, the lunch topic left behind them, but it wasn't entirely free from his thoughts.

If I were you, I'd fix that situation.

He hissed a frustrated breath. He wanted to fix it. And now, with the scent of her hair still in his nostrils, he wanted to fix it right that minute, right there in the woods—but there was no fixing this mess. Not in his position.

Melizan's words circled back to him. *Eventually, we all have to take a chance on someone.* He knew he was in trouble if he was even considering advice from his sister. Taking any more chances was the last thing he needed. Knight Commanders didn't take chances. They eliminated them.

CHAPTER 39

Bristol's spirits lifted when Tyghan said he would send squads to comb lands beyond the borders and inquire in other kingdoms for any sign of her father. He was doing more than he promised, using the kingdom's knights and resources to help her. The squads would be able to cover far more ground than the two of them could—and their questions would plant seeds. *Gold. Reward.* She saw the fae's attention spark at the mention of those words, branding the name Logan Keats into their minds. Eventually, someone would hear something. Someone would come forward.

As she waited for news, she threw herself into her training, hoping that if she couldn't be the savior of one thing at the moment, she could be the savior of something else. She was no longer faking her commitment to the cause—it was hers now too. She especially embraced her weapons training. Tyghan's words had provoked her. *The trows are good at killing.* She was determined to be better.

As busy as her days were, her nights . . . were inexplicably fuller.

It was a strange line she and Tyghan walked. By day they were still demanding Knight Commander and novice. By night they were something different, though she still wasn't sure what that was. Every night his first words to her were always stiff, like he had forgotten how to have a simple conversation that didn't include ordering someone around. But he was finding his way. Bristol was too. Words came easier, the stiffness melting away. She counted every conversation as a victory. He was learning to be not just civil but engaged. And so was she.

Bristol didn't think he was having these nightly talks with other recruits, but she couldn't be sure. He had mentioned making obligatory rounds. Was that all she was? An obligation? Part of his job? Was what she felt between them all in her head?

Tonight, the moon was already high in the sky, and she assumed he wasn't coming at all. She distracted herself with other thoughts, especially her sister Cat, wondering how she was handling the burden of holding everything together in Bowskeep. Cat was organized and capable, but it wasn't just about having money to pay the bills—it was about having someone to lean on. Bristol had always been that person. She crouched low with a handful of pebbles, pressing them into the soil near the base of a tree. First a *C*, and then a—

"What's that?"

She gasped, and the pebbles in her hand spilled as she jumped to her feet. "Can't you be a little noisier on your approach?" she snapped. "Or do you enjoy watching me jump?"

Tyghan shrugged. "Maybe a little. You do it so predictably."

He was not getting much better at compliments. His attention shifted to the pebbles pressed into the soil. "*C I*?"

"It was going to be *C K* before you snuck up on me. My sister's initials." She knelt to pick up the scattered pebbles. Tyghan stooped beside her to help gather them, his shoulder brushing hers, the small touch sucking up every ounce of her attention, even his woodsy scent making her heady.

"And you're doing this exercise *why*?" he asked.

"I was thinking about my sister. It was a quirk of hers when we were growing up and always on the move. She pressed stones into the dirt to create her initials, then wondered if they'd still be there if we passed through again. At campgrounds, rest stops, anywhere. A little piece of herself left behind in some hidden corner. Sometimes we teased her about it."

Tyghan pressed the last stone into the dirt to complete the K. "Nothing wrong with wanting to leave something of yourself behind."

"I suppose not," Bristol mused, a familiar melancholy roosting in her chest. She stood and brushed the dirt from her fingers. "But her initials were never there when we came back. I always felt bad about that, but it didn't stop Cat from doing it at the next stop, or the next."

"Why didn't she just carve or paint her initials, so they'd be permanent?"

"No, it always had to be little stones. She said they were fragile, movable, like a human life. They could be scattered anywhere—"

For the first time it hit Bristol. Maybe Cat wasn't leaving the stones so they could stay in place, but so she could imagine where they had gone. Where a piece of her had gone. Maybe she was imagining a different life for herself and what it might look like—the same way Bristol did. A faraway place where a stone might land and stay forever. An ache pierced her throat.

Tyghan still waited for her to finish her sentence. She swallowed away the ache. "My sister Harper has her quirks too," she went on, to cover for her lapse. "She smells books before she reads them. Every time. It's strange, I know. And she buys a lot of used books."

"What about your quirks? You have any?"

"Plenty, I'm sure, but that's a story for Cat and Harper to tell."

He crossed his arms. "But they're not here, and you are."

She knew the first quirk her sisters would immediately blurt out because it made them shiver. "I like spiders," she answered as she sat on a fallen trunk, "and I give them names so my sisters won't smash them with a shoe. It's much harder to kill something once you know its name. Howard was the last one I saved." She told him that it became her unofficial job to retrieve and take spiders outside if one got in the house. "Both of my sisters are terrified of them, but they've always fascinated me. Spiders are loners and artists, and they work so diligently weaving their webs. Did you know their silk is five times stronger than steel? Can you imagine a sword made from it?" She glanced sideways at him, her brows arched. "Just saying. Something you might want to look into. And the shrouds they create for their victims—there's something elegant and respectful about it. Killing isn't a thoughtless act for them; it's a well-conceived process."

Tyghan sat down beside her. "Or calculating."

"Completely," she said with admiration.

"Does the moth caught in the web also think the killing is elegant and respectful?"

She shrugged. "I wouldn't know. But it's better than getting plastered on the grille of a truck."

"Dead is dead," he answered. "There's nothing elegant about it."

His expression grew hard and distant, and she wondered if they were still talking about spiders.

It was only a few seconds later that he said he had to go.

She didn't see him again for two days.

CHAPTER 40

Tyghan scanned the shadows. He hated this silent, dark forest. It breathed. It watched. It was deadly still. Even the horse's steps were silenced on the soft loamy trail. There were no speeding truck grilles here, or spiders lying in wait, only a hundred other ways to die unexpectedly and painfully.

Only Melizan didn't seem bothered by the gloom. "Any news from the outliers?" she asked, riding up alongside him after tiring of Quin's company on the trail.

Tyghan shook his head. "No news that was helpful. The others knew as little about Willow as the sheriff did, and no one's seen her since the day we took Bristol."

"What about Princess Georgina? She was always a nosy one, in everyone's business."

"She refused to meet. Too busy."

A wry smile twisted Melizan's lips. "I suppose you can't force a princess, can you?"

"Yes, I'm well aware of that fact, Your Highness."

She chuckled. "Well, Georgina always comes to the Beltane Eve celebration. You can question her then."

Tyghan wasn't so sure. The princess no longer came to Samhain after harvest. One year, she would skip Beltane, too—and this year

Beltane Eve was more critical than ever. "If she comes. She wants nothing to do with Elphame anymore."

"It's that mortal husband of hers. I would demand her presence if I were you."

"She's not one of my subjects, but Eris has sent a request asking for her presence."

"Ask? What an enormous waste of time," she sniffed. "I should have been queen. There'd be no asking."

Melizan always made demands sound so simple. Georgina was heir to the throne of Gildawey. Forcing her hand, if it was even possible, would not endear Danu to her mother, Queen Alise of Gildawey. And currently, Danu was pressing for more Gildan long swords. It was the favored blade of battle, and with Danu forces growing these past months, they needed more. Forged with ancient techniques and unknown metals, they had an enduring edge so sharp, it could cut a beast in half like it was butter. It was ironic because the Gildaweyans rarely engaged in battle, but they continued to pass along their revered talent through the generations. Making demands of the princess right now might interfere with other negotiations—which weren't going well. Queen Alise was already annoyed with Eris's constant requests. "I'll tell you what, Melizan. Go ahead, take my crown. Maybe your demands would hold more sway than mine."

Melizan frowned. "What's this? You're ruining all the fun, Tyghan. I come to you expecting a good fight."

"Today the fight's gone from me."

"Then maybe I should take the throne. Are you not sleeping?"

Tyghan's eyes narrowed.

"Ah, there it is. The deadly hallmark cut of the Trénallis eyes. I knew the fight hadn't gone far. It's no secret what demon steel does to a mind. At least not anymore, but no one has betrayed your secret. Not everyone is a traitor, brother."

"I'm sleeping better," he confessed. "Of a thousand demons, I think I only have a few hundred more to go." His forced nonchalance fell flat, and he swallowed. "I haven't had any tormenting me for several weeks now," he said more quietly. "I guess the doors have become harder to find."

"Well, that's not surprising, at least not with a stone-hard head like yours."

He looked sideways at her. "Am I really as nasty as you make me out to be?"

A cynical puff of air escaped her lips. "And then some."

They rode along silently, Tyghan pondering the truth of it. "My mother loved you. You probably should have been queen."

"We both know that titling me as a Danu princess was a kindness from her and purely symbolic. Without the royal Trénallis blood in me, I'd never get the support of the council—at least not as long as you and Cael are alive."

"Thinking of remedying that?"

"Always thinking. I promise it won't be too painful."

"Nice to know."

"Your mother was a good woman. Not many would title their husband's bastard. That's why I fight for Danu—well, I like fighting too—but it's for her. Not for Cael or for you. And I can't forget that it was my father's death that broke her."

"Many deaths broke her."

"She cared too deeply. That's why I will never break."

"Warm blood does run in your veins too, Melizan—at least one or two of them. We do have the same father."

She sighed as if disappointed by this fact. "Yes, there is that, I suppose. Though I see nothing similar about us. I still contend, better ice than blood."

"Why can't you just admit that you love me?"

Her upper lip wrinkled, and she shivered. "Because brothers and admissions are boring, and secrets are infinitely more entertaining."

That was the line he and Melizan always navigated, the blood bond of their father, the veneration of his mother, and the secrets his sister loved to keep.

They finally emerged from the suffocating silence of Bleakwood

Forest, but even without the thick cover of black trees, darkness hung in the air. The gray sky writhed above them like a muscled god about to strike.

Up ahead, high on the Mistriven Cliffs, they spotted their destination, Skyborn Palace. Palace was a generous name. It was a long, dreary thick-walled fortress that overlooked Balor Pass, the long finger of the Mirthless Sea, and the kingdom of Fomoria. Mistriven was the only kingdom in all of Elphame with such a vantage point—one that could actually spy on Fomoria, at least to a limited extent.

They were greeted at the base of the cliffs by a contingent of jumpy guards who escorted them up the long, zigzagging trail to the palace.

"I don't like this," King Merriwind said, wringing his hands. "If they should see you—"

"You're king!" Melizan said, breathing in the vista, like it was beautiful instead of forbidding. "You never take visitors?"

"Not anymore. And especially not anyone from Danu."

Tyghan's eyes swept the horizon. "Today is your lucky day, then. You don't always want to cower in Fomoria's shadow, do you?"

"We don't cower—"

Tyghan's icy stare pinned the king to the buttress he huddled beside. "You cower, Merriwind. You're weak. I'm giving you the opportunity to grow a spine. Be the kind of leader your mother was, one who watched for threats from the northern seas. Now, go inside, put a warm shawl over your lap, have your tea and biscuits, and leave me and my officers to save your worthless ass."

The king scuttled off as told, disappearing into the fortress without a whimper.

"That was harsh," Melizan said, with a happy tone of approval.

They stood out on the wind-battered battlement, gusts sweeping up the cliffs, stinging their faces, and whipping at their clothes.

"Down there," Quin said, pointing out a thin copse of trees at the base of the sheer drop of Balor Pass. "With a little invisibility, it would give us added cover until we reached their forests."

"Skirting the caves at low tide would be better," Melizan said.

Tyghan frowned. "Advice from Cosette, no doubt. But if she gets caught in the tide, she isn't going to drown. Or be pulled to the depths by merkind."

"Every piece of advice from Cosette is not designed to kill you, Tyghan."

"We'll consider it."

Most of Fomoria was nestled between steep, barren crags. There was no easy way into the center where the castle nested, not to mention, they didn't know where Cael was being held prisoner. Wherever he was, Tyghan was certain it was not at the castle anyway, which, at one time at least, was excessively grand. Fomorians and their paranoia never allowed for outsiders to cross its threshold.

Without a final decision made on where and how they should access Fomoria next, they decided to set off on a trail that ran along the southern border where dark, undulating clouds had been spotted in the sky by shepherds from the northern Wilds. It likely wouldn't lead to finding Cael, but several sightings of restless dead in one area could mean the portal was nearby. They left instructions with King Merriwind to post a twenty-four-hour watch on the battlement to report any activity along Balor Pass. "Anything at all, even the smallest movement," Tyghan ordered. "I want every bird, buck, and shadow documented."

"But—"

"It is not a request, Your Grace," Tyghan said, stepping closer.

Merriwind bobbed his head, eager for them to be on their way.

From the start, their trail was plagued with icy winds, making it even more miserable than Bleakwood Forest.

"Damn northern seas. Stir up a warm breeze, would you?" Melizan grumbled.

"That would defeat the point of a small party," Tyghan answered. "We want to slide through here unnoticed, don't we?"

She pulled her cloak tighter, spitting out a frustrated hiss. "We wouldn't be freezing our asses off and searching for that self-centered dolt if he'd used half his brain instead of his cock to make decisions."

She'd get no argument there from Tyghan. Cael slipped out of the palace without a full contingent of guards for a clandestine rendezvous—that wasn't with his betrothed—but he had done it dozens of times without incident.

"Regardless," Tyghan answered, "he was plucked from his path with pinpoint accuracy. Someone knew exactly where he would be and relayed that information to Fomoria."

But who? From Stable Master Woodhouse, who prepared his horse, to Madame Chastain, who gave him a requested potion before he left, to Eris, who rearranged his canceled schedule, to his First Officer, who had to postpone their meeting, to Cosette, who was the last one to see him sneak down a back trail. For most, their loyalty was beyond suspicion. But Cosette was merkind, as were most of those who frequented the waters of Fomoria.

"You're going to have to make your peace with Cosette," Melizan snapped, as if reading his mind. "We're discussing marriage."

Tyghan's jaw clenched. "Having an affair is one thing, but binding your crown to merkind is another. They bring the art of betrayal to new levels."

"She's a fucking knight sworn in your service. What is the matter with you?"

"She was the last one to see Cael."

"So what if she was? That's not proof of anything!"

There was definitely more hot blood than ice in her veins, at least when it came to Cosette, but Tyghan didn't get a chance to respond.

"*Ahead*," Dalagorn whispered.

Tyghan spotted the torn flesh and dark glistening puddles at the same time—and then the pink skinned carcass of a lamb.

The *shing* of four swords cut the air and they moved into formation. Tyghan lifted his free hand, ready to call to service whatever other energies he might need. As they rounded the bend, the trail opened up onto a meadow—and sweeping carnage.

Pieces of sheep, horses, and shepherds were strewn everywhere—the leftovers. The attack was finished. It looked like the aftermath of a feeding frenzy by drunk animals, but they weren't feeding. The restless dead were gathering. They were gleaning body parts. Choosing bones, heads, and sinew to create their own bodies. Parts of the field were burned, and the nauseating scent of burnt flesh and fur choked the air.

Quin got down from his horse and knelt beside the headless torso of a ram and placed his hand on its belly. "Twenty minutes at most. We just missed them."

It was uncertain if their small scouting party of four would have survived such an attack—especially a surprise one. It only took a few restless dead to wreak so much devastation, especially against unarmed shepherds and sheep—but it just as well might have been a massive flock of creatures.

For hours after their discovery, they searched the area from land and air, hoping to make another sighting of the swarming creatures or find evidence of a portal, but the countryside only held a false veneer of serenity. Maybe that was the most unnerving.

It wasn't the first bloodbath any of them had witnessed, but the image of the pink skinned lamb swam in Tyghan's thoughts, making his stomach muscles knot. The wanton pillaging was not something he would ever get used to. By the time they got back to the palace late that evening, Tyghan was set on stepping up the training. The recruits were far from ready for an encounter with the dead—especially Keats. She would be a lamb in their sights.

CHAPTER 41

Bristol's breath rolled in dark clouds in her chest, her eyes locked with Tyghan's.

They'd had a rough afternoon. Tyghan was always a relentless taskmaster, but that day he'd been worse. She wondered if a gremlin had crawled beneath his skin when he was in Mistriven. He pushed them past their limits, barking orders at every turn. She was relieved when the day was finally over. They were all tired, battered, and bruised as they gathered up their jackets and packs. She slung her arm over Avery's shoulder in commiseration as they limped away, but then Tyghan ordered one more round in the maze.

She whirled to face him. "I think we're all done for the day."

"No. You're not." He stood there, rigid, a scowling pillar of stone.

"Don't you ever relax? Chill?"

His scowl remained unchanged.

"*Chill* means—"

"I know what it means," he answered.

"Judging by your tone, I can confirm that you don't! *Chill*."

A chorus of breaths sucked in around her, but Bristol was too tired and testy to back down.

Tyghan stepped closer, towering over her. "And judging by your tone, I can confirm you're about to do two more rounds."

Bristol hooted. "And I can confirm that you're completely delusional."

His brows pulled down, his bearing like a dark storm ready to strike. "Is that so?"

It was only a matter of seconds before she learned it was not wise to throw down a gauntlet to a fae king in front of his officers. Or other recruits. Or maybe anyone. Ever.

He surveyed the surrounding recruits and proposed Avery do Bristol's additional rounds. Avery paled.

"She will n—" Bristol watched the officers close in. This was a battle she wouldn't win, not without it costing Avery or the others something. She should have thought of that. "Let them all go for the day," she said instead, "and I'll do three."

He nodded in agreement. "See? I know exactly how to *chill*."

When he turned, she flew a bird at his back.

Later that evening, when Tyghan arrived at the grove, Bristol greeted him with one word. "Ass."

He grinned, unfazed. "But a high and mighty one?"

God, she hated his smile. It was a curse. She rubbed her sore thighs and worked to stay angry. "You are so full of yourself."

"Yes," he agreed. "On the training grounds, where I have to be. But not here. If I were, I'd make you do laps right now."

"In this?" she said, lifting the chiffon of her dress. Her eyes narrowed. "I'd like to see you try."

The grin again, like he was considering it. "I'm sorry I was tough on you today, but on the training grounds my words are never challenged—"

"But—"

"Never. Not because I'm an ass, which I'll admit to. The truth is, sometimes I'd like to call it a day as much as any of you. Maybe more. But the battleground is no place for second thoughts or second opinions. Hard, split-second decisions must be made, and I or my officers are the only ones who make them. No one else. Orders must be followed swiftly, or we're all in trouble. We're in a fight for our lives, and time isn't on our side. The daily drills, who do you think it's all for? The officers? *Me?*"

She restrained an eye roll. His sarcasm was not necessary. She didn't need to be reminded how much practice they all needed. And she especially hated that his logic was sound. A hard day was not justification for mutiny. Still, she couldn't bring herself to admit it. "Let's talk about something else, all right?"

"Fine." He studied her, that maddening confident air in the tilt of his head and piercing gaze that made her traitorous stomach turn to warm jelly. "There is something I've been meaning to ask you."

"Yes?"

"What's a laundromat?"

She raised a skeptical brow. "You're kidding, right?"

"No. You've made me curious."

"You've never read about laundromats in one of your *modern works?*"

"I guess not. Is it like a washhouse?"

She scoffed at the notion of a mere washhouse and motioned to the bench. He was so annoying, and difficult, and—she swallowed. And undeniably . . . a lot of other things she mused on in the middle of the night. She silently swore at herself. *Don't go there, Bristol.*

He sat down beside her, and she leaned back, thinking, her palms resting on the cool marble. He remained quiet, patiently watching her as she mused.

When she spoke, she didn't hold back. She loved laundromats, and she sold their magic to him like she was a seasoned vendor at a fair, waxing poetic. "A laundromat's . . . a wondrous place of new beginnings. A place where miles and miles of roads, wrong turns, and mishaps disappear like magic. And not just your own wrong turns, but everyone's. Laundromats are full of people who are hoping for clean slates. And they get them for a reasonable price. The air inside is warm and velvety and hums with the promise that all will be well. When I was a child, I used to love the jingle of our coin can when my mother shook through it for the proper change. I loved the sound of sneakers, zippers, and buttons banging in dryers. I loved the swish of the washer as it twirled with soapy bubbles and my favorite jeans. Those sounds made everything new again."

He looked at her strangely for a moment, like her cheese wasn't sitting quite level on her cracker. Maybe she had oversold it a bit.

"That's what you like about them, that they offer fresh starts?"

"Yes," she answered. "There's a lot of value there for just a few quarters. Hard to beat. And on a cold rainy day, nothing smells better, except for maybe a coffee shop."

"Those smell good too?"

"The best ones do. Like I told you, you've been visiting the wrong places." She told him about her favorites: a tiny seaside bistro in San Diego; a mountain café just outside Denver; and of course, Déjà Brew, the coffee bar where her sister worked. She described their muffins and cinnamon cakes, the bins filled with dark roasted beans from all over the world, the sweet, steaming milk. Sometimes as she spoke, he studied her so intently, she wasn't sure he was listening to what she said at all. The smoldering behind her ribs would make her forget what she was going to say next, but he always managed to fill the clumsy silence with a new question.

"With all the towns you lived in, did you have a favorite?"

"Probably when I was young, but I learned not to get attached. We never stayed anywhere for long."

"But did you ever *want* to stay?"

A surprising stab twisted in Bristol's chest. *Maybe. Yes.* But she shook off the pain as she had learned to do. "Staying was never an option. I took in the pretty sights, the pretty people, the pretty things, like they were paintings in a museum. Look, but don't touch. Take the memory with you, and that's all."

"Was that enough?"

She shrugged. "It had to be. I didn't have a choice."

"The trows?" he asked hesitantly.

She nodded. "We were a family. Hunting one meant they hunted us all. We all paid the price."

CHAPTER 42

Bristol's day had started out reasonably well, but by midmorning, dread beaded on her brow. Esmee was finishing up her last lesson—a lesson about time. With each new word, the walls closed in and Bristol's back grew damp.

"The mortal and fae worlds move at different speeds," Esmee told them. "I like to use the analogy of dropping two downy feathers from a cliff at the same moment. They'll drift to the ground at varying rates of speed depending on air currents and by the chance of how they tumble. But one will always land later and farther from the other. If you drop them again, they will fall in an entirely different pattern. It's impossible to predict their paths. Time falls in the same way, but there are two times a year when mortal and fae timelines are in sync—Samhain and Beltane—which you might know in the mortal world as All Hallows' Eve and May Day. A single day is a single day in both worlds."

Bristol edged forward in her seat.

"Beyond that, time is erratic," Esmee continued. "A century or a minute can distance one world from the other. While fae can always return to the time of their own world, only a timemark allows mortals to move safely back to theirs. When the—"

"A *what*?" Bristol called out.

"A timemark," Esmee repeated. "The ancient relics fashioned by the mages of Gorias. Time still moves at different rates, but the relic marks your place in time when you leave, so a week passing here will only be a week passing there if you return. That's why you all received one, just in case you have more mortal blood in you than you think."

"I didn't get one," Bristol said in a panic. "I didn't get a timemark!"

"Of course you did. A small gold piece with a hole in the middle. It looks a bit like a coin."

Terror clutched Bristol's throat.

A coin?

She gasped.

Don't lose it. It's your ticket back to this world.

She jumped up without explanation and ran all the way from Ceridwen Hall to her room, throwing her door open. Her chest burned from her wild dash. She ran to her backpack and dumped it on the floor, frantically scattering crumbs and wrappers, searching for a glimmer of gold. "*It's not here!*" Her hands desperately ruffled through tampons, toothpaste, and packets of oatmeal, and then when she sent a granola wrapper flying, she spotted the tiny round piece of gold. She grabbed it, clutching it to her belly. A hoarse sob tore loose from her throat.

Damn you, Tyghan! Why didn't you tell me?

But he had.

It was only a brief mention, and she'd been so overwhelmed by everything else at the time, she hadn't realized the importance of it. The fox emerged from its hole and nibbled the crumbs she had scattered, then scurried back to his den. With her heart still hammering, she searched for a safe place to hide the timemark where no careless hand or hungry fox could make off with it.

Without it, she could lose her old life—and her sisters—forever.

She knew all the best places to hide things in a motel room—in the zippered cushion of a chair, inside the rod of a shower curtain, under the cover of an ironing board. Her room contained none of those things. She flung open her wardrobe and searched for a place there, then spotted her old sneakers at the bottom. She pulled up the insole of one, and slid the coin beneath it, then safely tucked both sneakers back on the top shelf, hidden from view.

"Everything all right?"

Bristol whirled.

Hollis stood in her doorway, the other recruits just behind her. They ambled farther into her room.

"You gave us a bit of a scare," Julia said.

Sashka beamed. "But, boy, can that lady run."

Bristol swallowed. "Sorry. It's just that I wasn't sure if I still had the timemark—and I think I might have a little mortal blood in me."

"That could put a scare in anyone, couldn't it?" Avery said.

Hollis shrugged. "None of us know for sure what skeletons are in our family tree. It's one of those things families tend to bury. We all have a few bones in our closets, and one or two could be mortal."

"Did you find it?" Rose asked.

Bristol nodded.

"Good. Problem solved," Julia said. "Let's go to the dining pavilion before afternoon lessons. You're going to need food after that sprint."

They left for the pavilion, but as they walked, Bristol wasn't thinking about food.

Hollis's words burned behind her eyes. *We all have bones in our closets.* Bristol had more than a closetful—she had a whole house full of them. And she could guarantee that every one was mortal.

CHAPTER 43

C at? Harper?"
Bristol sat on the floor in Tyghan's study calling through the portal, staring at the small view of her mudroom, but was only met with silence. It was the second time her sisters weren't there, and her heart sagged, but at least it still looked like the same mudroom, the same broom and dustpan, the same overflowing baskets of laundry. That much was reassuring. They were probably already at work or school.

She left a note on the washer instead.

> *All is well. Still searching for Father. Off to investigate*
> *another promising clue today. I'll check back again soon.*
>
> *I love you both,*
>
> *B*

With Tyghan gone again on kingdom business, it was left to Cully to escort Bristol to a bridge on the north side of the city. Eris said a merchant there claimed to have encountered a tall, haggard mortal on a deserted trail that ran through the Bollybogs three days ago. The word *haggard* caught Bristol's attention, because most fae were fastidious, even their simplest attire always clean, neat, and pressed. She clung to this detail, because if her father was running from trows, there was no doubt he would be haggard. Knights had already searched the bogs, with no result, but Bristol wanted to question the merchant to see if the man he saw was actually her father. Even a possible sighting offered hope.

Mug Ruith Bridge was by far the widest of the many bridges she had seen. It had three rows of shops and homes divided by two busy avenues wide enough for carriages and wagons. Still, they exited their carriage on a street near the bridge, since there was nowhere to park. Inwardly, Bristol grinned, amused that even fae had parking problems. Maybe some annoyances were as universal as roaches.

While she was riveted by the sights on the bridge, Cully ambled along with his hands in his pockets, bored, not appearing to notice anything.

She paused to gawk in a shop window at pinky-sized sprites weaving ribbons as they danced in circles. In another shop, she spotted beautiful woven scarves that reminded her of her mother's work. Cully was several paces ahead before he even noticed she was lagging behind, but he didn't complain, and just slowed his pace.

Their destination was a shop of poisons at the other end of the bridge. She had just dragged herself away from ogling a self-pouring teapot, when a cloaked passerby stepped in her path. She mumbled an apology as they did a little dance back and forth trying to walk around each other, but the next thing she knew, her sidesteps led to her being backed down a dark alleyway.

"Excuse me," she said firmly, realizing this maneuver wasn't an accident. She tried to shove past him, but only found herself pushed deeper into the darkness, trapped in a corner. "Get out of my way before I—"

"Bristol, Bristol, is that any way to talk to an old friend?"

The voice. She froze and peered into the shadows surrounding his face. He pushed back his hood and smiled, revealing his signature charming grin that turned every woman's head in Bowskeep. His blond hair was still cut close on the sides, and on top, a loose strand tumbled over his brow. His warm brown eyes danced with amusement.

Not him, too.

Sweet fuck, all of Bowskeep was infested with them. Her knees turned liquid, but then old resentments ignited and firmed them to steel. Anger had become her new best friend. "What are you doing here, Mick?"

"Business," he answered.

"Sure you are. Giving bike tours in Elphame now? I suppose that's why you rushed off without saying goodbye?"

"That's right. The more intriguing question is, why are *you* here?"

"None of your business. But I'm guessing you already know why."

His nose wrinkled, and he nodded in a way that was grossly superior. At one time she'd thought that expression was purely sympathetic. What a complete mess she must have been not to see it before. But maybe when a person was hurting, good sense wasn't as important as stopping the pain. And she guessed he knew that.

"Yes, I know why," he answered. "Rumor is you're looking for your dead father."

"Another rumor says he's not dead."

"Who told you that?"

"Again, none of your business."

He leaned closer, taking a slow, deep breath like he was possessing every inch of her. Or maybe trying to determine what she was. *Yes*, she thought, *I'm mortal, you ass. How could I not see that you weren't?* Even without fae powers, she could sense the glaring magic all over him now. It wasn't a scent as much as it was a weight pressing down, a presence that consumed the air and space around her.

"Go home, Bristol," he said, the glimmer in his eyes turning threatening. "There's nothing here to find."

"Why would you even care why I'm here?"

"Women like you just end up getting hurt in Elphame."

"Women like me end up getting hurt in Bowskeep, too."

His grin returned. "Are you saying you missed me?" He leaned forward in a swift move, his hands pressed to the wall on either side, caging her in. "I could fix that. We had some good times together. I seem to remember you enjoyed it. How about a quick one for old times' sake?"

Bristol smiled, meeting his dark, burning eyes, which loomed far too close to hers. "Really, Mick? You have time for that? To use and dump me again? You are amazing. I was in a weak state when I met you before. I'm not weak anymore. Get out of my way."

He didn't move, like he was searching for another one of the slick lines he once used to sway her, or he was planning something more devious. She had never seen such emptiness in his eyes before. Like the curtain had been pulled back and there was only a hungry void behind it. He was someone else entirely—or maybe this was who he had been all along. Her skin prickled. *Unseelie*, she thought. That was what she saw. She pressed back harder against the wall.

"Be careful how you speak to me," he whispered, his finger grazing her cheek. "One day you may regret it." The threat in his whisper was blade sharp. *Be careful.*

She wasn't sure what she was going to do next if he didn't move, except perhaps knee him and hope he didn't turn her into a goat or worse, but then he heard the faint *click* and looked down at the switchblade in her hand.

"Remove your finger from my cheek," she said, "or lose it."

He smiled. "That little thing? You think *that's* going to stop me?" He chuckled. "You have no idea what you've gotten yourself into, Bristol. You're in way over your head. But I always liked your style. Your passion." His gaze devoured her mouth, then drifted lower.

Her grip tightened on the knife, but then there was a shout from the other end of the alley. Someone called her name. She saw Cully running toward her, and in that same instant, Mick vanished. Gone. The same way Willow had disappeared. She sucked in a startled breath.

"Who was that?" Cully asked when he reached her. "He disappeared before I could get a good look."

An illusion, she thought. An illusion she shamefully fell for.

She stared at the space Mick had just occupied, his warmth already gone, the alley suddenly not so dark, like he took the shadows with him. "No one important," she answered, not wanting to reveal her embarrassing error in judgment. "Just a passing stranger."

Which is exactly what he was.

CHAPTER 44

T hat's enough!" Tyghan said. "Out! I have other places to be!"
The army of tailors gathered up their supplies and hurried
out the door. They had been in his room for almost an hour,
fretting over fabrics, buttons, and cording. They already had his mea-
surements. Tyghan didn't know why they had to be there at all. Eris
had probably made them nervous. He'd been fretting over every detail
of Beltane Eve, determined to make it perfect, as if Tyghan's jacket
made the difference between success and failure.

He faced his mirror, thankful for the quiet, and raked his hair back
into place. There was no place he had to be. Only a place he *wanted* to
be, even though he told himself he wasn't going. *Not tonight.*

It wasn't a wise course of action.

Not going, he repeated as he dressed, fussing over which shirt to
wear. But then, as he tugged on his trousers, he thought, *Why shouldn't
I go? I'm king, after all. I can go wherever I damn well please. It's my duty
to look out for Danu's interests*—and Bristol definitely fell in that cate-
gory. He was only keeping an eye on her. A prudent move. "Duty," he
whispered as he closed his door behind him.

But he knew it wasn't duty. Bristol had gotten beneath his skin in
ways he tried not to think about. Maybe, he reasoned, he only wanted
to make sure he hadn't been so hard on her that day, that she packed

up and left—promise or no promise. Or that he was simply making some aspect of this world pleasing for her. Eris *had* advised him to be civil. And fae recruits often grew homesick. He saw that in her eyes when she spoke about her sisters. She worried about them. Bristol wasn't the oldest, but she was clearly the alpha, the protector of the trio. On their first meeting, she nearly leapt over the table at him when she thought he was threatening her sisters. And she did leap into Elphame to rescue her father. It was in her blood—the passion of a knight—like Kierus had once been. Every aspect of her fascinated him.

That morning he learned from Avery that Bristol's birthday had slipped by unnoticed just after she arrived. She had turned twenty-two but said nothing to anyone, only in passing to Avery that her sisters would be unhappy about missing her birthday. They'd had something special planned for her. Avery said that in the mortal world pretty cakes were a tradition on birthdays, but at nightly festivities, there were always long tables of extravagant cakes.

Instead, he fished a polished stone from the river. He headed to the groves, the stone in his pocket, and wondered what she would think of the Danu birthday tradition. He found her strolling among the willows.

"So what are you and the trees talking about tonight?"

He noticed the smile that sprung to her face when she saw him. Heat spiked in his chest.

"You," she answered. "They're sharing all your secrets."

"I wouldn't believe everything they say. Trees tend to be gossips."

"I find them quite reliable."

"Did they tell you what's in my pocket?"

Her brows rose. "We were just about to get to that."

He pulled the stone from his pocket. "It's for your birthday." He explained its significance as he pressed it into her palm. "Whatever strengths the stone has, they'll be yours on your birthday and every birthday to come. But first you need to close your eyes and let its power flow into you."

Her left brow quirked into a question. "My birthday was weeks ago."

He cupped her hand in his. "It will still work. I'm king. I can stretch the magic a bit."

She snorted and closed her eyes. "I'm not feeling anything yet. How long will it take for the power to flow?" she asked.

He stared—her eyes shut, her shoulders relaxed, her face glowing in the moonlight with amusement, playing along with him. *Until tomorrow, the next day, the day after that*, he wanted to answer, so she'd remain there, her hand wrapped between his. But instead, he slowly pulled his hands away and said, "It's done."

She opened her fist and smiled at the small white stone shimmering with a single fleck of blue at its center. "It's beautiful." She skimmed her finger across it. "Will I be able to lift a car over my head now?"

"Probably not. It's a moonstone. But it will strengthen your intuitions and help you follow your instincts. I'll bring you the car stone next time."

"Thank you." She continued to admire the stone, turning it to catch the faint light of the moon. "I'll have to fish stones from the river to take back to my sisters when I leave."

"You miss your sisters."

She glanced up, as if surprised he had noticed. "Yes, I do. We've never been apart much, and I worry about them. But they're both strong and smart. They'll be fine. Though Harper is rather defenseless when it comes to a good book. They've given her a deep-seated belief in happy endings."

"But not you?"

Her expression sobered. "Happiness is slippery. I savor the moments I can." Her eyes rested in his for a long moment before she dropped the stone into her pocket. "What about you? Do you miss your brother?"

Tyghan coughed. *Miss his brother?* It was mostly a holiday not having him around—except for the extra duties that now fell to Tyghan. "Sure I do," he answered.

A skeptical puff of air escaped from her lips. "Well, that was convincing." She relaxed against the tree trunk, her hand grazing one of the weeping branches. "I've told you about my family. Tell me about yours. You never talk about them."

Tyghan's neck tensed. "You don't want to know about them."

"Yes, I do. Think of it as another birthday gift."

"It's not your birthday."

Her left brow arched.

He struggled talking about his family. They were complicated. He eyed the path that led to the festivities and rubbed his neck. Maybe now was a good time to go.

"What's your brother like? Funny? Serious?"

Tyghan squinted, like the sun was in his eyes, deciding whether to answer. He stepped over to a half-buried boulder and sat. "Cael is arrogant, petty, demanding, and a literal royal pain in the ass."

Bristol shrugged, unfazed. "So he's a lot like you?"

Tyghan glanced down, trying to restrain a smile, but sewed on a sour face when he looked back up. "I'm a coddling nursemaid compared to my brother."

"So you say. I'm not convinced." She sat down next to him. "I guess I'll find out once we rescue him."

"Assuming we do."

She sighed, and he wasn't sure if it was because of the dismal odds or his dismal attitude, but she rolled past it. "So, continue. Tell me more about your family."

And he did.

It wasn't as painful as he'd thought it might be. Maybe it was her flippant attitude that made it all seem like a minor topic and not a hushed court secret. The gentry instilled that in him from the time he was a small child, the way they whispered in dark corners about his family like there was something shadowy and tragic about them. Something cursed. "It's only my brother, my sister, and me, and we all have different parentages." He explained that his mother, the queen of Danu, didn't have much luck in her marriages and was married four times. "Her first husband was a prince from Amisterre. He died only days after their marriage by falling on his own sword." He told her about the speculation that erupted and how his mother remarried quickly to dispel the rumors. "Within the year, Cael was born, but then his father died in an unfortunate encounter with a sandpit when Cael was only a baby."

He continued with the account of the queen's third husband becoming sick with an unknown ailment just days after their marriage, then wasting away and dying in a matter of weeks. "Which brings us to husband number four—my father. He came to the marriage with a daughter in tow. Melizan was five years old at the time, and I was born several months later. Our father lasted a bit longer than the previous spouses, but he died in another accident when I was seven. He was attacked in the Wilds by a crazed stag. At that point, something in my mother died, too. At least that's what Eris tells me. I was too young to fully understand. Eris said she became convinced she carried a curse that would bring ruin to her children as well. She walked into the woods one day to save us from similar fates, and she never came back. My brother was only twelve at the time, and was crowned king a week later, with Eris as regent. I was the spare, trained and destined to lead the order of knights as Knight Commander—until six months ago, when Cael was captured. I pity his captors."

"The fact that they took him and not you is telling. Maybe they considered you a worse lot of trouble."

Against his will, he smiled. "I can't argue with that. Actually, Cael does have his finer points. He loves parties and gatherings and never saw an invitation he didn't like. Anything to take him away from the throne. He's a social charmer. He can turn it on and off like a faucet. He mostly keeps it on for the far-flung gentry. It makes him a favorite among them, and that comes in handy in dealing with the other kingdoms."

She rubbed her chin. "Important point. You're definitely not the charmer of your family. How is Cael closer to home?"

"Stingy with his charm. Pain in the ass. Oh, I said that already, didn't I? Bears saying again." She was quiet, and he knew he had said too much. "But I don't want you to think he's not worth saving."

"Noted," she answered. "I suppose none of us would be worthy of saving if only judged by our worst qualities."

CHAPTER 45

The grove murmured. Swayed. The leaves sighed. It had become accustomed to the girl and her nightly visits. Dancing. Reaching. Hoping. The trees swallowed her up. Welcomed her. She reminded them of a boy who once climbed their limbs, a boy who fell in love beneath the boughs of a forest, too. They remembered the boy, because trees never forget—not the touch of mortals, creatures, or gods.

The girl's steps were soft. The trees felt them in their roots, in the swish of fallen leaves, in her tiptoe hope. The god's steps were heavier, but no less hopeful, a deep wanting the trees understood, the yearning for a season to pass—or begin.

But then they sensed another lurking nearby. Watching. Not with hope, but with the deadness of winter. The leaves trembled, quaked as warning. But the girl didn't notice. Neither did the god. For them it was only spring.

⸙

The music was hypnotic, the air fragrant, heady.

Bristol twirled in the moon shadows, her steps matched in time with a phantom.

A phantom that made every part of her feel alive.

She looked at the weave of branches above her, at the blanket of stars beyond, and felt a whisper-soft caress near her ear, barely there, but as powerful as a storm. Her eyes fluttered shut, willing that invisible caress to touch her in other places. Her neck. Her lips. The buttons of her dress . . .

Her fingertips tingled with want. She longed to run her hands over a burning bare chest, her nails across the hard muscle below.

Music pulsed beneath her skin. Something else pulsed low in her gut. The drumbeats. The air. The back twirling against her own, even the sweat on her brow, was an elixir consuming her, seducing her. Holding back was torturous, yet exquisite, like hot metal being burnished to a sharp point. The music slowed. Their movement slowed. The blinking of the stars paused, waiting, every inch of the universe ready to ignite.

Silence.

Second after second passing.

Tyghan, she whispered in her head, hoping he could hear her.

And then the bows plucked, the fiddles crooned, the drum resumed, and so did their movement. It was a dangerous, teasing dance. But she yearned for more. A dance that would drown her completely, until she couldn't breathe at all.

With each step, it grew harder not to want more of everything.

But she understood, too—maybe in a way that no one else could.

The exposure.

The risk.

The safety of invisibility.

It was a line she had walked her entire life.

Small steps.

She swayed.

She swallowed.

She ached.

Give it time.

And she whirled in his arms again.

CHAPTER 46

It was dawn, the air still dewy with mist. Madame Chastain neatly folded her hands in front of her, trying to restrain her growing irritation. Knights straggled into the rotunda, slouching into chairs. *Late, every one of them*, she thought, but with the king still not present, she could hardly chastise them. She wasn't sure whether to blame it on the approach of Beltane and the lack of sleep—even the most disciplined of knights weren't impervious to its allure—or simple weariness.

She had seen it in Eris last night as he lay in her bed, uncharacteristically quiet. Eris was a learned man, and though she'd had three husbands and a forgotten number of lovers, none were as skilled and knowledgeable in bed as Eris. He knew how to please a woman, and it brought him joy. But last night after their lovemaking, instead of being talkative and invigorated as he usually was, he lay quietly staring at the ceiling. When she asked what was wrong, he sighed and answered, "Just wondering how many will go home tomorrow."

The review meeting was long overdue, and the question weighed on them all. Finding a candidate who was bloodmarked was their only hope of stopping Kormick. And with less than two months until the Choosing Ceremony, nerves were frayed. Eris held so much hope for this newest recruit, but the High Witch was against it from the start.

The daughter of a traitor and a ruthless monster? That was not an auspicious birthright. She warned Eris, but he ignored her. It turned out her fears were unfounded. Miss Keats was mortalbound, no ability in her, but she didn't have the heart yet to tell Eris—at least not until he found someone else he could pin their hopes on.

More footsteps echoed through the hall. Cael's First Officer, Sloan, arrived and took a seat beside his two senior knights. Melizan and Cosette strolled in behind him. Eris rushed in on their heels, and finally, a good four minutes later, Tyghan arrived. Sloan sniffed at Tyghan's tardiness. Melizan whispered to Cosette, and they both laughed. The rotunda door boomed as Dalagorn shut it. Tyghan was disheveled, his hair windblown, as he took the last remaining seat at the round council table, Kasta on one side of him, Glennis and Quin on the other. It was not like him to be late, and the High Witch wondered if his night torments had returned.

※

Tyghan surveyed those at the table, then met Sloan's scornful gaze. He knew Sloan resented his position as king. Sloan believed the council had moved too soon to crown Tyghan after Cael was taken. With the power balance spinning out of control, the council was desperate to name another king quickly. *What kind of nation has two kings?* Sloan had protested vehemently. *Cael is still alive!* The council argued that they didn't know with certainty if Cael was still alive, and if he was, whether they would ever get him back. The Fomorian king's word was as trustworthy as a hungry wolf with a lamb in its sights. They maintained that in these trying times Danu needed a strong leader with the full title and power over the nation. Tyghan would relinquish the title of king if and when Cael was returned safely.

But Tyghan was sure it was Sloan's loss of position that provoked him most. He was used to being the king's First Officer. Now Kasta held that position, along with all the power that went with it. Sloan took orders from her now, instead of the other way around.

Tyghan looked away, refusing to be drawn into Sloan's pettiness.

He was glad that review meetings were generally short—he was already losing patience with this one. Once Madame Chastain called the meeting to order, Esmee and Olivia took over, reviewing the recruits' progress on basic magical maneuvers—from simple levitations to summoning blinding mists. Their recommendations, as usual, fell into three categories: keep a recruit for further observation, advance them to join the ranks of knights-in-service, or send those with no potential back home. Sloan's three recruits, while deemed not to be bloodmarked, were excelling and advanced to the garrison, along with one of Melizan's. No one objected when one of her other recruits was recommended for dismissal, but Eris winced when Olivia began reporting Keats's dismal attempts at even the simplest magics.

"Her field training has been dismal, too," Sloan complained. "Let's cut our losses now and be rid of her."

Tyghan's hand moved ever so slightly on the table. Kasta didn't miss a beat. While the king had final say, protocol required he stay out of deliberations. She leaned forward in her seat. "No," she said firmly. "It's too soon to send her home. There is still—"

"It's not too soon if she isn't showing progress, and she isn't," Sloan argued. "Time is valuable. Why waste our energy—especially on the traitorous spawn of Celwyth?"

He spit out the last few words with accusation. Challenge vibrated across the table, and Glennis's hooves scraped the stone floor like she was about to leap at him. Sloan's knights bristled, sitting forward in their seats, ready to meet her.

Review meetings were often tense, but rarely erupted into physical confrontation. Eris stood, trying to draw their attention. "But she is precisely the one who may have the talents we need for—"

But Sloan wouldn't let it go. "What talent? The talent to betray us? Who will get stabbed next? Haven't we all learned our lesson by now? Send her on her way before—"

Melizan sighed. "Oh, Sloan, hush. Let Tygh keep his little troublemaker for a few more days. Besides, we're all keeping an eye on her. She'll be gone soon enough."

Sloan's chest rose with indignation, his gaze meeting Tyghan's, but he finally conceded with a stiff nod. Even he didn't want to tangle with Melizan, and her last words, uttered with certainty, had probably appeased him.

The rest of the meeting passed quickly, and as soon as Madame Chastain declared it finished, Tyghan bounded out the door.

Kasta caught up with him. "Last one in, first one out? Madame Chastain was barely holding her tongue at your lateness."

"Eris and I were cornered on our way to the meeting by three council members. They were furious because they found out about Bristol's parentage. They demanded we get rid of her."

"*Rid?*"

"They didn't specify how. They just want her gone. I suspect they found out through Sloan's loose tongue. *Fuck.* By tomorrow the whole council will know. Break his nose or a rib during officer drills today, would you?"

"Gladly," Kasta said, chuckling to herself as if already imagining how she would do it. "But really, Tygh, why not send her home? We need to concentrate on the few we have left who have potential to be knights-in-service or bloodmarked. She was a good find on Eris's part, and the team has tried to work with her, but Sloan's right, she's not showing any promise."

"You're harder on her than the other recruits."

"We have to be. She's failing."

"She's good in some field drills."

"Some? Is that your standard now? That's not close to enough, and you know it."

Tyghan was silent, his thoughts tangling as he wrestled with the truth. He searched for a way to quell Kasta's line of thinking. Anything. He finally glanced over his shoulder to be sure no one followed too closely. "We need her. Even if she has no special ability, she still has value. She's our last resort. She is Maire's daughter."

Kasta's expression was blank, not grasping his point.

"A *hostage*," he whispered. The word jolted him. Spoken aloud, it sounded far more sinister than it had when it was only a distant thought in his head on Bristol's first night there.

Kasta's lips parted. "Oh." A crease formed between her brows as she weighed this new possibility. "Not a bad strategy, but it won't work. Maire's a heartless monster drunk on power. She'd sooner eat her young. She won't care."

"She was a mother, too. For over twenty years in their world. That has to mean something, even for her."

"Or it could backfire and unleash her full fury. Right now, she might just be doing Kormick's bidding. Give her a reason to fling wide the gates of hell, and who knows—"

"I said it was a last resort. If we—" Tyghan's frustration mounted. "Danu is never going to bend a knee to Kormick. I can't let the rest of Elphame be put at his mercy, either—and I won't let my brother die to do it."

"C'mon, Tygh, you don't even like Cael."

"He's still my brother."

Kasta cringed.

"You might not like it, but he's the familiar one," Tyghan said. "And when the world is upside down, even powerful queens and kings search out what they know. That's what they want right now—not more change. We've been negotiating for weeks with Gildawey for more long swords, and they still haven't agreed to send them. The queen said that if even Danu could fall victim to Fomoria, what was the point of more swords? And we need more swords. *Gildan* swords. Even if we manage to shut the portal, we still have the Fomorian army to contend with. We need a commitment of troops from all the kingdoms. We aren't going to get that without Cael. Besides, I made an oath."

"You were mostly unconscious when they crowned you."

"I remember enough, and it's an oath just the same."

A dubious *hmm* rolled from Kasta's throat. "Are you sure that's the only reason you want to keep Keats here?" She hesitated, then cleared her throat. "I wasn't spying, Tygh. Just doing my duty and checking up on you, but . . . I've seen you dancing with her."

Tyghan's pace slowed. He thought he'd been careful, but Kasta knew him too well. She could detect the telltale signs of his invisibility, the stir of dust near his feet, the blur of his breath in the air. Still, he answered, "That's impossible. I never danced with her."

"Seriously, Tygh? You're going to pull that with me? Remember who you're talking to—the toddler you turned into a frog."

"I changed you back."

A puff of air escaped her lips. "It was Eris and four sorcerers who finally changed me back because you couldn't remember how. I had to eat flies for a week! But I never held it against you because *I know you.* You were only curious. Tell me . . . is that all this is now? Curiosity?"

Tyghan twisted his head to the side like he was cracking a bone in his neck. He put his hand up in lieu of an answer. Everything she said was true. Kasta, Glennis, Quin, and Kierus had been with him almost since the cradle. Nurseries, school, tutoring by Eris, advanced train-ing tournaments from Danu's greatest warrior gods—and everything else—for their whole lives. They finished each other's sentences and completed each other's magic spells. They were scolded and punished as a unit, for whatever one did, the others were always complicit.

That all changed six months ago. Tyghan had changed. He could never go back to who he was.

"It's not what you think," he said, trying to sound indifferent. He explained that a few nights after she arrived, he left Bristol at the hazel grove, but when he looked back, he saw her dancing near the cliff with her eyes closed. "I was curious, watching her getting close to the edge but never going over. I wondered if Eris was right and she did have special instincts, and then I worried that she'd go over the edge and break her fool neck. I glamoured myself invisible and stepped between her and the ledge as a safeguard. When she stepped toward me with raised hands, I raised mine and then—"

"You were suddenly dancing."

Tyghan nodded.

"For how many nights now?"

"All right. A lot. What do you want me to say, Kasta? It's only dancing. You've seen me do it hundreds of times."

"Not in six months. And not like this." She paused, then added, "The other officers are noticing, Tygh."

He knew. Quin had spotted him watching Bristol from afar and said, *Be careful with that one.* And Dalagorn and Madame Chastain had made vague jabs about his late arrivals to festivities.

"It's only the season. You know what Beltane does to everyone. You could throw me down right here on this path and have your way with me, and I'd let you."

She snorted at the blatant lie. There had never been anything between them and never would be. They were only friends and fellow knights together—though some knights were more than friends. Kasta and Kierus had been occasional lovers, but Kasta was devoted to her knighthood in a singular way, while Kierus navigated a wider path. Tyghan had always thought something lasting might develop between them. He'd been wrong about that, too. When it came to Kierus, he'd been wrong about everything.

Kasta dragged her palm over her forehead like Tyghan was giving her a headache. "Have you thought about telling her the truth about her parents? Who they really were?"

"Are. They still *are* the enemy. Kierus is still a traitor facing a death sentence. Tell her that if we do find him, he faces the worst punishment Danu reserves for traitors like him? That we have a thousand archers waiting for a chance to put an arrow through Maire's heart? That it's not fucking trows she spent her whole life running from, but us? You think she'd help us then? We can't afford truth."

Kasta winced. Said aloud, every truth was far more damning, and she agreed, these were things that Bristol could never know. "How long can this go on? You're already juggling the impossible, having to decide between the Choosing Ceremony and your brother's life. Can you really juggle one more impossible thing? It's dangerous to be involved with someone you might use as a hostage."

"We're not involved. We talk. That's it. We've never—" He shook his head, leaving Kasta to fill in the blank.

"Talking can be far more intimate than screwing. Call it whatever you want, you're *something*—and it's not fair to Elphame or Danu."

"I would never break my oath. I'm not like Kierus."

"I know, but you also know what the council will think if they find out you're entangled with Maire's daughter. They're already on edge, and they'll fear history is about to repeat itself. I mean, Tygh, *her*, of all people? There are a hundred women in court who would have you. Take one of them to bed. You have to keep your position secure. And then there's Sloan." She rolled her eyes. "Ho! He'd be a horse in a pasture of clover at dinnertime. He'd gorge on the rumors and spread them like manure until you—"

"I know what they'd all think. Let me handle it, Kasta. And don't say anything to anyone about us dancing."

CHAPTER 47

W alk away, Tyghan. Walk away like you never found me.
The words haunted him. They were the last ones
Kierus ever spoke to him.
Walk away.

But now he was thinking of Bristol. It was one thing to manipulate someone you hated. It was another to manipulate someone who had pledged to help you. Someone you liked—more than liked. It was a hard thought for him to consider, much less admit, even to himself.

It was only supposed to be one dance. *One.*

He had pushed the thought away again and again, trying to find ways to discount it, but he couldn't anymore. It wasn't the season. It had crept up on him, maybe from the moment he first saw her in the inn, the way she stood her ground even when she was terrified, meeting his stare like she was planning how she would take him down. Then the nerve she conjured when she came back to the inn to bargain with him, afraid but still not cowering. His whole ride back to the palace he kept seeing every color that had swept through her eyes, the storm she navigated but refused to surrender to. At the time it had infuriated him—but captivated him too. Then, once back in Elphame, it was a word here, a glance there, lingering instead of leaving, conversations that went from angry to easy—conversations he had hungered for. *Still* hungered for. He wanted to know the things she contemplated, questioned, believed. The things she said made him wonder in a way he hadn't in a long time. She made something dead in him come alive again.

Now his thoughts drifted to her as easily as opening his eyes. As he ate his breakfast, he wondered what pizza tasted like. As he lay in his bed, resisting sleep, he'd see the pale freckle in the hollow of her throat. He'd relive every word between them. Even her name haunted him. *Bri.* A name he now longed to say out loud. Feel the sound of it on his tongue. See her reaction. She invited him to call her that from the first day they met, but now it seemed too late, too intimate. At night, as he drifted to sleep, he'd see her lips, her lashes, and remember the touch of her hand in his as he helped her up from the ground, or her arm brushing his—however briefly—and the burn it left behind, not just on his skin but deeper inside him.

The season, he told himself repeatedly. But the season had never done this to him before.

There are a hundred women in court who would have you.

But he didn't want them.

He wanted Bristol. Only her. In every way, he wanted her.

It was as simple and as complicated as that.

It made the charade of searching for her father more unbearable. Tyghan already knew Kierus would go nowhere near any city. Most likely he was headed for the Wilds and, eventually, Balor Pass that led into Fomoria. That's where a company of knights were watching and waiting to trap the man she desperately hoped to rescue.

Her of all people.

Kasta may have been the most direct, but she wasn't the first to warn him. He was courting disaster, and he already had enough of that to deal with. He didn't need more.

Walk away.

But he hadn't walked away then.

He wasn't sure he could now.

CHAPTER 48

The ancient barn creaked, not with age but wonder. Who was this new visitor? The barn was probably the oldest structure in all of Elphame, its mortar made of magic, its beams woven with enchantment, every stone hand hewn by the gods themselves. The gods revered and depended upon their horses, and great care was given to the quarters that housed them.

Bristol listened to the barn's sighs, the curious *hmmm* that circled around her ankles like an invisible tide, the whispers that might have been mistaken for wind whistling across a floor. She sensed as soon as she walked through the door that this was no ordinary barn, if, indeed, it could be called a barn at all. Each stall was constructed with beautiful carved stones depicting a weave of leaves and berries, drawn bows, beetles, antlers, and hands holding fruit—a stone forest that was both alluring and foreboding. Enormous iron chandeliers shaped like tree branches hung from high beams above the main walkway. Rear doors in the stalls led to a meadow, and the smell of sweet green hay permeated the air.

She had arrived early, and Master Woodhouse, the stable lord, emerged from an oak tree near the entrance to greet her. He was a spriggan, she guessed, like Avery, though considerably older, judging by the mottled lichen on his cheeks and the thick mossy vines that trailed down his hunched back. Since she was early, he offered to give her a tour. He was noticeably proud of his position and his charges, and he told her the long history of the Tuatha de horses, the famous processions they led, the battles they helped win, the heroes and gods who had ridden upon their backs, the important roles they played in shaping Elphame.

"And here," he said, once they circled around and came back to the first stall, "is August, King Tyghan's horse. Only His Majesty rides this one. Finest steed in all the land. No one will argue that."

Bristol eyed the enormous white horse. The horse eyed her back, his huge black eyes sizing her up, fire glowing somewhere deep in his pupils. His nostrils flared with a dismissive snort, and he ran through the rear door to the meadow.

Master Woodhouse chuckled, the heavy vines trailing over his shoulders briefly flushing a brighter green. "Don't take it personally. August tends to be standoffish. He's a one-person horse, and maybe a little full of himself. He's faster than the others and knows it. And of course, he knows Beltane is coming, and he'll be center stage in the pageantry—which reminds me, I have grooming to tend to. You'll be all right waiting here on your own?"

Bristol nodded, and he shuffled away. She was uncertain why Tyghan wanted to meet her here. He never met her anywhere during the daylight hours. Last night at Sun Court, Rose and Sashka bemoaned that the officers would soon be culling recruits, and they worried about their prospects. Bristol had performed more poorly than either of them. Was that why Tyghan wanted to meet with her at dawn? To break the news personally?

Heavy footsteps sounded outside the entrance. Tyghan rounded the corner and then came up short when he saw her. He'd been in a hurry. She wasn't sure if that pleased her or she should be concerned. But the look on his face—if only for a moment—made her belly rush with warmth. It was real. Unplanned. No pretense. He was relieved she had come. *No, this king is not sending me home.* He brushed the hair from his forehead, and the look in his eyes lasted a split second longer, but then the pretense returned, as predictable as daylight, like he wasn't allowed to be happy about anything.

"You're on time," he said formally, the stickler Knight Commander once again. "Good."

"What's up?" she asked.

His head cocked to the side as he thought for a moment, tripping on the phrase. As well versed as he was in so many things, it made her smirk inside when something she said made him stumble. It evened things out a bit. If only she could drag him into her world for a day or two and confound him completely.

"Up," he finally answered, like he got it. "Extra training. Sticks, to be precise." He led her outside to an adjacent structure—an indoor training ring. He explained that sticks were an ancient defense art that all fae were taught, because even if caught unawares in the middle of a wilderness, a stick was always a readily available weapon. Even though most fae possessed magics, so did the enemy, and very often, the physical world was the last defense one could count on.

"I'm not saying your father didn't teach you well, but there's always more to learn, and extra practice might help."

Help with what, he didn't need to say. She wasn't excelling at anything else, and sticks were something she at least fared decently at during field practice.

The ring was large, meant for horses. Far larger than what they needed, and she wondered if he chose this place to practice because it was out of the way and no one would see them there—like a faraway grove under the cloak of darkness. She tried to be understanding about his wariness after the horrible betrayal he had suffered, but how long could this last? Yes, his trust had been shattered, but still, she was growing impatient. Hadn't she proven herself trustworthy?

Once inside the building, he turned, and his right hand casually swiped the air. The stone walls on either side of the wide entrance spread, block by block, erasing the door. It was the first time she had witnessed him perform any magic other than disappearing at the inn. Apparently, he did know how to do more—and with very little effort.

A burst of anxiety swept through her. Just when she thought she was getting used to this world, something like this would set her off-kilter, reminding her she was not one of them.

"I don't want to be interrupted," he explained when he faced her. "There are—" His expression changed, maybe because of her own. "What's wrong?"

"I'm wondering—" The question on the tip of Bristol's tongue seemed utterly absurd—yet nothing about this world was conventional . . . so why not ask anyway and sound ridiculous? "Madame Chastain told us on our first day that the first Tuatha de were gods. She showed us some of them in a misty vision. I guess what I'm trying to ask, is that what you are? One of those gods? I mean, not a *God* god. But one of them?"

His eyes lit up, and a small chuckle shook his chest.

"Really," she said. "I want to know."

He shrugged. "Depends on who you ask. If you ask Eris, he'll say yes, at least as the gods are now. If you ask my fellow knights, they'll laugh, but out of respect call me a demigod. If you asked the real gods, they'd say I was an amusing distant descendant. I'm not a creator, only a manipulator of what already is. My talents pale next to theirs, but as Tuatha de go, I'm of the line of Lugh, and have my fair share of . . . abilities."

"But why bother with something as crude as sticks, when you can do something like that?" She motioned to the stone wall.

He gave the wall a fleeting glance, like it was nothing. "When I'm facing an enemy, our magics may be in direct opposition to one another, gaining me little ground. Sometimes reaching for the tools of the earth is what tips the battle. There is power in the creations of the mother god Danu. There always has been."

He explained how his magic worked, drawing on the energy inherent in everything, the soil, the air, water, sun, plants, even the distant stars, and focusing, bending, expanding that energy for a single purpose. When surrounded by a vast army, focusing energy on them all at once was close to impossible, especially when some of them held the same powers that he did. He said that even spoken words had energy and power in them, and directing that energy through incantations was what Madame Chastain and the other sorcerers were trying to teach the recruits. "I'm sure eventually Madame Chastain will teach you all the different kinds of magics, but we can't discount the power of flesh, and steel, and heart. They have a magic of their own, and every magic has its place."

He told her that even the great gods, when they roamed these lands, cherished a plow in their hands, the warm sun on their backs, the weight of a spear held high overhead, and the mist of the sea in their faces as they rode over waves in golden chariots. These simple actions fed their strengths, too.

As he spoke, he seemed like someone else, maybe the someone he used to be before everything went wrong for him, someone relaxed and fun and thoughtful, someone who paused and contemplated the world in thoughtful nuance and not angry absolutes. That was how their conversations always went at night. He unfolded like a rare night bloom, but now to see him talk this way in the light of day for the first time, forgetting to be irritated, or in a hurry, or circumspect, his voice easy, and his hands relaxed at his sides—it stirred a hunger inside Bristol for more of this person he kept hidden.

"Danu's gifts come in many forms," he continued, "from grand to humble—including sticks." He motioned with his head to the two wooden sticks propped up against the wall. "Should we give it a try?"

"What about invisibility?" she interjected awkwardly.

He tensed, his stance more cautious. "What about it?" he asked.

"Do you draw on energy for that too?"

"Invisibility is the opposite of glamour. Instead of drawing energy to yourself, you are essentially letting it go. It's why it's not too useful in battle. Your senses and other powers are less sharp."

"You feel less?"

"Sometimes."

"I can see why you'd avoid it, then. I wouldn't want to feel less. I'd rather feel . . . more."

Her eyes rested directly in his, unblinking, hoping for an acknowledgment of their covert dances. Maybe on some level, she wanted proof
that she wasn't imagining it all.

He was quiet, and she wondered if he perceived her hidden meaning. But he only answered, "Understandable. Shall we start?"

Bristol nodded, and pushed away musings she'd been having for
weeks, especially at night when she crawled into bed and wished she
wasn't alone.

She removed her jacket, tossing it on a bench. "I haven't had a formal lesson in over five years," she warned.

"That's all right. I'll walk you through it."

He grabbed both sticks and threw one to her. They took it slow at
first, simple drills to warm up. Left. Right. Block. Jab. And then faster.
It all came back to her. There was something graceful about it, almost
like a dance, but powerful and dangerous too. The raw wood dug into
her palms. Sweat beaded on her brow. They moved on to more complicated moves, rolling, swinging, and springing back to their feet.

Later, when they combined exercises, he used the same move that
had landed her on her back before—hooking her around her knees.
Bristol cursed at herself for literally falling for it again and promised
herself it wouldn't happen a third time. She went on the attack, and
then he stopped the exercise, showing her where her footwork was
catching her up, and explained that her eye work was revealing too
much to her opponent. "Never take your focus off their face, but see
everything else at the same time. It's not hard to do."

Easy for you to say, Bristol thought.

"Only look away if you want your opponent to think something is
there."

The exercises sped up, their sticks meeting, the sound cracking the
air, her eyes locked on his while anticipating his sidesteps, his lunges,
and noting his fighting idiosyncrasies.

"How am I doing?" she asked breathlessly.

"Good. But you should never—"

And then she jabbed him. *Hard in the gut.* He doubled over, falling to one knee, holding his side and wincing.

She stepped closer, hovering over him, and smiled like a hunter viewing her fallen prey. "And never get caught up in conversation with your opponent? It's terribly distracting. Sticks 101, Your Majesty. I think you might be dead."

He lunged upward, and she stumbled back several steps until he pinned her against the wall, his stick pressed across her shoulders, his chest heaving against hers. "And never fall for a feint." His voice turned husky. "Who's dead now?"

But she had no answer. No words. Everything inside her melted into something hot and messy and hungry.

She was certain he wasn't thinking about sticks anymore, either.

His breath was warm, his lips only inches from hers. No invisible veil between them. Her skin burned where his knuckle grazed her skin. The heat that swelled in her every night when unseen palms pressed to her own was now an inferno.

And she wanted more.

"What's stopping you?" she finally whispered.

The moment stretched tight, his body leaning in, his hips barely brushing hers. The fire inside her spread, begging to explode.

He swallowed. She could almost feel his heart pounding in his chest, but then he shifted his grip on the stick. He blinked and stepped back, releasing her. "Let's give it another try," he said, shaking his head.

She stared at him, her lungs hollow.

She wasn't ready to move on. Not this time. "Give what another try?" she asked. "We're simply moving on after what just happened? Are you denying there's something between us?"

There, she'd said it. It was out in the open now. There was no going back.

His voice turned sharp. "We're practicing sticks. That's all."

That's all? Bristol searched for words, her mind a jumbled whirl. Was he trying to convince himself or her?

He walked away and picked up the stick she had dropped, then held it out to her. "Well?"

That was it? Back to practice, as if nothing just happened? Like all the past nights of dancing and wanting didn't exist? Like he hadn't felt anything just now? How long did she have to pretend?

He waited for an answer, as steady as a pillar.

"I'm done for the day," she said.

"You can't—"

"I can do what I want. I'm *done*. Go find yourself another training partner."

He turned away and then back toward her, as if wrestling with a thought, and for a moment she was sure he was going to say something, *explain*, but then his shoulders squared, and he remained silent.

She walked back to the bench and snatched up her jacket. "You know, you aren't the only one who's been wounded."

His gaze became ice, the armor he kept in easy reach back in his grip. "Really?" he said. "And yet I don't see any scars on you. Where are they?"

His easy malice snatched away her breath. If he couldn't see her scars by now, he wasn't trying. "You can be sure, my scars are in places *you* will never see." She turned to leave but was stopped short by the solid wall. "The door," she said, still facing the stones.

There was a slight shuffle of footsteps behind her, and the wall retreated, the entrance reappearing.

She glanced back before she left. "And just so you know, I won't be at the hazel grove tonight."

"Good. The sooner you join the rest of us at festivities, the better."

Never missing a beat. Like he hadn't lingered there with her every night. Like they never danced at all. Like he hadn't felt the want between them. Maybe she *was* just an obligation in his rounds.

Her temples blazed. "Of course, Your Majesty. I have no good reason to dally. You can be certain I'll never be late again."

She stomped out the door, heading back to her room. Why did she even bother? Danu was just like all the other places she had skimmed in and out of her whole life. A stopover and nothing more. Deeper relationships were pointless. The last time she let her guard down, Mick had dropped her cold. *Fool me once*, she thought, as angry with herself as she was with Tyghan.

She felt a gaze on her back as she walked away, but she didn't look back. She was done with that, too.

CHAPTER 49

It didn't take much for Leanna Keats to decide it was a good time for her family to move on.

The crowds are thin here.

The shoppers are tightfisted.

The sun's too hot.

Moving on did make things easier in some ways. It hid your mistakes, and Bristol had made plenty. It wouldn't be the first time she had imagined a bond where there was none—when she imagined something more when there was only something less. Maybe all of it was her own delirium, a need to connect to something more meaningful. Something lasting. Something worth staying for.

We're practicing sticks. That's all.

It shouldn't have bothered her, really. From her first relationship at fifteen in the back of a van, to her last a few months ago with Mick, her life had been punctuated with breezy interludes that had all the nuance of a vending machine sandwich. Fast, easy, and forgettable. But what if you didn't want to forget? What if you still wanted more?

Let's go to the shore. Some salt air would be nice.

I hear the crowds are good at the Surrey Fair.

Move on.

It's a good time to move on.

Her mother's infuriating ways called to her. Maybe they always had. Move on. *Run.* Why was she fighting the urge?

Move on, because there was no good reason to stay.

Bristol lifted her hand to shade her eyes, swallowing away the knot in her throat. Storming down the path, she changed her direction and headed to Thistle Lookout instead, the highest point on the palace grounds. She would be late for her morning lesson at Ceridwen Hall.

Not that it mattered. She had memorized to perfection every incantation that Madame Chastain taught her, every subtlety, inflection, and syllable, even adding some flair. Working a booth at a fair was as much about theater as product, and she loved watching her father entice a crowd, splashing paint over a canvas as they watched with rapt attention, adding in captivating words to cinch the deal. She had acquired some of his knack for drama.

Now when Madame Chastain said she was impressed with Bristol's diction and passion, there was no charity in her words—she meant them. But regardless of the polished delivery and the flourishing hope that ensued, the ultimate result was always the same. Nothing. Even Madame Chastain seemed puzzled. Polish and flair could only carry one so far— all cons were eventually run out of town—especially when hard results were so vital to a whole kingdom.

From Thistle Lookout she could barely see the distant peaks of Amisterre, the nearest kingdom to Danu. There was no guarantee there would be trows in Amisterre either, but there certainly were none here. Why not take a chance? She had nothing to lose. Danu only offered up dead ends. She needed to go. But therein lurked the dilemma. Madame Chastain's strategy had worked—Bristol cared about the future of Elphame now. Maybe it was the impressive art collection at the conservatory, the paintings by Degas and O'Keeffe she had never seen before that left her speechless, or maybe it was the stunning vistas, the landscape dabbed with new radiant colors she had no name for.

Or maybe it was all the hopes her fellow recruits pinned on this world, the secrets they confided because she was a friend, the fresh starts they hoped to find, just like her. Or maybe it was little everyday things that snagged some soft part of her, the mischievous sprites who tangled her hair in gusts of wind and fits of laughter, then came, penitent, to smooth it down again and bring her thimbles of nectar as gifts of contrition.

Maybe most of all, it was that this place had taken in her father and nurtured him as one of their own. This was where he learned to paint, perhaps studying with the likes of da Vinci. Where he learned to make scepters of sticks for his daughters and gave them the skills to use them. So much of who he was had been woven into him here and, in turn, woven into Bristol. *This world is part of me too.*

It was these things that made her reluctant to leave. Even the scowls of lords and ladies seemed like a strange upside-down victory, because whichever of their delicate toes she had stepped on, she had stopped caring. She'd give the trows that much; they gave her a reckless heart and reinforced her back with a ribbon of steel by robbing her of a place to belong. They weren't going to steal away her father too—not without a fight.

Her eyes narrowed, trying to guess how far away Amisterre was. The human eye could see as far as two hundred miles from high peaks in clear conditions, usually far less—oh, the trivia she learned from her father as he explained the effects and tricks of the atmosphere on the human eye, and how to convey that onto a flat canvas. Step by step, he taught her the mathematics of perspective that the masters used.

She eyed the sun. She eyed the Wilds. Tonight, she would eye the stars. Her mother had loved the darkness of night above all and taught her about constellations and how to chart a path by them. Where did her mother learn such skills when she was unschooled in so many others? Some questions came too late. Some questions weren't even allowed to be asked. Whatever the answers, they had died with her mother.

Bristol guessed that Amisterre might be as far as two hundred miles away. A long way to go in one night. But there might be ways, and that was something a Keats was good at finding. Ways. Somewhere out there, between all the wild places, her father might be hiding, waiting for someone to rescue him. And that someone was her.

CHAPTER 50

W hen Bristol arrived at Ceridwen Hall, the door was locked and a note was pinned to it.

No one is late for my lectures.
Especially not you, Miss Keats.

Master Reuben may have thought he was punishing Bristol, but it was a welcome gift instead. She waited in the hall until the other recruits were done with his lecture, and then they walked to the training grounds together.

"Everything okay?" Julia asked.

"No," Bristol answered. "But I'll explain later."

"I wish I would have been late and locked out," Avery said.

Hollis drew in a shocked breath. "What? And miss Master Reuben's tedious droning?"

Avery's eyes became bored moons. "He lectured about dreamwalkers and how to keep them out of our heads—the *whole* morning."

Bristol had heard about dreamwalkers, mostly innocent nighttime wanderers who stumbled into your dreams. She'd take one of them inside her head over Reuben any day. "Sounds like a dreamy lecture. Glad I missed it," Bristol said.

They all laughed, but when they reached the training grounds, Sashka let out a long miserable moan. The maze was back.

"Not again," Julia commiserated. "I thought we were done with that wicked beast."

The recruits climbed the stairs to the observation deck. For the last two weeks, their lessons had involved weaponry and maneuvers on horses, which resulted in fewer scrapes—and concussions. The last time they'd been forced to navigate the maze, Avery was knocked out cold by a swinging tree limb. She had to be carried away.

Avery sighed, and the tangle of leaves in her hair drooped as she took her seat. This maze was triple the size of the others—and more ominous. A twisted canopy of trees hunched over it like conspiring withered crones, blocking much of it from view, but not so much they couldn't catch glimpses of shadows slithering within.

It ultimately came back to this—finding the elusive door, reaching inside for a stubborn sleeping talent, and coaxing it to life. Nothing was more important.

Of them all, Bristol guessed that maybe Julia or Rose was blood-marked, or—it was impossible to tell really. Each had their strengths and moments they shone. Even the officers, who scrutinized every breath they took, seemed undecided. But they were all still there, so that was something. It boosted their spirits, like they were meant to be together. Like they had become something bonded and unbreakable—though it didn't erase the worry. Maybe it only elevated hope that one of them had this forgotten ability to find invisible doors to other worlds.

Bristol glanced at Avery and wished she could ease her despair. Avery probably had the least confidence of them all, though she had become whip fast at deploying earth elements—churning up choking whirlwinds of dust and whispering stones to rise up and fly—but so far only enough for a distraction, not destruction. Day by day, they had come to know one another better. Sometimes their late-night dancing together spilled into later sessions in one of their rooms, eating, discussing Elphame, Danu, and, inevitably, the various inhabitants they encountered there.

Bristol discovered they were often just as surprised by this world as she was, even Julia, who had studied Elphame extensively as part of her research at the University of Paris. "Being told about a world and actually seeing it are two very different things," Julia told them.

They'd all been raised in the mortal world, and though they knew of Elphame, they had never visited. Still, their families managed to instill a reverence for their homeland, and none of them had hesitated to say yes when Eris approached them. Julia had wanted to come since she was a child, and her great-aunt had encouraged her, always claiming Julia was destined to play an important role in Elphame. But between studies, romantic relationships, and responsibilities at the university, time had slipped past her until finally, when Eris asked her to come, she knew the time was right.

Rose was excited by the adventure from the start—and the chance to freely use her shape-shifting abilities at last. *To be my real self*, as she phrased it. Though she loved to play the piano, flying through the skies was her true passion, and it was never easy to explore the world as a sizable hawk in the heart of London, where she lived. Rose reminded Bristol of Harper in so many ways—from her soft brown skin to her huge dark eyes, to the way she settled into Danu so quickly. A noticeable difference, though, was their voices. Harper had no problem with volume, while Rose's voice was soft and angelic, and when she was worried, it became a whisper that was barely audible.

In a moment of courage, Bristol had leveled with them about not being fae when they tried to convince her she would get better at magic. She didn't swear them to silence, but she knew they wouldn't tell.

Maybe that was why Rose's worry turned back to trows now. She scooted closer to Bristol and whispered, "Is that why you were late to class? Was it *trows*?"

"No," Bristol assured her. "I was—" She was still not ready to re-hash her morning with Tyghan. "No," she repeated. "I haven't found any trows yet."

"Is it wrong of me to hope that you don't?"

Bristol had no reply. It was something Harper might have said.

Instead of an answer, she shifted her attention to the maze below that was still transforming with its twists, turns, and hidden surprises, a churning forest eager to eat them up like little snacks. "So, will one of us finally make it through that monster today?"

Rose nodded and grabbed Bristol's hand. "Yes," she replied confidently. "I think today is the day we will beat that beast."

CHAPTER 51

Tyghan walked the course with Kasta, getting it ready for the next round of training sessions. They added new obstacles, like sinkholes and alluring creatures to send them to their doom—anything the recruits might encounter in the deep Wilds that surrounded Fomoria. The recruits groaned when they spotted the maze, but better for them that they fail there than in the Wilds.

Tyghan glanced up at the observation deck for a second time. Bristol was there, ignoring him. As she should, he reminded himself.

What's stopping you?

He almost hadn't stopped. He had ached with the need to close those few inches between them. He wanted to finally taste her lips on his own, to explore the softness of her mouth with his tongue, to feel her body against his without the dull veil of invisibility between them. He wanted to touch her in a real way and was already leaning in . . . but voices rose in his head, as unwelcome as the demons that haunted him in the night. *Walk away. You're already juggling the impossible. It's not fair to Elphame. Can you really trust that she is that different from Kierus?* And then a clear *Stop*. Because if he was forced to make an impossible choice, he would choose Elphame. Because his oath was fae law.

Stop because if he made a careless slip and Bristol found out who her family had really been running from her whole life, she would never help them. *Stop* because eventually the nation she was working to save was the same one that would kill her father and mother and that would end whatever he was hoping to start.

A simple task, Eris had claimed. Find a door and shut it. But Bristol made it complicated. And being involved with her only made it more so. It was anything but simple.

But it was done now. There was no going back. She was hurt and furious, and he was glad. It was done, *done*, a recurring beat in his head. He had nailed that door shut, so it was impossible to open it again. He glanced up at the deck, for the last time, he told himself.

Bristol and the other recruits were immersed in conversation except for Julia. Her eyes were trained on him like a cat transfixed, and she didn't look away when he spotted her. She wanted him to know she was watching. That she had been all along.

Last night he was standing on the lawn near Sun Court when she surprised him by stepping into his line of sight, then pointedly turned her head to where he'd been looking—at Bristol, who was laughing and dancing with Hollis and Rose, her aqua dress swirling into the air like a wave of frothy water.

"A very pleasant view, Your Majesty," Julia said, like she had caught him in the act of something lurid. "I've grown fond of her too."

"Is there something I can do for you, Julia?" he asked, hoping to hurry her along.

"You know my name?" she replied, and laughed. "I'm surprised. We've barely spoken. Most of my interactions have been with your officers or Eris. He's probably told you a few things, but I'm sure there's a lot you don't know about me. Let me introduce myself more fully. Julia Maëlle DuJardin. My family settled in Avignon centuries ago. A war in Elphame made them flee into the mortal world, and they never returned. They became farmers—among other things. And though I may be new to Elphame, I can trace my lines all the way back to the goddess Brigid. My parents were careful about such things, as were their parents."

"Impressive," Tyghan replied, doubting her claim but wishing she would hurry and get to her point, because he knew there was one coming.

"So as you might guess, I'm quite invested in this world—every bit as much as you are. Of course, these past decades I've poured my energies into my work at the university, and I admit my extensive repertoire of magic was largely unpracticed, given that I lived in the mortal world, which is why I am here. Thankfully, I'm quickly making up for lost time."

"Julia, if you don't mind, I have other—"

"You should know, I'm not bloodmarked. I confess, I've known from the beginning. I won't be opening or closing any doors for you—but you needn't be dismayed. I'm still quite powerful."

Her focus purposely turned back to Bristol, who was spinning, carefree, raising her hands with Rose, unaware she was being watched. "I know who the Butcher of Celwyth is," she said bluntly. "And the Darkland monster."

Julia had his full attention then.

She laughed. "Don't be so surprised, Your Majesty. I'm a scholar, and research is second nature to me." Her smile faded to a grim line. "I can also see how events might play out. How Bristol's role in all this might change into something else. No doubt, you have too. It's a dangerous game you're playing. I urge you stop." Her cat pupils narrowed to sharp points. "More than urge."

Her eyes were unflinching, waiting for him to respond.

"That sounds more like a threat than a suggestion."

Her smile returned. "Take it as you will."

"Why don't you leave kingdom business to me, Julia, and spend more time actually showing your power on the training grounds instead of spouting boastful claims to me."

Her chin dipped in a nod. "As you wish. Good evening, Your Majesty."

But as she left, he saw the bare swipe of her hand at her side, the hint of claws on her fingertips. Immediately the ground beneath his feet rumbled upward, like a plow furrowing the earth, and he stumbled back on the lawn. She disappeared into the night before he even got back to his feet. He had meant to talk to Eris that morning about her, but then the council members had pounced upon them.

"We're ready," Glennis said, interrupting his thoughts. "Should I call them down?"

Tyghan nodded, looking up at the observation deck. Melizan, Cosette, and Sloan, who didn't usually watch from the deck, had taken front-row seats, most likely taking careful notes to cull a certain recruit from the pack. Bristol sat two rows back talking to Rose, oblivious to her possible fate.

From here forward, Tyghan would stay out of it. At least that was what he promised himself.

Are you denying there's something between us?

His chest burned. He forced himself to look away from Bristol. *Done*, he reminded himself as he walked away.

Whatever the others decided, even Sloan, he would abide by it.

CHAPTER 52

It skulked through the air discreetly, the scent of decay, sulfur, and scheming. Just as magic had a scent, so did mayhem. But the air was electric at the training grounds. Anticipation for the maze was at a thunderous pinnacle. No one noticed the creeping mayhem that was as quiet as a spider spinning a web.

Except for Madame Chastain.

She nudged Olivia and Esmee where they all stood together in the shade of an oak observing the proceedings from afar. "Watch," she warned.

Bristol and her fellow recruits milled near the starting position, waiting to see who would go first, but then there seemed to be a sudden discussion going on between Madame Chastain, Tyghan, and Kasta. Other officers joined them.

"Relax for a few minutes," Cully told the recruits as he left to see what was going on.

"Probably a last-minute change," Glennis added, and followed after him.

Avery blew out a ruffled breath. They were all stressed, and waiting only made it worse. They wanted to get this over with. Sashka shook her head, then did the angriest handstand Bristol had ever seen.

"I wish I could do one of those," Hollis mused, shaking her head. Her pink curls shivered on her shoulders.

Julia stood nearby with rapt attention, watching the distant discussion. Bristol wondered if she was able to read lips.

Rose wandered over by the middle entrance to the maze. She raised her brows mischievously to Bristol. "Maybe I'll just scout out a few things while they figure out what they want for lunch." She slipped inside, unnoticed. Bristol didn't know if scouting ahead of time was cheating or not, but if it helped Rose get through the maze, she didn't care.

Bristol looked back at the knights, who were now turning, fanning out, searching for something, and then a shout came from Olivia, who was some distance away on a knoll. "Shadow!" she yelled, and pointed to a small rowan bush near the far corner of the maze. Pandemonium broke out. Knights ran for weapons.

The sun was high. Shadows were everywhere. Bristol didn't understand why one shadow caused such a disturbance.

Julia watched, her gaze frozen. "It's unanchored," she said.

Bristol still didn't know what that meant—but then she saw it. The shadow tucked beneath the bush moved, traveled across open ground to elude its pursuers, like it had a mind of its own.

"Clear!" came a call overhead. Everyone stopped running, and Bristol looked up just in time to see Melizan standing at the edge of the observation deck, a golden spear poised in her hand. She threw it with lightning speed, its whir razor-sharp, cutting the air just over Bristol's head with precision. It hit its target, landing in the middle of the shadow, appearing to pin it in place.

And then something happened.

The shadow transformed. It grew in volume, no longer a flat darkness staining the ground, but taking shape. Human shape. The knights ran over, a few kneeling beside it. Bristol and the other recruits walked closer to see what was happening. By the time they reached it, the figure was fully human—a Danu knight—with the spear piercing his chest.

Dalagorn dropped to his knees and wept. Quin stepped close behind him, squeezing the ogre's broad shoulders.

Tyghan cradled the young man's head in his lap. "It's all right, Liam. Shhh. You're home."

"Nisa?" Kasta asked.

"At peace," Liam answered. "She slit her throat." Tears rolled from the corners of the young man's eyes. "As I should have done. I was too slow. I'm sorry. I failed you."

"No, Liam," Glennis answered. "We're the ones who failed you. We—" Her voice broke, and she pressed her palm to her mouth.

Tyghan's eyes glowed with heat. He briefly closed them, like he was shutting down his fury. He brushed stray hair from Liam's brow. "Go to your deserved rest, my friend. Paradise awaits you."

"I'm sorry," Liam repeated, still struggling to speak. "I'm sorry I failed you." His eyes closed, but with his last bit of life, he said softly, "Run . . . *run now*."

CHAPTER 53

Tyghan laid Liam's head down gently on the ground, then rose to his feet, searching the sky. "Get the recruits underground!" he shouted.

Bristol's heart thudded. She saw it too. A small black cloud undulated in the distance. It was moving closer.

Horns sounded, piercing the air with warning.

Kasta, Glennis, and Quin were all moving, shouting orders as they went.

Tyghan swiped his hand overhead, leaving claw marks across the bright sky. Black, churning clouds spilled through the jagged tears like bubbling ink, until, almost instantly, the sky was dark and charged with webs of lightning. Bristol froze, stunned in the midst of the chaos. Booming cracks of thunder shook the air. Tyghan shouted more orders to Sloan and his company, then swept his palm upward in an angry motion, commanding the elements around him into more impossible things. The ground rumbled, and huge, spiked crystals broke through the soil, creating a sharp, deadly rampart.

The knights' white steeds arrived in seconds, already summoned from their stalls, and knights mounted them with swords and spears in hand. Archers spilled out onto the grounds, taking positions at the spiked barriers.

"Hurry!" a knight yelled to the recruits and ushered Avery and Sashka toward an unknown destination.

Cully tugged on Bristol's arm to get her attention and waved to Julia and Hollis. "This way!"

But Julia ran in the opposite direction. "I can help!" she shouted.

Cully called her back, and that was when Bristol broke free too. Rose was still in the maze.

She ran toward the middle entrance. "Rose!" she called.

Didn't Rose hear the pandemonium? The horns and shouts? Unless she did and couldn't find her way back out. Bristol raced inside, still shouting her name. Without the team to activate the obstacles, there were no poles jamming into her gut, but the trees themselves were alive, branches and vines batting and clawing at her as she passed. She ducked, she rolled, but one hit her square in the head, making her stumble. She kept running, her forehead stinging, and when she swiped something from her eyes, she saw blood staining her fingers. She ran faster, certain Rose was in trouble. She was a shape-shifter, after all—she could have changed into a hawk and flown out.

Only a short way into the maze, the deafening sounds of battle began screaming overhead. Whatever the creatures were, they were already there, and their shrieks of attack were horrific. Bristol glimpsed dark, fleeting shadows in the overhead canopy as she ran. The screeching of creatures, the ringing clash of metal, and the shouts of knights were a thunderous din around her. Pieces of creatures fell onto the pathway, and sprays of blood rained down. The heavy stench of burnt flesh hung in the air, making Bristol gag. She swallowed and kept going, rounding turn after turn, desperate to find Rose. She finally spotted her hanging upside down beneath a tree. She was tangled in vines, her arms and legs pulled in awkward directions. At first Bristol thought she was dead, but when she called her name, Rose's eyes weakly opened.

"I couldn't get out," she said, the small effort making her wince.

"Shhh," Bristol ordered and got to work, pulling on the vines around Rose's face and neck first, but they returned as fast as Bristol pulled them away, determined to keep their prey. Bristol finally resorted to biting and breaking through the tangled mess. The vines wept with red sap and reluctantly shrank back until Rose fell free. She coughed and choked and finally managed a deep breath.

"Can you walk?" Bristol asked.

Rose nodded, but when Bristol took her by the arm to help her up, she cried out in pain and clutched her arm to her stomach. There would be no flying out for Rose.

Bristol managed to get her to her feet, and Rose limped forward, her leg injured too, but as they headed down the path, a creature fell in front of them, blocking their exit. The beast was mortally wounded, snapping at the air and kicking its clawed hooves. One of its thick-skinned wings flapped wildly. The back half of the creature was missing entirely, and Bristol imagined Kasta's enormous sword slicing through it. How long would it take to die? They needed to get past it.

And then Bristol noticed something else—it had a saddle. *This creature once had a rider.*

She held her finger to her lips and listened for other sounds, afraid the rider might be in the maze with them, but with the melee above them it was impossible to detect anything.

"We have to go," she whispered to Rose. "The other direction. There's another way out. This time we're going to find it."

The sky teemed with sharp-clawed hyagen and the hideous restless dead who rode on their backs. Tyghan, Quin, and Kasta fought side by side, the swarming cloud of beasts darting around them, while the dead wielded their scythes and swords. As they fought, the knights dodged still more creatures that rained down around them, already dead from the web of lightning overhead. While Tyghan worked to maintain the electrifying force above them, he also fought off attackers, slicing them in two with single sweeps of his sword. Their putrid black blood spurted through the air, showering down on the archers.

"Below you!" Kasta shouted.

A demon on a hyagen had swooped low and now lunged upward toward Tyghan. He sent August into a spiraling maneuver, but the creature rose up too rapidly, knocking Tyghan from August's back. The hot sting of a claw slashed his thigh as he tumbled through the air. The sharp ramparts below were coming up fast to meet him. Tyghan couldn't fly, but he was able to slow his descent by summoning an updraft. It gave August time to dive and swoop beneath him, catching Tyghan, and now they were the ones flying upward to the creature, who had moved onto Glennis.

She battled two at a time, her swords swinging and reflecting flashes of lightning. "Glennis, *east!*" Tyghan yelled, freeing her to fight the creature on her right as he took on the other. He cut his unsuspecting target in half, sending rider and steed into a free fall, until both were skewered on the ramparts below. Glennis lunged and speared the demon she battled between the eyes and on her return swing lopped off the wing of its hyagen. The creature's screech split the air as it plummeted to the ground.

Sweat trickled down Tyghan's face as he battled one creature after another. It was the largest pack he had ever encountered, but finally the onslaught seemed to thin. Then he heard a familiar voice. On its heels, the power of spellwork slammed into his back. It jostled Tyghan momentarily to the side of his saddle, but that was all. It was only weak magic, which was why the dead loved their scythes more. Another slam. They served as distractions as Roleck moved in, aiming his curved blade at Tyghan's head. August knew what to do. The horse banked and spun, and now Tyghan's sword met the scythe.

Roleck smiled. "So good to see you again, young prince."

It was the fourth time he had encountered Roleck in battle. The previous three times, Tyghan had killed him—as much as you can kill the dead. The thing about the restless dead was, they still held on to every one of the vanities they'd had while living, pride foremost among them. Roleck loved being recognized, so the details of his face never changed, even if his body did. Being recognized made him feel like the ultimate victor—even over his past defeats. He would always come back, and he loved to remind Tyghan of that fact, showing off the power he still possessed with a few jabs of magic, but it always came back to the blunt force of swords and spears. There was something satisfying and certain about controlling the forged elements.

Roleck liked to prolong their encounters, circling, dipping, and rising. It bought him time to recall his visit to Tyghan in the middle of the night, when he had wandered through Tyghan's mind like a landlord, staking a claim to every secret room within, and this time was no different. "How did it feel, Tyghan, to have me sifting through your thoughts? Powerless? Violated?"

Maybe Roleck brought that question up repeatedly because he knew Tyghan was still scarred with the memory. He had flinched the first time Roleck taunted him, still raw and sick with the encounter, but since then Tyghan had learned to bury his emotion. Today his expression remained unaffected. "Not so powerless. I easily cast you out. You were the weakest of them all."

Roleck ignored the dig, boasting about his thick, muscled shoulders instead. "And look at the new body I fashioned. What do you think?" Roleck crowed like a rooster as his long arms viciously swiped the scythe toward Tyghan again.

Even though the faces remained the same, the bodies did change. This one was grotesquely muscled and misproportioned, Roleck's head looking tiny atop the thick neck.

"Impressive," Tyghan answered.

Roleck still knew mockery when he heard it, and his ire surged. "There's a body waiting for you," he growled as he maneuvered around Tyghan, trying to find an advantage. "One day you'll be fighting beside me."

Tyghan had had enough of Roleck's banter. He swept the sharp tip of his sword across the hyagen's throat and, on his backswing, charged forward. In a vicious swipe, he parted Roleck's small head from his neck, sending both rider and beast plunging to the ground.

He looked down at the crumpled, bloody bodies.

Fighting beside you? "Not today."

He searched the ramparts for another familiar adversary but didn't see Braegor's distinctive red hair below, nor had he encountered him yet in battle. Braegor was another of the restless dead who came with every wave of attacks, even more persistent than Roleck, usually hunting down Tyghan and his officers first.

Tyghan circled through the air, surveying where he was needed next, but the battle was waning. The first casualties were the restless dead who didn't make it through the web of lightning. Their charred corpses had fallen to the ground like fried locusts. Some of the other restless had fled, with knights in pursuit. The remainder had been killed in battle—or were about to be.

A skirmish still hovered past the back side of the maze. Melizan and Cosette were taking on three last attackers, skillfully beating them back. Melizan paused for a heartbeat to allow one to advance, and when he did, Cosette surged upward, skewering him tail to neck like a roasted duck. The other two turned in retreat, with Melizan and Cosette in close pursuit. The attackers wouldn't make it more than a few hundred yards. His sister and Cosette were a formidable team. *Dangerous*, as Melizan liked to remind him.

He circled around, making sure no one else needed him. This was the first time a squadron had dared to venture deep into the heart of Danu. What prompted this attack? Kormick's warning not to challenge him at the Choosing Ceremony was clear. As the date drew close, did he think Tyghan needed a reminder of his strength? Wasn't holding his brother hostage assurance enough? Or did he suspect something? Kormick always denied he had anything to do with the restless dead, preferring to play the virtuous but maligned ruler, one more than worthy to rule Elphame. And yet every kingdom that defied him had borne the brunt of their attacks until they conceded to Kormick's demands.

Tyghan patted August's neck. "Let's go down." As August banked, Tyghan spotted Cully propped up against a pillar of the observation deck, his chest soaked with blood. Madame Chastain and Eris knelt at his side, furiously working on him. A nudge from Tyghan's knee sent August into a nosedive.

As soon as he reached the ground, Tyghan jumped from August and ran to Cully, dropping to his knees beside him. "What happened?"

Madame Chastain sighed and sat back on her feet. "Not to worry. Bleeding's stopped now. He'll be fine."

"Fine, Tygh," Cully repeated, a sloppy grin on his face. "You heard her. Jogged left when I should have jogged right. But the bugger's dead. I won in the end."

"Fine, except for the mess you've made of my robe," Madame Chastain said, looking at the spurts of blood trailing across her lap. "And look at the mess you've made of the counselor."

Eris's crisp white tunic was equally soaked with blood. "Stop talking," Eris told Cully. "Save your energy. A pallet's on the way for you."

Madame Chastain glanced at Tyghan, her eyes and the subtle shake of her head saying what her words concealed—it was close. They almost lost him. Elven were quick, usually able to avoid injury entirely, but they were bleeders.

Tyghan nodded. "Any other casualties?" he asked as he scanned the grounds.

"Two archers. Cut clean in half from behind. There was no saving them," the High Witch answered.

Tyghan's nostrils flared, suspecting Braegor as their killer. Just as in life, it was his specialty—stealth and stalking. He was there somewhere, hopefully dead on a rampart.

"Other than that," the witch added, noting Tyghan's bleeding thigh, "there are some claws to be dug out and slashes to be mended." She eyed Cully with an accusing stare. "And of course, potions to prepare to restore buckets of lost blood."

Cully sat forward, ignoring Eris's order to be quiet, or perhaps too woozy to remember it. His head wobbled unsteadily. "I can walk. Keats is missing. Glennis said she saw her run toward the maze. That's where I was going when—"

He fell back, fainting, just as his pallet arrived.

Missing? Keats was missing?

Tyghan turned, looking at the maze. His temples pounded.

He lifted his hand to swipe the trees and shrubs away, to find her *now*, but caught himself. She might be trapped in a snare inside the maze.

Instead, he ran, praying to Lugh that he wasn't too late.

CHAPTER 54

The crash of swords, the yelps of beasts, the heavy thud of fallen bodies, and the whining clamor of things dying pierced the air around Bristol. Her throat burned as she helped Rose through the maze. Rose leaned on a pole they had yanked from the shrubs, her other arm tucked painfully to her stomach. Bristol gripped her by her waist, trying to steady her, knowing she was in terrible pain.

And then the noise around them stopped. They both froze, wondering at the sudden quiet. Bristol's ears pounded with the eerie silence.

Except for a rustle. And then a *crackle*. Like bones. Or knuckles.

Something was in the maze with them.

The rustlings got closer.

Bristol held her finger to her lips and tried to convey to Rose with her eyes that they needed to move faster. Rose nodded, and they shot out, no longer mindful of the noise they made, racing down paths, brambles scratching their arms. Bristol pulled Rose along, sometimes dragging her, turning unknown corners out of desperation and hope. But the sound within the maze grew louder too.

Breaths.

The crunch of footfalls on leaves. It was stalking them.

Bristol hugged Rose closer to her side, almost carrying her, and then on the last turn, the exit was in sight. They'd made it. The open land-scape behind the maze was visible through a narrow break in the hedge.

But then a shadow. A grunt. A thump—

A creature sprung into their path. Or a man. Bristol wasn't sure. All he wore were tattered pants that barely went past his knees and a sword that was sheathed on his back. He was grossly muscled, his chest broad, with thick, bulging veins on the surface of his skin as if it had been turned inside out. His hair was wild and flaming red, and deep, dark sockets surrounded his burnished yellow eyes. His hand curled into a tight fist, the bones cracking with anticipation. But it was his expression that was the most frightening of all. A smile curled the edges of his thin gray lips, more distinctly human than the rest of him.

"Do you know me?" he asked.

It could speak. And its voice was strangely refined. Like the overed-ucated voice from some stuffy documentary.

Dread crept down Bristol's back. She nudged Rose into position be-hind her, grabbing the pole from her hand in the process. The creature's eyes narrowed as she held the stick in a blocking stance. "You need to step aside," she told him calmly. "We're on our way out."

"Do you know me?" he asked again.

Should they turn and run in the other direction? But the entrance was too far, and Rose too weak. They would never make it. She whispered, "Can you run just a little farther past him—run for all you're worth?"

"Yes," Rose whispered back.

"On my signal," Bristol said.

"Do you not have ears, girl?" the creature yelled. "I asked you a question! Do you know me!"

Bristol eyed him. Swallowed. Tried to make sense of his question and why it mattered. It clearly was very important to him. He was set on an answer. She had no idea who he was. "The cable man?"

"Braegor!" he snarled. "And I promise you'll never forget my name again."

He advanced toward them, and that was when Bristol's attention jumped to a place just past his shoulder. "There you are! Maybe you can tell this creature—"

He barely glanced back, but Bristol used the split second to charge as she yelled to Rose, "Now!" She jammed the pole into his gut just below his ribs. Other than a slight grunt, it had zero effect except to enrage him. His huge arm swung, hitting Bristol's stomach, sending her flying down the path. She slammed onto her back and struggled to draw a breath. Rose made it past him, but he reached out a long arm, grabbing her and lifting her by her throat. Squeezing. The crackling splintered through Bristol. Was it his knuckles—or the bones of Rose's neck?

She gasped for breath and then screamed, "No!" scrambling for the pole, and then charged him again. When she had sparring practices with her sister, most body parts were off-limits, especially the head, but if you were fighting for your life, the head was fair game, especially the—

She hit his shoulder first—a feint so he would turn his head, and then, with every bit of strength she possessed, she plunged the end of the pole into his eye socket. He screamed and flung Rose's limp body away. She fell with a thud not far from the exit.

Get up, Rose! Run.

But she didn't move. Braegor stood between them as he thrashed and wailed. A foul gelatinous substance flowed from his socket.

"Rose!" Bristol screamed. Her lifeless body remained still. Sick heat flashed over Bristol's skin. *Rose.* This couldn't be happening. She couldn't be—

Braegor roared and yanked the stick out, throwing it aside. He held the side of his face, alternating his focus between Bristol and Rose with his remaining eye, the ghastly ooze escaping between his twisted fingers.

Bristol stared back, ready to run, her head throbbing with rage and fear, but she wanted him to come after her, not Rose. "Do you know my name?" she screamed. "*Do you know it? It's* Bristol Keats! And I'm guessing after today, you'll never forget it either!"

But there was no time to run. In a single leap he was on her, his momentum throwing her back several feet. He landed on top of her chest, his weight crushing the air from her lungs. His hands wrapped around her throat, squeezing—but slowly—like he was drawing energy from her death and wanted to make it last.

Ara cantu mai yuroneis. Tera ohm anasie te elufarra. . . . She couldn't speak, but she repeated her memorized incantations in her head, hoping maybe this final time, her effort might work. It didn't. Instead, the edges of her world turned gray. The thin smile of the creature blurred. *Ara cantu—*

But then she saw something behind him. Movement. A flash of color. Someone. The world was bobbing, fading.

The creature laughed, thinking it another trick.

He didn't turn to see what Bristol saw.

CHAPTER 55

B raegor!" Tyghan yelled.

The creature was quick, turning as he sprung to his feet. In the same instant, he drew his sword, and the point now rested on Bristol's throat.

"How fast is your magic, Tyghan?" Braegor asked. "Fast enough?"

Tyghan froze, fearing that the slightest movement or expression from him would send the sword plunging downward. *No*, Tyghan thought, staring at the tip of the blade grazing the soft hollow of Bristol's throat, *not fast enough*. Braegor had nothing to lose, while Tyghan had everything. A word, a flinch, anything that hinted of invoking magic could be disastrous. There were some wounds even he and a whole kingdom of sorcerers couldn't heal.

Braegor laughed. "Ah, look at you now, young Tyghan. Where did all your swagger and strength go? It seems I found your weakness. You look like a young buck with his antlers stuck between two trees. Those sharp antlers you love to show off are worthless to you now, aren't they?"

Braegor had never had the upper hand in their encounters, and it was obvious he was relishing the rare moment, seizing a fraction of his power back. He'd once been a feared and powerful mage, commanding armies and kings. His name was revered in history books simply for his cunning and sway, but death made a servant of him like all the other restless dead, and no amount of knowledge or infamy could make him more than he was now—a creature let out of his prison to serve the will of another.

Tyghan tried not to look at Bristol, to stay focused only on the mage. "How many times have I killed that putrid body of yours, Braegor?" he asked. "Four? Five? Go ahead, kill her. She's nothing to me. Only a novice, and not a useful one at that. Her death will make the news of me killing you that much more noble. Kingdoms will sing ballads about me—especially Greymarch."

At the mention of the word *noble*, the muscles in Braegor's neck writhed like snakes beneath his skin, but then his single eye gleamed with amusement and swiveled downward at Bristol. "What do you say, *Bris-tull Keats*?" His tongue flicked out as he enunciated her name, mocking every syllable. "Are you nothing to this great god of Danu?"

Bristol's throat throbbed where he had crushed it. It was hard to speak, her lungs empty. Her head swam, but she was conscious enough to hear Tyghan's words, and to see the gleam of a sword over her neck and feel its prick.

"Answer me!" Braegor demanded.

"Nothing," she rasped. "I am nothing to him."

Tyghan remained frozen. He knew Braegor's attention was divided, the word *noble* still seething in him. It was probably the one piece of truth Tyghan spoke that would bite deep, a word that Braegor would never get past. A blacksmith's apprentice from the kingdom of Greymarch was the one who had exposed the mage's treachery, resulting in Braegor's subsequent beheading. That apprentice was honored with the title Noble, which in Greymarch was the highest title that could be granted, just below Sovereign, a title that even Braegor had never achieved.

"Noble!" Braegor bellowed. "It means nothing in the end! A title that crumbles with the ages like the paper it's written on." He glanced at the tall hedges surrounding them. "And this? Another useless contrivance," he snarled. "What need do you have of a training ground?"

"Knights are always in need of training. So many of you to kill. And we're so good at it."

Tyghan had two thoughts in his head—keep his eyes off Bristol and keep Braegor's ego inflamed long enough to find a way to disarm him, or long enough for Kasta or Quin to come along and spear him. Braegor's inflated self-regard was his weakness, and talking about his bygone power was his passion. Tyghan guessed it made him feel like his former greatness was still within his reach. Maybe that was what made the restless dead so restless, always reaching for their innate magics that were now as dead as they were. All they could draw on was the spellwork they had mastered in their former lives. Only the power of words was able to transcend death.

Usually in battle, Tyghan couldn't be bothered with Braegor's pointless chatter, but now he tried to draw it out. There was nothing else of value he could offer Braegor. No deals for the restless dead. The mage was bound to the Darkland monster, and her commands were bound to Kormick. Braegor was a mere—

Tyghan glimpsed a shimmer of bright green advancing behind Braegor—emerald green. His lungs constricted. *Cosette.* What did she think she was doing? She crept along as silent as a fish in water, but even with a single eye, if Braegor looked down, he would see her bright reflection in his sword. She was going to get Bristol killed.

"Have you not learned?" Braegor asked. "So many of us—that is exactly why we will win. An unlimited army is the strongest one."

Cosette lifted her finger to her pursed lips.

Tyghan's mind reeled, quickly trying to revise his plan. He was desperate to keep Braegor's eyes fixed on him now, but he forced his tone to remain slow and insulting. It was a game Braegor thrived on and had spent decades perfecting.

"Win what, Braegor?" he said. "You can't win back your former glory. You'll always be less than half the man you once were, and you'll always— Oh, excuse me. I stand corrected. You're not even a man anymore, are you? You're only an ugly creature who stitches together bodies so you can jump at a monster's commands. What a life you have."

Cosette gripped her sword with both hands and lifted it over her shoulder.

Braegor's head tweaked slightly to the side. Suspicion inched across his hideous face.

Now, Tyghan thought. But Cosette stood, poised.

"You're full of talk today, aren't you?" Braegor said. A small laugh hissed through his lips. "You wound me, Tyghan. You take me for a fool?" His knuckles crackled as they tightened on the hilt of his sword.

Now! Now! What is she waiting for?

Braegor smiled. But he couldn't resist. He had to see first. He turned. He had to—

Cosette swung, silent and strong. Her aim was deadly accurate, as if she had measured every crooked vertebra in his neck. Braegor's head flew with the force of the blow, and his body and sword spun upward, caught in the maelstrom.

Tyghan leapt, his back barreling the torso aside, and grabbed the sharp blade with his bare hand before it could fall onto Bristol.

CHAPTER 56

Bristol's gaze swam in cool blue pools. They kept her from sinking back into the murky world that still pulled at her. Her throat scratched and clawed its way to speak. Only hoarse sounds came out.

"Quiet," Tyghan ordered. He hovered over her, his black hair hanging in damp strands. His hands were wet and warm against her neck. She reached up, feeling slippery liquid between their skin and he placed her hand back on her chest.

"It's my blood, not yours," he said. His hands applied gentle pressure to her throat. "Lie still," he added when she tried to move. He seemed to be searching for something. "Nothing's broken, but there's bruising and swelling."

Blurry faces bobbed just behind him. Melizan, Kasta, Eris, Cosette. They looked on as Tyghan's hands circled behind her neck. She tried to speak again. "Rose—"

"Esmee and Olivia are with her," Kasta said.

Tyghan's fingers spread wide over each side of her neck, his face tense with concentration, and he drew them toward each other. He repeated the motion several times, his eyes never leaving hers, like that was part of the magic to keep her from drifting away. He murmured words with every pass of his hands.

The pain subsided. His thumb skimmed the length of her throat as he whispered more words. Her lungs were finally able to expand with full breaths. The blurriness retreated. She placed her hand over Tyghan's, her fingers lacing with his, his blood warming her skin. "Rose? Is she alive?"

"Yes," Madame Chastain said, elbowing her way in. "Of course she is." She pulled Tyghan's hand away. "Go let Esmee see to your hand. I'll finish here."

But Tyghan didn't leave. His attention remained locked on Bristol. *Go ahead, kill her. She is nothing to me.*

Nothing? That was not what Bristol saw in his face. She saw worry. Fear. Need. She saw him wanting to lean in. Hold her. Kiss her. Stay. She saw everything that was true and real between them resting in his eyes.

Or maybe she was truly delirious now, a lack of oxygen muddling her brain.

But Anastasia Wiggins had said it and so had he—fae couldn't lie. *She is nothing.*

Kasta tugged on his arm. "Come away, Tyghan. Leave this for Madame Chastain."

Like Bristol was some messy inconvenience.

Tyghan stood and walked away.

CHAPTER 57

First-year knights swarmed the grounds as Sloan and garrison commanders directed their efforts to dispose of bodies and kill hyagen that still lingered. Their screeches lanced the air like the battle was still on.

The stench had been horrific, but Tyghan noted it was now gone. Probably thanks to Melizan. She had the least tolerance for the smell of rotten flesh hanging in the air.

Kasta led him directly to Esmee, who had just finished bandaging an archer's shoulder. "You don't have to wait," Tyghan told Kasta as Esmee worked on his hand, but she stayed close by his side as if he were a child she couldn't trust.

Dalagorn, Quin, and Glennis walked over like they had nothing else to do. Had Kasta called in reinforcements?

"That was some catch you made," Quin said. "I don't think any magic could have acted faster."

"He was motivated," Glennis added with a hint of insinuation.

"Though gloves might have been helpful," Esmee complained. "I'm a physician, you know? Not a god. You could have lost those fingers."

Dalagorn grumbled under his breath. "Damn fool."

"You saw too?" Tyghan asked.

"Everyone saw," Kasta answered, shooting him a warning glance.

"We were hanging back," Glennis explained, "waiting for Cosette to make her move."

All of them watching. Did they see the terror in his face? What was it Braegor said? A young buck stuck between trees? He certainly wasn't the picture of the hardened Knight Commander they expected.

"Almost done," Esmee said as she wove the skin on his palm back together. She did it faster than Tyghan could have done it himself, and healing your own wounds was never recommended. Scattered concentration, especially with bad injuries, could result in unfortunate outcomes.

Finished with the weaving, she examined his leg next, probing the slash for hyagen claws. When he winced, Esmee applied more of her soothing balm.

Unlike Madame Chastain, she had a distaste for pain. While she wrapped his wounds with bandages, Tyghan surveyed the carnage around them.

"Do you think Liam was the herald for the attack?" Glennis asked.

Tyghan remembered Liam's last tormented words. *I'm sorry.*

It was every knight's worst fear, being used by the enemy to spy on your own, kept from death in a limbo world, every part of your humanity stripped from you but your consciousness. That's what the claws did, their poison *almost* killing you, leaching flesh and bone into a nether existence until you were truly only a shadow of who you once were.

Quin nodded confirmation. "The timing wasn't coincidence."

None of them blamed the young knight. He couldn't control where the shadow took him or what it saw, but whatever was witnessed was relayed back to Kormick, and the Fomorian king didn't like what he saw—the intense training of hundreds of knights at the garrison.

"He thinks you're going to challenge him at the Choosing Ceremony," Quin said.

"And he will," Kasta replied. "He has to."

Glennis cringed. "But what if we don't have Cael back by then?"

"We'll have to see how things play out," Tyghan said, not committing to a course of action. He already knew that anyone was expendable to keep Kormick from ruling Elphame. Including Cael. But letting him die would also serve a demoralizing blow to all the kingdoms. If even the most powerful Elphame nation was at Kormick's mercy, what chance did any of them have?

The knights exchanged tense glances, knowing a decision regarding Cael would have to be made soon.

Esmee broke the tension as she continued to wrap Tyghan's thigh. "Rose is a scrappy little thing, isn't she? Olivia took her to the treatment chambers. Her neck wasn't badly hurt, but it appears she tore a ligament in her shoulder and cracked her scapula, and with her being an avian shape-shifter, we have to treat her bird bones carefully or she'll never fly again. I'm certain Olivia will do a fine job of it."

Tyghan wondered if Bristol had injuries other than her bruised neck. Did she break anything? He didn't know what else Braegor might have done to her before he got there. What if—

"There you go." Esmee admired her work and patted Tyghan's arm. "Done."

He eyed the excessively large bandage on his hand.

"Fingers are a tricky lot to heal," Esmee explained. "And you managed to nick tendons. Leave the bandage on a bit longer than usual—at least until morning."

"He will," Kasta answered.

Tyghan noted Melizan and Cosette lingering on the periphery of his officers and as soon as Esmee stepped away to treat other injuries, they moved in.

"Looks like your troublemaker's going to be all right," Melizan said.

Tyghan nodded. "I think so."

Melizan cleared her throat and angled her head toward Cosette. "A thank-you might be in order."

Thank Cosette. He knew he needed to, but it pained him. He had a deep-seated distrust of all things Fomorian. The early Fomorian sea gods were the ones who brought merkind with them to Elphame. And Cosette was still a suspect in Cael's disappearance.

"You took a chance, creeping up like that," he said instead, once again the hard-nosed commander. "He might have seen you."

Cosette grinned. "I calculated the risk, costs, and my skills. Trust me, Your Majesty, very little chance was involved. And looking at the outcome, I'd say I judged wisely." She eyed his bandaged hand and bloody trouser leg. "But I suppose you did your small part too. More or less. You were a useful distraction."

A win for Cosette. "Well done," he conceded, knowing she was right. "Thank you."

Cosette and Melizan paused and exchanged a glance.

"Something else on your mind?" he asked.

Cosette pursed her lips. "We're suspicious. Keats managed to make it to the end of the maze. She almost made it out." She explained that when she and Melizan were fighting above the south end of the maze, there was a moment when she had a clear view below her. "Keats was running, practically dragging Rose at her side, but she hit every turn on cue like she had it memorized. How would you explain that?"

Tyghan couldn't explain it. "Maybe Rose—"

"No," Cosette replied decisively. "It was all Keats."

"No one coached her ahead of time, if that's what you're implying," Kasta countered.

Cosette's jade eyes narrowed. "Cool your claws, Kasta. We're only wondering if you checked her for ticks when you brought her here."

"No. And I don't need a first-year officer checking up on me. She was on the horse with me the whole time when we went through the forest, and when Dalagorn shot the pods into the shadows, we were well clear."

"We're not wondering about ones she might have acquired in the Wilds," Melizan clarified. "We mean before that. In the mortal world. A tick that was purposely placed there."

"That's impossible," Quin rumbled. "In the mortal world? How would—"

Melizan's brows rose. "It's not inconceivable, considering."

They were all quiet, stunned by the possibility.

Considering.

Considering who her parents were.

🐝

Bristol was well down the footpath with Avery and Hollis, all of them eager to check on Rose and the other recruits, when Kasta called to her, telling her to wait up. She was flanked by Tyghan and Quin, with several officers following on their heels. Their demeanors were solemn, and their steps driven like a new battle was just beginning.

"That looks ominous," Avery said as they approached.

Bristol sighed. "I disobeyed orders by going into the maze, and you know how they are about orders."

"But you saved Rose," Hollis argued.

The group stopped a few feet away.

"You two can go on your way," Tyghan said. "We need to talk to Keats alone."

Avery and Hollis didn't move. "It's all right," Bristol told them. "I'll be along." She hoped.

"Call if you need us. I'll hear," Hollis said before they left, like she was leaving Bristol with a pack of wolves.

"You seem well recovered from your injuries," Melizan said once the others were gone.

Bristol was sure they weren't checking up on her neck. "What's wrong?" she asked.

Kasta edged forward. "Nothing is wrong exactly, but—"

Cosette elbowed her way past Kasta. "We're wondering if you had any ticks on you before you got here."

Maybe Bristol was still wound tight from her experience in the maze, Braegor's oozing eye still fresh in her memory. Or maybe it was Tyghan's blood that still stained the front of her shirt that left her on edge. Maybe she was still crazed with worry about Rose and simply had no time for their nonsense. But something inside her snapped. She was tired of being sniffed at like she was an unwashed mutt.

A messy inconvenience. Tired of being nothing. Now was not the time—

"No!" she shouted. "Believe it or not, we do bathe in my world! Regularly! I do not have any vermin—no lice, no fleas, no ticks! And if my scent isn't to your liking, you can just cover your sensitive noses that have no place in my business to begin with. If you had any sense at all, you would know now is not the time to be asking me this! I'm not—" Her voice cracked. God, she hated it when that happened.

Tyghan stepped forward, his hands raised in a gesture of truce. "Keats," he said softly, "we're not talking about vermin. A tick is something else here. It's a weapon. You probably saw Dalagorn shoot some into the forest when you came. They make the dangerous creatures scatter and clear the path—they don't want to encounter a tick even for a few minutes. It settles deep beneath the skin. It doesn't hurt. You can't even feel it. Do you have anything on you, something small that you might mistake for a birthmark?"

They all stared at her, waiting. She remembered Dalagorn shooting his small innocuous arrows into the shadows, and then the skitter of something in the leaves and the squeal of creatures running away.

"Lots of people have birthmarks," she answered.

"But do you?" Melizan asked.

She'd always had it on her lower back. It was pale, a tiny thing, smaller than her fingernail. Cat and Harper called it a ladybug. It was cute, they said.

"It's only a birthmark. I've always had it. It's nothing new."

"How long?" Tyghan asked.

"*Always*. It's always been there."

Cosette sighed. "May we see it?"

Bristol took a step back. This was ridiculous. *No.* All this fuss over a tiny mark that was little more than an overgrown freckle?

Her chest tightened. They waited expectantly, including Tyghan.

She spun, her pulse racing, and yanked her shirt loose from her trousers. She lifted it partway up her back. Before she even exposed a few inches of skin, there was a gasp.

A hiss.

Then words she had never heard before that sounded like curses—and a few that definitely were.

Deivdas.

Kerdah.

Blazes.

Fuck.

Tyghan stepped close and pulled her shirt down. "We've seen enough."

Bristol whirled around. Her heart banged in her chest. "What is it?"

Tyghan shook his head. "It's not a birthmark."

CHAPTER 58

They reconvened in Madame Chastain's treatment chambers and Tyghan summoned the High Witch and Eris. The whole walk there, Bristol demanded to know what they saw, but Tyghan only said they would show her when they were in the privacy of the treatment chamber. Once there he continued to delay her viewing it, but she insisted.

"Would you like everyone to leave first?" Madame Chastain asked.

"No," Bristol answered. What was the point? They already saw part of her back. Why not see it all? Dispel their doubts. Maybe it was only a bad bruise from when Braegor sent her flying to the ground. She landed hard. Her throat may have been healed, but she still had plenty of scrapes and cuts. Or maybe it was one of the branches that hit her as she was running through the maze. She and Rose were both battered by the trees tasked with their destruction.

Kasta held a mirror in front of Bristol, and Glennis angled a floor mirror behind her. While Madame Chastain snipped away the back of her shirt, Bristol was silent, her legs heavy and numb. She wished someone would laugh or that they would at least stop looking so solemn. My god, they had just had a battle with monsters. Of course she had cuts and bruises.

"It's only a birthmark or a bruise," she said again, trying to convince them, but her stomach churned.

She listened to the snip of the shears, and the chamber air chilled her skin as her shirt was peeled back. The High Witch stepped aside so Bristol could have a full view.

She stared silently, her lips trying to move. Cold sweat sprung to her chest. She looked away. "Get it off," she whispered.

"We will. Just give us—"

"Get it off me! *Get it off now!*" she screamed. Panic gripped every part of her. She wanted to run, scratch it off, tear her skin away, but there was nowhere she could go that it wouldn't follow. Her arms shivered. The room was tilting, and she dropped to her knees and vomited.

CHAPTER 59

T yghan stepped toward Bristol, but Dalagorn held him back. "Let the witch do her work."

The knights were ordered to the far side of the room while Madame Chastain and Eris coaxed Bristol over to the exam table, promising her they would take care of it. Bristol lay face down on the same table where the High Witch had dug claws from Tyghan's shoulder just weeks ago. He understood the claws. This he couldn't understand. He'd never seen a tick that large. He hadn't thought it was even a possibility. Madame Chastain stood back for a moment, eyeing the creature, and shook her head.

"She fainted from pain when we came through the portal," Kasta whispered to Tyghan. "It had to be that thing."

Tyghan remembered Bristol pressing her hand against her lower back on her first night there. He'd thought it was only a backache because she was unaccustomed to riding a horse. He had removed ticks from creatures before, even one from August's fetlock. None of the ticks had ever been much larger than how they started out—about a half inch across and still only a smooth, pale shadow beneath the skin as they fed on their host's magic, sucking up their innate abilities until someone removed them. The black shadowy creature buried deep under Bristol's flesh covered her whole lower back. Its crooked legs were as thick as an ogre's thumb and twisted across her spine. Its body alone was the size of his palm. The dark shadow shifted beneath her skin like it was settling in with a tighter grip. It knew it was being watched.

Bristol clutched the end of the table, her knuckles white, her hands shaking. The knights looked on in shocked silence. Even for them, it was horrific to see the creature squirming inside her.

Madame Chastain stepped over to where Tyghan and the others stood. "That thing has been on her back for years—long before she got here. I suspect that traveling through the portal into Elphame made the tick swell with twenty years of suppressed magic. I'm going to need help. See if Olivia, Esmee, or Reuben are available yet—or get another healer from the city."

Tyghan sent the guard posted at the door to find them. With several injured in the battle, sorcerers with expertise in the healing arts were stretched thin. Even so, Tyghan had never seen the High Witch ask for assistance.

"It must have been Kierus and Maire who did it," Cosette said. "No one else in the mortal world would have access to a tick."

"What kind of parent would do that to their own child?" Quin asked.

"A desperate one," Tyghan answered.

But Melizan voiced the truer answer. "A ruthless one."

The same kind of ruthless person who would stab a fellow knight, Tyghan thought. One who would stab a friend. A brother. Because that was what they had been. As close as brothers.

He knew Kierus as well as he knew himself—at least he used to think he did. Did he ever really know him at all? What did he miss? His last moment with Kierus replayed behind his eyes as it had at least a hundred times before. He saw the unexpected embrace, the swiftness of Kierus's hand, and then the blade piercing his side. The angle. The precise intention. The vicious upward lift. The shock he felt. The disbelief. The cold dampness of his knees as he fell onto the muddy floor of the forest. The fiery heat of the demon blade burning inside him, abandoned in his gut. The gush of warm blood through his fingers as he gripped his side.

Walk away.

And that's what Kierus did, without ever looking back.

"But why would they do it?" Glennis wondered aloud. "What purpose—"

"Risk," Tyghan said. His focus locked onto Bristol's shaking hands. "Navigating a mortal world with a fae child is dangerous when you're being hunted by two very angry and powerful kingdoms. It's impossible to know when or where a child might use their magic and expose them. The tick eliminated the risk."

Kasta shook her head, her lip twisted with disgust. "At least Eris must feel validated. She may be bloodmarked after all. Maybe in the end, this is good news."

"Hmm," Melizan mused. "Maybe . . . maybe not."

Olivia hurried through the door and went straight to the exam table. She and Madame Chastain conferred and gathered supplies from the High Witch's stock, and Eris stepped away so he wouldn't break their flow of energy once their work began. The witches took positions on either side of Bristol and rubbed oil on her back.

The strong scent of cloves and roseclaw permeated the room. Olivia chanted a calming spell: "*Ara mei ash a ash. Ara mei ash a ash.*"

Madame Chastain chanted a summoning spell: "*Ecktay ano umalu o nei. Ecktay ano umalu o nei.*" The edges of the room dimmed, and the air pinched tight, as light, sound, and scent were focused deep within Bristol's skin. Her face dripped with sweat, and Tyghan's fingers curled to fists. It took every ounce of his effort not to go to her side. *Do something.* But he couldn't. Any movement would interfere with the witches' magic. It was already circling the room.

"Your job is over, pet," the High Witch cooed as she gently pressed near one of the creature's legs. "You are sated. It is over. It is time to rest. Time to let go."

Tyghan saw the dark shadow wriggle beneath Bristol's skin. One leg emerged, and then another. The knights breathed in as a whole, waiting. The High Witch took hold of the leg, gently coaxing it out, but then the other exposed leg retreated back beneath the skin like it sensed a trap. Olivia continued to chant and rub in more oil. Madame Chastain's grip tightened on the remaining leg. "No, my pet, this way. This—"

The creature writhed, jerked, the leg thrashing back and forth, and then its screech shattered the air, flinging Madame Chastain across the room into the wall, a torn piece of the black leg still wriggling in her hand. Bristol arched backward, screaming in pain as the tick's fiery blood trickled over her skin. Tyghan ran to her side, but she had already collapsed, unconscious. The smell of her scorched flesh choked the air.

"It was coming," the High Witch said, hobbling back to the table. "But this—"

"No more," Tyghan ordered, waving her away. "You're going to kill her."

"Agreed," she said, staring at the tick that was now deep beneath Bristol's skin again. "No more today, except to heal her burn." The High Witch ordered the knights and others back to the other side of the room, but Tyghan's feet remained planted at the head of the table. Olivia prepared a potion and held its amber smoke beneath Bristol's nose to keep her in a deep sleep, then she and the High Witch got to work on the burn left by the tick's powerful blood. They whispered healing words into circles of salve in their palms, then rubbed them over the blistered flesh. It stopped oozing, and the flaming redness faded.

Olivia applied more balm and bandaged the burn, then repaired Bristol's shirt. The High Witch stepped over to Tyghan and whispered that they'd given her something for the pain. "She'll be all right— except for the tick that won't release her." She shook her head like she was trying to make sense of it all. "That tick is a greedy miser with a fortune of gold it can't spend."

"What do you mean, gold?" Tyghan asked.

"Over twenty years of magic," she answered. "He wouldn't give it up. He's drunk on the magic's beauty, though he has no actual way to use it. I've never seen anything like it." She ran one of her long, slender fingers across her brow, thinking. "We're going to need the Lumessa to consult on this. She was here when the first ticks were created. She may know—"

"Impossible. She's at Mount Nola. She can't—"

"I know where the Lumessa is. She may need the healing waters, but we need her. She might be able to tell us how to proceed."

"She's there because she's dying."

"Which is all the more reason for you to make haste. I'd suggest you take your best to help retrieve her."

Tyghan's attention darted back to Bristol, still mercifully unconscious. He couldn't leave now. "I'll send—"

"*You*," the witch said. "It must be you. Your personal effort—an apology—will appease her. She'll come."

Jasmine. All Tyghan wanted to do was avoid her. She was Madame Chastain's mentor and the previous High Witch of Danu. She was celebrated for having served in that position longer than any other witch or wizard—for over six centuries—earning her the esteemed additional title of Lumessa, the "wise one"—and Tyghan had insulted her. More than insulted. He'd made accusations. He had done the unthinkable and pointed his finger at her and raged. She and the Sisters would probably aim to kill him on sight, or at least maim him, before accepting any apology.

Madame Chastain noted Tyghan's hesitation. "An apology isn't so hard."

"You mean groveling."

"Exactly. It's an art you should learn, the sooner the better. Or . . . we can leave the creature in Miss Keats's back?"

He was ready to argue, but the alternative sobered him. "I'll go."

"Good. Go tonight. And use her earned *title*, not her name. It won't be easy to get her back here. She can't ride a horse. And a carriage?" She bit her lip, thinking it over. "I'd suggest you use some clever magic to ease her journey. I'll leave that to you. I'll have her suites at the conservatory readied. And the Sisters', too, of course."

How long would this take? He could make the ride to Mount Nola in a matter of a day, but returning with a fragile passenger and hostile escorts? He laid out a tentative plan in his head and turned back to Bristol, now lying peacefully on her side, lost in Madame Chastain's potion-induced dreamworld. "I'll gather my crew after I take her back to her room. No one is to enter her chambers while I'm gone without Kasta's approval." The High Witch nodded, and he gently scooped Bristol into his arms, but as he did, he paused, noticing her hands for the first time. The white half-moons of her nailbeds had changed. They were now a deep vivid blue—and pointed like the arm of a star. Or a claw.

Olivia leaned close. "More of her magic was released into her blood in the struggle with the tick," she explained. "She's definitely not mortalbound."

CHAPTER 60

Tyghan laid Bristol on her bed like she might break. She didn't
stir as her head sank into the pillow. He wouldn't be there when
she woke, and that thing would still be on her back. What would
she think? What would she do? Scream and shake like before? Would
anyone be there to comfort her? *He* should be there.

His blood still stained her shirt. He'd speak to Kasta before he left.
She'd make sure her clothing was taken care of, and that Bristol lacked
for nothing.

He lingered, knowing he was wasting precious minutes. The sooner
gone, the sooner he could return, but instead of leaving, he knelt beside
the bed and drew her hand into his. He pressed her knuckles to his lips,
then looked at the pointed blue moons on her nailbeds. *She's definitely
not mortalbound.*

But what was she?

The confusion in Olivia's eyes, and the uncertainty in Madame
Chastain's voice, crawled over his skin. They knew the change meant
something, but didn't seem to know what that was. They'd both be
searching through their histories and grimoires late into the night. Or
maybe that was why Madame Chastain sought the Lumessa's help—
because only she could explain what it meant. *Claws.* He was certain
the possibility was running through their minds. The claws of what?

He thought back to that moment in the forest when Maire walked out of the cottage, half-naked, a blanket clutched around her body, her long copper hair cascading over her shoulders. She raked it back with lovely fingers and pale nailbeds the color of pearly seashells. Not blue. Maybe she glamoured them, but not likely. She didn't care what Tyghan thought or what he observed. All she said was, "Get it over with, Kierus. We have to go." And she'd gone back into the cottage.

Tyghan placed Bristol's hand back at her side, then ran his finger over a small cut on her brow, making it disappear. He wished he could do more.

Grovel.

He would crawl on his hands and knees if that's what it took. And it likely would.

CHAPTER 61

"Here you go." Winkip placed parchment on the table in front of Kierus. "Write your message."

Kierus balked at the tiny sheet of paper. "Is parchment so expensive?"

"You insisted on actual paper, and small messages are easier to conceal and pass. We have someone inside the palace who will leave the note for your daughter."

Inside the palace? Kierus wondered. "Who—"

"The *who* is not your concern. Just that they can get the job done."

Kierus understood anonymity, but he still wondered who in the palace would have dealings with trows. Was a pouch of gold their only motivation? Or something more? Either way, they were a Danu traitor, which shouldn't have been any of his concern, more his good fortune. Still, it nudged something inside him, something old and buried, but not entirely forgotten. A virtuous oath from a different lifetime. "It's more than just a note I need to send. I need to speak to her face-to-face."

Winkip shook his head. "That would involve additional risk."

"Like the risk I took to save your king's son? She's my daughter. I will see her."

Winkip's stony expression remained unchanged, but Kierus knew he wasn't pleased. "Use caution with your words," Winkip ordered.

"No one should know the note is from you in case it's intercepted. And don't mention trows."

Kierus could manage that easily enough. No one would even know the note was for Bristol—except the person who delivered it. Who was that? The question still niggled at him. Could it be Fritz? He could access the palace. But he had sworn to guard the house in Bowskeep with his life. He would never break his promise to Kierus.

He finished the last few words of the note and dusted the ink with powder before handing it to Winkip. The doorward tucked the note in his vest. "We'll get word when it's been delivered. It may take a while."

"How long?" Kierus asked.

"We don't know. The note will pass through several hands. Our primary contact said access to your daughter is limited. Someone is always with her."

Limited. Kierus knew Tyghan's ways, but he knew his daughter, too—far better than the young prince did. She'd find a way out. A way to reach him. He'd explain everything, so she would know the truth. The real truth.

CHAPTER 62

Ivy flew into Tyghan's path, intercepting him.

"Your Majesty!" she said, breathless. "I heard from Stable Master Woodhouse that you were back. The counselor wanted me to warn you as soon as—"

"Stop!" Dalagorn complained, trying to dodge her wings. They were still flapping, batting him in the face. "Slow down."

Ivy eased out an even breath, and her wings settled. She told them there was a council meeting in session. "Eris wanted to stop it, but there was a quorum and—"

"In the rotunda?" Tyghan asked calmly, though his aggravation was already spiking.

She nodded.

"Thank you, Ivy," he answered. "How's Cully?"

Her face brightened. "Still recovering," she answered. "But back to light duty!" Just as quickly, her lashes lowered. "I mean, I believe he's doing well—at least according to the High Witch."

"Good," he answered. He expected nothing less. Cully was strong, and after his close call with the restless dead, he would be twice as clever and fast. "Would you check in on the Lumessa? Make sure she has everything she needs? She's in her suite at Celwyth Hall. I want her to be able to receive Keats as soon as possible."

"The *Lumessa* is here? At the conservatory?"

Tyghan nodded. And the Sisters. And their damn wolves. And some newly acquired welts on his arms he hadn't had the time or inclination to heal. It was a very long two-thousand-mile ride, and an aberrant council meeting was not something he wanted to come home to.

"And Keats?" he added. "How is she?"

Ivy's face darkened. "I'm not sure. I haven't seen her since you left. She hasn't left her room."

♟

Lord Csorba pounded his fist on the table. The towering candelabra in the center trembled under the force of the blow. "And I say, kill her!"

"What's this?" Tyghan asked, walking into Lir Rotunda with his officers on his heels. Their heavy boots echoed across the dark slate floors, and the grumbling that circled the room instantly quieted. Tyghan noted the fullness of the chamber. It wasn't just the high-ranking ten who met every week but, disturbingly, all thirty members of the council. Every head turned toward Tyghan as he pulled off his cloak and threw it onto an empty chair. "A full council meeting without the king? I've only been gone four days. You couldn't wait?"

"An emergency council meeting," Lord Csorba answered.

"And just what is this *emergency*?" he asked, as if he hadn't heard the words *kill her*. He wanted Csorba to say it to his face.

Lord Csorba reached for a stack of papers, but Tyghan stepped forward, his hand angrily swiping the air. Papers on the table flew in an explosive, angry gust, swirling to the floor as a blast of heat flashed across the room. Hair, fur, and robes ruffled in the wake of Tyghan's fury. "I don't need to see your papers!" he shouted. "I asked you a question, Csorba! Kill who?"

"I think you know who he's talking about," Lord Alistair said, rising to his feet. "That woman. The one you scooped up and so gallantly carried to her chamber just days ago."

Lord Alistair wasn't even there at the time, nor Csorba, but the rumors had obviously been passed around like a dish of licentious candy.

"I carried her because she was unconscious," Tyghan countered. "She couldn't walk."

"Anyone could have taken her."

"And I happen to be anyone. Am I not, Lord Alistair?"

He reluctantly dipped his chin in acknowledgment.

"Then sit down," Tyghan ordered. Lord Alistair complied, sinking into his chair.

Tyghan's searing gaze circled the table. "Who called this meeting?"

"I did," Lady Barrington replied. She shrugged dismissively. "Someone needed to. In light of the direct attack on the palace and the recent developments—"

"Call it what it is, Lady Barrington!" Tyghan said. "You're plotting to kill a recruit who might very well be our savior. I'd call that kind of plotting treason."

Lord Csorba came to life again, empowered by his fellow council members. "Savior!" he spat, the word sounding like poison on his lips. "Our reasons for calling the meeting are not treasonous but sound and judicious! This recruit you brought into our midst hasn't been seen in four days. Not a glimpse! She conspires, I tell you! We all know where her true loyalties lie. And now we know there's magic within her that could be devastating for Danu. Why wait until she's mastered it so she can kill us all? Her absence from festivities speaks for itself! She is not one of us!"

Before Tyghan could respond, Eris jumped to his feet, his face contorted with rage, a rare sight on the reserved counselor. "I told you, Csorba! Miss Keats is in shock, not conspiring. Four days ago, she believed she was mortal. An inconsequential birthmark on her back has transformed into something ugly and frightening. She's barely eaten in four days and is hardly in the mood to be entertained by your fatuous antics at festivities! I will not tell you again, stop with your conspiracy theories or—"

"Or what? What will you do, Eris?" Csorba snarled back. "Throw your useless book of rules at me?"

Eris's eyes were sharp glass. "Laws set down by the gods? They are what we live by, Csorba. Don't underestimate my power to use them."

"Careful, Lord Csorba," Melizan warned. "It's not just his book of rules you need to fear. I'm sure Madame Chastain has another mirror in need of garish decoration, and Eris does hold sway with her."

Madame Chastain shot Melizan an icy glance.

"Stop," Sloan groaned, finally joining the conversation. "Everyone, just stop. Let's not be hasty with all this talk of killing the girl. She may prove to have no useful magic at all—just a hideous creature on her back. On the other hand, she might turn out to be useful in another way. As a hostage."

The room quieted. "Only as a *last resort*, of course," he added.

Tyghan stared at Sloan, the air punched from him. Those were his exact words. And Sloan had just proposed them in front of an entire council that was ravenous for action. Tyghan's eyes darted to Kasta, ready to accuse her. Sloan didn't choose those words by chance. She shook her head in denial, her brows pinched with confusion.

But if she didn't tell him, who did? She was the only one—

"Actually, I'm surprised it hasn't been said before now," Sloan continued. "Surely, it's occurred to someone else as a way to save Cael. She is the Darkland monster's daughter, after all. And Kormick only wields power by the monster's hand. Without her, he is only a demigod leading a limited fae force. What about you, Tyghan? Didn't you think of it as a way to save your beloved brother too?"

Every muscle in Tyghan hardened to stone. Sloan knew it had occurred to him. Tyghan reluctantly nodded. "Yes . . . I thought of it."

The words were barely out of his mouth when whispers of approval circled the room. *He has a plan. A backup plan. A good plan.*

"Of course you thought of it," Sloan added. "Any good strategist would."

"But I only thought of it as a last resort."

"As it should be," Sloan agreed, but the hint of a satisfied smile creased his eyes.

The seed was planted, the damage done, Tyghan thought. Keats would now be viewed less as a helpful recruit than as a game piece to be moved and sacrificed at their command.

Tyghan looked back at the rest of the council. "I don't want any more talk of killing Bristol Keats. Do you understand, Lord Csorba? She made a sworn promise to help Cael and Elphame, and I will consider any more conspiring behind my back an act of treason—and take appropriate measures. Don't forget, I am the king until my brother returns, and I hold all the power that goes with the title. Power I will *use*."

Silence gripped the room. Lord Csorba sat quietly, but his hands were still curled into fists on the table.

"May I suggest," Lord Alistair said, "that if she might be used as a hostage, perhaps we should all take an oath, here and now, that this information won't be discussed with anyone outside this room? It wouldn't bode well for any of us if she found out what might be her fate."

Tyghan nodded, eager for this proposal to be adopted, and for Sloan's loose tongue to be squelched. A round of *aye*s circled the table, and Tyghan hoped he would never hear the word *hostage* again.

When the door was sealed and Tyghan and his officers were safely ensconced in the counselor's study, Eris whirled, facing Tyghan. "A hostage? Have you gone mad?"

"Early on, it occurred to me. When I was frustrated and desperate. But—"

"The council is still desperate! Can't you see that?"

"It's not a bad idea," Quin said. "As a last resort—"

"Tygh did take an oath to do everything in his power to save Cael," Kasta reminded him. "And by your direction, Counselor."

"A hostage trade. That's all we're talking about," Quin added.

Glennis winced. "I don't think it's a good idea."

"She is not a hostage!" Eris hissed. "She's here by her own free will. We cannot violate that."

"We're not using her as a hostage!" Tyghan yelled, trying to end the runaway speculation. "I said it in a private conversation with Kasta. After the review meeting, I was thinking out loud, trying to find ways to make sure they couldn't send her home. Sloan is trying to undermine me." He turned to Kasta. "How did he find out?"

"I don't know. I swear I said nothing. Maybe he thought of it on his own. It's not a completely unique thought—and he is a talented strategist."

"More like a conniving weasel," Tyghan answered. "And his smug smile was as good as a wink to let me know I was being watched." Tyghan hissed, wishing he had something to break—like a neck. Sometimes he had to remind himself that they were both on the same side. He turned to Madame Chastain, more questions burning inside him. "Why hasn't Keats left her room? Or eaten? Is she ill?"

"No. She hasn't left for the exact reasons Eris stated. She's still coming to grips with having a creature on her back—one that her own parents placed there—not to mention that she's not who she thought she was. Nor are her parents. That would take anyone time to get used to. Her fellow recruits come by every day, hoping to visit with her, but she won't see them either. They're afraid she plans to leave. But in Avery's vernacular, she said Miss Keats just needs space. That means time alone. I agree. We all need to give that to her. Especially you, especially after today. We need to give all these wagging tongues a chance to cool." She eyed Tyghan's dusty, travel-weary clothes. "When was the last time you wore your crown?"

He hesitated, unable to remember. "I wear it in the throne room. There's no need—"

"Wear it tonight," she snapped, but then her countenance softened, perhaps seeing Tyghan's grow harder. "And one of your formal jackets. I take it the Lumessa accepted your apology?"

Tyghan sighed. "I may have raised my voice—"

"You what?" she shouted, throwing her hands up in the air, her ire returning as quickly as a crow to carrion. "I told you—"

"She didn't give me a chance to apologize! But she's here. That's all that matters."

"How so?"

"She agreed to come for Bristol's sake. Because she's Kierus's daughter."

Madame Chastain nodded. She understood the clemency the Lumessa would afford Tyghan because there was something she cared about more than what angered her. Kierus was the only child she had ever raised, and by extension, Bristol Keats was a product of her devotion and patience. Raising a mortal child in Elphame was not easy, especially when you ultimately lost him to the world he came from.

"I'll go check with the Sisters and see when a meeting can be arranged," Eris said. He pulled Tyghan aside before he left. "Cael and Elphame are foremost in all of our goals, but I don't want her sacrificed on a whim, just because she's Maire's daughter. That is not what I brought her here for. Do you understand? We are not Fomorians. We are Tuatha de. Our gods and laws matter."

Eris paused as he unlatched his door and leveled a warning glance at Tyghan. "The last time I arranged a meeting, the Lumessa's business with Miss Keats was cut short—by you. Do *not* cut it short again. And stop thinking out loud. You're the king, dammit, and anyone could be listening."

They all stared at the door after Eris slammed it behind him. He was the quintessential peacekeeper, and always deferred to Tyghan, but now twice in one hour he had not only raised his voice but cursed at the king.

Madame Chastain shook her head. Only she understood the true reason why.

CHAPTER 63

Bristol sat in the wide nook of the window, her arms hugging her knees. A blanket she'd pulled from her bed circled her shoulders and twisted around her feet, and her hair was a swirl of neglect. She leaned her head against the wall and stared out the window at the hazy expanse of the distant city, tiny figures on tiny horses navigating tiny streets.

But mostly she saw other things.

Twenty-two years was a lot to sift through. Truth and lies had been longtime partners, and they'd played a glorious good trick on her.

For four days her attention drifted from the bed to the ceiling to the past. She fingered her way through memories like slips of paper, memories she had folded and tucked neatly away in hidden places. Now they fell loose, in disarray around her, small bits she tried to make sense of, until one would catch her by surprise with its sharpness, a paper cut slicing into her skin.

Come away, child. Come away from the tree.

She was four years old when she wandered into an overgrown park, wild with weeds and abandon, not far from their motel.

But, Mama, it whispered to me. It wants to give me something. It's asking me to—

Come away, child! Now! Do as I tell you!

Her mother's voice was harsh, and her cheeks were flushed with fury. Bristol ran into her arms, crying, not sure why she was scolded.

Leanna Keats scooped her up, squeezing Bristol so tightly she couldn't breathe. Her mother ran the whole way back to their motel chanting jibberish, then frantically rubbed herbs into Bristol's hair, like she was washing away invisible dirt. That very hour, they packed up their van and left for another city. Any city. It didn't matter which one, as long as it was far away.

Come away, child.

It was her mother who was fae.

Her *mother*.

She had repeated that revelation often over these past days, thinking sense would come from it. A burst of enlightenment. Instead, she had to painfully sort through memories that didn't come easily. But they were there, tucked into deep dark places. Maybe some things she had chosen not to see as they were. Things she didn't want to remember. Like the way her mother would stare vacantly across the room and slide her thumb along her fingers, a phantom motion, like she was kneading something between them—the same movement she saw Madame Chastain use before she summoned magic. But there was nothing magical about her mother, no chanting, no spells, no supernatural scents that hinted at anything beyond the ordinary.

Cinnamon toast, meadow grass, campfires, powdered doughnut, orange soda, the oily trace of long hours in a beat-up old van, and the joyful whiff of rose oil after a long bath at a motel, those were the scents of her mother. Everyday scents. If her mother knew any magic, she never used it—at least not that Bristol ever saw. Maybe because it would have led other fae to her—the ones she was trying to escape from. How had Bristol not seen the signs? But it was the only life she had ever known, the truth of her world, and her mother's quirkiness was as much a part of it as washing up in rest stop bathrooms, and sleeping like a tangled litter of pups stuffed in the back of their van.

Maybe sometimes you couldn't see truth until you gained distance from it. Fae and magic hadn't even existed in Bristol's mind. And that wasn't by accident. It was by design—her parents' design.

Memories flooded back. The things she had ignored—or was trained to ignore. The simple things her mother didn't know. Civics. Riding a bike. How to step into an elevator and make it move.

Then there were the things she and her sisters never questioned, like how their mother's hair color would change overnight, though she never went to a salon. Or the strange desperate language she spoke in fevered dreams, her father waking her with a gentle shake. Covering for her.

They both lied. And to cover up who they were, they placed a—

Sour saliva swelled on her tongue. It was one of the reasons it was hard for her to eat. Every bite would also feed the creature on her back so it could go on sucking away more of who she was. Madame Chastain told her the tick had probably been there since she was a baby—a way to keep her magic stunted and concealed. Going through the portal made the years of repressed magic explode within the tick. The High Witch had never dealt with anything like it before and said she had summoned someone of exceptional skill and experience who might be able to get the tick to release its grip on her.

A tick. Ugly vermin deliberately placed on her. Her own parents did this. And they never told her.

And then another memory. One that faded in, out. A hazy slip of paper cutting her over and over again. A recollection so blurred she wasn't even sure it was true. Toddling into the bathroom and screaming. Her mother not looking like her mother. Her father scooping Bristol up and carrying her out of the bathroom.

It's only a costume, darling. Mama's playing dress-up. She'll take it off. Only a costume.

Bristol asked Madame Chastain if she had known her mother. "No," the witch answered, "she wasn't from Danu."

Maybe her mother did grow up in a small town with a rotten family just as she claimed—a rotten fae family. All her fellow recruits were born and raised in the mortal world. There seemed to be plenty of them there. Or did her mother and father meet in Elphame? Or maybe they—

This was the game Bristol had played for the last four days—or maybe it had been her entire life. The truth had become as twistable as the balloons molded at street fairs into different creatures for the price of a coin. It was pliable between skilled fingers and could be anything you wanted it to be. How skilled her parents were.

If I'm bloodmarked, I got it from her, Bristol thought.

If.

But now, with her mother dead, Bristol would never know for sure. Unless she found her father. Surely, he would know. If he was alive. Now even Willow's "truth" seemed suspect—as did every truth of Bristol's entire life.

Just that morning another question broke through the dull clamor in her head, and she asked Madame Chastain, "How did you *really* find me? In the whole mortal world of small towns, I doubt you were sitting on a street corner in Bowskeep looking for recruits."

Madame Chastain shook her head. "No, we weren't. It was Freda who noticed you. She learned about our search. She also knew your mother was fae, and one day she saw a car headed for you and your lightning-quick move on your bike between two parked cars to avoid it."

Bristol remembered that near collision vividly, the car turning a corner too fast. Hearing the screeching tires before she saw it coming at her. Even she had wondered how she sensed that narrow space between two parked cars was there for her to escape into. She was looking in the other direction at the time but managed to swerve into the tiny gap without so much as scratching either car. *Desperation and luck*, she had called it at the time.

But even Freda, whom Bristol barely knew, suspected it was more. Leave it to a librarian, especially a fae one.

Bristol also asked the High Witch about the art her father claimed to have found at a swap meet. "Did he steal it from Jasmine?"

"We don't know. She wouldn't say. He mattered to her more than a piece of art."

More loose ends that didn't add up.

Bristol rubbed her temple. At least her headaches were subsiding. The aspirin she'd brought from home didn't touch them, and Madame Chastain gave her a smoky green liquid to drink instead. The witch said that because of the changes within her body, the aspirin was probably no longer effective for her. Changes. It made her nauseous.

Bristol noticed another tray of food that had been left on her table while she slept, but meal after meal, she fed most of it to the fox. She spoke to him often now. He was her new confidante.

Watch this, she would tell him, and say, *Treima,* the command to die.

From a distance she would snuff each candle on the candelabra that lit her meal with a simple motion of her pinched fingers and one quiet word. And then with a chant, *ante feru lask*—blaze bright—and the swift gathering of her hands, ignite them all at once in a burst of fire. It came easily. The chant she had memorized that she thought was useless—because she was useless—now worked because of the small amount of magic-rich blood that had leaked back into her from the injured tick. Her own magic it had stolen.

Now, as soon as she levitated a piece of food, the fox came running, ready to grab it before it ever hit the floor. *You'll get fat,* she warned him. But of course, he wouldn't because he wasn't real.

Was she?

She was a sudden stranger to herself, blurred and unfamiliar.

It was frightening to be one thing for your entire life, and then find out you were really something else. It felt like part of her had been erased. Madame Chastain asked if her sisters had similar birthmarks. They didn't. They both had skin that was as flawless as a fresh canvas. No freckles, no birthmarks. But she knew she needed to tell Cat and Harper about herself—except the thought overwhelmed her, made her tired, made her crawl into a ball in her bed and go to sleep. She didn't want anything to be different between them. She wanted it to be how it had always been. The Keats sisters sticking together and making their life work.

Her mother lied to her.

Her mother was fae.

It came back to that again.

And if Leanna Keats could lie, it meant all fae could lie—including Tyghan.

Did that make her happy or angry?

The mixed feelings sat heavy in her chest. She wasn't sure what to think anymore. *She is nothing to me.* He'd lied. Hadn't he? She remembered the touch of his hand on her neck when he healed it, the gentleness of his fingers on her skin, the real fear in his eyes. There was purity in those brief, anxious minutes, something truer than all the words that had passed between them. And yet he hadn't come to see her, to check on her . . . in how many days? Maybe the truth lay there.

Nothing. It was how she felt. Floating in some in-between world.

A creature owned part of who she was. Revulsion swept over her again, the flash of that moment when she saw the hideous beast on her back. It was still there, refusing to let go. She reached behind, her fingers tentatively skimming her spine, afraid the tick might bite off a finger. But every time she checked, it was always the same. Her skin was smooth, the creature deep inside her. Hiding. Determined.

She shuffled from the window seat back to her bed and curled into the mattress, letting it swallow her up, sliding her hands beneath the pillow where she wouldn't be able to see the sharp blue moons of her nails, nails that belonged to someone she didn't know.

CHAPTER 64

The tiny gray mouse scurried along the hallway, hugging the wall, its whiskers twitching nervously. When it reached the outer walkway, it circled in place, its fur becoming pink curly hair, its tiny legs transforming back into long, lithe limbs.

"The attendant just left," Hollis said, brushing a curl from her brow. "It's clear."

The five recruits rushed down the hall to Bristol's door, and Avery tapped lightly. They'd been turned away multiple times by Kasta and the High Witch. Now was their chance.

There was no answer to the tap, so Avery knocked a bit louder.

"Bri!" Sashka whispered against the door.

Nothing.

Julia finally banged on the door, saying they had nothing to lose. "Bri!" she called. "We need to see you!"

"We have a surprise!" Rose added. "Let us in!"

Bristol was half sleeping, half searching her locked-away memories when the knocking began. She hoped it would go away. She was a mess and didn't want the others to see her, but when she heard Rose's voice, she crawled from her bed.

When she opened her door, the recruits swarmed in like bees around a flower, but Bristol was no flower. Sashka wrinkled her nose. "You haven't seen this side of a bath in days, have you?"

"We'll fix that," Avery said, and disappeared into the bath chamber.

Bristol heard water running. "No, I can't—"

Julia grabbed her hand and gave it a reassuring squeeze. "We heard about the tick. It will be taken care of in due course. In the meantime, you—"

"Need a bath!" Rose finished, and hugged Bristol with one arm, the other still in a sling. "You'd think with all the sorcerers around here someone could fix a simple broken shoulder, but I guess my bird bones are trickier than most."

"But you'll be all right?" Bristol asked.

"Yes. I'll be flying in no time. Esmee says so."

"It's ready!" Avery called from the other room.

If moving things along quickly was their strategy to distract Bristol, it was working, but when it came time to disrobe, she hesitated. She didn't want them to see her back. Their chatter quieted, and Julia held up her cloak as a curtain while Bristol slipped into the tub. A rainbow of colors swirled on the surface of the water. Bristol dipped below the long river of purple bubbles, working hot soapy water into her scalp. When she surfaced, Sashka and Hollis were holding up swatches of shimmering forest green brocade and gold satin.

"What do you think?" Avery asked.

"Hopefully you like them, because it's too late to switch," Rose said.

"We thought these fabrics would complement your hair and eyes," Hollis added. "We had to choose for you since you didn't come for the fabric selection. The tailors are eager to get started. Our dresses are going to be extra special, and Beltane Eve is only a few weeks away!"

"What are you talking about?" Bristol asked.

They explained that the Beltane Eve celebration for the kingdom courts was usually reserved only for royalty and select nobles—the only time the monarchs all got together—but this year Danu was bringing recruits to the celebration at Timbercrest Castle as a gesture of reassurance so the other kingdoms would know that Danu was not giving up the fight.

"*Us* as reassurance?" Bristol said. "Are they that desperate?"

"I know. Right?" Sashka laughed. "But I guess they think we performed admirably in the surprise attack."

"Julia did manage to kill three of those foul-smelling creatures," Avery said. "And the rest of us helped the archers or finished off downed demons. We never did go underground as they ordered."

"Scandalous, aren't we?" Hollis added, and fluttered her lashes. "Master Reuben would have self-combusted if he had seen us."

Julia's mouth twisted in a crooked smirk. "The truth is, we're far from being the answer to their problems yet, but in one evening of tipsy revelry, the gentry won't know if we're skilled or skilled impostors. And Danu is hoping to rally support from the other kingdoms by instilling confidence in a positive outcome."

"Hmm," Bristol mused. Smoke and mirrors, her father called it, the many cons she saw on the fair circuit, a way of molding the truth to fit hopes and desires. The fae of Elphame needed heroes, and for one night that was what they would be. An illusion. It was a con Bristol understood with new clarity. She sank lower in the water.

"So . . ." Julia said, taking Bristol's hand from the side of the tub, looking at her blue nailbeds. "What is this? Looks like you're fae after all."

"So they tell me," Bristol answered, and pulled her hand away, submerging it beneath the rainbow swirls.

"And you're not happy about that?" Sashka asked. She ran a finger along her jewel-colored jawline. "Blue is a lovely color."

Bristol shook her head, unsure how to answer. "I don't know what to think. Or what it means. The High Witch didn't know either. She just called it irregular. I do know I'm not happy that I have an ugly creature living inside me. Or that my parents put it there."

"Why would they do that?" Avery asked. "Why suppress your magic?"

"Because they were hiding and running in a mortal world, and I guess they were afraid my magic would betray their secret."

They all weighed in, talking about what it was like to grow up among mortals, the many things about their lives they kept secret from others. "Sometimes it was hard, but at least I knew who and what I was," Sashka said.

"And there was a whole community of fae where I lived, so we had each other," Avery added. "I wasn't the only one with a crown of moss and twigs."

Hollis shook her head. "I'm sorry you found out this way. I can't imagine the shock—and it's understandable why you've missed training and classes."

Rose leaned forward, her hands gripping the rim of the tub. "But you're going to stay, aren't you? We need you."

Stay? Bristol hadn't thought about staying or leaving. For the last few days, time had stopped for her.

"We'll let you finish your bath in peace," Julia said as she stood. "If you need help, let us know. In the meantime, we brought some food—your favorites. We'll go lay it out in the other room."

Bristol finished washing her hair, and she had to admit the floral scent of the soap did lift her spirits—or it at least made her think about something else for a change. For days her mind had been stuck in a dark spiraling whirlpool with no beginning or ending.

When she finished dressing and emerged back into her bed-chamber, the first thing she saw was the recruits lounging around on her forest floor carpet with a blanket of food between them like they were on a picnic. The fox hovered just outside their circle, waiting for handouts. The second thing she saw was her favorite foods, just as they promised. Stuffed figs, spiced kumquats, soft warm rolls drenched in thyme butter. Bowl, after basket, after platter. Everything she loved.

Her chest swelled, aching that they knew her so well. That they barged their way in. That they knew how much space to give her—and not give her. That they were able to find that delicate balance between pushing in and stepping back. That they were far better at this friend thing than she was, but they didn't hold it against her. They were helping her along.

Avery patted the carpet next to her. "Sit."

Bristol did.

And she ate, mostly forgetting about the freeloader on her back. Her stomach rumbled to life, and she sampled everything.

Hollis delicately licked her fingers as she finished off a handful of sugared borage blossoms. "You know what I miss most about the mortal world?"

"Television!" Sashka blurted out.

"No! I was going to say tacos."

"Yes! Tacos!" Avery agreed, licking her lips. "And guacamole! But I do miss my shows too. I was almost finished with *Starlands*. I'll never know who—"

"It was Fremont Bellows who did it," Rose said.

Avery screamed and threw a pillow at her, and they all laughed.

"We're not missing much drama, though," Julia said, lounging on her side like a lioness. "Considering there's quite a show going on here every night."

"And an encore of drama during the day. Worse than the teachers' lounge," Hollis added.

"Has something been going on?" Bristol asked.

They exchanged furtive glances. "Well, there's been a lot of angry whispers among the lords and ladies, and this morning our classes were canceled," Sashka explained.

"Olivia was *not* happy," Avery continued. "She let it slip that the council called an emergency meeting in the absence of the king. It gave the unfortunate appearance of a conspiracy."

"What do you mean, in his absence?" Bristol asked. "Where is he?"

Hollis said that he'd been gone ever since the battle. He was sent away on kingdom business. "Madame Chastain needed him to personally retrieve a powerful sorceress, but she didn't say why."

"Apparently there was some sort of bad blood between the king and this sorceress," Avery revealed in a hushed tone, "and he had to do some groveling to get her to come. We heard he just returned this morning."

So that's where he's been, Bristol thought. Kasta told her everyone who asked to see her, but she never once mentioned Tyghan. That was why. A weight lifted inside her. He wasn't avoiding her, but was off on kingdom business—and it appeared to be an errand run for her benefit.

Sashka rolled her eyes. "I can't imagine him groveling for anyone, though."

Neither could Bristol, but she knew how rumors could spread and grow. "What are the gentry whispering about?"

Rose looked down at her lap. "You," she said softly.

"They're afraid," Julia clarified.

"Of me? Because of this thing on my back? Do they think I'm a monster now?"

"No," Julia answered. "And you are *not* a monster. It's your absence, hiding away in here. They wonder what you're doing. They wonder what you've become. Rumors are cruel, and they're imagining the worst."

"They're not used to battle so close to home," Hollis added. "The attack left nerves raw."

Bristol bit off a corner of her lemon popover. Apparently, she wasn't the only one reeling from sudden changes. She swallowed. "Then I guess I should attend the festivities tonight. To put their minds at ease." But the thought of being under scrutiny immediately made the popover stick in her throat.

"You're going to stay?" Rose said, her long lashes casting a shadow under her eyes. The others waited for her answer too.

She was either fully in or she wasn't. She took a sip of sparkling wine to wash down the popover. And then chugged back another long drink. She licked the sweetness from her lips. "I made a promise just like the rest of you. I never planned to leave until our goal was accomplished."

She would stay and see this out, not to mention there were now even more answers she needed from her father, and she was going to get them—one way or another.

"Yes," she answered. "I am absolutely staying."

CHAPTER 65

Bristol had promised to meet the others at Sun Court as soon as dusk rolled in, but now it was well past dark. She had fussed over her dress, her hair, even the hollows of her cheeks that she feared made her look more sinister. *They're imagining the worst.*

She ate more food, but of course that wouldn't instantly fill out the few pounds she had lost. The fox sulked nearby as she ate the last stuffed fig. She changed her dress three times, nothing improving the sharpness of her cheekbones, and finally settled on a pale blue chiffon dress with lacy sleeves of swirling flowers. It was the cheeriest dress in her wardrobe, a piece of spun confection plucked from the sky. Surely it could dispel the whispers. She was not a monster.

And if she was, she was no more a monster than any of them.

She glanced at her hands, now glamoured to look as they had before.

The others had given her a quick tutorial on glamour when she hesitated because of her nailbeds. "Glamour's easy," Julia promised. "We can teach you in ten minutes." She said she used glamour all the time in the mortal world to transform her cat eyes, and Sashka explained how she would change her butterfly-blue skin to a nice warm brown.

"Once you get the hang of it, it becomes second nature," Julia said. "You'll hardly have to think about it. The power is inside you. You just have to bring it to the surface." They made her stand up, and Julia touched her finger just under Bristol's chin, lifting it slightly. "Think about how you want your nails to look. Now pull back your shoulders and settle into your hips, your ribs. Feel the weight. Own what's inside you. Every inch of it. Breathe deeply. Now focus your eyes a hundred miles away, a hundred years away."

"Focus through my chamber wall?"

"Yes," Hollis answered. "It's not a place you're seeing, but a distance. You own all that space from here to there. Breathe in and believe it. Say the words *mahr credeigm*, and let the power inside you do the work."

Bristol thought she was getting more of a poise tutorial than anything magical, but she did as they said, walking around her room, chin up, her eyes focused a hundred miles away, ages away, seeing highways and landscapes and time blur past her, the nameless towns, motels, missed chances, and meadows that shaped her for better or worse, and she owned it all—instead of the shadows owning her. When she looked at her hands, she was stunned—they appeared the way they used to look. In her shock, they reverted back, but after a few more tries, she was able to maintain it. They were right, the deception of simple glamours was frightfully easy. That was how her mother had done it for all those years.

"Not many can see through it, unless they really make an effort, usually with an incantation," Avery said.

"But that's considered quite rude, like peeking up someone's dress," Julia added.

Now, with dress, hair, and even glamour in place, Bristol still found herself pacing the floor, reluctant to leave. *He just returned this morning.* Now that Tyghan was back, would he come looking for her? But it was late now, and he still hadn't come. She remembered when she lifted her shirt on the foot trail, the gasps, the curses.

Was he as repulsed by the tick as the rest of them? "Of course he was," she whispered. Who wouldn't be? She lifted the skirt of her dress and slid her palm across her lower back. She wasn't able to bring herself to look at the dark stain again, the twisted legs and body that pulsed in time with her own heartbeat, but her skin was smooth beneath her fingertips. She swallowed, forcing down the woozy sensation, and tried to imagine the tick wasn't there at all.

She skimmed her wardrobe again, eyeing the cloak Esmee gave her—an invisibility cloak similar to the one Kasta placed on her shoulders for their ride here. While invisibility could be practiced and learned by most fae, for those with mortal blood in them, invisibility was not always possible. Suddenly, becoming invisible was the most important thing in the world, and she desperately wanted to wear the cloak to the festivities, but being seen was the whole point. She closed the wardrobe door before she changed her mind.

She walked out the door, her head held high, focusing on her destination at Sun Court, but she only made it as far as the upper gallery that bordered it. When the first few heads turned her way, she couldn't bring herself to walk down the grand staircase, and slipped into a dark alcove instead. Only for a few minutes, she promised herself. She checked her hands. Two of her nails had reverted. She tried to focus a thousand miles away, to a lifetime ago when she was just Bristol Keats, part-time student, part-time assistant manager, full-time sister trying to keep her family together. *You are the strong one.* For tonight at least, she would believe it. When she looked back down, the sharp blue moons were gone, and her attention jumped back to the revelers below. There was something different about them tonight.

A current of uneasiness ran beneath the gaiety of swishing satins and tinkling crystal. It flowed just under the laughter, the dancing, and the arrogance. These powerful beings were afraid, the kind of fear that could never be admitted. It was disturbingly familiar to her, pricking memories of her parents rushing to pack up, her father's foot pressing steadily on the gas pedal as miles sped past them in a desperate blur. She saw it all differently now. How hard it must have been for them to run with three children in tow, to tack on smiles, pack favorite snacks for the road, keep their voices light. But the lightness always had an edge, the sun catching it like broken glass. That's what she saw now, an undercurrent of broken glass beneath the merriment. Was it because of the attack on the city—or because of *her?*

Now she had to force herself to become part of it, smiling, dancing, and using a shimmering dress to cover all the broken pieces inside her that they might see.

"Finally emerging from your dark cave, I see."

She swept her hands behind her back. Reuben came out of nowhere, like he'd been stalking her.

"Hiding something, Miss Keats?" he taunted, blocking her escape.

Bristol's back stiffened. "No."

"One wouldn't know it by the way you've skipped required festivities—not to mention your classes. You certainly won't be allowed back for my lectures. You may as well pack your bags. It's time for you to go."

He said it so smoothly. Soundly. His voice held all the conviction of a done deal. *You are dismissed. Go.*

"I'm not going anywhere, except to join my friends." She took a step forward, daring him to block her passage.

Reuben stepped aside with a sweeping gesture, a sneer twisting his lip. "Go home, Miss Keats. You don't belong here. Go now, before the choice is taken from you."

Bristol moved past him, her thumb casually swiping her fingertips, silent words hidden on her tongue. As she walked away, Reuben didn't notice the hem of his robe was smoldering, but he would notice the flames soon enough.

She paused at the top of the stairs and lifted her chin, looked a hundred miles away, a thousand miles, even past Bowskeep, and made her way down the grand staircase.

CHAPTER 66

Quin swigged back the contents of his glass and slid it across the table to Dalagorn for a refill. They had already killed off one ogre-sized flask of whiskey and were starting on another. It had been a long, dry journey to bring back the Lumessa, and they were making up for lost time. Glennis didn't touch goblin whiskey but was gleefully sipping honeysuckle wine while she downed a whole leek pie.

"We're way ahead of you," Quin said, noting Tyghan's untouched drink.

Tyghan shrugged, his mind elsewhere.

They were tucked beneath an arbor in a dark corner of Jasper Court. Cully sat across from Tyghan, showing off his lightning ability to catch cherries between his teeth that Glennis was happily pelting at his face.

"Hey, Cully," Kasta said as she joined them. "Ivy's looking for you. It seemed important. Something about Beltane Eve. She's over at Middle Arch."

Cully scrambled to his feet, stumbling on his chair and righting it, Glennis still pelting him with cherries. "I better see what it's about," he said, and hurried away.

Quin snorted. "She really looking for him?"

Kasta smiled. "No, I just wanted his chair."

They all laughed, and Dalagorn poured Kasta a glass.

"What is it her parents don't like about Cully?" Glennis asked between bites of pie.

"No wings," Quin answered.

Kasta grinned. "Elven have their qualities. Look how quick he is with cherries."

Glennis shook her head. "They should just run off and marry. Her parents will come around."

"A pixie come around?" Dalagorn scoffed. "They're far too proper." He extended his little finger like he was holding a cup of floral tea instead of whiskey. "Especially not Lord Hambry. That stubborn coot . . ."

Tyghan slowly spun his drink, the conversation around him fading, of no more interest to him than the music and the ringing of goblets raised in greetings. The distant torchlight shimmered on his drink's amber surface. *Space*, he thought. *She needs space.* It was a strange term, especially since she was closed up in her room. His farm had space. The seaside had space. Her chambers were finite and small. How long would she need that space?

They're afraid she plans to leave.

He was certain she wouldn't leave. She believed in promises.

But maybe that had changed.

I have no good reason to dally.

No reason.

But Tyghan wanted there to be a reason. Gods help him, *he* wanted to be that reason.

His hand tightened on his glass.

He wanted her. *He wanted her deeply.* He'd been warned he needed to shake the idea from his head, but he had already tried too many times—on the ride to retrieve the Lumessa, and on the ride back.

Maybe it was seeing the tip of Braegor's sword pressed to her throat, and the sheer terror that had gripped him. Maybe it was their almost kiss in the barn and the scent of her skin so close to his it made him dizzy. Maybe it was the ache in his chest when he laid her unconscious

on her bed and knew he wouldn't be there when she woke up. There
was something about the desperation of that day, almost losing her, the
near finality, that turned hazy thoughts into sharp and bright ones.

He didn't just want her, he *loved* her. And he had for a long time.

Even now, all he could think about was how she was feeling. Maybe
he should take her some food? But Kasta already told him attendants
were delivering trays to her five times a day, and they mostly went untouched. *Just give her space, Tygh.* It seemed to be a new phrase they
were all using. Especially in regard to him.

But he didn't want space between them. He was tired of everyone's
warnings. Tired of the council. Tired of paying for his brother's sins.
He wasn't Kierus, and he wasn't his brother.

Kasta tossed a stray cherry at Tyghan to get his attention. It landed
in his glass, splashing whiskey onto the table. "Look at you. All dressed
up like a king."

Tyghan glanced down at his formal black jacket. "Even kings must
sometimes appease counselors and High Witches."

"But no crown?"

Tyghan leveled a glare at Kasta. He could only be pushed so far.

"All right," she answered. "But have you at least been out on the
grounds talking to anyone yet? Making your presence known? I think
that was the point. It's your first night back. Your subjects might find it
reassuring to see their king walking among them."

Tyghan fished the cherry out of his drink and ate it, then spat the
pit off to the side. "You're my subject. And you see me. Are you reassured?"

Kasta grunted.

"Let him be," Dalagorn said. "Four days with those Sisters looking
over our shoulders is enough to make anyone hide in a corner. Even an
ogre. Even a king."

Quin hissed. "And those damn wolves of theirs. I still feel their hot
slimy mouths on my skin. Every time I made a quick move, I had a
bracelet of teeth around my wrist." He chugged back his drink, but

mid-swig he stopped and set down his glass. "Well, would you look who Hollis is talking to? Someone's not hiding in her room anymore."

Tyghan's eyes shot up and followed the line of Quin's gaze. Bristol came in and out of view as partygoers passed between them. She was seated at an overlook about twenty yards away. Julia and Sashka sat on either side of her, the other recruits standing around her.

"That's a good sign," Dalagorn mused. "She's adjusting."

"You mean getting used to the overgrown tick inside her?" Quin said. "Who could ever get used to that?"

Glennis frowned. "None of them are dancing. Usually they—"

"They're not dancing because she's not dancing," Tyghan said. It was obvious to him. "They're creating a protective buffer around her. Look at the gentry."

The lords and ladies near them were staring, shaking their heads. Wings flapped with contempt. Lips turned hard, holding back curses. Did they think her oversized tick and potential magic were a threat? But a few, council members like Lord Csorba and Lady Barrington, stood a bit farther back, smugly eyeing her, with another secret warming their hearts. They saw something else. *Hostage.*

Tyghan's focus returned to Bristol. In just a few days, she had become thinner, her eyes darker. Her neck was stiff, like she was using every bit of strength she had to keep her chin held high in the middle of the surrounding scrutiny.

"It's her first night back since the tick was discovered," Kasta said. "They'll move on to some other juicy news to entertain them, especially now that she's not hiding in her room."

Tyghan wasn't so sure, and then he spotted Reuben descending the grand staircase in a rush, his long hair streaming behind him. His black eyes gleamed and were hotly focused in Bristol's direction.

"I don't like what I'm seeing," Tyghan said, heat already burning his temples.

The others spotted Reuben too. "Neither do I," Quin and Kasta said almost simultaneously. "We'll go—"

Tyghan was already standing. "I'll take care of this," he said, and left to intercept the sorcerer. He stepped into Reuben's path long before he reached Bristol, making him come to a startled stop. "Something on your mind, Reuben?" he asked.

"Nothing to trouble you, Your Majesty. I only need to talk to one of the novices," he answered, and tried to sidestep Tyghan.

Tyghan blocked his path again. "Talk to me instead."

Reuben's brows pulled down with discernment. Anger trembled across his upper lip. "She has to go!" he snapped. "Look what she did!" He grabbed the bottom of his charred robe and shook it in his fist, black flecks of burned cloth flying loose. "I know it was her! If not for my amulets, I might have been burned to a crisp!"

"She hasn't been able to perform the simplest of magics, and now you're claiming she set you afire? Did you see her do it?"

"No, but—"

"Look around you, Reuben. How many here have you crossed? Too many to count, I'd say." And then pressing closer, Tyghan added, "Stay away from my recruit."

"*Your* recruit?"

"That's right. Mine. Don't look at her. Don't touch her. Don't even think her name. Stay away from her. Do you understand?"

Reuben dropped the hem of his robe, and his chest puffed out, awareness spreading over his face. "Yes. I think I do," he answered. His chin dipped with wooden acknowledgment. "I serve at your pleasure, Your Majesty—until your brother returns."

CHAPTER 67

T he whispers were hard to ignore. At least half of those shooting
Bristol sideways glances were capable of lethal magics, not to
mention the garden variety of mortal threats like a knife in the
back. She managed to force a smile, but trying to keep her thoughts
focused as she spoke with Julia was impossible. When the chatter
spiked, she thought, *Not again.* Wasn't her presence there enough to
quell the rumors? *I am not a monster.* And then the crowd rippled
like a disturbed school of fish. Someone was pushing through them—
toward her.

Bristol braced herself for another angry face, like Reuben's. Or
maybe Lord Csorba or Commander Sloan this time. They had all made
their disapproval of her known.

Avery and Hollis shifted their positions, fortifying their protective
wall, but then her stomach sank when they stepped aside too, the wall
vanished, and someone stopped in front of her.

It was Tyghan.

He was dressed not like a Knight Commander in leathers and weapons, but like a king. He wore a formal jacket, the same midnight black
as his hair. Silver threads embroidered the cuffs and collar. It was the
first time he actually looked like a king and not some roguish soldier,
except now he was the picture of a formidable monarch, his expression

severe, like he was there to start a war. The crisp, tailored edges of his formal attire emphasized his power.

The crowd went silent, waiting.

He didn't speak immediately. He stared for a long, uncomfortable moment.

Fire ignited in her chest, and she wasn't sure if it was from the dangerous figure he cut or because it felt like he was devouring her with his gaze. She was too afraid to entertain the latter notion. She'd gone down that empty road too many times, and the hurt of it was still fresh.

"Welcome back, Your Majesty," she finally said, trying to break the awkwardness.

His attention shifted to Julia. "I'd like to steal Miss Keats's company for a few moments, with your permission."

Bristol sat straighter on the bench. *Permission?* This was getting odder by the moment, and yet there was a long, strained moment between him and Julia. Her cat eyes narrowed, passing some sort of judgment.

When she finally nodded, Tyghan extended his hand toward Bristol. "Would you join me for a dance?" He said it loud, so everyone would be sure to hear.

Bristol eyed his hand, his gesture visible to everyone around them. His palm was turned upward, not a hand to pull a fallen recruit off the ground for more drills, but a hand offered as an invitation. Every head in Sun Court craned forward, and the crowd pressed a step closer. Bristol's hands remained on her thighs, her fingers squeezing her knees. *Dance?* What was this very public performance all about? What was he trying to prove? She didn't want to misunderstand his motive and imagine one thing that was only something else. The crowd watched, breathless. "Here? Now?" she whispered. "I don't think—"

"The king of Danu wishes to dance," he answered, again, loud enough so that everyone heard. "With you. Here and now." He waited, his hand still extended.

Bristol's blood surged at her temples. It was definitely a show, but why?

Sashka poked Bristol with her elbow, like she wasn't paying attention. "The king is asking you to dance."

So he was. Bristol didn't want to create another kind of spectacle by refusing him. She placed her hand in his. "Showing off your rank?" she whispered as she rose.

"Sometimes that's what it takes," he answered.

Chatter erupted around them, ruffling the air like a brood of clumsy mud hens trying to take flight.

"Let's go where we'll have more space," he said.

Somewhere dark and out of the way? Bristol wondered. *A place where they wouldn't be seen?* But he led her down a short flight of stairs to the sprawling central plaza where it was guaranteed that virtually everyone on the palace grounds could see them from the surrounding overlooks.

"Are you sure you want to be seen with me?"

"Too late, Keats. I think we've already been seen."

"You're taking your chances. I hear they're calling me a monster."

"I don't listen to what they say. Neither should you."

As they approached, the crowd in the plaza thinned, dancers stepping back to the perimeters. When they reached the center, he stopped and faced her. "You're well?" His voice went from commanding to soft, like it was only the two of them alone at the hazel grove.

Suspicion poked her. "What's this all about?" she asked.

"My question? I thought it was fairly direct. I'm wondering how you're feeling. Does it require a translation?"

"I'm well enough, considering," she answered, and glanced sideways at the ogling partiers.

"Ignore them," he said. "Just look at me. Be with me. Nothing else matters. We've done this before, but now we'll do it better."

"You're not denying we've danced before?"

"No." His eyes were cold steel. "I'm through denying a lot of things. And I'm through dancing under the numb veil of invisibility. I want to feel every step. With you." He lifted his palm into the air.

Her heart pounded in one continuous beat. She hesitated, then lifted her palm to meet his. Their hands circled the air.

And their dance began.

Familiar. Natural. Turning. Dipping. Swaying.

But strange. New.

Touching.

Skin to skin. Face to face.

Not a phantom dance, but the real thing.

The drums beat through her veins. *Their* veins. Synchronized. The world a blur around them, the same as before.

Only better.

His eyes remained fixed on her. *Watch me. Ignore them.*

"Why tonight?" she finally asked. "Why dance with me now? Only because you're king and can do whatever you want?"

His hand slid lower on her back, tugging her closer. "Yes, because I *am* king," he answered. "And I'm trying to prove something—and I want them all to know it."

But the way he said it, it sounded more like a personal confession to her.

Murmurs followed them as they circled the plaza, but for those few precious minutes, she stopped caring, stopping hearing anything but the music and the sound of their feet moving in time, together.

This feeling. This was what she had imagined. Craved. Not just being held in his arms, but seeing him, his hair falling over his brow, his gaze truly resting in hers.

I want them all to know it. Know what? The question burned in her. Only that she was well? Or something else?

When the music stopped and another song began, others joined them. First Melizan and Cosette, then Avery, Glennis, and Sashka. A steady flood followed, Kasta, Quin, Julia, Dalagorn, and Hollis— more and more until the plaza was full again, full of laughter and noise like on any other night, and the whispers receded. She danced with others, Avery, Sashka, Cully, but she and Tyghan always returned to each other, ending each dance in each other's arms. As the hour grew late, knights began slipping away. Dawn and duty came early for them. Even the Knight Commander had to retire eventually, and Bristol and Tyghan departed with them, dancing from plaza, to lawn, to hallway, their movements slowing, until they were finally in front of her chamber door. Alone.

"We're here," he said gently.

Bristol's hands slipped from his shoulders, and Tyghan's returned to his sides.

Now that they were alone and the message sent that he could dance with anyone he chose, was the performance over? Would they go back to what they were?

The boldness he'd had out on the plaza was left behind. As king, he was trained for public gestures and demands. They were far easier than intimacy. Here in her dim hallway, he was someone else, someone as uncertain about life as she was.

"It's late," he finally said. "And we rise early. I should go." But he didn't move.

"Is that what you want?" she asked. "To leave?"

"No," he said softly.

"Then don't."

And she opened the door behind her and pulled him into her room.

CHAPTER 68

They stumbled into the dark, and she stopped only a few steps from her bed. When she turned, he was still in the middle of the room, left behind in her fevered trail. A sliver of light illuminated his form, his black hair iced with the moon, the rest in shadow. But the blue of his eyes cut through the darkness, something simmering in them that she couldn't read.

"Bri," he said, unsure, as if testing the name on his lips. It made everything in her go liquid, and then he said it again, slow, more certain. "Bri . . . are you sure you want me here?"

She stared at him. She wasn't sure of anything. Not here in Danu or in Bowskeep or anywhere. *But this.* This she wanted more than her next breath. "I'm sure I want you. That's all I know. I want you . . . here and now."

His chin lifted, like her words were something solid that pushed against him, pushed him away, and for long seconds, fear struck her that her want for him was so great she had misread his intent, his touch, even his words—but then he crossed the room, his steps deliberate and slow. He stopped in front of her, and his hands rose to gently hold her face, but instead of leaning into her mouth, his lips met her jaw and slowly grazed upward to her cheekbone as light as a passing shadow. His breaths were husky, uneven, betraying his desire. "This," he

THE COURTING OF BRISTOL KEATS

whispered. "This is what I wanted to do that day in the barn. I didn't want to stop. I shouldn't have stopped."

"Why did you?"

"Voices in my head," he answered. "My own. Others. Ones I should have ignored. The only voice I'm listening to now is yours." His lips traveled to the corner of her mouth, waiting. "The only thing in this world or any other that can stop me now . . . is you."

Her breath hitched in her chest. "Then nothing is stopping you."

With those words, his want was unleashed, as great as hers. His fingers curled through her hair, tilting her head back, and he pressed his lips against hers, pausing like he was soaking in her touch, but then his kiss grew hungry, his tongue searching, demanding. He tasted of whiskey and cherries and magic, and she was dizzy with his scent. His teeth nipped at her lower lip and his fingertips were fire against her cheek. Waves of heat engulfed her, and she slid her hands beneath his jacket. His chest trembled as she undid the buttons of his shirt, his breaths growing heavy. He reached down, pulling and lifting her upward, her legs circling him, both of them caught in bunches of silk tulle and satin, the room tilting, spinning, his mouth discovering hers again and again. They bumped into the wall, a nearby painting clattering, and they laughed against each other's lips.

"Your laugh," he whispered. "Every time I hear it, it fills me with something I can't describe."

"You've never heard me laugh before."

"At Sun Court when you danced with your friends. I watched from a distance, wishing you were laughing with me. I drank in every syllable from your throat."

His confession, the things he had felt all along but kept hidden, undid her. It was a vulnerability she understood too well, like all the times she held back and pretended she didn't care for him. Her eyes stung, and she blinked.

"Then you have to promise to make me laugh more often—and laugh with me."

His hips were still pressed against hers, and even through all the layers of crushed fabric between them, she could feel the enormity of his passion pressing against her.

"I'm not very good at laughter," he answered, his voice hoarse.

"Then show me, Tyghan," she whispered. "Show me what you're good at."

His grip on her thighs eased, and her feet slipped to the floor. He gently turned her, so she faced the wall, and his fingers pulled on the laces of her dress. The fabric loosened, tug by tug, slipping from her shoulders, and she tensed, remembering her back. He pressed close, sweeping aside her hair, his lips hot against her neck. "Shh," he said. "It's all right. You're beautiful just as you are. I want you just as you are."

And she believed him.

It was a soft sound, a whoosh, her dress falling to her ankles. The only undergarment she wore was a wisp of fabric between her legs, and he slipped that free, too. Now his lips trailed her bare shoulder and she turned. His breath caught as he took in her body. He lifted his hand, gently caressing her breast like she was a rare jewel. Needles of heat pulsed low inside her, and her breath skipped. She wanted more, more of his touch everywhere.

"Your turn," she said, and she slipped his jacket and then shirt off. She struggled with the top button on his trousers, and he eagerly took over, shedding them in seconds. Now it was her turn to take him in and she did, her eyes skimming the muscles of his chest, the ridges of his abdomen, and his obvious hunger just below that. She inhaled sharply because, for a few seconds, she had forgotten to breathe.

He smiled. "There's still time to turn back."

"Not a chance," she said, and their mouths met again, their bare chests touching, hot, damp, skin against skin, and they moved through the darkness, until she felt him lifting her, and then the bed cool beneath her back, his weight pressing into the downy mattress beside her, the soft creak of the bed shivering through her bones, all of it real, and not a dream.

He explored her body with his hands and his mouth, leisurely, like he was claiming every inch of it—or surrendering to it—her throat, her belly, her thighs, and all the places between. Her head swam with every caress, her skin trembling, her thoughts tumbling in a blur as she ceded every inch to his touch. She eagerly explored his body too. Her lips skimmed his chest, and she breathed in his salty scent, her fingers sliding over the hard muscle of his belly, even the roughness of his scar, every touch a declaration, *for this night, you are mine*, and then lower still, taking him into her mouth. His head tilted back, his breath catching, and she soaked in his moans, kissing him deeper, harder, but then he mumbled a curse like he was losing control, and she was beneath him again, his eyes sinking into hers like he wanted to stay there forever. "This too," he said softly, "getting lost in your eyes, and never finding my way out again. This is what I wanted. I wanted you. I'm sorry I took so long to say it."

"And I'm sorry I didn't tell you that I imagined this very moment at least a hundred times."

"You can stop imagining," he whispered, then kissed her, his mouth tender, and she thought she might weep with the sweetness of it. She reveled anew in the soft warmth of his lips, in the taste of his tongue exploring hers. And then he moved down, his lips perusing her breasts, his tongue circling, as if every part of her was a miracle. He listened to the small sounds escaping from her throat, her uneven breaths, like they were a roadmap, lingering when she moaned, his mouth sliding to other places, and then between her legs, his tongue teasing, his mouth merciless, until he brought her close to an edge, air stopped up in her lungs, sound snagging between gasps, every part of her on fire, her need for him so great she couldn't breathe.

"I need you in me," she whispered. "Now." He moved atop her, nudging aside her legs with his knee, his hand sliding beneath her hips, pulling her impossibly closer, whispering her name against her lips. And then he pressed forward, gentle at first, but then deep, hard, a powerful force cleaving her in two, his hunger consuming. Her back arched, her hips meeting him, wanting it all, and he pressed deep inside her again and again, his breaths quivering against her temple. The sharp fullness of him, the burning heat, the rumble in his chest, it pushed her over the threshold she was teetering on, and the fiery throb between her legs exploded, rolling in wave after wave, devouring her so completely, growls rolled from her throat and through her clenched teeth. His arm tightened around her and his chest shuddered, halfway between moan and scream, halfway between pain and pleasure, pushing deeper, plundering every inch of her, until finally a last savage groan vibrated from his throat, and she felt the hot hiss of his breath on her cheek.

And then the room grew quiet again, and between them there was only the sound of their gentle panting, air filling their lungs again, as he relaxed against her.

And finally, laughter, soft and wondrous.

CHAPTER 69

Kierus trudged through the forest, finally coming upon the abandoned cottage. He thought after so long, he might have forgotten the way, but there it was, still standing, tucked deep in the Wilds, the shadows so thick, even monsters didn't pass this way. It was mostly unchanged. The thatch roof sprouted with ferns and weeds. The shutters hung from broken hinges. He'd expected it to be in ruins by now, but then again, here in Elphame, only six months had passed, not the lifetime he and Maire had created together in the mortal world.

He noted that the dark door of the cottage was ajar, beckoning him in, just as it had then.

Whether it was six months or twenty-three years, their first day together was still as fresh to him as yesterday.

He remembered they had stripped slowly, undressing like it was a formal ceremony. A charm, an amulet at a time, a belt, a sword, a knife, a garrote, a shirt, a dress, until they were each left with a single amulet around their necks, mutually agreed upon to protect them from spells the other might cast. Her amulet hung from a thin gold chain and rested between her breasts. Lovely breasts. Kierus had drawn a deep breath. She smiled at his eagerness, which was impossible for him to hide.

Their first stilted steps toward each other were a strange combination of wariness and barely controlled lust. The lust won out. If she got the upper hand and that was how he was to die, Kierus couldn't think of a better way.

They took their time, savoring each other's body like it was a last meal. Which in both of their minds, it probably was. Later, when they finished, she rose to dress, while Kierus lay back on the bed, his skin damp, his chest still heaving, the taste of her skin still in his mouth. He wasn't sure he could even stand.

It was only supposed to be one day, one time. Her back was turned as she pulled a stocking over the leg he had just caressed. His knife was within reach, she unaware, the perfect moment, but he couldn't do it. He wasn't sure why. It was the plan. Their business was done, and he knew she was plotting to be rid of him so she could get on with the business of terrorizing Elphame, but then when she turned, he stopped thinking about his knife and asked, "What's our hurry?"

She met his gaze for a long while, and her silence became a growing blaze inside him. "No hurry," she finally answered.

One day turned into five, five days into ten.

They lay on their backs, both exhausted, she tucked into his shoulder. "What if we don't go back?" he asked.

"And do what?"

He rolled to his side and lowered his mouth to hers. "This?"

On the fourteenth morning, he asked again, "What if we never went back?"

"Kormick will hunt me down eventually, and I will pay dearly for my long absence."

"Haven't you ever wanted to be something else besides the Darkland monster?"

She laughed. "Is that what they call me? I like it. It's better than what I was called before."

She had told him of her years growing up in the Darkland Forest at the hands of her uncles and cousins. It was not something anyone would want to go back to.

"What about you? Don't you love being the renowned Butcher of Celwyth?"

"It wasn't something I ever planned to become. It just happened. Others told me what I was good at, and I wanted very much to please them. Fit in. But at one time I wanted—" He let the thought trail away, dismissing it with a shake of his head. But she pressed him, and he told her how he had grown up in the upper halls of a museum where he met great artists and watched young artists blossom. He had studied with them, until he was drawn into the knight's service.

"Do we always have to be what we were? Only what others planned for us?" he had asked. "Do you think it's possible to start over—to leave the past behind and become something else?"

"You're very good at what you do," she said, running a lazy fingernail down the center of his chest.

"I want to be better at other things."

"You're a dreamer, Kierus. They'll find us, and I will be forced to kill you, or you will kill me. One of us will be dead, and the other left with fond memories. We'll live on through them. That's something. Let's not ruin these moments with maybes." And then she lowered her mouth to his.

But on the sixteenth morning when they woke, she whispered in his ear, *"What if we didn't go back . . ."*

They set their plan and spent five more days preparing, she closing the Abyss door and then every other door out of Elphame she could find to make hunting them down harder if not impossible; he, selling what few valuables he had to the trows. A knight's Gildan sword, especially his, was worth a small fortune. They were minutes from leaving for good, everything prepared, when Tyghan rode up outside their cottage.

Kierus tried to shake the memory away, but still found himself turning from the cottage door to look back at the clearing where he and Tyghan had confronted each other.

A season had passed now, a new forest blanket of detritus was laid. Spring grass and fiddleheads pushed through pine needles and alder leaves, but the crooked weeping trees, the fallen worm-eaten trunks, the slumbering rounded backs of half-buried stones, remained the same. The blood may have been gone, but it was all still dark and stained in his mind, a violent storm . . . a tempest.

He still heard the *thump* at his back as he walked away, the sound of Tyghan falling to the ground.

And now Tyghan had his daughter.

Well played, prince of Danu. Well played. But this battle isn't over yet.

CHAPTER 70

B ristol had never woken up next to someone in her bed before, and she wasn't sure what to do.

It was strange to see Tyghan sleeping beside her. *Sleeping deeply.* There was something so intensely personal about it. And trusting. Maybe that was what was so strange, to see him lying in her bed, serene and vulnerable.

His head was half-swallowed in pillow, a hint of day-old beard shadowing his face, his hair a tousle of black waves. She wanted to run her fingers through them again, but his breaths rose slowly, lazy as a summer breeze, and she didn't want to wake him. When he was awake he was always a flurry of motion, plans brewing behind his eyes like he was wrestling with a thousand thoughts.

Now he looked like he might sleep all day. After the night they'd had, she guessed it wasn't surprising. Sleep played little role in it. They moved from bed, to wall, to bath chamber, claiming every corner of her room like they were conquering the world, and maybe for those few hours, they were.

He lay on his stomach now, one arm wrapped around his pillow, the other wrapped around her, the sheets kicked off and huddled near his feet, spent and exhausted. Should she slip away and dress? Were there rules to these things? She had no idea. Her previous encounters were mostly rushed. Mornings were never involved, and beds rarely were. A stuffy panel truck in a swap meet parking lot, or the couch in Sal's storage room that Mick opted for, were not exactly places to linger.

But here . . . she wanted to soak in every detail, remember every touch and sound. The taste of his lips on hers. The feel of his muscles beneath her fingertips. She wanted to capture every color and nuance in her mind like a painting that would last forever.

Dawn peeked through cracks in her drapes, golden fingers reaching through the room. The light outlined Tyghan's bare back like delicate gilding. Soft shadows settled in the dip of his spine where it trailed down to the rise of his—even that was magnificent. What would Michelangelo have called it? Gluteus maximus? It seemed a more fitting name than ass. She felt only a sliver of guilt, ogling him as he slept.

Or maybe not a bit guilty.

She had already seen everything, after all—including the full length of his scar. In the middle of the night when they lay on their backs, resting and talking in the golden candlelight, she'd studied the wound's twists and jagged turns, like a long drunken seam in perfect silken flesh. This was not the result of a quick desperate stab. It was a vengeful story at every turn, a cold-blooded message not meant to be forgotten. And she knew he hadn't.

Does it still hurt? she had whispered.

No, he answered—too quickly.

But she already knew fae could lie. Perhaps it wasn't his flesh that hurt, but something deeper inside him that could never be mended.

His fingers twitched against her side, and she wondered if he was dreaming, soaking in something more pleasant like their long bath together, dipping beneath the water, his mouth on hers, oxygen an afterthought, rising again with deep breaths, his face glistening in the flickering candlelight, water dripping from his chin.

Heat stirred between her legs. Maybe she was the only one soaking in the memories of last night. Finally, at some late hour, they had gone back to bed—to actually sleep.

His arm was heavy across her ribs, and she liked the feel of it tucked up warm against her breasts. She rolled over, settling in against him to get more sleep, but then there was a knock. Her eyes shot open.

"*Tyghan*," she whispered, rolling back to face him. He didn't move.

She nudged his shoulder. "Tyghan, wake up. There's someone at the door."

He stirred, rolling to his back and stretching, and when he finally focused on her, he smiled. "More? Don't you ever rest?"

The tap came again, more insistent.

"Did you hear that? Someone's there. Go to the bath chamber while I answer it."

He leaned over and leisurely kissed her. "There's no laws against what we've done. It's encouraged even. Babies, you know? There are never enough in Elphame."

She pushed him away and sat up. "There will be no babies!"

His brows pulled down in mock offense. "Are you a goddess who sees into the future now?"

"I am the goddess of birth control pills—surely you've read about those in your modern works. Now, hurry, go. I don't want awkwardness, or more gossip. There's already way too much of that going on around here. And we don't know who's there."

"I could make myself invisible?"

"Would that work?" she asked hopefully.

"Maybe. Depending on who's at the door. Should I answer it first and see?"

"Go!" she ordered, pointing to the other room.

He rose from the bed and frowned. "Kings aren't usually banished to bath chambers."

"In my quarters there are no kings, only guests—now go. Hurry."

His eyes brushed the length of her. "I think I was more than a guest last night."

Heat rushed through her, like he was touching her in all the ways he had the night before. He was far more than a guest; he had said and done things that no guest ever would, and she wanted him to do it all over again. She saw in the glint lighting his eyes that he knew it, too. The arrogant bastard.

The tap again.

"Please, Tyghan."

He grinned and nodded, snatching his scattered clothes from the floor before retreating to the bath chamber.

She yanked the sheet from the bed, wrapping it tightly around her as she hurried to the door, but before she reached it, the door swung open. Madame Chastain burst in carrying a small tray. "Forgive the early intrusion. I thought perhaps you were sleeping and didn't hear me." She walked past Bristol and set the tray on the table.

The High Witch was the last person she'd expected to see. She had certainly never brought her breakfast before.

"Is something wrong?" Bristol asked.

"You've been summoned. The Lumessa is feeling well this morning and will see you."

"Oh," Bristol said numbly, trying to shift gears from a mostly sleepless night to an unexpected morning. Summoned?

"Quickly," Madame Chastain ordered as she poured Bristol's tea. "Eat. Get dressed. Her windows of health are small. I will escort you."

"Of course," Bristol answered, and dutifully sat at her table. She took a hot apple bun from a basket and slathered it with sweet butter, suddenly ravenous, but then she spotted Tyghan's shirt crumpled on the floor beside her chair. She nudged it beneath the table with her foot, eyeing Madame Chastain, who had already turned her attention to Bristol's wardrobe. She flung open the doors and methodically searched for clothes, laying them out on the nearby chaise in precise order—underclothes, creamy tunic and trousers, a long green jacket with wide embroidered lapels, and a pair of soft doeskin boots. All of it understated but tasteful, as if she wanted Bristol to make a good but humble impression on this powerful sorceress. "These should do nicely," she said, turning back to Bristol.

"Thank you. Should I—"

And then the sound of running water roared from the bath chamber.

What part of being quiet didn't he understand? Bristol sipped her tea, hoping Madame Chastain wouldn't say anything.

The High Witch closed the wardrobe doors. "So, *this* is where he is. Eris has been looking all over for him. I suspected as much."

Her tone was edged with something sharp. Was the High Witch one of those voices who tried to dissuade Tyghan? Bristol set her tea down. "Is *this* a problem?"

The witch's left brow rose. From her morning lectures, Bristol knew what would come next. A calculated silence. Five precise seconds to make her words punch a little more deeply. "Not as long as your sworn commitment doesn't falter if this dalliance should sour. Broken promises are not looked kindly upon in Elphame."

Dalliance? Yes, she was unquestionably one of the voices. "Broken promises are not looked kindly upon anywhere, Madame Chastain."

"Indeed." She sighed and crossed the room before Bristol could reply and pushed open the drapes, letting morning flood the room.

Bristol let the inference rest, wanting to get out of there as fast as possible. She left her breakfast half-eaten and hurried to dress, but as she sat on the chaise pulling on her last boot, a voice that was supposed to be quiet filled the room.

"How long will this meeting take?"

She and Madame Chastain both turned to see Tyghan standing in the entrance to the bath chamber. His hair was still wet, and he wore his formal jacket from the night before, his bare chest in clear view beneath it.

Bristol blinked, unsure if she wanted to melt beneath the chaise or grab his shirt from the floor and throw it in his face.

But Madame Chastain didn't flutter a lash. "We're subject to the Lumessa's timing, Your Majesty. The meeting will take as long as it will."

"Can I—"

"No. She requested to meet privately with Miss Keats."

"Did you remind her of the purpose and parameters of this meeting? The removal of the tick only?"

Parameters? Bristol wondered. What did he think this sorceress would do to her?

"I did, but we must trust the Lumessa's judgment in this matter."

Tyghan's eyes turned to ice, but Madame Chastain met his gaze, unblinking.

He looked at Bristol, the anger draining from his face, the confidence from moments before vanishing. Something else filled his expression now, something disturbed and serious. Was he worried about the outcome of removing the creature from her back? Or was it something else?

"I'll be in the throne room," he said to Madame Chastain. "Have one of the Sisters bring Bristol to me as soon as the meeting is over."

He shot the witch a stiff glance as he strode toward the door, but stopped first where Bristol sat, and leaned over. His lips lightly brushed hers. "This is not a dalliance," he whispered, and then he was gone.

CHAPTER 71

Like the palace and university, the conservatory was built over millennia. It began with the humble workshop of the goldsmith Creidhne, a god able to weave thin fibers of gold into fine ropes and jewelry. His workshop eventually grew to include many types of artisans because the Tuatha de revered all aspects of art in their world. Art was a gift of Danu, just like the sacred talismans, to strengthen mind and spirit. The expanding grounds became a place for anyone, who by invitation, mistake, or the will of Danu found themselves in Elphame, to study and practice their art. Even mortals like Leonardo da Vinci.

It was now a sprawling, busy complex with four floors and numerous wings named for goddesses and gods. The top floor, named for Aine, the goddess of light, was accessible only by invitation.

And Bristol was invited.

The sweeping granite staircase that led to this floor was guarded by a white wolf. The beast lay halfway up on the landing, lounging and bored, her belly and throat exposed—unless someone even eyed the first step with any amount of intention.

Bristol had witnessed a student test the drowsy animal during her first tour of the conservatory when he had lifted a foot to the stairs. His boot and the first step never connected. She didn't actually see the animal leap—it happened so fast—but the tearful young man found himself on his back, pinned to the floor by razor-sharp teeth around his throat.

Even with an invitation, Bristol was wary.

"You're sure she knows?" Bristol asked, motioning to the wolf.

"Her name is Kayana," Madame Chastain said. "And yes, she knows."

The wolf didn't so much as bare a tooth as they walked up the steps, lying in a patch of morning sun like an old hound dog on a porch warming its bones.

When they entered through the double doors at the top landing, Bristol was surprised to see so many visitors wandering the length of a bright glass-roofed cloister, engaged in brisk conversations or studying sculptures and paintings. To Bristol, it looked like a busy museum on a free admission day. About halfway down the corridor, a group was gathered, and as she and Madame Chastain approached, one of them turned, sensing their arrival.

Bristol suppressed a gasp. "What's *she* doing here?" she whispered.

Madame Chastain was unruffled. "The Lumessa? This is her home. I thought you understood—"

"No one told me who she was, and she doesn't look ill at all."

"Appearances can be deceiving."

Something Bristol already understood too well. She had always thought herself savvy, but there were cons, and there were *cons*. Between the sheriff, Willow, and now her parents, she was getting a whole new perspective on "appearances."

The Lumessa held out her hand as the final space between them closed.

Jasmine. Her father's foster aunt.

The one she all but stole the art from at the Willoughby Inn at their first meeting.

Jasmine took hold of Bristol's hand, her fingers surprisingly strong. "Bristol," she said. And then again, slowly, softly, *"Bristol."* Like there was a whole history between them, like she was soaking in memories that Bristol didn't have, like the art didn't matter but their mutual bond did.

Something inside Bristol swayed, like she was about to open a forbidden door, and all the secrets her father had gone to great lengths to hide would rush out, toothy and deadly. But Jasmine was not a "so-called" aunt. Not a scam or a hit man. She was the real deal, the aunt who had raised her father in Elphame.

"Jasmine," Bristol returned.

Two of the guests watching the meeting gasped.

A stout ogre-ish fellow in a mauve velvet suit and ruffled cravat stepped forward. He had furry pointed ears similar to Mae's and a disposition to match. He corrected Bristol like she had made a tactless blunder. "The *Lumessa*, you mean."

Evidently, no one called her by her familiar name except for a select few.

"She spoke correctly," Jasmine said, then proudly introduced Bristol, like she was a long-lost relative. Bristol saw their surprise. More introductions followed, and Bristol was just as surprised to learn their names. Raphael, Henri, and maybe most surprising of all, a squat, plain man with long sideburns and a rumpled gray coat but an easy smile, Robert Kirk. She had read about him in Anastasia's book. He was a scholar whose death was shrouded in mystery. Some believed he had actually disappeared into fairyland. Bristol knew the answer to that mystery now. She couldn't wait to tell Harper. And was this *the* Raphael?

Before she could find out, Jasmine said her goodbyes and excused them both.

"I'm sure you have a lot of questions," Jasmine said as she led Bristol away. "We'll take a look at the tick soon, but first, let's go to my apartments and talk—the talk we should have had before."

Before everything went wrong at the inn.

Before Tyghan appeared in the dining room and started yelling. Was that the "out" he had with the Lumessa? The reason he had to grovel?

As they walked, Jasmine explained why she wasn't able to see Bristol sooner—that she hadn't been well for a long time. "When one spends six centuries as High Witch of Danu, curses are bound to catch up with you." She said that she and the Sisters had purged them regularly of course, but even the smallest of curses left marks. "They accumulate. I have good days, like today, but the bad days are winning, I'm afraid."

"Who would curse you?"

She laughed. "Anyone and everyone. Enemies and comrades. Probably strangers too. Many hard choices must be made as the High Witch of a powerful kingdom. They do not please everyone. Some choices I made did not even please me. I served nine different crowns during my service."

"Isn't it the king or queen who has to make the unpleasant choices?"

A wry smile twisted her lips. "The administration of a kingdom is a complicated thing."

"Meaning you had to do the dirty work?"

Her head dipped thoughtfully, but it wasn't exactly an answer. "Here we are."

She motioned to a circular foyer that led to double doors. Engraved in the marble over the door were the words, *Celwyth Hall*. Bristol had heard the name whispered behind cupped hands more than once. *The Butcher of Celwyth*. Did he live here?

"I've heard mention of a butcher of—"

"There is no butcher here, nor has there ever been. Celwyth is my family name and the architect of the conservatory. Pay no attention to the chinwag of court. Gossip is a favorite pastime of the idle."

With a small motion of Jasmine's hand, the double doors swung open.

They then stepped into yet another hall, this one a stark contrast to the one they just came from. It exploded with texture and color, reminding Bristol of an antiques shop overflowing with mismatched treasures. She looked up. Staggering tapestries that depicted pastoral scenes, or dancing gossamer-winged fae, or sweeping bloody battles hung from walls that were two stories high. Paintings hung in the spaces between tapestries, and scattered pedestals held towering sculptures of kings, queens, and creatures. Brass teapots, copper cauldrons, a life-sized wooden horse, and other collectibles were arranged throughout the room, and overstuffed chairs with colorful pillows were scattered between it all. Everywhere Bristol turned, there was something else to see, and this was just the first room.

"It's a lifetime of collecting the things that please me the most. And the Sisters," Jasmine explained. "They're eager to meet you too, but first things first."

She drew Bristol to an alcove by a window that held two blue silk chairs, and they sat. "I promised to tell you about your father. Where should we start?"

Bristol wasn't sure. There was so much she didn't know. "The beginning, I guess. How he came to be here."

Jasmine's long pale finger rested on her lower lip as she thought. She nodded, like his beginnings were playing out in her mind. "It came as a surprise to us all. Your father stumbled into our lives just after I passed the position of High Witch on to Madame Chastain, and the Sisters and I were getting Celwyth Hall in order. A fairy brought your father to court, offering him as a gift to the queen. Of course, everyone was horrified. Taking mortal babies had long been outlawed, but in some of the remote Wilds of Elphame, it still happened. The queen brought him to us to determine his parentage and return him, since the fairy couldn't remember where she had gotten him, but it was no easy task. He was only a babe barely walking and not yet talking."

Jasmine smiled, her gaze lost somewhere in time as if she was remembering him toddling about. *She loved him.* Bristol's eyes stung, and she struggled to keep the ache in her throat from turning into something loud, messy, and embarrassing.

"Even his clothing gave us few clues. He wore the sweetest little white frock, but it was difficult to trace." She said she and the Sisters spent three years searching for clues before finding out where he came from. "It was a mention in an old mortal newspaper about a missing boy. But I'm afraid, by then his parents were long dead. As you've probably learned by now, time in Faerie can pass quite differently from the mortal world."

Bristol leaned forward, her attention gripped by the old newspaper article. "You found out who his parents were?"

Jasmine nodded, and as she explained, Bristol floated in a strange timeless space, connected by her own lifetime of questions, her father's shocking journey to Elphame, and the truth that began over a century ago—with his parents.

In 1890, Sanjay Kumar was the handsome son of a wealthy Mumbai merchant. When he finished his university studies, he entered the family business, and on a trip to Boston with his father, he met Catherine Brennan, a young woman newly arrived from County Derry in Ireland. She was working as governess for the business associate hosting the Kumars for the summer. Love bloomed quickly, Sanjay sweeping the lovely raven-haired Catherine off her feet, and by the end of the summer, they were married. Sanjay stayed behind to look after his father's interests in Boston, and before long, the couple was blessed with the impending arrival of a baby. It was while on a picnic with friends, two summers later, that their beloved child disappeared. One minute he was there, toddling across a meadow high with summer grass, and the next he was gone. Vanished. A brigade of searchers couldn't find a trace of the boy, and after a few months, the search was abandoned, believing an animal had taken him. The heartbroken couple returned to Mumbai a year later. By the time the Sisters discovered the parents' identities, they'd been dead for half a century.

"Sanjay and Catherine," Bristol whispered to herself. *Indian and Irish.* That's what her father was. What *she* was. At least one half of her. And Cat and Harper, too. Bristol leaned over, pressing her palms to her eyes, drawing in deep breaths.

"Are you all right, dear?" Jasmine asked.

Bristol nodded, her eyes closed, still hiding her face in her hands. The knowledge soaked in, like water on parched ground. She needed to tell Cat and Harper as soon as possible. They deserved to know. She opened her eyes. "Did he know?"

"Yes, we told him when he was seven," Jasmine answered. "But I'm not sure he grasped it fully. Danu and this life were all he had ever known. He knew of course that he was different, that he was from the mortal world, but he never talked about it, or even asked questions. He wanted to run and play and study and be all that his friends were. He had to work twice as hard at everything, of course, being mortal, and even then he was never quite like them. But he had other qualities that served him well. He excelled in his own ways."

"What was he like?"

At that point, the Sisters joined them, swarming in at Jasmine's call. Like Jasmine, they were older women, but vigorous and strong. Two of them wore swords on their backs like they had just come from a formal—or deadly—event. They shed their armor and weapons, letting them clatter onto a nearby sofa, and eagerly greeted Bristol. She was awed as she met them all, her father's other aunts, Adela, Camille, and Izzy, the women who raised him, and they all had plenty to say. He was the delight and bane of their lives. *Oh, the troubles he got into. He was so curious. So talented. So sweet. So mischievous. A hellion. A darling.* So much of everything.

Her father was the son they never had, the son who came to them late in their lives, the one who toddled and tore through Celwyth Hall, with occasional breakage. They laughed, they told stories, they showed her his paintings that hung throughout the halls of Celwyth. Paintings he had signed. *Kierus.* Bristol ran her finger over the name, feeling the light texture beneath her fingertip. He had left the name behind, too. "That's what you called him?"

"Yes," Camille said. "It means wanderer."

A fitting name, Bristol thought. "He was an artist here, too?"

"For a time," Jasmine answered. "Until he was drawn into the knight's service."

Bristol whirled from the painting to the aunts. "My father was a *knight?*"

Camille sighed as if she didn't approve. "It was what he wanted."

"At least for a while," Adela added.

Bristol noticed their dispositions change, their smiles retreating.

"Was he happy as a knight?"

"He appeared to be," Izzy said.

"Then why did he leave?" Bristol asked. "Was it trows?"

Bewildered lines wrinkled their brows. "Trows?"

"He didn't tell us he was leaving at all, or why," Jasmine interjected. "There were no goodbyes. It happened suddenly and without notice. Something called him to the other world."

Love? Bristol wondered. "What about my mother? Did you know her?"

"No," Adela answered. "We never met her."

"How old was he when he left?"

"Twenty-five."

Her father was forty-eight now, but only three years older than her when he left—and *a knight*—like Tyghan.

"Was he powerful? As powerful as the other knights here?"

"Very much so," Izzy answered. The others nodded in agreement.

Bristol shook her head, trying to absorb this new information. Then why was he so afraid of trows? She tried to conjure a picture of her father wielding a sword, shouting orders, riding a huge horse like August, throwing a golden spear, but the images wouldn't come. When she tried, all she saw were other things—her father concentrating on a new painting, swirling dabs of violet and ultramarine together with such concentration she could feel the cool shadows he was about to create; she saw him humming as he sawed wood to build yet another frame for a canvas; slathering gesso over raw fabric until it was smooth and perfect. She saw him playing a tune by the campfire as she and her sisters danced; she saw him collapsing in a heap at the top of the stairs after their mother died. Her father's world was small—painting, music, his wife and daughters. That was all. Not the world of knights. He had become someone else entirely. These women didn't know the man she knew. A question wormed through her gut.

She motioned to her back. "If he was so powerful, why would he have done this to me?"

Jasmine shook her head, her pale eyes glistening. The Sisters' expressions turned grim. Seconds stretched, like they were retracing their steps, wondering what became of this boy who left them without explanation, this boy they had raised and loved. "We don't have those answers," Jasmine said finally. "Maybe it's time we examine your back and give you the answers that we can."

Bristol sat on a stool, her shirt removed and her hair swept over her shoulder. She clutched a soft blanket to her chest. Jasmine did most of the examining, but she heard the low murmurs as the aunts consulted with one another.

"It will be painful," Jasmine finally said. "But I think we can remove it."

Think? Bristol had expected more certainty from the most experienced sorceress in Danu.

"The question is," she continued, "are you certain you want it removed?" She circled back in front of Bristol and took one of Bristol's hands in her own, examining the pointed blue moons again. She kept coming back to them, like they interested her more than the enormous tick on her back.

"Of course I want it removed."

"Hear me out," Jasmine said, still studying Bristol's hand. "This is unexpected. This trait is passed down through both parents, which means your father, while mortal, did have some trace of fae in him. We never knew this. It probably never would have manifested itself at all except that your mother was fae."

A vestige. She remembered Tyghan telling her that many mortals had traces of fae in them from somewhere way back in their lineage. It usually amounted to nothing. "What does it mean?"

"That's the problem. We don't know. By itself, probably nothing, but combined with your mother's fae heritage, we can't be certain. We do think it is likely that you are bloodmarked, but removing the tick will carry a small risk of death. You should also know, if we successfully extract it, and the magic in you is fully restored, there will certainly be more changes. Possibly profound ones."

Bristol swallowed. She didn't like the grim tone of Jasmine's voice. "What kind of changes?"

Jasmine shook her head gravely. "We don't know yet."

Bristol remembered the horror of toddling into the bathroom, her father trying to soothe her. *It's only a costume, darling. Mama's playing dress-up. She'll take it off.*

Only a costume.

But what if it wasn't?

She tried to remain calm as Jasmine studied her fingernails. Maybe she could become something even worse. Was that what Jasmine was trying to tell her? "And what happens if I don't remove it? If I let the tick stay there?"

"Ticks don't heal. Its torn leg will continue to bleed into you, but in very small amounts, enough for a few of your innate abilities to surface over the course of time. You may have seen this already?"

Bristol's mind tripped over the past few days. "I'm able to do a few spells now that I couldn't do before."

Jasmine went on to explain that even before the tick was injured, it probably released some magic into her from time to time in the interest of self-preservation, like when she was maneuvering on her bike in Bowskeep or even in the maze during the battle—just enough to ensure her survival—because if its host died, so would the tick.

A host. A sour taste swelled in her mouth. *She was a host.* An un-willing one. A host for a repulsive creature that used her for its own existence. But removing it meant she might become a hideous creature herself.

Bristol stood, her breaths coming fast now. She gathered her shirt, her jacket, rushing to put them on. "I have to think this over. I need time. I—"

"Of course," Jasmine said. "A decision like this needs consideration. While you think it over, the Sisters and I will continue to research the matter."

"But keep in mind," Izzy added, "with the Choosing Ceremony so close, Danu is running out of time."

CHAPTER 72

I have news."

"Daddy?" Harper asked eagerly. "Did you find Daddy?"

Bristol shook her head. "Not yet. I'm sorry. This is a big world. It's harder to search than I thought it would be—even for the fae who live here. But they're helping me."

Harper peered closer. "The room you're in is so dark. Are you still underneath that table?"

Bristol nodded. Cat and Harper leaned against the washing machine, staring into the portal. Bristol had called to them, and they stumbled into the laundry room, still in their pajamas.

"When are you coming home? That's the only news I want to hear," Cat said, with the same insistence as in their last conversation.

Bristol knew she was pushing Cat's patience, but at least with the sale of their father's painting and the advances on the Leonardo da Vinci sketches, money wasn't a pressing problem anymore. Financially, they could manage without her, but it wasn't only money they needed. They needed *her*.

Bristol eyed Cat, trying to decide how to deflect the question. Cat's face still glowed with the same demanding edge, but Bristol noticed the momentary dimpling of her chin, like she was trying to hold back.

Bristol quickly changed the subject. "So how much did you get for Daddy's painting?"

"Millions," Harper answered.

Bristol rolled her eyes. "Really, what did you get?"

"Five mil," Cat confirmed. "No joke. We're still trying to absorb it, too. But Sonja said it was legit."

Bristol shot out a barrage of questions, still skeptical. Cat explained that it was an anonymous buyer and Sonja was helping them figure out where to put the large sum of money. All Sonja knew of the buyer was that it was someone who was a longtime admirer of their father's work.

"So that's our big news. What's yours?" Harper asked.

Bristol was so stunned about the art, she almost forgot she had something important to share, the answers to a lifetime of questions. "I know who we are, at least partially." She told them the story of their father's origins, who his parents were and where they came from. "His birth name was Rían Kumar." She saw them both visibly sink lower on their elbows as the details unfolded, the news startling the strength from them as much as it had her.

When Bristol finished, Harper repeated the names Sanjay Kumar and Catherine Brennan several times. No doubt she was already making plans to research what she could about them at the library. By the time Bristol returned home, Harper would probably know where every Kumar and Brennan lived within a thousand-mile radius of Bowskeep, and be convinced they were related to them all.

"But that's only half the story. There's more. This part . . ."

This was the hardest part to tell. Bristol looked at her hands in her lap, at the sharp blue nailbeds that were impossible to ignore. The reminder that she would never be who she was again, that her parents perpetrated the biggest con of all on their middle-born daughter. Bristol swallowed, her gaze returning to Cat and Harper. "Remember that little birthmark on my—"

Cat began shaking her head. Her chin dimpled again. Tears puddled in her eyes.

Bristol paused, watching her recoil, the anxious tilt of her head, the rise of her shoulders like she was bracing herself. *Remember that little birthmark.* Something unspeakable crawled over Bristol's scalp. She watched every twitch of Cat's flushed cheeks, and it split something inside Bristol wide open. A suffocating awareness crashed over her. The secret glistened in Cat's eyes. Bristol choked on her words, struggling to make her mouth work again. "It— When— You knew? *You knew?*" She gasped for air. "Oh my god. Oh my—"

"I was going to tell you," Cat sobbed, her tears now streaming. "But I promised Daddy not to say anything unless something happened. And then you ran off—"

"Something happened, Cat! Something fucking happened! How could you not tell me? What else haven't you told me?"

"What's going on?" Harper wailed. "What are you talking about?"

"I only found out when I went back to school," Cat cried. "Daddy said—"

"That was over a year ago! You had a whole year to tell me!"

"I'm sorry. I—"

"*Sorry?* And you think that fixes everything? I have a fucking monster on my back, Cat!"

"You shouldn't have gone. I told you—"

"Maybe I wouldn't have if I had known! I had a right to know! I trusted you! I told you everything! And you told me nothing! Look at my hands!" Bristol shoved a hand through the portal, splaying her fingers wide. "This is what I am now, Cat!" Though she didn't even know what that was. No one did.

Cat and Harper stared at her hand, horrified, like they were looking at an animal's claw. Maybe that was exactly what it was—or would be.

Cat grabbed Bristol's hand, trying to pull it to her cheek. "I'm sorry. Please, Bri—"

Bristol snatched her hand away. "Get away from me! Get the hell away! I don't even know you!" She pushed and slammed her fist against the edge of the portal, trying to block out Cat's voice, and then to her shock, it closed. Disappeared. Just like that. The sounds, the sobs, the yelling—gone. The silence vibrated inside her.

She searched the wall, her hands trembling, trying to find the portal boundaries again, but it was solid. The portal had vanished, along with Cat and Harper, and no matter how she pressed and probed, she couldn't get it back.

CHAPTER 73

The throne room was dark and rough-hewn, an ancient strong-hold, one of the oldest structures on the palace grounds. The soot-dark vaults arched across the ceiling and splayed over the petitioners below like the protective rib cage of a beast—its heart a magical beat that made everyone speak in whispers. Deep windows set high in the walls let in the barest of light, and the rest was lit with torches. The walls breathed with memories, the blood that had been shed, the victories celebrated, the schemes of kings and creatures, the layers of history that were pressed into their seams. A young woman lurked in the shadows of the vestibule, oblivious to the murmurs of the walls, but the rough stone blocks felt every beat of her heart as she wrestled with her own unfolding history.

Bristol was still furious with her sister. It was one more lie, and this one, especially, was breaking her. How could Cat have kept this secret from her? Their father was persuasive, but Cat wasn't a child. They were both grown women. Cat should have known his promise was un-reasonable.

She leaned back against the cool wall. It felt like there was nothing she could believe in anymore. That everything and everyone had hid-den sides, her town, her parents, and now Cat. *Cat.* The one person she thought never lied. Bristol closed her eyes and saw her sister's glistening irises again, her cinnamon lashes spiked with tears. The secret had weighed on Cat. Bristol's heart wobbled against her will, but she was bitter and wanted to stay angry.

She better understood that protective armor Tyghan reached for again and again. It was a way to keep others at a distance and to shield yourself from more betrayal. She wanted Cat to worry and wallow over the secret she kept, wanted her to see Bristol's hand plunged through the wall in her every waking and sleeping moment, to feel the horror anew each time as she saw the half-blue nails that looked like the retracted claws of a beast—to ponder how deeply she had wounded Bristol. But the memory of Cat's tears made her heart wobble again. Damn the secrets, lies, and her stupid weak heart.

She rubbed her temple, reluctantly swallowing at least some of her bitterness. She'd let Cat stew for a while before she reached out to convey a message of understanding. The portal might be gone, but she knew Eris was quite proficient at sending letters.

She turned her attention back to the proceedings, watching from afar.

Fresh starts. That was what Bristol saw in each face as they left the throne room with a pledge from the king. Hope. It was a Faerieland type of laundromat. The stains, at least temporarily, washed away.

Bristol had never seen Tyghan wear a crown before, and it was strange to see him acting as a monarch—listening, questioning, judging. He had many sides to him, and this was one she hadn't seen. She watched Eris, Kasta, and the petitioners regard him, the way they listened and waited. He commanded their respect and she guessed he had for a long time, not just since he stepped up in Cael's absence.

For someone new to this role, he seemed made for it, but maybe being a king was not that different from being Knight Commander. Strategies and solutions were his stock in trade. Yes, he could be arrogant and demanding, but he *put the time in*, as Sal would say, wherever he was needed. Whether it was council meetings, working with recruits at the training grounds, traipsing around the countryside searching for her father, or this—meeting with fae eager to speak directly with their sovereign.

And now she was the one needing to speak with him. She would start with the easy stuff—the letter. Maybe she wouldn't bring up the tick at all, because what would he think if she told him she was keeping it?

She wasn't even sure if it was the right decision. It made her queasy when she thought about being its *host*, but she was just as sickened by the alternative—the unknown changes that removing it would bring. All she had done for her entire life was start over. She couldn't do it again. She had her sisters to think about. They were expecting her to return as she was, not as an unrecognizable creature from Elphame.

That damn gene train she always wanted to be on had taken a turn. It was too late in the game now for her to become something else.

But Izzy's words haunted her.

Keep in mind, Danu is running out of time.

She looked at her nails, letting the glamour recede until the sharp blue points showed again. Like a claw. She glamoured them back and slipped into the shadows, buying more time. She had to think this over.

CHAPTER 74

Tyghan's index finger tapped the arm of the throne like a persistent drip of water, his focus beginning to fade. What was taking so long? He should have heard something by now, or she should have come to him. Unless Jasmine had betrayed him. Unless she told Bristol about her father. Kasta's words nagged him. *Can you really juggle one more impossible thing?*

But then another thought arose, one that made his chest turn hollow. What if removing the tick was too much for Bristol? Her screams rolled through his head again, and the image of her convulsing body when Madame Chastain tried to remove the tick. What if it was too late? What if the tick had been there too long, was too deep inside her? What if removing it would kill her? Why hadn't he considered this before? Maybe even Jasmine wasn't skilled enough—

"Your Majesty, Lord Bowry is waiting for your answer," Eris murmured.

Tyghan blinked. He saw the room again, and the lord still awaiting his reply. He stood with his retinue just past the first step of the dais. Tyghan didn't hear what Bowry asked for, but why in Lugh's name did he need a whole contingent of aides to help him ask for it?

"Protection"—Eris nudged again, knowing Tyghan was distracted—

"seems like something we could accommodate considering his township's vulnerable location in the borderlands. Don't you agree?"

Tyghan cursed himself for not focusing. It was the first lesson he learned as a knight, and Lord Bowry had traveled far and waited a long time to see him. "Yes, of course," he answered and turned to Kasta. "Assign appropriate patrols to Rookswood."

Lord Bowry's pinched brows relaxed.

Fear. It owned the throne room that day.

Nearly every petition so far that morning was for protection. There had been no more demon attacks since the day at the training grounds, but shadows swirled in distant skies across the nation on a daily basis, and everyone knew the shadows were not flocks of birds. It was a warning. Braegor had seen the training grounds and reported that information to his master, but what he saw was not proof of any dark plans Tyghan was hatching. Danu had always had training grounds for knights. Still, the sighting was enough to put Kormick on the offensive.

Maybe it was time for Kormick's attentions to be divided. Tyghan would speak to Kasta about an organized campaign of rumors, spreading them to every corner of Elphame—from the mountains of Tattersky to the underwater caves of Gablerock—rumors of rampant magic and whole hidden colonies of bloodmarked. The more outrageous, the better. If there was one thing Kormick wanted, it was certainty. He was resolved to show up to the Choosing Ceremony unopposed and to the roar of cheers—not sounds of resistance. Rumors might keep his focus scattered.

"You are most gracious, Your Majesty. Thank you." Lord Bowry bowed, but as he turned to leave, the aide at his side stepped forward.

"Your Majesty, if I may add something else?"

The man's eyes were sunken. Tyghan nodded for him to continue.

"My son is missing," he said, his voice rising. "He was up on the roof repairing the rushes. He's a good boy, thirteen, not quite a man yet, but—" The man stopped, his lips pressed together in concentration, and it took a long, strained moment for him to continue. Curious whispers circled the cavernous hall.

"He was taken," he continued. "We know. By them. We found his pouch of twine and shears tossed to the ground. His sister had seen a flock in the western sky only minutes earlier." The man took a step closer, his hands clutched in front him. "I know there is no saving him. I know what they do. But if you or your knights should encounter my boy—he has green eyes, curly red hair, freckles—I pray that you will make his end as painless as possible, that you would smile and say the gods' blessing to ease him into the next world, so he knows paradise awaits him, so he will know he is not blamed for what they've done to him." With his last few words the man broke down, his chest shaking and his hands coming up to hide his face. One of the other aides held him as he struggled to regain composure. And that was when Tyghan noticed the rest of their faces, the loss etched in them, the fear. These were not aides—they were villagers, farmers, merchants, who made the trek with Lord Bowry. Tyghan had been fearing potential loss all morning—these supplicants had already experienced it.

"Your son's name?" Tyghan asked.

The sobbing man swiped at his cheeks with the back of his sleeve.

"What's your son's name?" Tyghan repeated. "So I can inform my knights to give this young man the blessing he deserves in his final moment."

"Samuel," the man answered.

Tyghan nodded. He turned to Kasta. "Make sure every knight in the realm knows the name of Samuel from Rookswood, that they make his end quick and they comfort him and ease his passage to the next world."

"It is done, Your Majesty," Kasta answered.

The man thanked them and was led away by his friend, still choking back sobs.

But as the next petitioner was ready to step up to the dais, another from the Rookswood contingent, a sturdy man with thin graying hair, boldly stepped forward and blurted out, "Do not give in to them, Your Majesty! We know what they've done to the other kingdoms, broken the laws of the gods and decency, terrorizing and murdering to achieve their goals—and now stealing away a king, your *brother*. We know the choice you face, but Danu is the last hope for Elphame. Once they have the Cauldron of Plenty, we will forever be at their mercy. Do not bow to their demands, or we are all lost."

The room reverberated with silence. Tyghan stared at the man, caught off guard. He couldn't answer him truthfully, because whatever he said today would be fodder tomorrow in every village and hamlet— but bowing to Kormick's demands had never been an option.

Tyghan chose his next words carefully. "Danu is continuing to weigh its options. We will follow a course of action that serves the common good."

The man's eyes narrowed as Tyghan spoke, like he was measuring the import of every word and the length of pauses between them, like he heard the ticking clock pounding in Tyghan's head. "I understand, Your Majesty . . . I understand. And if you think we must bend our knee to Fomoria, then that is what we will do." His gaze rested heavily on Tyghan's, his face sharp with discernment, and he nodded.

Tyghan dipped his chin slightly in return.

The next few petitioners had easier requests to address, but it was the last petitioner who stepped up to the end of the line who drew Tyghan's attention.

He hurried through the other requests, a yes, a yes, and an easy no—a request to paint his portrait as the new king of Danu.

And then finally, the last petitioner stepped up to the dais and bowed deeply. Bristol's loose chestnut hair fell in waves over her shoulders he had caressed just hours ago. She stood tall, serious, her eyes as deep and dark as a night sea. Her full lips were half-parted, and her chest rose in careful breaths. She didn't need to petition him for anything. He'd give her the world if she asked for it.

His temples pounded. Was there something so grave on her mind that she felt the need to address him formally?

"Clear the room," Tyghan said to Eris. "I'll hear this request in private."

Bristol shook her head. "It's not necessary to—"

"It will only take a moment," Tyghan said.

Lingerers in the vestibule were ushered out, and the king's aides left with them. The entrance doors closed with a heavy *thunk*.

Tyghan leaned back in his throne, bracing himself. What did Jasmine tell Bristol? Did Madame Chastain make it clear it would be treason to share certain information about Kierus? That the survival of Elphame hung in the balance in this matter?

Bristol's eyes rose to meet his, and she grimaced. "I feel foolish now. My request is trivial compared to the ones I just heard. Well, except sitting for a portrait." She rolled her eyes, a smile pulling at the corner of her mouth.

Relief flooded Tyghan's chest. "Yes," he answered.

"Yes, what?"

"Yes, whatever you request, it's yours."

"I want to send my sisters a letter," she said.

"Done. I'll have Eris arrange it. When do you want—"

"Wait," she said as if remembering something. "There's more, actually." Creases around her eyes deepened. "Something more important. I have good news and bad news to share with you. Shall I get the bad out of the way first?"

Tyghan leaned forward. "Are you all right? Did you—"

"I'm fine, but . . . I still have the tick. Jasmine said she could remove it, though it would come with a small risk of death, you know, that fine print sort of thing? Worse, though . . ." Her words came out in a breathless string then, as she explained to him about the fae vestige from her father's line, and removing it might result in profound changes. "It could be far more than these marks on my nails." She bit her lower lip. "I don't want to become something else, Tyghan. I can't go back to my sisters as something else. Jasmine tried to hide it, but I saw the look on her face. She was afraid." She paused and drew a deep breath. "It's something I at least need a little time to think about. I hope you understand."

Tyghan stood and walked down the dais until he stood in front of her. He gently lifted her face to his. "No one's making you remove it or even asking you to. I promise. It's your decision." His thumb brushed her cheekbone. "And the good news?"

She shook her head and stepped away, circling the space in front of the dais. "More bad news first, I'm afraid. I lied to you. That day you caught me in your room? I wasn't lost. I snuck into your suite and found your study."

"I don't allow anyone in my study."

"I know that. It was . . . obvious."

"Then why did you go in?"

"I was following a sound—I thought it was my sister singing. It led me to a portal."

Tyghan remembered Daiedes's account of what happened. The snake made no mention of a portal, only her wailing. He had claimed she was bewitched. "There is no portal in my study."

"I guessed you didn't know, especially after—" She tiptoed through her next words. "After seeing the abandoned state of the room, but yes, I can assure you there's a portal. I talked to my sisters through it. At least there *was* a portal until an hour ago. And that's the good news—I was able to close it." She repeated herself, as if to make sure he understood the significance of her confession. "I *closed* a portal. It's gone."

Tyghan followed Bristol up the stairs to his study. *Dammit, why didn't I clean the room?* It wasn't the mess that bothered him. It was the madness. Eris liked to call him a god, but this, *this* had made him powerless. The demon blade Kierus shoved between his ribs had reduced him to something base and brutish. Less than an animal. He couldn't bear to see the study, much less clean it up, and he didn't want anyone else seeing it either. But Bristol already had. And now to go in *with* her? She reached back and grabbed his hand in the dark hallway so he couldn't back out.

"I'll get it," he said when they reached the door, trying to pretend it didn't bother him. He pressed the latch, throwing the door open, and was immediately hit with the familiar scent of dust and despair.

Bristol didn't seem to notice and pushed past him. "It was over here." She dropped to her knees and felt beneath the table, pressing her hand to the stone wall. "The portal was smaller than a dinner plate." She explained the sounds that led her to it and how she made it disappear. As she spoke, he tried to concentrate only on her, but the room swam around him, the marks on the walls, the shadows shifting, waiting to come to life, the—

He leaned clumsily against the desk, his hand knocking books to the floor. "I think I—"

Bristol grabbed his arm and guided him toward the door. "We'll talk downstairs."

CHAPTER 75

They took the stairs slowly. Bristol held Tyghan's arm securely, though if he were to tumble, she wasn't sure she could keep him from falling. By the time they reached the last step, he seemed recovered. He wouldn't admit that anything was wrong and tried to slough it off as simple fatigue, but the trickle of sweat at his temple was telling. He went to the basin in his bath chamber and splashed his face with water. "I didn't get much sleep last night. Not that I'm complaining. It was more than worth it."

When he pulled the towel from his face, Bristol stepped in front of him. "Please, Tyghan, share with me. What's going on?"

He shook his head. "I told you, it's only—"

"Stop. I know it's hard for you to talk about. It was hard for me to tell you about keeping the tick. I was afraid you'd think I was letting everyone down. And it was even harder to admit that I lied to you. But I needed to take that chance. After last night . . . my god, Tyghan, we were *intimate* with each other."

He smiled. "Many times, but who's counting?"

"Tyghan, I'm serious. Can't we be intimate about this, too? Can't you trust me enough to tell me what happened in that room?"

His smile faded, and he tossed the towel onto the basin, but she saw the slight tremor in his hand. He quaked at a memory he couldn't bring himself to share. The line of his jaw turned sharp, like he was bracing himself for a blow. His gaze grew distant, reaching for that safety net he returned to again and again.

"Please," she whispered.

"It's not—" His head tilted to the side like he was working out a knot in his neck, and his blue irises filled with cold resistance . . . but when he looked back at her, he swallowed and his eyes filled with surrender instead. He grabbed her hand and led her to his sitting room, motioning for her to sit on one of the sofas.

He didn't join her. Instead, he grabbed a green apple from a bowl on the credenza and spun it in his hand, using it as a distraction as he paced.

She waited patiently as he gathered his thoughts. "Does it have to do with the scar on your side?" she prompted.

He swallowed and words finally broke loose, at first stilted, but they came.

"Yes. The steel . . . it was practically a myth. Rare. A blade forged by . . . a thousand demons. The restless dead had been banished to the Abyss for so long, no living fae had ever actually seen such a blade, much less been stabbed by one."

He spoke like he was talking about someone else, like he was only relaying the stuff of legend, but then he slowed, his voice growing unsteady, the memories slicing too close. "When the dagger draws blood, it allows every demon who helped create the blade passage into its victim's mind."

"And you were its victim."

She saw the despair in his eyes, and her stomach clutched. *What has he been through?* A long silence swallowed him up, like the shadowed world that tormented him had grabbed hold of him again. His free hand curled into a fist.

"The blade opens a thousand different doors for them to walk through," he continued, "one at a time so they can draw the agony out. Each demon brought a new nightmare to torture me. They taunted, tempted—" He drew a deep breath. "They made their torments and depraved desires my own. That was the worst part. Their sick thoughts became mine. Their pain became mine. They crawled beneath my skin, through my belly. I felt them choking me, suffocating me, laughing at me. They sliced me wide open while they whispered their darkest plans for every inch of my flesh."

A sheen of sweat lit his brow. He leaned on the credenza for support. "They slipped in when I slept, so I tried to stay awake. The books helped, but eventually I'd succumb to exhaustion. Some nights as many as four or five of them would come, one after the other, and I was powerless to stop them."

He began pacing again, saying that Madame Chastain gave him every potion that she, Olivia, and Esmee could think of to help him, but they said there was no cure for the dark magic of demon steel. It had to run its course—if he survived it. They put a special collar on him to prevent him from using any kind of magic that he might accidentally conjure when battling the demons in his mind. His friends took turns sitting with him. "But one night, as I wrestled with a demon, I almost choked Quin to death. That was when I barricaded myself in my study. Every demon only got one shot at me. That was why I marked the walls, I guess as a way to keep my sanity, proof I had survived a hundred visitations and I could survive a hundred more." He sat down opposite her and set his uneaten apple on the low table between them. A silent storm rolled through him, and she wondered what nightmares he wasn't able to share. "Some nights, I didn't want to survive at all. I wanted to give up, give in."

"But you didn't give up."

He shook his head uncertainly.

"What happened to the friend who stabbed you?"

"He walked away. Disappeared, while I bled out on the forest floor. Now . . . he's dead to me."

As he should be, Bristol thought, *though the traitor deserved a far worse punishment than simple escape.* "Why did he do it?"

Tyghan leaned forward, his arms resting on his legs. "He changed sides. He joined up with the enemy, and I—" He cleared his throat. "I got in his way."

There was a bottomless loss in his voice. Loss of a friend. Loss of trust. It was the most desolate sound Bristol had ever heard, worse than her father's sobs. "I'm sorry your friend did this to you."

"I am too."

"How many more demons do you have to go?"

"A few hundred, maybe more, but I think I've managed to purge the power of the steel." He looked up from his hands woven in front of him, forcing a smile. "Or as Melizan puts it, my head has turned as hard as stone, and even demons can't get through the doors anymore. I haven't had any visits for months now." He motioned upward toward the study. "I'm sorry you had to see that."

"I could help you clean the room? Put it behind you?"

"No," he said, shrugging like it was a trivial matter. "I'll take care of it. I've just been busy."

Bristol knew it was more than that. There were hundreds of servants at the palace who would happily take care of it. It was a reminder he wasn't ready to shed yet. Or maybe he thought it was too soon—that more demons might still come. That his stone-hard head wasn't as impervious as he wanted it to be.

His brows rose. "And now we've given that subject more attention than it deserves." He stood and crossed to where she sat, pulling her to her feet. "Let's go tell Eris and the others about the portal and see what they say. It might have been a burrow."

"A burrow?"

"A type of portal made by small animals like mice or hares that can wind in a lot of directions, just like their underground burrows do, but they only pass into the mortal world, not into the Abyss. There's probably dozens of them on the palace grounds. But being able to detect one is still a good sign, and if you can close one kind of passage, you might be able to close another kind, too. Eris will know."

Small animals? Bristol's heart slammed against her chest. *Shit.*

The image of two beady eyes flashed through her head.

Angus.

If a ferret could have a shocked expression, Angus had worn it when he saw her peek though the portal. Then he scurried off, looking as guilty as a dog sneaking off with a holiday turkey. *The portal belonged to Angus.* Did he create it? What sort of creature was he?

Her parents claimed they swapped one of her mother's scarves for him in a supermarket parking lot before Cat was born, which at that point in time would have made Angus fifteen, but Bristol had read ferrets only lived for about eight years. When she confronted her mother about this, she had simply said, *This particular breed lives much longer*, but she couldn't seem to remember the precise breed of their long-lived ferret. Neither could her father.

Was Angus a pet her father brought with him from Elphame when he left? She remembered Angus studying her as she waited for Harper. How he often studied them throughout the years. The girls used to joke that he understood everything they said. Now she wondered if he actually did. Was he one more thing that wasn't what it seemed? Bristol raked both of her hands over her scalp, feeling like her head might explode.

"What's wrong?" Tyghan asked.

"Ferrets," she answered. "What about them? Could they make a hole like that?"

"Some, I suppose," he replied cautiously. "Why?"

She told him about their pet ferret, Angus, and his penchant for disappearing. Several times through the years, they'd thought he was gone for good. "Maybe he was a pet my father brought from here. But why a burrow from our laundry room to your study?"

A muscle in Tyghan's jaw twitched, and he was slow to answer, appearing to be just as perplexed as she was, but then he smiled. "Who knows? Maybe when you left, your pet was worried about you and he did his best to follow. And burrows aren't an exact science. Like I said, they wander in a lot of directions. It's hard to predict exactly where they'll end up. He did get somewhat close to your room."

"I guess so," Bristol answered absently, now preoccupied with trying to sort out memories of Angus and his exploits.

Tyghan took her hands in his. "Let's move on from burrows. Besides being able to close them, is there any other magic you're able to do now that you haven't mentioned?"

"Like what?"

"Like setting robes afire?"

Bristol wrinkled her nose. "He told you."

"No, he practically spat the news in my face."

"I promise you, he deserved it," she grumbled.

Tyghan grinned. "I don't doubt that, but be careful. Reuben is powerful and petty—and he does love his expensive robes."

"Better his robe than his hair, right? I considered that too."

He laughed. "Then I suppose I should be glad you showed restraint."

"Look there. You're good at laughing after all."

His gaze swam in hers, easy and comfortable, like she was a warm oasis. "I'm learning. I have a good teacher. Any other new talents I should know about?"

"I'm getting better at levitation."

Tyghan pulled her close and skimmed a hand low across her back. "Trust me, you've already mastered the knack of that."

He reached up and lightly trailed a finger across the hollow of her throat. Her blood ignited and an exquisite fiery throb clutched low in her belly. Her lashes fluttered shut for a moment and she gasped. "How—" She swallowed. "How do you do that?"

"I have a few skills you haven't seen yet too. Want to see more?"

His lips met hers, and they decided their news and Eris could wait for another hour.

Or two.

CHAPTER 76

Eris sat forward on the fallen log, his arms resting on his thighs, listening to the hum pulsing through the forest. Even the wood sprites were rejoicing, as if they had heard the news too, though it was still a carefully guarded secret. But joy and hope were contagious, and the hum elevated his own high spirits.

It had been two weeks since he and Dahlia confirmed that only the animals that made the burrows—or those who were bloodmarked—could detect and close them. Bristol had found and closed three more burrows since then. With her newfound skills, it seemed all six of the recruits were shining, growing together in strength. He watched them laughing and hugging over their newest success. They were executing team advancement drills through the forest, competing with the officers, using elemental magics, spells, or brute force to knock the other team to the ground. After five rounds, the recruits were ahead three to two.

"You do know the officers are letting them win," Dahlia said.

"Yes, I do," Eris answered. "Nothing wrong with that, just this once. It's boosting their confidence, and week's end is Beltane Eve. Tyghan wants them to swagger into Timbercrest Castle like they own the place."

Like joy, confidence was contagious too, Eris thought. They needed the other kingdoms to believe defeat of the Fomorians was possible. Their commitment of forces and weapons was more crucial than ever. Even if Bristol eliminated the portal to the Abyss along with the restless dead, they still had Kormick's fae army to contend with. Fomorians were desperate and dirty fighters, and with the restless dead fighting their battles, they had no casualties. Their numbers had continued to multiply. Danu needed the other kingdoms to believe victory was possible—that their combined resistance could turn the tide. Fomorians had controlled Elphame once, in the long-distant past. It had been a disastrous reign of oppression and hunger, and the Tuatha de suffered greatly under their rule. Their ways were volatile and erratic, and always cruel. This time, Eris was certain, it would be far worse, not just for Elphame but for the mortal world, too. Kormick's hunger for control was too great—he wouldn't stop with just one realm. Talks, letters, and pleas to the other kingdoms for support were getting them nowhere. They needed to see hope with their own eyes.

Dahlia sipped her tea as she eyed the recruits. She and Eris were there to watch them in the field and offer criticisms and incantations in order to fine-tune their burgeoning skills. "A burrow is a far cry from a portal," Dahlia reminded him. "They're temporary and eventually crumble shut on their own. A portal does not. We have to let her attempt the real thing."

Eris sighed. He didn't need a reminder. The dilemma was, there were only a handful of portals left, thanks to the Darkland monster, and no kingdom would be willing to sacrifice one near them. Many fae were tied to the mortal world on a daily basis; there were hobs, brownies, and gentry who kept a foot in both realms. To cut them off even further would disrupt commerce in both worlds—and anger monarchs they needed on their side. The solution, of course, was to have Bristol open a new portal of her own, and close it as practice. But so far she hadn't been able to accomplish that.

In this regard, both Eris and Dahlia were mostly helpless. There were no incantations to recite, or potions to offer, no ancient grimoires to study, no instructions of any kind, for that matter, to make her innate

ability as a bloodmarked show itself, beyond what they had already
done. It was like Rose shape-shifting to a hawk or Julia to a lion—it
was an instinctual calling. Bristol needed to hear the whisper of Brigid
through the millennia—to feel the quickening in her blood.

The Lumessa said Bristol's innate abilities would continue to bleed
out of the injured tick in small amounts. All they could do at this
point was offer Bristol gentle prodding to coax her ability to the surface. They gave her a tella stone to sleep with, and another for her
pocket to sharpen her connections with those who came before her, to
help her recognize another language humming through her veins—
that is, if the language wasn't some butchered message inside her.
There was still some question as to what Bristol actually was. When
Eris and Dahlia consulted with the Lumessa, she said it was unclear,
but Eris had noticed the skittish glances between the Sisters as they
listened on.

"If she had the tick removed . . ." Eris mused.

"That subject has already been broached. Miss Keats and the king
both say no. Even the Lumessa is not in favor of it yet."

Why? they both wondered. It was unsettling. The Lumessa herself
believed the risk of death was small. Was it only because Bristol was
afraid of what she might become? Or because the Lumessa was?

Dahlia grimaced as if remembering something else. "Miss Keats
came to me with questions. And she's questioned a dozen others. I don't
like it. She learned that her father was a Danu knight and asked if I
knew him. She assumed that since he's been in the mortal world for
twenty-four years, that was how long ago he left here."

"What did you tell her?"

"That I didn't know him well—which is certainly a version of the
truth. But her questions aren't going to stop."

"I know, Dahlia. I know." Eris dragged his palm over his brow. "She
came to me, too. Everyone's been advised how to respond."

They watched Tyghan approach the recruits, congratulating each
of them on their drills, and then he grabbed Bristol's hand. He pulled
her a short distance away into the shade of an oak tree before drawing

her into his arms and whispering into her ear. She laughed and pressed her hands against his chest until he pulled her tight and kissed her. A prolonged kiss.

Dahlia huffed. "And that. He should at least keep his public displays in check. It is not wise. It could—"

"Why is it not wise?" Eris asked. "They're lovers."

The High Witch replied with silence.

"Love is not a bad thing, Dahlia," Eris added. "He's learning to trust again."

"Is that really prudent at this time? What if he lets his guard down and tells her everything?"

A weight pressed down on Eris's shoulders. He shook his head. "No. I've spoken to him. He knows there is too much at stake. He's a king first. He wouldn't jeopardize the future of Elphame."

"It's still a risk. Besides being Maire's daughter, she was raised in the mortal world in a very mortal fashion. I've had enough interaction with her to know she's an outlier at heart and always will be. Her ways are not our ways, not to mention lovers have quarrels. We need her. If things shouldn't work out between them—"

"Let's believe that they will." He reached over and pulled Dahlia's hand into his lap.

She snatched it away. "Please. We don't want to create talk."

Eris suppressed a moan. "Dahlia, my love, I can assure you, everyone already talks about us. We've been together for almost eight years. When will you believe that I would never betray you?"

"Why wouldn't you? Because I might turn you into something dreadful?"

"Because I *wouldn't*. There is not a creature in all of Elphame that could turn my head from you. I am the scorched earth, and you are my rain."

She looked sideways at him, both brows arched and one corner of her mouth curved upward, but Eris knew that was her version of *I love you, too*. Maybe one day she would actually say the words to him. He was a patient man.

A thunderous gallop of approaching horses roared through the air, commanding everyone's attention.

It was Quin and three knights from the garrison.

Eris could already tell by the troubled expression on Quin's face that it wasn't good news, and he wondered how long it would take Tyghan to pull away from Bristol to speak with him privately. What excuse would he give her this time? There were endless things he couldn't discuss in front of Bristol—the kinds of things Dahlia worried about—but so far Tyghan had maneuvered well around difficult questions. When he didn't let his temper get in the way, his foresight and acumen were impeccable. Eris took great pride in that.

Kasta, Dalagorn, and Cully were already breaking away from the recruits and heading over to Quin. It was news they were all waiting for. Dahlia sucked in a disapproving breath as she and Eris rose to join them. "What are we doing, Eris?"

Doing. After eight years together, he and Dahlia had a canon of inflection between them. He knew what she meant, and heard the dirty nuance behind *doing*.

"We're trying to save our world in the most honorable way we know how."

"But is it? Honorable?"

Eris winced, and left his answer at that.

CHAPTER 77

Bristol leaned into Tyghan's embrace, not trying to hide anything from anyone anymore. She happily breathed in the dust and sweat on his skin, and the scent of pine and juniper ground into his clothes from when she sent him crashing to the forest floor during drills. The dirt smudge across his cheekbone somehow managed to make him even more handsome.

"You were ruthless today," he whispered in her ear. "Will you be that ruthless tonight?"

She plucked a piece of grass from his hair. "Is that what you want? Not an ounce of mercy?"

"I don't need sleep," he whispered as his mouth met hers.

But she knew by tonight, it would be she who was at his mercy. His mouth knew every curve, every dip and hollow of her body, every quivering nerve, and he seemed to take great pleasure in helping her discover them all, too. His hand discreetly eased beneath her shirt, his thumb stroking her breast, fanning embers already burning inside her.

The sound of galloping horses interrupted their kiss, and they both looked to see who it was. Quin was back. Bristol wondered what had taken him so long. After only a few days of making Cat "suffer and stew," Bristol broke down and wrote Cat a letter, one with far gentler words than her parting ones had been. She was eager to hear everything

Quin had to say. Eris already told her Quin wouldn't be speaking to her sisters—the fewer who knew Danu knights were in Bowskeep, the better—that he'd only be leaving the letter in their mailman's bag. As the Choosing Ceremony drew near, it seemed everyone was growing more cautious, guarding their actions like spies were everywhere. Still, she wondered if Quin had seen her sisters. "Let's go see if—"

Tyghan cut her off. "No. I'll speak to Quin."

"But—"

"Melizan's waiting for you and the others over in the meadow, and you know how she loves to be kept waiting."

Bristol sighed. Weapons training was scheduled for the afternoon. Melizan had taken a keen interest in the recruits' ability to wield swords and spears, where she said their skills were sorely lacking. It was true. They were all much more intrigued with learning magics and practicing quick evasive maneuvers than the tedious art of throwing and stabbing. But Tyghan's words stuck in her head. *Sometimes reaching for the tools of the earth is what tips the battle.* Or saves your life. "All right," she said reluctantly, "but ask questions. Make sure they got my letter."

"I will," he promised, and gave her one last kiss before he left.

She lingered—at the risk of enraging Melizan—watching Tyghan walk away, his woodsy taste still on her lips. Even with all the shocking truths she had learned since she came to Elphame, these last weeks were as close to perfection as any she could remember. Her purpose and power were growing, and she and Tyghan grew more inseparable every day. It seemed that once he shared his darkest secret with her, there was no distance between them anymore. The final veil was lifted.

Of course, there was still a lot to learn about each other, but they were gaining fast ground on that, often staying up until the very late hours talking. A week ago, as they were drifting off to sleep, he had mused aloud, *When this is all over, I want to visit Bowskeep with you. Smell all those laundromats and coffee shops you told me about.* She had laughed but spent the rest of the night thinking about what he said.

When this is all over. Like there was a sequel to this odd story of theirs. A part two. Like they had a future together. No more fresh starts but a chance to water a seed, to let something grow and bloom. The thought had consumed her ever since. She wanted to bloom with Tyghan and see what transpired. Longings she had kept at arm's length—like permanence—took root, because with each passing day, she was finding it harder to imagine her life without him.

Every day, he left more of his clothing and personal belongings in her room, until soon she thought another wardrobe closet would need to be brought in to hold them all. Waking up with him at her side, his arms and legs tangled with hers, now felt as natural and welcome as the sun on her face. She wondered if Madame Chastain had stopped thinking of it as a mere dalliance. What she and Tyghan shared was anything but casual and fleeting.

And even though she still had the tick, she was learning to ignore it. She hadn't looked at it in the mirror again since the first time. Maybe she was deluding herself, but there was a steady trickle of magic still flowing into her from the injured tick, and her skills continued to inch forward. She hoped the most important skill—finding and closing portals, not just burrows—would be next.

In the meantime, she and the other recruits had great fun using newfound skills. With just a twitch of their fingers, they would yank up a bit of carpet to trip officers as they walked by or steal food and drinks from unsuspecting gentry at evening festivities, rarely spilling a sip or crumb. It was all in the name of practice, of course, since being able to summon defensive weapons or obstacles in dire situations was crucial to a successful mission.

They were all excelling, and Bristol wondered if the others had been holding back for her sake, or maybe somehow each of their strengths grew along with her own. It was like they were a confluence of swift streams that had become a powerful river. Avery was now able to coax trees to sprout new limbs for climbing, and great ferns to unfurl from the ground to provide cover. Rose was flying again, her eyesight keener than ever, able to spot and warn them about distant objects, and Sashka's quick leaps and maneuvering skills made it almost impossible to corner her. Of course, Julia was as fierce and cunning as ever, and Hollis's courage had blossomed tenfold. She was no longer afraid to assume her furry four-footed self. In a forest—or the empty halls of a large palace—it made her close to invisible, her light footsteps undetectable. Even the smallest opening was accessible for her. What a strange, unexpected group they were, all so different. Maybe that was what made them strong.

When this is over. She left for the meadow to join the others, grabbing a flask of sparkling wine from a supply basket on her way, and let her mind wander, just as Tyghan's had, imagining him meeting her sisters, and the places in Bowskeep where she would take him. Sal's, for sure. Maybe she'd even let him make his own pizza. The thought made her laugh, the powerful king of Danu fumbling behind the counter with pepperoni and olives. And then she imagined him scrambling for words when he one day met her father, because her musings included that, too. Certainty that her father was alive budded in her like spring. She would find him. Was it the fae magic in her veins telling her this secret? Or was it just common, everyday hope? Maybe hope was mortal magic. She would take either kind.

♟

Tyghan glanced over his shoulder to make sure Bristol didn't follow.

"What took you so long?" he asked Quin.

"We stalked and waited and turned the house inside out for three days. There was no sign of that oversized rat, but he had been there. I heard the younger sister say that Angus was missing again. That's what they call Fritz. The older sister said he would turn up eventually. That he always did."

"You're sure it was him and not just an ordinary ferret?"

"There were signs. Hidden symbols he left at windows and doors, even the front steps, to alert him to intruders."

"That slimy weasel," Kasta hissed.

Just as they had thought, it was no ordinary animal that had created that burrow into Tyghan's study. Fritz was a shape-shifter who was more comfortable in his ferret skin than his human one. He was supposed to be dead—at least, that was what they'd been led to believe. He had once been a knight of Danu, until he took over the duties of doorward at Celwyth Hall. He joined the search for Kierus when he disappeared. They had found Fritz's bloody cloak in the forest and thought he was another casualty of the restless dead.

As a warrior, Fritz was brawny, powerful, and fierce, but not half as agile and sneaky as his sleek ferret form. And he had watched Kierus grow up at Celwyth Hall. No doubt an emotional investment over time made Kierus become more to him than just a resident of the manor.

"That's how Kierus stole the art," Quin grumbled. "He had Fritz get it. No one else could access Celwyth without detection."

"What about Kayana?" Cully said. "With her wolf nose, I'm surprised she wasn't able to sniff him out."

Tyghan's nostrils flared. "Maybe she didn't try." He couldn't shake his suspicions that Jasmine had aided Kierus.

"No," the High Witch said emphatically. "The Lumessa would never break her oath to Danu."

Tyghan wanted to believe she was right, but his belief in oaths and loyalty was strained since Kierus had stabbed him.

"The four knights we left behind will keep watch," Quin said. "Fritz will show up eventually."

Fritz had a sixth sense about him. He sniffed trouble coming. It didn't surprise Tyghan that he had vanished. But protection was in his blood, whether a doorward at Celwyth Hall, or doorward for a small, run-down house in Bowskeep. That was probably why Kierus left him behind—to watch over his daughters and protect them from mortal threats—but even Fritz was no match for a squad of powerful Danu knights. He'd be lying low for a long while. The knights Tyghan assigned to stay in Bowskeep were also there to protect the Keats sisters in case anyone else came nosing around.

"Bristol's sisters didn't see you?" Kasta asked.

"No," Quin answered, "but we saw them both reading the letter on their couch. Halfway through, the older one burst into tears. That must have been some letter."

Tyghan wouldn't tell Bristol about the tears. Only that the letter was safely delivered.

"What about Keats?" Quin asked. "You think she knew about Fritz?"

"How could she not know?" Dalagorn replied. "Over all those years, he must have shape-shifted in front of them."

"No," Tyghan said. "She's the one who brought him up, wondering if he could have made the burrow. I saw the shock on her face. She had no idea he was fae. Even now she still thinks he's only a fae ferret—not a shape-shifter."

Quin shook his head. "I'll give this much to Kierus, he was clever. I guess if he could deceive all of us, he could deceive her, too."

Kasta's face darkened. "Not clever enough. Kormick managed to track the family down."

"Hmm," Eris mused. "Over twenty years in the mortal world is a long time to be on the run. I'm guessing he and Maire got sloppy."

Tyghan had a hard time picturing Kierus being sloppy about anything. He remembered how methodically he dressed, every button in order, top to bottom, his trousers tucked precisely in his boots, how he insisted on sharpening his own blades until they gleamed, how when he hunted boar, his aim was so exact, it was rare his javelin didn't pierce a beast straight between the eyes. His kills were always clean and quick. He had earned his title as butcher. Kierus wasn't sloppy.

"Or maybe they weren't tracked down by Fomorian scouts at all," Madame Chastain suggested. "Maybe Maire simply grew tired of Kierus as she did with other lovers and returned to Kormick of her own accord. A dalliance might have been all she had the patience for."

Tyghan knew her last comment was directed at him as a warning, and he glanced at her sharply, ready to shut her down, but her eyelids hung half-mast and her brows were pinched with worry. He bit back his reply.

"Whatever the reason," she added, "we can't have Fritz flitting in and out of the palace at will. I would suggest you have a talk with Daiedes this evening."

Tyghan nodded. On that much he and Madame Chastain agreed. He had already planned to make the snake's hungry dreams come true and give Daiedes permission to pounce and feast on any ferret who might venture into his chamber or onto the palace grounds. Fritz's excursions were about to come to an end.

Tyghan turned to leave, but one of the garrison knights stopped him. "Your Majesty, the commander asked me to report that a scouting party is late returning to the garrison. They were due back last night. We have two squads searching for them now."

Two squads? Any number of things could delay a scouting party. It wasn't that unusual. "Have you seen evidence of an attack? Blood? Riderless horses?"

The knight shook her head. "No. But our last communication with them was a note carried by a rook. It only said they were in the Whelky Lands following a lead and they planned to return last night."

The Whelky Lands stretched the entire length of the northern border of Bleakwood. That was a long expanse to get lost in—and to search.

"Who was leading the party?"

"One of your officers." She hesitated, then added, "Officer Dervy."

Glennis. All the officers served rotations at the garrison. This last week was her turn.

"No doubt they're holed up in that inn near the border that Officer Dervy claims serves the best leek pie," Tyghan answered.

Quin and the others voiced agreement, but knew as well as Tyghan that Glennis would never return late from a scouting expedition for any reason under her control, especially not for a leek pie.

"Tell the commander to double his search efforts," Tyghan ordered. "And to keep this information quiet."

CHAPTER 78

When Bristol reached the meadow, weapons practice was on hold. "They're having an afternoon *repast*," Sashka explained in the haughtiest tone she could conjure, daintily dabbing at the corners of her mouth with a lace napkin. She used it to gesture toward Melizan and Cosette, who sat on the opposite side of the meadow in the shade of an oak tree.

With blankets spread for picnicking, and light filtering through the trees to dapple the bright green meadow, Bristol thought it could almost be a Seurat painting—except for the sharp and deadly weapons lying about.

"I don't even know what a repast is," Avery said between bites of a raspberry cream horn.

Rose laughed. "It's what you're shoving in your mouth right now."

"We call it a snack where I come from," Hollis answered. "But it's served with coffee, not tea."

Julia sighed. "Oh, how I miss my afternoon espresso with a cinnamon palmier. My local bistro always saved the same corner table for me. It was a nice tradition I miss."

"My afternoon repast was my boyfriend, Wynn," Avery stated matter-of-factly. "Usually in the barn. I miss that tradition too. Wynn wasn't happy when I left, but I promised him I'd be back in time for harvest."

Sometimes Bristol forgot that the others had left lives behind, too—routines, traditions, and people who were waiting for them to return. That they missed parts of their old lives like she did, including things as ordinary as doughnuts and coffee. Her heart tugged with thoughts of her sisters. She hoped her letter had smoothed things out with Cat.

Hollis made a place beside her for Bristol, and she joined them on the blanket, surveying the food laid out in the center. One thing the fae always had in abundance was food, at least as long as the Cauldron of Plenty remained in safe hands.

"I think their repast is just frustration eating after us whooping their asses today," Sashka hooted, still exhilarated by their triumph over the officers in drills.

Across the meadow, Melizan and Cosette paused from their repast and turned their heads toward Sashka. Even from thirty yards away, their stares were numbing.

"Oh shit," Sashka mumbled, and glued her gaze to her lap like she wished she had already mastered the art of disappearing.

The others broke into muffled fits of laughter.

"I don't think they heard you," Hollis said unconvincingly, which made them laugh more, but they all took note and were careful to keep their voices low as they continued their chatter.

"They are quite the item, aren't they?" Avery said.

"A powerhouse," Bristol agreed.

Hollis frowned. "I wish I was somebody's item. What about Quin?" She fanned her hand in front of her like just the mention of his name seared her skin. "I love that he's shorter than me and I can kiss the top of his sexy head. I mean, I could, if we were an item. But he's twenty-six. Do you think he's too young for me?"

A discussion of their four-year age gap ensued, and everyone agreed that four years was a trifle.

"My mother was five years older than my father," Bristol added.

"And it worked out for them." But then remembering their last fateful argument, she added, "Mostly."

"Well, speaking of items . . ." Sashka said. They all looked at Bristol in unison, like they had planned for this conversation to land on her.

"Me?" Bristol answered innocently.

"Yes, you," Rose said. They inched closer to block out Melizan's and Cosette's sensitive ears. "You can't evade us any longer! We want details!"

"Juicy details!" Avery added.

Sashka's brows shot up. "Is he a good kisser?"

"Do you love him?" Avery asked. "Have you told him? Has he told you?"

"No. I haven't— We—"

"You don't love him?" Hollis gasped. "Then he must be one helluva kisser."

"Is he?" Sashka asked again. "A good kisser? What is it like?"

Bristol swallowed a groan. Madame Chastain had given them all a lecture about keeping their heads about them during Beltane. Julia had said it was similar to spring fever in the mortal world, but here the pull was much stronger and could overtake your good sense. *Just keep your head about you, and you'll be fine*, she told them. But the season crept into everyone's bones just the same, even Julia's, who danced continuously with Lord Fently last night until they both disappeared into the shadows. She arrived at drills late, her hair disheveled, but with a smile on her face.

Sashka drew in an eager breath. "And what about his—"

"Holy hell, Sashka! Yes, he's a good kisser," Bristol said, wanting to avoid the rest of her question. "And no, I haven't told him I love him."

"But do you?" Rose asked again.

Bristol exhaled a long breath. Rose always asked everything so innocently, like there were simple yes or no answers.

Julia eyed Bristol, waiting, too, but her expression was filled more with concern than curiosity.

She wanted to reply but wasn't sure how. *Love* was a strange word. Bristol didn't quite trust it. It was used every day to place value on the simplest, most trivial things, from pizza toppings to overpriced party dresses to well-worn sneakers. Her mother had claimed Bristol's father was the love of her life, and yet she had left him—and left him broken. What kind of love was that?

Bristol knew she loved being with Tyghan. She soaked in every minute they were together, and when they were apart, she couldn't wait to be with him again. His gaze was fire inside her. His kiss. Just thinking about it made her blood race. She would never tire of his lips on hers, or his hands exploring her body. Or the way he studied her like he had found some fascinating treasure. And there was no denying, their lovemaking was great and getting better by the day. She was learning things. So was he, both of them eager to please the other.

But it was their small moments together that whittled to her core: the crook of his little finger hooked with her own as they walked to drills, his laugh that came more often now, the way he would notice a wayward strand of her hair and tuck it behind her ear, the sound of his breaths beside her as he slept peacefully, his hand gently sponging her back as they bathed, his caress, slow and tender, the way they talked in the middle of the night, wanting more of each other than they wanted sleep—all these moments, they filled an emptiness that had lurked inside her for too long.

Whatever she and Tyghan had, she liked it a lot, and she didn't want to muck it up with a confusing word that came with expectations. She just wanted to watch what they had change from one wondrous thing into something even better. *When this is all over.* All she knew was that being with him made everything inside her feel warm and right, and— she hated to admit—slightly giddy. A burning anticipation ran through her every time he walked into a room, every time he glanced her way with some silent message simmering in his eyes. A wordless message meant just for her.

"There's something I like about him. Something that I like *a lot*. Way more than warm cheese puffs," she answered, and then pointed her finger at the tray between them, levitating a cheese puff into the air, flicking her finger so it flew up a good four feet, then tumbled down, straight into her mouth. Everyone cheered at her levitation prowess, which was what Bristol had hoped for, a distraction that would change the topic.

"I bet he's way more tasty, too," Sashka said, still pushing the subject.

Bristol only raised her brows in a vague reply.

"Looks like repast is over," Avery announced.

Their heads turned. Melizan and Cosette walked across the meadow toward them, their golden spears casually resting over their shoulders. They stopped a few feet away from the recruits' picnic blanket, surveying them all with smiles that chilled even the nearby trees.

"So, who's ready to whoop our asses?" Melizan asked. "Sashka, how about you? You want to go first?"

CHAPTER 79

The valley rumbled, stretched, the earth awakening after almost one hundred years of sleep. It nudged the stone at its center awake, too. It was nearly time. The stone felt the new grass, the rabbit holes, the tree roots cleaving new paths, the sun, the shadows of clouds. It felt everything within its circle of power, but also beyond—it felt the gentle plod of *footsteps . . . footsteps*. It listened. More would come. They always did, and then the stone would know. It would choose.

Bristol stood on the southern crest of the valley, the breeze whipping at her hair. For a week the team had conducted drills in various terrains, but Tyghan scheduled a break to bring her to the valley and view the stone at its center. Bristol hesitated before saying, "That's it?"

"Not impressed?"

"With such a lofty name, like the Stone of Destiny, I think I expected more. Something fancier? It's just a plain gray rock."

"That's all it is. At least until Danu's magic shakes it awake."

Bristol hoped Tyghan wasn't offended by her lack of awe, but the stonework at the palace was so impressive that she had imagined that the stone that chose a new ruler for all of Elphame would be something equally magnificent. The dull flat rock was no more than a few feet across, and barely peeked above the earth.

"What are all those other stones surrounding it?"

"It's called the Mother Ring. Willing kings and queens stand within its circle and when the one destined to be Elphame's next ruler steps onto the stone at its center, it sings out, proclaiming them the ruler of Elphame and caretaker of the Cauldron of Plenty. But if no one steps forward . . ."

He left the thought dangling.

"Except for Kormick," Bristol finished. "That's the only way the Stone of Destiny would choose him."

Tyghan nodded. "And he'll be defending the inner circle and the stone with his legions."

Maybe not, Bristol thought. Not if she closed the Abyss portal. She eyed the huge expanse of the surrounding valley, the waving grass, the bluebells and buttercups, the oaks standing like ancient sentinels on hilltops. The valley was too beautiful to be scarred with war, but she knew it wouldn't be the first time. Olivia and Esmee had covered the history of kings and queens fighting for the right to rule—though none before had a limitless army of demons at their disposal. That changed everything.

Tyghan grabbed her hand. "Come on," he said, motioning to a nearby oak. "Before we eat lunch, let's rest in the shade of that tree."

She pulled back, eyeing him suspiciously. "Somehow, when you say rest, I don't think it means *rest*."

He flashed a devilish grin that told her all she needed to know.

"I'm wounded," he said, his hand pressed over his heart. "Are you calling me a scoundrel?"

She shrugged. "Depends. Just what do you think a scoundrel is?"

"A lovestruck ass?"

Lovestruck. Even though he was teasing, the word fluttered inside her. She scowled to hide the woozy feeling. "Out here in the open? The others will be along—"

He took a step closer. "No, they won't. I told Quin we wanted to be alone. It wasn't a request. It was an order."

Her brows shot up in mock surprise. "So you're saying the Knight Commander lured me here for his own wicked passions?"

"That's exactly what I am saying. Do you object?"

"You're a master schemer," she said and began unbuttoning her shirt. She slipped it off, and knew he was hoping her bra would be next.

"Master schemer," he repeated. "Is that another one of those titles you've given me?"

"Yes, and quite fitting, I think. But I'll admit, sometimes I'm amused by your devious ways."

He grunted. "Last night your chamber walls were shaking with your amusement."

"Braggart."

His jaw tightened and his demeanor changed from shameless lust to something else, and he stared at her oddly. "Do you only love my devious ways? What about me, Bristol? Do you love me?"

She blinked, taken by surprise. He wasn't teasing or playing a game anymore. His voice was tender. *Do you love me?* It was the last thing she'd expected to tumble past his lips. Love? His eyes shone, bright as the sky above him, waiting for her reply like she held the key to his next breath.

The answer pulsed inside her.

Tyghan had settled deep into her marrow, and she couldn't picture her life without him. He made her laugh, and—

"It's taking you an awfully long time to answer. Should I be worried?"

He truly sounded concerned, and she smiled. "Yes, Tyghan. I love you. Not just the devious you, but all of you."

He beamed like a happy schoolboy, like it was the first time he had ever heard the words. Like he could breathe again. But then he just stood there smiling at her.

"And?" she prompted. "Do you have something you want to say to me in return?"

His brows pulled together, perplexed. "Like what?"

"You arrogant bastard," she said, trying to hide her smile. She threw her shirt at him and ran. He chased on her heels, but she wasn't going to make it easy for him.

He caught her arm, and she felt herself spinning, both of them tumbling, but he turned to take the brunt of the fall. She landed on his chest, but then he rolled until he straddled her, bracing an arm on either side of her shoulders.

His expression turned solemn, his laughter and play set aside. His knuckle grazed her jaw like her skin was a delicate flower petal. "Yes, I do have something I want to tell you. I love you, Bristol Keats. I love you more than anything I've ever loved in my life." His lips met hers, and he whispered against them. "I loved you since that first day we met—"

She couldn't restrain a laugh, and he pulled back. "What?"

"You did not!" she said, still giggling. "You wanted to throttle me."

He cocked his head to the side. "All right, maybe it was a week later," he conceded, "but it's true. I loved you early on, before I could even admit it to myself. I was lost to you after that first night we danced. And it wasn't just lust." He traced a finger down her chest until he reached her bra and then slipped his hand beneath the silky fabric, caressing her breast. "But I'll admit to plenty of that, too." She shuddered and felt his growing desire pressing against her.

His hand moved from her breast to her chin, cupping her face, and he leaned down, kissing her cheekbone, her temple, her brow, and then he pulled back to look into her eyes again. "You frightened me, but I still craved every part of you—your voice, your touch, even your silences. You weren't afraid of them. You weren't afraid of me. I loved the way you shared your life. You've made me care about laundromats, the seashore, coffee houses, and maybe even that nasty thing you call pizza."

"Whoa," she said. "You love me that much?"

He smiled. "You made me want to share my life, too. Something I couldn't do before." His black hair tumbled over his brow, and his blue irises were a world of sky swallowing her whole. "I want to share my life with you, Bri. All of it."

She didn't have to parse out exactly what that meant, because they were kissing again, touching, needing, peeling clothes away, the meadow a soft bed beneath them, the sky a blanket above. *I want to share my life with you, Bri. All of it.*

She wanted that too. And the thought didn't even make her afraid.

He looked into her eyes again, like nothing else in the world mattered but them, and she wondered how she reached this place, the miracle of it. The *nakedness* of it.

Not just the nakedness of skin touching skin, but a deeper kind. A place of vulnerability and trust. Layers peeled away. *Love.* God, she loved him, and she wondered why it took her so long to say it, so long to move past the fear. They both helped each other reach this place.

He smiled, studying her. "What are you thinking about?"

"The miracle of nakedness."

He didn't scoff. He knew what she meant, and his mouth met hers again, as tender and soft as a cloud.

CHAPTER 80

It was well past midnight when the Sisters finally tucked into their evening meal. They had been in their library, researching the full scope of Elphame histories and studying the grimoires of every faerie kingdom.

The Sisters were silent as they ate, the grim clinking of their knives and forks against the fine porcelain dishes the only chatter in the room.

Izzy finally broke their silence. "Why didn't you tell Bristol the truth when she was here?"

"The girl was already scared witless," Jasmine answered. "She doesn't need to know yet what she might become."

"*Will* become," Adela added.

"We'll continue to study the matter," Jasmine countered. "It's complicated. We can't be certain."

"We'll have to stop her heart to get that tick to release her," Camille lamented. "It's the only way."

Izzy sighed. "But only for a few minutes."

Camille dabbed at her eyes with her napkin, then openly wept. "I saw Kierus in every one of her expressions. She's a good girl. I can tell."

"But Kierus was a good boy. Until—" Adela didn't have to finish. The Sisters had already talked the problematic knot dry, dissecting how everything had gone so terribly wrong.

"You can't keep putting off Madame Chastain. What will you tell her?" Camille asked, her voice shaking.

"Nothing," Jasmine said firmly. "Only that we're studying the matter. What Bristol does or doesn't become will remain with us for now."

But Jasmine already knew with certainty what Bristol would become and the only way to prevent it. Stop Bristol's heart when she removed the tick, and never start it again.

CHAPTER 81

D ammit, Eris," Tyghan hissed quietly so no one else would hear. "*Relax*."

Eris resumed his fussing, making sure every detail was perfect. Tyghan had never been nervous about a procession before. As a prince of Danu and Knight Commander, he'd made the entrance to Beltane Eve every year, walking behind his brother without a thought as to who was watching. He never cared. But this year was different. Every extravagant detail was a reminder that the stakes were different. A reminder that he was not Cael and every eye would be on him.

"I'll relax later," Eris answered and swiped the back of Tyghan's coat one more time, removing wrinkles that even he knew weren't there.

"Good gods, Counselor," Melizan moaned from behind them, waiting for the procession to begin. "Enough. You can't make a silk purse out of an ogre's ear. He's going to have to go down that staircase as is."

"Nothing wrong with an ogre's ear," Dalagorn huffed.

"Nothing except for the warts," Quin said.

Dalagorn growled. "My mother loves my warts."

Cully stroked the smooth pointed tips of his own ears. "I agree with your mum. They're adorable. In a gnarled sort of way."

Eris sniffed, annoyed by Melizan's comment. *As is?* He went to great lengths to make sure the most impressive attire was created for the entire party—especially the king. Tyghan cut a perfect picture of power and grace in his sharply tailored black coat. The gold and silver embroidery that trailed down the front borders honored the nine sacred trees of Elphame, and his crown of gold leaves was the stunning final touch against his black hair. And Tyghan's eyes, well, they alone always commanded attention—

The counselor tripped on his thoughts. While Tyghan's steely blue eyes commanded attention, they could also turn menacing, and right now, they were cutting a hole through Eris. Perhaps Melizan was right in this case, that it was time to step back, and so Eris did, hoping Tyghan's scowl would fade to something less lethal before the herald blew his trumpet. He craned his neck to see the back of the foyer, where Esmee, Olivia, and Dahlia were making sure the recruits were in place.

Miss Keats always softened Tyghan's disposition. If only she could walk down in front of the king, but there was an order to these things Eris had to follow: royalty, the king's officers, senior council members—no one else. Adding the recruits to the end of their procession would certainly raise brows but would make a statement, too. The king of Danu could spurn protocol in favor of the interests of Elphame. But letting them go first, that would be going too far. Ignoring tradition had its limits. But maybe if he—

The trumpet blared. The roar of guests down below in the Timbercrest Castle ballroom quieted, and the herald announced the Danu Nation.

Danu was the twelfth and last kingdom of Elphame to arrive. Pixies, fauns, and sorcerers, ogres, wizards, and wild things, stopped middance, midflight, midbreath when the herald's trumpet blew. Sloshing goblets stilled. Beltane Eve was a night of indulgence, but more importantly, news. Queens, kings, and gentry quieted with anticipation when the herald announced the Danu Nation, not just because of their power and position among the kingdoms but because of the many rumors— that the young king had been stabbed with demon steel and survived it, that he was planning to defy the Fomorians, that he was Lugh, the sun king returned, fully a god and ready to take revenge against Fomoria—or the pettiest of rumors laughed behind cupped hands—that he had grown a spiked demon tail since being stabbed. Of course they had all watched Tyghan grow up, witnessed him trailing behind his mother and brother, but he'd been only a boy, getting into trouble the way many fae children did, or later they saw him as the Knight Commander who favored the dark corners of a room. They didn't pay him much attention, as the young prince preferred.

But they paid attention now.

"King Tyghan Trénallis of the Danu Nation!"

Tyghan's eyes skimmed the crowd, a colorful blur, then his gaze rose above them to the knotty branched chandeliers that held hundreds of flickering candles and a few curious wild things, their fangs and leathery wings gilded in the light. But he felt the scrutiny of Elphame's leaders, the visceral pull of their presence, in a way he had never felt before, and it drew his attention back downward. He locked eyes with the shrewd elven queen of Eideris first, then the goblin king of Bleakwood, with his knobby little princes and princesses huddled around his knees. Next, he met the curious regard of the queen of Cernunnos, her antlers bejeweled for the celebration, her white stag at her side, and then he saw the hesitant nod of the ogre king of Greymarch.

All their faces held a similar question—even if they didn't mean for Tyghan to see it. Will you kneel to Kormick and keep the peace? Or will Elphame go to war? What can you do that we haven't already tried? If the most powerful kingdom in Elphame could lose their own king to Kormick, what chance did any of them have? As long as Cael was in Fomoria's custody, Tyghan knew none of them would attempt to challenge Kormick. He needed to convince them that Danu had a plan and they should join their smaller forces with Danu. Every sword, soldier, and spell counted.

Halfway down the staircase, he heard the next announcement, Princess Melizan of the Danu Nation. By the time he reached the bottom step and walked across the ballroom to the outstretched hands of King

Roderick of Timbercrest, the rest of the Danu party had descended. Almost all. The murmur of the crowd rose again, ready to resume the festivities, and of course comment on Tyghan's apparent lack of a demon tail.

King Roderick immediately tried to draw Tyghan into a conversation, but Tyghan stopped him. "Your Majesty, there are a few more we wish for Elphame to meet."

The leaves trailing over the spriggan king's shoulders fluttered with curiosity. "But I thought—"

The herald's trumpet blared again, and he announced, "The royal elite squad of the Danu Nation."

CHAPTER 82

There was a ruffle of surprise.

A hushed murmur rolled through the ballroom.

Whispers. But all eyes were focused on the top of the wide staircase.

Bristol smiled, but inwardly she snorted at "elite squad." *Smoke and mirrors*, she thought. That had to be Eris's doing. But maybe right at this moment, they did feel elite, like they could conquer the world. They stood shoulder to shoulder and then the drums thumped, the low beat skittering through Bristol's blood, empowering and primal, and the recruits began their descent. Halfway down the staircase, the hems of their lavish gowns rose, coaxed by a bit of ribbon and tailoring magic, and then six polished sticks flew through the air, launched by the officers at the bottom of the stairs.

The sticks spun, flipping end over end, seemingly suspended forever, then began their descent until one landed in each recruit's hand. Then the real fun began. Fiddles rang sharp, bows burning over strings fast and bright as they accompanied the drums. Bristol dipped and circled; Avery and Sashka lunged; Julia twirled, regally stepping between them. Rose and Hollis moved in, closing up the sides, all their sticks meeting with perfect timing, the loud crack of wood on wood sounding in the air, the *crack, crack, crack* of the traditional Danu dance reverberating through the hall—with unexpected modern moves woven in. There was a brief gasp of awe from below, but the recruits weren't finished. Their steps were flawless as they worked their way down the stairs, practiced to perfection, weaving in and out of each other, then dancing back-to-back, twirling to the music, their sticks meeting again and again in mock battle, and finally flying overhead as they tossed them to each other and, on the last step, threw them back to the officers before they took a flamboyant, and very immodest, bow. *Own the moment*, Tyghan had said, and they did.

The ballroom exploded with cheers, which were immediately followed by the roar of chatter as everyone discussed the surprising entertainment—and the delicious impropriety of it all. Eris had objected to their inclusion of the nontraditional steps at first. He said he never heard of street dance before, but after he saw the Danu gentry mesmerized by the recruits' unusual steps at nightly festivities, he agreed a few might be included.

The recruits proceeded straight to where Tyghan stood next to King Roderick so they could be introduced, as they had been instructed. Other than the dance on the stairs, Eris had fully choreographed every step of the evening—who they should talk to and whom they should avoid, what they should say, and what they absolutely shouldn't. By the time they reached their appointed destination, the elven queen of Eideris and the ogre king of Greymarch had already moved in to greet Tyghan—and await introductions to the elite squad.

"What an enchanting surprise," King Roderick said, the vines resting on his chest warming to a rosy hue as he cupped each of their hands between his own in traditional Timbercrest fashion. He lingered especially with Avery, curious about a fellow spriggan raised in the mortal world, but Kasta made sure questions were kept to a minimum. After a few niceties, Quin and the other officers stepped up to usher the recruits away to the banquet tables for refreshments, ostensibly so the monarchs could catch up on kingdom news. But in a quick moment, when Kasta strategically stepped between them and the monarchs, blocking them from view, Tyghan mouthed *beautiful* to Bristol. In a gesture of thanks, she touched the emerald teardrops adorning her ears that he gave her the night before, but he whispered, "No. *You.*"

He gave her a last nod before they were whisked away, indicating they had accomplished the task, but the buzz in the room already made that evident. King Roderick was dazzled by this elite squad, and others nearby stretched their necks to get a better look at them, though the recruits had done little more than a few fast steps on a staircase. The mystery surrounding them was as magical as any true talent they possessed. The officers kept up the charade, staying close at their sides as if the recruits were national treasures, behaving more like their assigned attendants than their commanders. Bristol noticed Hollis had managed to maneuver over to Quin's side, while Sashka was firmly pinned between Melizan and Cosette.

Cully fell into step beside Bristol. "Well done," he whispered. "Remember—"

"I know. Eris drilled us."

Cully smiled. "Sorry. He and Tyghan drilled the officers, too."

They were to maintain the mystery, let the word *elite* take on a life of its own, and not reveal any specific role they played in Danu to the hundreds of inquisitive nobles now gawking at them. That was Tyghan and Eris's job, to drop judicious details and discreetly explore possible strategies with monarchs, procure initial troop commitments while giving them vague but visible hope that Danu had a plan—which included this unusually skilled squad. It couldn't become common knowledge or even a certainty—only idle, drunken banter at Beltane Eve—because other Elphame rulers could be suspect, too. Even though they now shared a common enemy, they were not one big happy world. Seven kingdoms, no matter how reluctantly, had already agreed to Kormick's demands regarding the Choosing Ceremony, buying his lies in exchange for momentary peace. *Fear has a way of making lies seem virtuous,* Eris told them at his last briefing. *We need to win them back.* The sprite king had been the first to concede to Fomoria, and with his loose tongue, he was on the list of the few they were to explicitly avoid, even though every precaution had been taken, including a full array of amulets sewn into their dresses. Under protest, Reuben had grudgingly produced them on Madame Chastain's order. Bristol hadn't hidden her gloating grin as he handed them over. She was glad he was left behind at the palace. He had sniffed at that, too.

After a few encounters with probing gentry, where the recruits handled themselves admirably, the officers finally loosened their leashes and stepped away to get refreshments of their own. Sashka sidled close, happy to be rid of the iron watch of Melizan, and whispered, "We kicked ass, didn't we?"

"Yes," Julia agreed, "and then some."

And then some. Julia was not prone to hyperbole, but maybe she knew tonight was one night to indulge in a little bit of cockiness. Sashka and Rose glowed with their success, while Avery went off to delight in the wonders of the Timbercrest banquet tables. That left Hollis free to monopolize Quin's attentions—and he didn't seem to mind. It was a true celebration, their smiles all real, and they danced, they reveled, and Bristol waited for Tyghan to free himself from his duties so she could dance with him, too—until she spotted someone on the far side of the room—someone she'd never expected to see in Elphame.

Someone from Bowskeep.

CHAPTER 83

The Timbercrest gardens were sweet with the scent of honey-suckle. Bristol and Princess Georgina strolled along a winding path, will-o'-the-wisps twinkling between ferns and trees. It was entrancing, but positively the last place Bristol had ever expected to walk with Mayor Georgie Topz.

Bristol had spotted her mingling with four other princesses in the royal party from Gildawey. Georgie's long crimson curls had thrown Bristol off, but the way she tapped her hand on her thigh like she was listening to her own unique music caught her attention, the ever-abiding Topz energy that had a beat of its own.

When Bristol approached her, the princess suggested a walk, eager to escape her royal duties. Once outside, she shed her glamoured hair, too. It was her mother's idea—the queen disapproved of her blunt blond cut. "Unbecoming of a Gildawey princess," she said, imitating her mother's queenly air, but the roll of her eyes was pure Mayor Topz. "And how is Elphame treating you?" she asked.

"It's been rocky, but things are going better now," Bristol answered. "I worry about my sisters, though. Have you seen them?"

"Yes," she reported cheerfully. "Quite a bit, actually. They're doing well. Harper's always lugging armfuls of books in or out of the library—

she's on a research binge, it seems—and Cat's been in town several times driving her new little car. Looks like they came into some money? I'm guessing that's because of you."

"My father, actually. Sonja was able to sell his painting for a lot more money than we ever dreamed."

"Hmm. Isn't that . . . fortuitous."

Bristol thought it suspicious too, and still wondered about the anonymous buyer. But right now it was helping her sisters, and it might be months before the da Vinci sketches were certified authentic and money came in from them. She had other matters that were far more pressing than unknown buyers who had money to burn. "I never would have guessed that you were fae. You act so . . . mortal."

Georgie laughed. "I've been in Bowskeep for a long time."

"Do you ever use magic there?"

She grimaced like she was sharing a dark confession. "Occasionally, like when I see a bit of paint chipping on a storefront, but I was never much of a student of magic. Most of my magic is the mortal kind— cooking up creative solutions that don't break the bank."

"What about my family? Did you know my mother was fae?"

"No. I don't go snooping into anyone's past, just like I don't want them snooping into mine. But I suspected she might be by the way she acted. There were a few telltale signs, like those scarves of hers, the colors and patterns were very similar to those of the northern lowlands. I never try to see through anyone's glamour, though. None of my business."

"What made you leave Gildawey?"

She laughed. "A tall, handsome mortal. Sixteen years ago my mother sent me to the mortal world on holiday, thinking it would get my head out of the clouds and prepare me for my future role as queen—which I had no interest in. Instead, I met Charles. The rest is history. And with four sisters to step up as queen, it's not like I left her high and dry."

"You gave up everything for him?"

"What did I give up? The gossip? The games? The secrets? The long curly tresses and a crown that gave me a headache? I truly love Bowskeep, and I gained a man who adores me and puts up with my chickens. I'd say I'm the winner here."

"When do you go back?"

"Tonight. I've done my daughterly duty, and I have a town to run. Plus, Faverolle chicks are due to hatch. I don't want to miss that. How about you? When are you coming home?"

"I'm not sure."

"Because you're part of the king's *elite squad*? Just what does that mean? You're a knight now?"

"No. Not exactly. I— Well . . ." Bristol stumbled, searching for words that weren't too revealing. "I'm afraid I can't say."

Georgie nodded, a frown pulling at the corner of her mouth. "Secrets. They've drawn you in already." She stopped and grabbed Bristol's hand, holding it tightly between her own. "Elphame's problems don't have to be yours."

"This time, I'm afraid they do."

"Squabbles between kingdoms? One or another is always beating their chest."

"This time it's more. The mortal world may be at risk too, not to mention, I made a promise."

"A promise," she repeated, nodding, as if understanding its weight. Her brow wrinkled. "Anything I can do?"

Bristol shook her head. "Just keep an eye on my sisters until I get home. That would give me peace of mind."

"Of course," she answered. "And I'll speak to my mother about the Gildan blades Danu requested—see if I can persuade her to step up production, though I'm not exactly on her hit parade at the moment. I'll do my best."

"The king would be very grateful."

"Just remember, you have a home and family waiting for you. Sal, too—it's the busy season. They gave you a timemark?"

"Yes."

"Good. Don't lose it." She hesitated for a moment, then added, "And you and the king. What's going on with that?"

Bristol's mouth fell open.

"You thought I didn't see? His eyes all but blinded the rest of the room when he spotted you at the top of the stairs."

Bristol's cheeks warmed. She had seen it, too. "I suppose we're an *item*, as my friend Sashka likes to put it," she admitted. "But we're not supposed to flaunt it tonight."

"Item?" Georgie huffed out a sharp breath. "Like something on a grocery list? I don't think so, unless it's one of those decadent hot chocolate desserts from Starky's Bakery on Main Street."

Bristol laughed, remembering the molten ganache cake Starky's was famous for. "Maybe it's something more like that."

"And how do you expect things to work out for you two?"

She searched for a clever reply to stop Georgie's musings, but instead a flood of unforeseen words stormed through her head. *I want to share my life with you. All of it.* Words that had nothing to do with going home. What should she tell Georgie? Expect?

Love. Another word sneaking in. It took root the moment she and Tyghan had said it to each other. Love. It was a big, dark door that led to imperfect meanings. Maybe she had been testing the meanings all along, trying to find one that best fit her and Tyghan. A definition that was practical. Solid. But what they had together was neither of those sturdy, reliable things. It was reckless and passionate, fragile and tender—and it was outrageously delicious, like a steaming chocolate cake. It was all the things that could spell disaster. But it made every inch of her feel alive in a way she never had before, so she didn't care.

Georgie's brows rose, still waiting for an answer.

Bristol knew her long silence spoke volumes, but she wasn't ready to admit anything. She shrugged. "No expectations."

The mayor's lips pursed to the side like she was looking the other way on a parking violation. "I understand," she answered. "Shall we continue our—"

A strange silence suddenly fell. They heard the distant echo of the herald's trumpet and the dull roar of the ballroom instantly stopped like the party was over. And then the herald's faint announcement. They both tweaked their heads to the side, confused, wondering if they had misheard.

"It can't be," Bristol whispered, but they both spun and ran back to the Timbercrest ballroom.

It was late, almost the midnight hour, the reverie a loud tipsy roar, wild things darting like drunken spring swallows overhead, when the herald's trumpet blew again. Bewilderment washed over the crowd. All the kingdoms of Elphame had long since arrived. Tyghan, Kasta, and Quin were in deep discussion with the king of Greymarch and the queen of Boghollow. Eris and Madame Chastain were equally engaged with the goblin king and queen. Everyone looked to the top of the staircase where a commotion was stirring, and then the herald announced with a stammer, "King—King Kormick of Fomoria."

Tyghan was sure the herald had made a mistake, but then a tall figure stepped out of the shadows. His blond hair and scarred face were unmistakable. He wore a long, formal, bloodred coat with swirling black cording. His crown was black, too, a circlet that glimmered against his golden hair. No doubt, every polished button on his coat bore an enchantment of protection—and retribution—for unwelcome magics.

Hushed gasps rippled through the room. Everyone was instantly sobered by Kormick's appearance. Tyghan glanced to King Roderick, who was moving through the throngs toward the bottom of the stairs to receive the Fomorians. As he passed he whispered, "I had no idea he was coming. Fomoria's never come before."

Tyghan hissed. He turned to Kasta and Quin. "I'll stay here and keep him at the bottom of the stairs for as long as I can. Find the recruits and usher them out—discreetly—and apprise them of new protocols. I don't want any of them interacting with Kormick."

Kasta and Quin melted back into the crowd.

"Restraint, Your Majesty," Madame Chastain whispered from behind Tyghan. "Any fight—magical or otherwise—in these close quarters could prove disastrous. Six of those warriors behind him are formidable wizards with itchy hands."

Tyghan's hands itched, too, a ball of vengeful energy at his fingertips begging to be released, but Eris echoed the High Witch's message of restraint and added, "Remember, he still has Cael."

Kormick ambled down the stairs, soaking in the hundreds of eyes fixed on him like he was already the king of Elphame strutting before his subjects. A dozen of his bull-chested warriors trailed behind him.

When he reached the bottom stair, King Roderick stepped forward to greet him, but Kormick brushed him off and walked straight toward Tyghan, who stood dead center in his path.

The two powerful kings met eye to eye, chest to chest, neither willing to give up ground. Tension wound tight, knights from every kingdom stepping into place to protect their monarchs.

"What are you doing here, Kormick?" Tyghan asked.

"Fomoria is a kingdom of Elphame," he said, a smug smile curling his lips. "Why wouldn't I be here? I came to celebrate Beltane Eve with all the other kings and queens of faerie." But there was no celebration in his dark eyes as they scanned the silent hall. He waved his hand in the air. "Please, resume the party," he called. "Dance! Drink! Isn't that why we're all here?"

The chatter and music resumed immediately to mollify him, though certainly conversations now jumped in a new direction. *Is Timbercrest Castle surrounded by the restless dead? Do we dare leave?* Those who had stepped back inched only slightly closer, still wary of the animosity blistering the air between the two rulers.

"You're not a recognized kingdom of Elphame, Kormick. Fomoria has never contributed a single tithe to the Elphame union except a tithe of chaos."

"That will be remedied soon enough. Elphame is about to change for the better. And if you behave yourself this time, your brother will be back home before you know it."

Tyghan trembled with rage. *Behave?* But he knew the game Kormick played, trying to find out what the Danu Nation was up to, and he swallowed his burning impulse to throttle Kormick. "I already offered to settle this matter with single combat—just you and me."

Kormick's lip twisted with distaste. "Such an antiquated concept—and barbaric. It's beneath me. Let's try to be civilized, shall we? And not ruin the party with talk of tithes and combat. It will all be settled soon enough. Now, if you'll excuse me—"

Tyghan saw his knights moving through the hall gathering up recruits. Quin and Kasta ushered Sashka and Rose out the door. Cully was leading Hollis out to a private place where they could speak freely. There was no sign of Julia, Avery, or Bristol. Tyghan needed to keep Kormick occupied a little longer.

"Where's your demon charmer tonight?" he asked, trying to prick Kormick's cool exterior and delay him. "You didn't bring her along to entertain everyone? Pluck a few eyes from sockets and juggle them?"

Kormick stopped short, the first sign of rage blazing in his eyes, his voice low and full of threat. "Do not push me too far, Trénallis."

"What are you afraid of? That everyone will find out your little secret? Too late for keeping up appearances. We know where the demons come from—and who controls them."

"You know nothing. And I won't have you spreading lies about me. Remember who still has your brother."

"I have no proof that my brother is even alive."

"You have a king's word. My word. That's all you need."

Tyghan bit back a laugh, even as his fingers curled into a fist. "Your word is worth as much as a—"

"Well, hello, Your Majesty! Welcome!" Melizan crooned as she stepped between them with crystal goblets of golden wine in each hand. "Excuse my brother. Where are your manners, Tyghan?" She held one of the goblets out to Kormick. "A little something to revive you after your long journey?"

Kormick smiled, his full attention raking over Melizan's dipping neckline, her bosom glistening with golden oil that hadn't been there just moments ago. The heady scent of bergamot filled the air. "Princess Melizan. Always a delight to see you."

He took the goblet from her and held it up to the light, judging it for poison. Melizan stepped closer, wrapping her hand over his, and brought his glass to her mouth, taking a generous sip. She licked her lips seductively. "I can assure you, it's delicious—and safe."

The distraction gave Tyghan a moment to scan the ballroom again, but the crowd had milled closer, blocking much of his view. Eris stood some distance behind Kormick and showed his open palms, indicating recruits were still missing. Where could they be? Maybe they had spotted Kormick and left on their own?

Melizan tried to coax Kormick to dance with her, but he said he had kings and queens eager to speak with him yet. He kissed her hand. "But I promise to dance with you later." More revelers stepped up, coached by Eris, to keep Kormick at hand, but his warriors were spreading out, weaving through the throngs.

From behind, a hand caught Tyghan's arm.

"What is—" The question froze on Bristol's lips as the view became clear. She stopped short, staring at Kormick. Her eyes creased with confusion as if she wasn't sure who he was, though his black crown made it obvious.

Kormick opened his arms toward her, expecting an embrace. "Bristol, so good to see you again."

Her confusion deepened. "*Mick?*"

"Hmm, yes." His finger traced the line on his face that traveled from his forehead to his jaw. "A scar like this attracts attention in your world, so I concealed it, but in Fomoria we wear them with honor. But it's the same me. Though here you must call me Your Majesty."

Bristol took a step back, her head shaking. "You—" She turned and left, pushing her way through the crowd.

Tyghan watched her leave. *She knows the king of Fomoria?* "You've already met?" he said to Kormick, struggling to keep the strain from his voice.

Kormick laughed. "You thought I wouldn't investigate Bristol and her sisters, too? I can assure you, you're wasting your time. All purely mortal. Useless. None of them have their mother's talent."

"I'm not investigating anything. She's only here to find her father."

"Who we both know is dead. My first order of business in that shabby little town was to confirm it. A nasty encounter with a car, I understand. Such a dangerous world. But surely that news made you as happy as it made me. I know what he did to you."

"If it made you so happy, why didn't you kill him as soon as you found Maire?"

Kormick shrugged. "The give and take of life. We all have to strike bargains. His death wasn't as important to me as Maire's compliance. I needed her more than I needed to kill off her frivolous affair with your knight."

Tyghan turned to leave. Kormick deluded himself that he was projecting an image of a just and fair ruler to Elphame—his ego demanded it—but privately, he didn't bother to maintain any pretense of innocence, and a conversation with him was only going to spiral downward. The restraint the High Witch had ordered was getting harder for Tyghan to come by. But only two steps away, Kormick crowed a few last words at Tyghan's back, eager to fan the flames he had managed to ignite in just a few minutes. "My brief time in Bowskeep wasn't a complete loss, though. I understand why you're using Bristol. She's a passionate creature, isn't she? We had some tasty moments together. I hope you're enjoying my table scraps—"

Light exploded behind Tyghan's eyes. He spun and swung. His fist sent Kormick flying backward, tumbling across the floor, his crown sailing in one direction, his goblet shattering in another. Partygoers screamed, tripping over robes and gowns in a rush to clear the center of the room. Knights drew swords, and Kormick's warriors rushed forward, but in a quick magnanimous gesture, Kormick lifted his hand to stop them. He did it swiftly and elegantly, like he had rehearsed the moment, orchestrating every step. He swayed and got to his feet, grabbing his crown and putting it back atop his head. "Go on, everyone. Back to your party.

Please. I don't want trouble. King Trénallis and I simply had a small difference of opinion. Continue on. It's Beltane Eve, after all."

Hobs hurried forward to sweep broken crystal and mop the wine. Swords were hesitantly sheathed. Music resumed, a pluck at a time, but most kept their distance, hugging the perimeters of the ballroom. Tyghan still waited for Kormick to retaliate, but he only wiped the blood from his lip with the back of his hand and staggered forward until he stood almost chest to chest with Tyghan once again.

"Thank you," he whispered. "I have witnesses now. You've just confirmed to a roomful of royals that you're the king with violent impulses and that I'm the clear choice to rule Elphame. It will make the transition so much smoother. My reign will be welcomed with open arms." He tugged on his cuffs, smoothing out imaginary wrinkles, before he left to join the party. "And just a bit of advice, Trénallis—no charge. I would send Bristol home sooner rather than later. If Maire finds out that you have her daughter, you can be certain things won't go well for you."

A thousand thoughts blazed through Tyghan's head, not the least of which was how he would make Kormick suffer once he had his brother back, but his expression remained cool, ruinous. "The fact that you haven't already informed her that Bristol is here tells me it wouldn't go well for you, either."

The smugness drained from Kormick's face. "I guess when it comes down to it," Tyghan continued, "even you can't be sure how a monster will react when a bargain she's made has been compromised."

CHAPTER 84

Melizan's fingers dug into Bristol's upper arm. "Slow down," she ordered. "Smile. Members of the elite squad do not get flustered—they get even. You're the one in control. Say it. Believe it."

Bristol obediently slowed as they passed guests already buzzing with gossip. "Right," she answered through a clenched smile. "I'm the one in control."

Melizan tightened her grip. "You don't believe me? You're the one with the upper hand now. You know something Kormick doesn't—you're bloodmarked. If there's one thing all fae hate—whether it's forest sprites, or the powerful malevolent kind like Kormick—it's secrets. And now, thanks to Kasta, other secrets are swirling all over Elphame and he's mad with curiosity. Why do you think he's here? Worse, the secrets are festering and multiplying in his own imagination. Those are the most treacherous kind. Remember that. Secrets are power."

"I detest secrets. I've been running from them my entire life."

"Is that what you plan to do now? Run?"

"*No.*"

Melizan smiled. It was a short answer, but Bristol's tone held a lethal edge. She pulled her closer like they were best friends. "Good. Now, how is it that you know Kormick?" she asked.

"I don't know Kormick," Bristol answered. "I knew a slick-mouthed thirty-year-old cyclist named Mick who gave tours on the coast. He showered me with attention just after my father died, and I fell for it. Then he disappeared entirely. That man in there, he—"

"He used you," Melizan finished.

"For what? A quick screw in a storage room?"

Melizan laughed. "People glamour themselves for far less. But for him it was probably a spicy diversion while he tried to find out if you were bloodmarked."

"Just because my mother was fae? How would he even know about her? And why the king? Doesn't he have slimy minions to do his bidding?"

Melizan walked cautiously around the question. "Kings don't leave important work to underlings, and when there's a desperate race all over Elphame to find another bloodmarked, not a single stone is left unturned."

"That's what I feel like right now, a big stupid stone. And an angry one."

"Anger is good. Rage is better. It sharpens the claws."

"Anger and rage don't begin to describe my state of mind right now. That sick bastard—" Bristol drew in a sharp breath. "My god. My sisters. What if he—"

"I don't know what he did with them when he was there, but right now, your sisters are well guarded. Tyghan posted four knights at your house as soon as he found out you were bloodmarked."

Melizan watched the fire in Bristol's cheeks fade. Her voice went flat. "My sisters need to be guarded. What have I done?"

"The good news is, Kormick had no suspicions about you, or he wouldn't have left any of you in that drab little town of yours. And you haven't performed any magic since yesterday, so I'm certain he didn't catch any scent off you, especially not in a full ballroom."

They reached Melizan's guestroom at the end of the hallway, and she pulled Bristol inside. "You only have a few minutes to get yourself together. We need to go back before you're missed and everyone assumes Kormick scared you senseless. The show must go on."

Melizan crossed the room to her dressing table and grabbed a vial. She lifted the stopper and sniffed the contents. "Gardenia will be perfect. And a bit of hyacinth. Some rose, too, I think." She chuckled. "Kormick will hate it. It should make it easy for you to avoid him." She dabbed a bit on each of Bristol's wrists and another dab on the cleavage just above her dipping neckline. "There. You're a spring bouquet. Positively not his favorite."

"And bergamot is?" Bristol said, eyeing Melizan's chest.

"Exactly," Melizan answered, and smiled. "Word does get around."

A furrow creased Bristol's brow. "How do you do it?" she asked. "Smile? Laugh? Pretend that none of this matters to you?"

Melizan placed the vial back on the table. "You're not a good listener, are you? I don't need to get rattled. I get even. Now, on to other matters." She drew the dagger sheathed at her side. "The High Witch needs a lock of your hair so she can keep tabs on you—just in case." She explained the power of freshly cut hair. "The magic only lasts two or three hours at most or they would have done it earlier. Quin and Kasta are doing the same with the other recruits. Just a bit of insurance in case you should be lured away."

"I have no intention of being lured anywhere."

"And yet I lured you right here to this room, no questions asked." Melizan turned the dagger in her hand so the blade shimmered in the candlelight.

Bristol swallowed, eyeing the knife, then reached out and grabbed the blade from her. She cut off a lock and handed it back to Melizan.

"Make no mistake," Melizan said as she tucked the strands of hair into her pocket. "We may all belittle Kormick to vent our anger, but he's not in his current position because he isn't smart, ruthless, and powerful. He's a demigod, same as Tyghan. You'd be a fool to under-estimate him."

Bristol barely nodded, her eyes narrowing.

"Well?" Melizan demanded.

"Believe me, I don't underestimate him, but now it will be his mis-fortune that he ever underestimated me. Let's get back to the party."

CHAPTER 85

When Bristol returned to the ballroom, her eyes landed on Mick first thing. He glowed with the attention of being center stage, his coat tailored to perfection, the deep jewel red fabric commanding and threatening. He was a strange mix of beauty and terror, his allure both riveting and deadly. She had seen the edges of that back in Bowskeep, a certain danger in him, but here it was unveiled in full splendor. He danced with a noble from the Silverwing kingdom who seemed equal parts frightened by and enthralled with her dancing partner. Maybe the danger he presented was a thrilling diversion for her.

But Mick wasn't without his weaknesses.

If there's one thing fae hate, it's secrets.

Maybe him most of all. Bristol remembered their last encounter in the alley on Mug Ruith Bridge. The urgency he tried to hide. *Why are you here? Who told you he was alive?* Secrets. Those burning questions had driven him to a dark alley in the middle of an enemy nation. When she told him it was none of his business, his control slipped. His charm vanished. His eyes lost their glamour. *Be careful how you speak to me. One day you may regret it.*

She regretted everything about him, especially her own weakness when she had let him into her life, however briefly. Now it was her turn to inflict regret.

Kormick is mad with curiosity.

He was about to get a little madder. She might not have his magical powers, but she could throw him off his game.

"He knows you're staring. Don't give him that satisfaction."

Bristol whirled.

Tyghan held out his hand to her. "We're not allowed more than one dance together, so let's make the most of this one."

That was Eris's counsel, too. He didn't want everyone to think Tyghan favored Bristol for any other reason than she was a valued part of the mysterious elite squad. He was to dance with everyone equally. And so was she.

"Of course, Your Majesty," she said, offering a small curtsy, knowing everyone's eyes were watching them—including Kormick's.

Tyghan drew her into his arms, just a bit closer than was proper, but among the fae, proper was a loose term. "I'm sorry about my rushed exit," she whispered. "He caught me off guard. I hope I didn't ruin the aura of mystery."

"You didn't ruin anything." He told her that Kormick's sudden presence had everyone so shaken most barely saw his fist send Kormick flying to the floor. "Which was pretty hard to miss."

"You did *what*?"

"He said things to provoke me, and it worked. He's trying to paint me as the aggressor to the other kingdoms."

"Surely the kingdoms know—"

"They know. His presence here is just a warning to them all that he's watching them. But it's also a sign he's concerned. Part of this is my fault—we've been spreading rumors to distract him."

Bristol smiled, her mind already toying with rumors of her own. "Our wicked minds think so much alike. What did he say to provoke you?"

"It doesn't matter."

But Bristol already knew the answer. She looked down, her cheeks burning. "He told you about us, didn't he?"

Tyghan lifted her chin. "Smile," he said, reminding her they were being watched. "It doesn't matter. He doesn't matter, at least not as far as you and I are concerned. He made no secret about using you. I'm sorry. I'm sorry you've been dragged into this. I'm sorry that I—"

"Smile, Your Majesty," she said, forcing one of her own. "Add a laugh, too. No apologies. He isn't worth it."

And then he was suddenly there. Kormick. Cutting in. "May I, King Trénallis?"

Tyghan's eyes went molten, betraying his relationship with Bristol. "No. Find someone else to—"

"Your Majesty," Bristol intervened, "of course I will dance with King Kormick. He and I have so much to catch up on. Don't we, *Mick*?" She leaned close and whispered in Tyghan's ear. "Remember, everyone is watching, and your elite squad is not afraid. You shouldn't be either. I've got this."

"I don't—"

She took Mick's hand before Tyghan could protest again, and Kormick pulled her away to another part of the dance floor.

"What did you say to him?" Kormick immediately asked her.

Bristol warmed inside. New secrets were already eating at him. "Nothing important."

"It must have been important enough that he didn't take another swing at me. What power do you have over him?"

"Oh, you'd be surprised."

"That's not an answer."

She smiled. "It's the only answer you're going to get."

Heat flickered behind his pupils. His beautiful blond hair tumbled over his brow. He tugged her closer as they spun on the dance floor. "Whatever scent you have on, you need to get a new one."

"Spring bouquet. I like it," Bristol chirped.

He frowned. "I thought I told you to go home. There's nothing for you here."

"Why do you even care, Mick? I mean nothing to you."

"You mean something. And I don't want you chasing after lies. Your father isn't here. I have it on good authority, he's dead."

"Well, aren't you a delightful dance partner? Always bearing such good news."

"I only come with the truth. I even asked around for you. See? I'm the honorable one after all, in spite of what Trénallis may have told you."

"Honorable? You must use that term loosely. Forcing yourself on Elphame as the new ruler hardly seems honorable."

"Not forcing—simply campaigning—as they all do."

But not with an army of demons, she mused. "How far will you go for this campaign?"

"As far as I need to go, as any good leader would. There are no limits or borders to prudent governance."

His need ran deep. She saw it in his eyes, the flame that ignited in them when he spoke of it. She had no doubt that the mortal world was in jeopardy too, just as Eris had already warned.

"Fomoria's been systematically excluded from the rule of Elphame for centuries," he continued. "Our turn has come. Trénallis and his kind twist everything. Is he the one who said your father was alive?"

Another burning question. It was definitely secrets that had driven him to barge in on the celebrations. Bristol paused as if carefully considering her answer.

Kormick's smile vanished, and he gave her a warning shake. "Tell me."

Only three small secrets, and he was close to unraveling—and she was only getting started. Maybe his agreeable facade required a strong magic he couldn't sustain. She had never tested him back in Bowskeep. She had only swallowed his lies. When grief consumed her, her caution disappeared.

"No," she answered with dramatic flair, hearing her practiced pitch in every singsong word she uttered, a story, a weaving, a splash of paint. A spider knitting a shroud. "It wasn't Trénallis who told me. It was Cael."

He laughed. "Cael? The king's brother? He's been in my custody for months. You'll have to do better than that."

"I'm well aware that you're holding him, but he told me in a dream. Cael is a dreamwalker."

Kormick huffed out a disbelieving chuckle. "No, he isn't."

Bristol eyed her hand resting on Mick's shoulder, his thick locks only inches away. The vein at his temple ticked with growing irritation.

"Interesting. That's what Tyghan said, too. He was full of denial. But the palace gossips say—" She shrugged, adding a secretive smirk. "Never mind. I think our dance is over. You go about your business, Mick, and I'll go about mine."

She saw it only briefly, his control snapping, a flash of fury, and in an instant, everything changed. He spun with her, as if it was a turn in the dance, but—

The room went dark. The dance floor disappeared. Everyone disappeared. Bristol's own breath disappeared. All she felt was the iron grip of Kormick's arm around her back, and the clutch of ice in her throat.

The thing Tyghan hated about being king was there was no slipping into the shadows. No magic on the sly. Even from the darkness of an alcove he couldn't watch without being watched, and there was no pretending he was happy about Bristol being in Kormick's arms. Anything could happen. So he openly stared, his eyes never leaving them.

Melizan, Eris, and Madame Chastain scrutinized their movements too, and from various positions around the room, so did Esmee, Olivia, and his officers. They knew what Kormick was capable of. He and Bristol circled the floor, other dancers instinctively staying clear. Bristol smiled, laughed, but Tyghan noted that with each movement of her lips, Kormick grew stiffer, his expression grimmer.

"Whatever she's telling him, it's not putting him at ease," Eris moaned. "Doesn't she know—"

"She knows," Melizan said.

What is she up to? Tyghan wondered.

"If they would stop turning, I could properly read their lips," Julia said, stepping up beside Tyghan. "They're discussing something about Cael."

Eris hissed. "This was not part of our plan. I don't like it."

"Kormick wasn't part of our plans either," Melizan replied, "and yet he's here."

"They've danced long enough," Tyghan whispered to Melizan. "Go over there. Cut in. He promised you a dance."

But before Melizan had even taken a step, Bristol and Kormick vanished. His warriors around the room disappeared, too. It happened so swiftly, many simply continued to stare at the empty space they had just occupied. Except for Tyghan. He cursed and turned immediately to Madame Chastain. "The lock! Give me the lock!"

"No," Eris said, stepping between them, lecturing him on the reasons why it was too dangerous for him to breathe the smoke.

Tyghan knew the dangers. He didn't care. He pushed Eris aside, his hand outstretched. Fire ignited from his fingertips. "He can't be far yet. Give me the fucking lock!"

By now, Dalagorn, Melizan, and Julia had closed in, providing a shield from curious eyes.

"Lower your voice," Eris said. "We don't want to panic the entire room."

Kasta and Cosette spread out to calm fears.

Madame Chastain already had her own ball of fire hovering over her hand, and she and Eris leaned close as she held the lock of hair over the flames. Each strand twisted and curled, turning to bright orange embers, and finally dissolved into smoke that she and Eris inhaled. "*Aramascue odemas*," they chanted as they closed their eyes. *Open my eyes as hers.*

"The garden," Eris said. "She sees trees, an arbor of wisteria nearby."

"And a fountain," the High Witch added.

Tyghan shifted from one foot to the other, barely able to hold back. The gardens were vast, with multiple fountains. These details were not helping. "What else? What else does she see?" he demanded.

"A stone bench . . ."

Quin was already distributing weapons. Cully strapped on his quiver of arrows. Partygoers murmured on the other side of the room as Avery and Sashka kept King Roderick at bay with cheerful small talk.

"She's looking down near her feet," Eris said, "She sees a red starburst—"

"Surrounded by a white circle of granite," Madame Chastain finished.

"*A terrace*," Cully said. "It's in the lower south gardens. I saw it when I was securing the grounds today. That's where he took her."

CHAPTER 86

B ristol's body jerked to a sudden stop, like she had crashed into a
wall. She gasped, drawing breath at last. Her skin was ice, and
she shivered beneath Kormick's hard grip. He loosened his hold
on her.

"We're done," he said, "only when I say we're done."

Bristol gaped at the unfamiliar surroundings—the nearby fountain,
the trees, the tile beneath her feet—and listened to the night birds—the
same songs she had heard earlier. She guessed he had brought her to
one of the hidden terraces deep in the Timbercrest gardens.

There was never a more perfect invitation to lash out and Bristol
jumped on the moment. "You stupid, arrogant—" She lunged at his
face, grabbing his hair, digging her nails into his cheek. "You scared the
shit out me just so you could—"

Kormick grabbed at her flailing arms, tearing her sleeve from her
shoulder as they struggled. He managed to get hold of her wrists, wincing as he yanked her hands away from his face. Strands of his hair
ripped free, still wound between her fingers.

He twisted her arms behind her back. "Have you lost your mind?"
he screamed. "Do you know what I could do to you?"

An angry welt on his cheek beaded with blood, and his face flushed
with rage. Panic gripped Bristol's muscles, her knees going weak. She'd

meant to be convincing when she attacked him, but didn't want to die in the process. He jerked her closer, his hips pressed to hers.

"I'm sorry," she said, true fear gripping her. "I was frightened. I didn't mean to—" She shuddered. "I'm very sorry."

His breaths calmed, and the rage in his eyes receded. "That's better," he said, appeased by her groveling. "I forget sometimes that your kind are unaccustomed to our ways, like leaping from one place to another." He freed her wrists, and she slipped her hands into her pockets, shaking her fingers free of his hair.

"Is that what that was? A leap?" she asked.

"It's known by many names. Wolfleap, nightjump. A dark-adieu is my preferred term. A quick movement over a short distance. Only the most powerful fae, like myself, are capable of it."

"I couldn't breathe."

"Only for a short time," he chided. "You lived, didn't you? Now, give me your hand."

"My hand?" She didn't have to feign fear. "Are you planning to leap again?" she asked.

"No, I'm planning to dance. As I said, we're done when I say we're done."

The pompous brute. This dance hadn't gone quite the way she'd planned. She considered setting his coat on fire as a distraction for escape, but she couldn't reveal her abilities and there was still more she needed to do. The deal wasn't done yet. She pulled her hands from her pockets, and he drew her into his arms, with only the music of the trickling fountain to dance by.

"There," he whispered. "Much better." His finger stroked her bare shoulder where the fabric had torn away. "It appears I've damaged your lovely dress, but I like it better this way."

Powerful fae or not, he was back to his game-playing self, trying to use her as he sought out information. "I'll be sure to tell my seamstress," she replied. "But we're not doing anything for old times' sake, Mick. So get it out of your head."

He laughed, his eyes still undressing her. "For now. Let's talk about something else. Tell me more about Cael and the palace gossip."

This was something he was more passionate about than his lecherous thoughts for her—and she would happily spoon feed it to him. But she couldn't seem too eager.

"It's not important. And I'm not sure I should be telling you—"

"Shall we take another leap?"

"No!" she answered quickly. "But I already told you, Tyghan adamantly denied the gossip."

"But?"

She frowned like she was still reluctant to share sensitive news. "But my seamstress said it's been a dark secret at the palace for years. It seems no one wants to admit they have a dreamwalker in their bloodline— something about nasty betrayals. But the gossip is pretty damning. Even Cael's nursemaid from when he was a child admitted to the palace chef that he was a dreamwalker."

"Courts love their gossip. How do you even know it was Cael you saw in your dream?"

"Dreams. He came to me more than once. And of course, I can't be certain it was him, but when I saw his portrait hanging in the palace, I gasped. Except for the filthy, ragged clothing he wore in my dream, he and the man in the portrait were identical."

"Ragged clothes?"

Bristol guessed that whatever state of repair Cael's clothes were in after being abducted, they weren't pristine and that Mick hadn't provided him with fresh ones during his captivity. "They were dirty and torn. His face was filthy too, so I could be wrong. The gossip could be wrong. But the dreams were real enough to me, so I have to stay and search for my father, at least for a while longer. There you have it, that's the reason I'm still here."

"What did Cael say to you in this so-called dream?"

"Only that my father was still alive. But he said it like he was surprised too. Maybe he discovered my father on one of his dreamwalks?"

And then in an offhand remark, she added, "I know. The High Witch chastised me for listening to gossip too. She said my dream was only wishful thinking and nothing more. Still, there's been hushed rumors circulating around the palace that he's been visiting others . . ."

Kormick didn't respond, but his fingers dug at her waist, and she knew by his silence that she had made the sale, that he'd be going home with a Keats painting and scarf he hadn't planned on buying. The deal was done. *Others. What others?* His focus was splintered, already consumed with what Cael might be telling them. His grip became a vise around her as they continued the pretense of their dance, and a new concern jolted her—that he wouldn't leave her behind. Her mind reeled, trying to think of an escape.

But then something else caught her attention.

A mouse.

It skirted the edge of the terrace, then stopped, sitting up on its hind legs. The white fur of its belly gleamed in the moonlight, and its shiny black eyes shifted from Bristol to the sky. She followed its gaze and saw a hawk gliding high above her, cutting through the light of the moon. *Hollis. Rose.* They were signaling her. Maybe—

The roar of a lioness shattered the silence as she leapt onto the edge of the terrace, crouched, ready to leap again. Kormick jerked Bristol closer. In the next instant, a circle of knights surrounded them, weapons drawn, spears and arrows aimed.

"Let her go," Tyghan ordered.

Kormick smiled as he surveyed the circle of knights. He turned back to Tyghan. "Is this really how you want it to go, Trénallis?" And with his last word, his warriors materialized, forming another circle just behind the knights, weapons raised, the wizards' hands poised for mayhem. "Now, this is a prickly situation, isn't it?" Kormick mused, his smile severe and smug. "It certainly could end badly—for one of us." And with a bare motion of his hand, like he was swatting away a gnat near his face, the moonlit sky behind him unfurled like spilled ink, a dark stain rolling across it until it was endless, a lethal black cloud of

the restless dead. It was both stunning and suffocating, and the growing breadth of it made the attack at the training grounds look like an
insignificant scuffle.

An inexhaustible army.

"Did you think I would come here without an escort?" Kormick
asked.

Bristol's gaze shot to Tyghan. "We only wanted to finish our dance
out here, Your Majesty. That's all. It's only a misunderstanding," she
explained, working to calm tempers like she was soothing a squabble at
Sal's on a Friday night. She also needed to preserve the precious ground
she had just gained—the freshly pulled hair in her pocket. "Right,
Mick? A misunderstanding. It's my fault, actually. I'm the one who
said I wanted to catch up, and the ballroom was so noisy. It was easier
to talk out here. Let's not make this more than it is." *My fault.* She was
offering Kormick a way out, because he would never give an inch to
Tyghan, but she also knew the secret she planted was assaulting his
thoughts. All he wanted to do was make a quick exit. *Who else had Cael
spoken to? What else was he saying? What was he revealing?* The burning
questions had probably already quadrupled in his mind. "*Please*," she
pleaded, knowing groveling was gold to him. "Let this go."

He eyed her for a long while, his grip on her still tight, then looked
back at Tyghan. "Go on, Trénallis. Go back to your party. Count this
as the last mercy I'm granting you. Take her with you. I have more
important matters to tend." He kissed Bristol's hand as a goodbye, and
with a bare nod, bid a dark-adieu. His warriors and wizards vanished
with him.

Quiet, sobering seconds followed as they stared at the retreating
cloud, everyone horribly aware they couldn't have survived such a
massive attack, but Bristol noted the low sounds too, a hiss from Quin,
Dalagorn cracking his knuckles, the quiet rumble from Kasta's throat,
the furious rage at their own glaring vulnerability they had yet to find a
remedy for. Kormick's power was staggering, and they had likely only
witnessed a fraction of it.

Once the menacing cloud was gone, questions were unleashed in a massive flood, a torrent swirling around Bristol from all sides, but Tyghan pushed past the others. "What the hell did—"

She held her finger to her lips, still wary of unwelcome ears hearing what she had to say. "No one say a word," she ordered. "Follow me to my room. I need to speak to you all alone."

"But—"

"*Now*," she said, because time was of the essence. Giddiness rose inside her, and she had to suppress a smile all the way back to her chamber.

Tyghan walked beside her, strangely silent as she had ordered, but whispers trailed behind her as the rest followed.

What did Kormick do to her?

I don't like this.

Could she be enchanted?

But the amulets—

Unless—

He's a demigod—

Secrets. Oh, how they all hated them.

But she was certain they'd find this revelation worthy of the wait.

The opponent's game piece had been played.

And now so had hers.

CHAPTER 87

The room bustled with impatience as everyone crowded in. Kasta eyed Tyghan as if to say, *She's the one giving orders now?* Esmee and Olivia immediately checked Bristol for enchantments, and Melizan and Cosette took up positions on the end of the bed, eager to watch a show.

As soon as Tyghan secured the door, Bristol whirled, facing everyone, no longer able to hide her excitement. She dug her hands into her pockets, and when she pulled them out, she stretched out her open hands for everyone to see. The faint strands of blond hair were barely visible against her palms. She looked at Madame Chastain. "Please tell me this is enough. It has to be enough."

The High Witch stepped closer, examining Bristol's palms. "Enough for what?"

"It's Kormick's hair, and it's freshly torn from his scalp. Now you can see where he's going."

"It's a scant amount, probably sufficient, but I already know where he's going. Back to Fomoria."

"Possibly," Bristol answered. "If that's where he's keeping Cael, because that is exactly where he's going right this minute. He's on his way to see Cael."

"Tonight? Why would he do that? He's had Cael for months."

Bristol smiled and glanced at Melizan. "Because he hates secrets, and tonight I told him one."

"What did you tell him?" Tyghan asked cautiously.

"That Cael is a dreamwalker."

Eris jumped up from his seat on the chaise. "*A what?* He is no such thing!"

"I know! But for the next few hours, Kormick doesn't know that. And right now, he's mad with curiosity. If you want to know where he's keeping Cael, now's your chance." She looked at her open palms strewn with blond hair.

Melizan hooted with delight. "What are we waiting for? Let's get to work."

Heavy sofas were pushed aside, a small table and three chairs pulled to the center of the room, and every hair was meticulously plucked from Bristol's hands like each strand was gold. Her pockets were searched for more.

Other than Tyghan, Quin was the most familiar with the Fomorian landscape, but Cully had an unusual eye for detail, so he was chosen along with Quin to inhale the enchanted smoke. The rest circled around them in the darkened room as Madame Chastain held Kormick's hairs to the flame hovering in her hand. Cully and Quin whispered, *Aramascue odemas*, and as the wisps of smoke curled upward, they breathed them in.

At first there was nothing.

Cully and Quin both reported there was only darkness, and more darkness.

The air wrung tight with the waiting, but Kasta whispered that darkness was to be expected. Kormick was probably riding his horse through the night sky at incredible speed.

Minutes passed with still nothing, and Bristol gripped the back of Cully's chair.

A crease deepened between Quin's brows. "Black. That's all I see."

Bristol's throat grew dry. Maybe a handful of torn hair wasn't enough?

"Wait. A ribbon," Cully said. "White in the moonlight. Balor Pass. Yes, it's the pass. Kormick's looking down at it."

"The sea," Quin intervened. "He's not going to his palace. He's passing over the inlet to the northern forests."

Another long, dark minute passed. Only forest and more forest. Madame Chastain was down to just a few hairs.

"A marker," Cully said. "Cross-stones. And now a village."

Quin cursed. "More forest."

"Queen's Cliff," Cully said. "He's headed for the cliff. I know it. There's nothing else in that direction."

"Just tell us what you see. Don't guess," Eris ordered.

Cully smiled, his eyes still closed. "There it is. Sheer rock. I see the fucking cliff."

Tyghan whispered that Queen's Cliff was an ancient rocky fortress built on the top of a mountain in the middle of a deep ocean inlet. Halfway up, the mountain was ringed with thick forests. Long ago it served as a lookout for the northern isles. Impenetrable. Harsh. Remote. The water that lapped its shores held all manner of deadly creatures. The fortress was mostly forgotten, and now absorbed into the northern border of Fomoria. It was considered a no-man's-land, but it could be a good place to stash a prisoner. Especially if you didn't care about their comfort. There was no escape, even without guards.

"He's getting off his horse," Quin said.

Cully and Quin described the path Kormick walked, a forest clearing, a tunnel through overgrown brush, a rocky plateau, the torches that were lit, the stone steps he climbed, the rough rock hallway, a door.

"I only see two sleepy guards."

"One of them is unlocking the door, taking the torch in."

"Kormick's stepping inside now."

Quin and Cully were both nodding.

"*What?*" Eris said. "What does he see?"

"Cael," Quin answered. "He's there. He's alive. They've got a collar on him."

"And he's squinting against the torchlight and cursing," Cully added.

"You can *hear* him?"

Cully laughed. "No. I just know a curse from his lips when I see one."

There was a cheer in the room, relief that Cael still had some surliness in him.

The rest of what they saw was inconsequential, Kormick apparently questioning Cael while a wizard rechecked the collar secured around Cael's neck to make sure he was not capable of any magic—including dreamwalking.

With the last bit of hair gone, the images faded, and Quin and Cully opened their eyes. "We got him," Quin said. "We know where he is, and we can get to him."

"An oath," Eris ordered, and before anyone left the room, they were all sworn to silence. Not even the council back in Danu was to be told what they had discovered—maybe especially not them.

Tyghan took Bristol's hand, holding it firmly while everyone else filed out of the room to rejoin the party in the ballroom. "We'll be along soon," he said as they left. His eyes were an unexpected squall, considering the good news. No one questioned him, but Bristol saw the puzzlement in their faces.

When the last person was out of the room, Tyghan closed the door and pulled Bristol into his arms. He held her so tight, she thought he'd never let her go. His breaths were rough in her ear. "I was terrified I had lost you. Afraid that he—"

He loosened his grip, his steel eyes cutting into hers. Angry. Sharp. "Never do *anything* like that again. It was too risky. Too—"

"Sometimes you have to take risks. Especially for a payoff like that." Bristol smiled, trying to ease his worry, to pretend she hadn't been scared out of her mind, but the chaos was catching up with her in the quiet of the room, pounding in her head. She tried to shake it off, move past it. "And really, what was it you said when we first met? None of this was more dangerous than crossing a busy street on a bike?" She let out a small laugh. "That was some street I just crossed. Right?"

A crease formed at the edge of his mouth, the closest thing to a smile she was going to get. He looked at her shoulder and the torn sleeve, the top of her bodice folded over like a broken wing. "He hurt you. Dammit, Bri, you're lucky he didn't kill you."

In the rush of events, she hadn't noticed the deep scratches where Kormick's nails dug into her skin during their struggle or felt the sting of torn flesh until now.

Tyghan raised a finger to her shoulder and slowly, tenderly, drew it across one scratch at a time. The stinging subsided, the flesh weaving whole once again. His gaze met hers, deep wells of blue swallowing her up. His fingers burned as they slid across her collarbone and over the hollow of her throat. The air snapped taut, Bristol's breaths quivering, Tyghan's growing heavier. Now her skin burned for a different reason.

His hand eased lower, his eyes never leaving hers, but she saw his control ebbing as he pulled the torn bodice lower, his hand hot against her breast, his thumb circling her nipple. Heat pulsed low in her groin, and her hips pressed forward against him. She drew in a shaky breath. "What about the party?" she whispered.

"What party?" he answered, and then his mouth came down on hers. Rough. Hungry. Like every emotion in him was tearing loose at once. They fell back against the door, his one hand sliding up her throat, the other pulling her skirts up, gliding across her hip, finding the warmth between her legs. She moaned, her head tipping back. Her eyes fluttered shut as she yanked at his belt buckle.

"Take it off," she gasped.

Their lovemaking was wild, urgent, like they were stealing back a lifetime together they had almost lost, every touch suddenly more precious than air. She fumbled with the button of his trousers, his shirt, too many things. They both began tearing off their clothes, seams ripping, buttons popping like rain across the floor, and when enough was ripped loose or tossed away, he pressed against her again, his fingers between her legs, stroking, caressing until she couldn't stand any more, and they slipped to the floor. He hovered over her, his teeth scraping her neck, her shoulder, his hand still teasing, her breath quivering, her hips pressing forward, and she groaned as his knee separated her legs and he plunged inside her. The darkness behind her eyelids pulsed with color. He was a storm devouring her, every thrust stealing her breath, and she wanted him to take more, take every part of her, take her until she couldn't breathe at all. Her hips pushed into him, her back arching, the burning heat throbbing between her legs reaching a crescendo, and every nerve in her exploded at once, wave after wave consuming her. A string of guttural curses streamed from her throat, and her screams brought on his, hoarse and feral, his thrusts coming harder. They were bound together in every way, and nothing could come between them. With his last forceful thrust, he finally relaxed against her, spent, his breaths still shuddering, raw and uneven.

It was only after, as they lay there, that she noticed her single torn sleeve still hung like a casualty of war from her shoulder and buttons from Tyghan's shirt lay scattered like spent shells across the floor. His chest was wet against hers, his heart still pounding, and he whispered against her cheek, "No more chances, Bri. Do you understand? No matter what happens. I will not lose you."

"You never will," she answered. "I'm not going anywhere. Not without you."

He tucked his head into the crook of her neck, every part of them entwined, and they held each other for another long minute, as if sealing a promise between them.

CHAPTER 88

The ballroom hummed with a new kind of excitement. Tyghan noticed a few brows rise when he and Bristol returned to the grand hall—both in new attire—but his knights and recruits were jubilant, and as it turned out, the Elphame gentry were elated, too.

It was true, they murmured. The mysterious elite squad had precipitated the hasty departure of King Kormick and his brute warriors. This squad had some kind of power over him. *Magic.*

At least that was how it was perceived, and no one tried to dissuade them.

As bad a turn as the evening had taken, and despite the momentary terror it had brought him when Bristol disappeared, it had ended up exceeding Tyghan's expectations for success. They almost had Cael in their grasp. Cully repeated over and over, *She's bloody brilliant*, among other adjectives that included *clever* and *devious*.

Tyghan noticed the lines in Dalagorn's face deepen when Cully said *devious*. It was a poor choice of words, considering who her parents were. Nerves still weren't healed in the wake of Kierus's betrayal, but he knew Cully only meant it as the highest praise. Bristol not only survived the physical attack she launched on Kormick, harvesting his hair in the process, but managed to send him scurrying off like a trained rat, burning with the lie she had told him. Tyghan had to admit it was both brilliant and devious, and he was eager to return home to work out the details of Cael's rescue, but first he had to garner more support from the other kingdoms. The Choosing Ceremony was only weeks away, and this was their last chance. He and his officers spread out.

It turned into an exceptional Beltane Eve. By the time they departed in the early hours before dawn, the Greymarch and Eideris kingdoms had committed troops, however small their numbers, for the Choosing Ceremony *if* Tyghan promised to show up and claim the throne. He couldn't reveal that by then it might be his brother claiming it, but he didn't think they would care which Trénallis brother showed up, as long as it wasn't Kormick ruling over them. Besides the commitment of troops, the queen of Gildawey had inexplicably agreed to step up production so that every knight in Danu would now carry a Gildan long sword before week's end.

But even with the positive turnaround, Kormick's show of power weighed on Tyghan. He still saw the endless army of restless dead, waiting to descend on them like a cloud of locusts and pick their bones clean. *This is a prickly situation, isn't it?* Kormick had enjoyed watching them stand there, slack-jawed and silent, so obviously defenseless. Rescues and weapons were all for naught if the portal to the Abyss wasn't closed.

On the way to Tyghan's farm, in the Wilds just south of Timbercrest, was a little-used portal. King Roderick wouldn't like it, but it was the one least likely to be missed—or noticed—by Kormick. It couldn't be put off any longer. It was time to give Bristol a real portal to practice on.

CHAPTER 89

The sky was still a deep purple, lavender just beginning to frost the tops of the distant tree line. Forest air full of mist dampened Bristol's hair.

Like all portals, the one in the Wilds beyond the border of Timbercrest was invisible. It was charted and mapped centuries ago, and most of those in Elphame knew its location—except for newcomers like Bristol. Everyone was overjoyed when she led them directly to it.

She couldn't exactly explain it, the how or why of finding it. It was nothing like the burrows. With them there was sound—the whisper of wind, the chatter of birds, or the gurgle of an unseen brook.

The portal today didn't whisper, sing, or chatter. It pulled. Bristol didn't understand it at first, the heaviness in her chest that grew to an ache. She mistook it for something else. A sadness, an unexpected longing, the kind of melancholy that crept up on her on lonely nights. Maybe it wasn't this way for all bloodmarked—maybe only for her—because she longed for her old world in a way she had never expected to. The familiar called to her. Small-town streets, cold pizza, traffic, stupid cell phones that rarely worked—the need to be there for her sisters to keep everything from unraveling. She slid from her horse, drawn toward a glade in the forest, and the others followed close behind.

"Here," she whispered, still uncertain, at least in her head, but somewhere else inside her was certainty. *Here.* The ache behind her sternum tightened, a fist squeezing bone. And then she knew—she was only a step away from home. Maybe not Bowskeep home, but the mortal world she knew, the world that held her past and all the secrets that had created her.

She put her hand to the air in front of her, and Tyghan grabbed her arm, holding her back. "Careful," he warned as she pressed her palm forward. A shiver of light cut through the air, like the sun peeking through a drawn curtain, and then it spread wider, revealing an enormous portal. A long alleyway with a busy city laid out just past its end rippled into focus. It might have been New York, Chicago, or some other big city she had never visited, but it was familiar—the mortal world—tall buildings, concrete, cars, streetlights. The world where her sisters were. The ache inside her pinched tighter.

It was only then that she heard the excitement erupt behind her. She had found the portal on her own. The ache receded as relief flooded in, and then a heady sense of control washed over her, control over something, *anything. Power.* It warmed her blood and tingled her fingertips.

Tyghan kept a firm grip on her arm, and she realized it was so she wouldn't accidentally tumble through the portal. *Her timemark.* She didn't have it with her. She jerked her hand back to her side, and the seductive warmth vanished from her temples.

"You found it!" Rose cheered, bringing Bristol back to what she had accomplished.

Hollis clapped her hands. "We knew you could!"

"Well done," Julia added.

The sky had lightened with the dawn, the joy easily seen in their faces.

"Now," Madame Chastain said, tempering the cheer, "let's see if you can close it."

Because that was really all that mattered—the whole reason she was here.

Bristol nodded to Tyghan. "You can let go. I'm all right."

He reluctantly released her arm, but looked ready to spring if she should lose her balance. People did tumble through portals accidentally, maybe the way her father had as a toddler.

She lifted her hand again, her palm flat, the portal visible once more. Power surged through her, the heady sensation returning. A thousand bees hummed in her blood, hot, eager, addictive. The burrows weren't anything like this. She thought about how she had closed them, pushing and tugging at the edges. This portal was far too large for that, wide enough for three horses to gallop through, and far taller than she could reach. What should she do? It had to be possible. The Darkland monster had closed dozens of them in one day.

She swiped her hand one way and then another. Whispered multiple spells. *Duseen o duras nay tulay—May this door be no more.*

Nothing.

She tried again, with the same result.

She closed her eyes and pressed both of her hands to the portal opening. Light streamed through her closed lids, circling her hands, warm and alive, traveling up her arms like it was reaching out to meet her. Like it knew her. She concentrated. The hum rose in her gut. The burn. She called on the powers of Brigid, claiming them as her own. Seconds ticked by. Heat glowed on her skin. Sweat trickled down her back. She was certain she had it. She was close. She rapidly brought both hands together, the way she summoned fire.

Nothing.

Not a hint of closure.

She returned her hands to her sides. Rolled her stiff shoulders. Wiped damp strands of hair from her face.

She focused on the ground, unable to look at anyone. *The tick*, she thought. Was the ugly beast holding back her power? And on the heels of that thought, she imagined her parents placing it there, on the tender skin of a baby. Her concentration scattered.

Tyghan gently stroked her back. "It's all right. We can try later."

But it wasn't all right. She saw the desperation in his face when she looked up. For god's sake, he was king and in three weeks would lead his knights against uncountable restless dead. They were facing a certain slaughter. *It wasn't all right.* She saw it in every pair of eyes fixed on her, their elation tumbling.

She shook her head, rejecting his offer. Now. It had to be now. "I can do this," she said, but doubt grew in her throat, a painful knot she couldn't swallow away.

She flexed her fingers at her sides, trying to relax. Every part of her ached. *There is always a way. Always a way.* The ache turned to raging heat.

There is always a way.

She whirled. "I need a minute," she said to Tyghan, but her eyes landed on Madame Chastain. "Just a private minute." As she walked past Julia and Sashka, she quickly whispered, "I need you to distract Tyghan. Whatever you need to do, *do it.* Don't let him look my way."

"What is it?" Madame Chastain asked as Bristol led her into the deeper shadows of the forest.

"I need you to do something for me that Tyghan would never do—because what he and I have is *not* a dalliance."

The High Witch's lips pulled in a tight line at Bristol's tone. Her fingers crackled with pending punishment. "And that would be?" she asked.

"You're a physician, accomplished in the healing arts. I assume that means you know where my heart is, my lungs, the essentials. That you know how to be careful in navigating them. I'm close to shutting the portal. I can feel it. I need you to stab me. Precisely. Prick that son of a bitch in my back so more of its blood is released. *My* blood and magic that it's stolen. I don't need much. Just a—"

"*No.* Absolutely not. You should have thought of that before. This is not the place nor the time—"

"And I say it is. This is exactly the place, Madame Chastain. Or I'm out. Do you hear me? *Out.* I've let all of you call every play. I'm calling this one."

Bristol eyed the two tiny knives sheathed on the medical pouch at the High Witch's side and turned before she could reply, lifting her tunic. "Hurry. He's not watch—"

A sharp pain pierced her shoulder, and she gasped.

"Breathe out," Madame Chastain ordered.

Bristol's knees wobbled, and she felt the witch's arms around her waist. "Steady," she said. "And now breathe in. Breathe through the pain. Breathe, Miss Keats."

But besides the stab in her shoulder, the tick clutched her, recoiling with its own pain, crushing her insides.

Bristol sucked in a shallow breath. "I can't—I—" *Focus. You can do this.*

Madame Chastain still gripped her from behind, keeping Bristol on her feet. "Another breath. That's right. Another—"

"Tyghan's turning," Bristol groaned. She forced herself upright, pushing away the High Witch's hands. But it was too late. In spite of Julia's and Sashka's efforts, Tyghan had already caught a glimpse of her.

"*What the hell is going on?*" he yelled as he ran over.

The stab was small as she had asked, little more than a deep prick, but the back of her tunic was damp with a stream of blood. "I'm fine," she said. "Just coaxing that creature on my back to give me what's mine. Let's get this done."

Tyghan cursed, grabbing her arm, but she shook free and pushed forward, still forcing in breaths through the spasms of pain caused by the writhing tick.

Uproar exploded around them.

Questions and shouts at her. At the High Witch.

Are you mad?

What have you done?

You stabbed *her?*

Eris was a swirl of commotion trying to calm everyone as he shouted too.

But Bristol remained focused on her steps, the thousand bees in her blood humming louder, stronger. She stopped in front of the portal, the growing buzz swarming hot in her chest. She looked at her palm, then punched it into the portal, her hand sparking with brilliant light. The shimmering light traveled up her arm, to her shoulders, and through her hair and lashes in blinding tendrils. *"Abiendubra,"* she whispered. *Sealed forever.* She closed her hand into a fist and pulled back, like she was yanking a sheet from a line.

And in a sharp, hot second, the portal was gone.

CHAPTER 90

Spirits soared as they headed to Tyghan's farm for the next Beltane celebration. Bristol hadn't realized how afraid she'd been of failure, afraid of letting everyone down, until she closed the portal and her fear gave way to euphoria.

The other recruits rejoiced with her, hugging and excitedly talking about the future as they rode together back to Danu.

"This is going to happen!"

"My family will be so happy."

"Mine too. They've wanted to come to Elphame for years."

"There is still a Fomorian king to defeat."

"We're going to whoop his ass, too."

"I hated him the minute I saw him."

"He reminded me of a professor I used to work with. It will bring me great satisfaction to see him walk off with his tail between his legs."

"Walk? You mean crawl—if he's lucky."

"He has a tail?"

"He won't be walking or crawling. I have an arrow whittled just for him."

"And another for the Darkland monster?"

"Yes, one for her too."

"Won't they have powerful wards protecting them?"

"All wards have their limits. Esmee and Olivia will find them."

The Beltane celebration back in Danu was completely different from the ball at Timbercrest. The first was for news and gossip, and the second was to usher in summer and celebrate the greening of pastures, the fertility of crops—and procure blessings from the gods for other types of fertility as well.

Extravagant gowns and gossip were left behind. So were ballrooms. In Danu, the festivities took place in the hills and farmlands. Sparkling banquet tables were replaced with rough-spun blankets and wooden tables carried from farm kitchens to share the first fruits of spring. Towering vases of flowers were replaced by wildflower posies hanging over doorways and chamomile woven into crowns.

Tyghan had a farm he only rarely visited, and the celebration began in his kitchen. Flour dusted Bristol's hands and Hollis's cheeks as they mixed ingredients and kneaded dough for bannock cakes. Julia shaped the dough into flat rounds, then fried them in a skillet. Sashka sat in the corner of the kitchen plunging a stick into a barrel of milk, which would somehow turn the milk into fresh butter, though Sashka remained skeptical. Like Bristol, she thought butter was only purchased at the market, already wrapped in pretty paper packages. Milk transforming into butter seemed like an odd, work-intensive kind of fae magic. All of the preparations happened under the gentle and sometimes amused guidance of Ahbriya, the urisk steward of Tyghan's farm. Like Glennis, she had beautiful curved horns circling her head. She had adorned them with bright, colorful ribbons in honor of Beltane. Bristol was sorry Glennis couldn't be there enjoying the festivities, too, but Cully said she was still out on patrol.

The rest of their crew was outside doing other chores. Rose and Avery were gathering primrose and rowan flowers, while Tyghan and Dalagorn gathered dead wood and brush in a copse by the river. It would be used for blazing bonfires later that day. The piles needed to be large and stacked high so they could be seen for miles from the hilltop and would burn well into evening.

"Here we go," Quin announced as he and Rose walked into the kitchen with baskets full of berries.

"I'll take those," Hollis said, wiping her dusty hands on her apron, though Quin was already headed in her direction. Julia, Sashka, and Bristol exchanged sly glances. It appeared that Hollis's interest in Quin might be mutual.

They had all managed to get a few scant hours of sleep in the early dawn hours, Bristol and Tyghan tucking into his small bedroom and smaller bed, which she didn't mind at all. She should have been exhausted, but Bristol couldn't sleep when she laid her head on the pillow. Exhilaration still raced through her. Victories were coming fast now. First Cael, then the portal.

When this is over. Now it seemed like it was possible. Both an end and a beginning were in sight.

"Sleep," Tyghan had whispered, then pulled her close. "It's going to be a long day yet." He gently streamed his hand across her brow and over her eyelids, repeating, "Sleep," and whether it was magic or just the contentment of his nearness, sleep had come, deep and full.

Tyghan dumped an armful of sticks into the cart they were loading for the bonfires. He had wanted to forgo the celebrations and get back to the palace to prepare—there was a battle looming. But honoring the gods was part of that preparation too, and once he opened the door to his farmhouse, he knew he had made the right decision. Every time he came to the farm, he always resolved to come more often, to take a greater part in the plowing of the fields, harvesting, and tending the cattle, but it never happened. Other duties always took precedent. Thank the gods for Beltane and Samhain, or it wouldn't happen at all.

He remembered when he was only six, still a dreamy child, and he saw Amaetheon walking waist deep through their golden field of ripe wheat. The seedheads were heavy, bowing and nodding, ready for harvest, but Tyghan thought even the seedheads knew they had a great god in their midst, and they bowed in reverence to him. It was the last time he had seen the god, though he knew Amaetheon still came. His steward had seen him twice in the years since.

"Will you help with the harvest?" Amaetheon had asked him.

"Yes," Tyghan had answered eagerly, though he wasn't sure he would be allowed to help at all. Prince or not, he was mostly a child underfoot.

Amaetheon waved him over and presented a golden scythe Tyghan hadn't noticed before. "Here, let me show you how." The tall god had leaned over him, wrapped his hands around Tyghan's, ensuring his grip, then helped him angle the blade, and they swung. In that manner, together they had cut and bundled a whole field of wheat in an hour, a job that would have taken days for an ordinary farmer. Amaetheon had pressed a ripe seedhead into Tyghan's small, blistered palm, saying it was a tithe for the Cauldron of Plenty.

"Come next spring," the god told Tyghan. "I will show you how to plow."

When Tyghan ran back to the farmhouse to tell his parents the wheat was harvested, they thought it was only a childish story—until they saw it. A few days later when his family returned to the palace, all Tyghan could talk about was becoming a farmer and returning to the farm in the spring.

His parents laughed and reminded him that the week before, he had aspired to be the Knight Commander of Danu and as secondborn prince, it was his birthright. He wanted to be a knight, too. He could be both, he told them, but for the next few months, his sights remained set on wheat, barley, and long days in the sun with Amaetheon. The god himself was going to teach him how to plow.

But Tyghan didn't return in the spring as he had promised the god. By then his father was dead and his mother gone, a broken shadow.

Life changed. He changed. His brother was crowned king. Scythes were forgotten. He threw himself into swords, spells, and strategies. Eris and Madame Chastain tutored him day and night. A Knight Commander was all he wanted to be, all he was destined to be, his whims of autumn abandoned. Change was inevitable. Everyone had to grow into what they were meant to be. He didn't regret it. Becoming a knight had been his first passion.

But what if you were forced to become something you didn't want to be?

Convince her. The tick must go.

After they had left the newly closed portal, Bristol had ridden ahead with her friends, all of them occupied with excited chatter, but Quin and Kasta had fallen back with him. "Are we supposed to stab her every time she needs a little more magic?" Kasta asked, a practical question that had even crossed Tyghan's mind.

"It's incredible what she did," Quin added, "but the restless dead pouring through the Abyss portal aren't going to wait politely every time we need to stick a knife in her back."

"We just had two victories," Tyghan answered. "Maybe we should focus on those before moving on to all the downsides."

"Ignoring downsides?" Kasta's lip lifted in a sneer. "That is not the Knight Commander speaking. That is a smitten—"

"Watch your words, Kasta," Tyghan warned between gritted teeth. "I am still king." He felt her seething beside him. By then Eris and Dalagorn had ridden up and joined in, advice and concern bubbling up around him.

She acted on her own.

We're not making the plans anymore. She is.

Rein her in. She must be under your command.

The tick must go. For Danu's sake.

For all of Elphame.

Control. That was what they really wanted. Complete control. It didn't matter that when Bristol had strayed from the plans, she'd met with success. She went against a direct order and danced with Kormick. She employed Madame Chastain in a plan no one else was privy to. It wasn't the unexpected plans as much as that *she* was making them. What else might she do without consulting them? And simmering unsaid beneath it all was the worry that perhaps she was too much like her father—or, worse, her mother. She was still an enigma to them. Part fae, part something else. She was an enigma to herself. He remembered the fear in her eyes that day in the throne room.

I can't become something else. It's too late.

But that was what they all wanted her to be. Something else. They wanted her to be like her mother, but not like her, too. They were trying to create something safe, controllable, but powerful—water that burned like fire.

That morning, as Bristol drifted off to sleep in his arms, Tyghan had stared at her shoulder, grateful she couldn't see the changes. Now was not the time to dampen her spirit, not when they were so close. Olivia had remained quiet when she healed the stab wound on Bristol's shoulder, but her concerned eyes had briefly met Tyghan's before fluttering downward. Later, when Bristol was out of earshot, Olivia still didn't mention it, perhaps knowing it was best left a quiet secret just between the two of them.

But stabbing the tick for more magic had come at a cost.

A faint line of golden scales now rippled along the blade of Bristol's shoulder.

CHAPTER 91

August huffed and pranced, a wondrous sight in his ribbons and braids. Bells jingled from his tack, and fire danced in his pupils. Children lining the road stepped forward in awe, then back with fright. Little fauns feigned bravery but hurried behind their mother's skirts when August whinnied, a deep, throaty reverberation that sounded more like a fearsome beast than a horse. Pixies sitting on tree branches that arched over the road were unafraid and threw flowers onto the path below them. August led the pageantry, as he always did, first between the bonfires, and then through the hamlet with the king riding on his back, acknowledging the cheers, but August knew, it was really him they came to see, the beast of legend and lore who bore kings into battles.

The girl rode on his back too, sitting just in front of the king, but he wasn't sure why. She was nobody of consequence, not even a minor royal. Master Woodhouse had wooed and cooed August as he groomed his fetlocks that morning, telling August to be kind, as if he suspected he might buck her. It was an amusing thought, but the steeds of the Tuatha de were royalty in their own right. They didn't stoop to such crude behavior, at least not in public ceremonies. But perhaps later—

"They love you, August," the girl whispered to him, patting his neck.

Of course they do, August thought, but it was nice that the girl acknowledged it, no matter how lowly a creature she might be. He could tolerate her presence on his back. And then, inexplicably, she scratched behind his ear, soothing an itch he didn't even know he had.

The note was secure in the intruder's palm. With so many away from the palace for Beltane, it wasn't difficult sneaking into Bristol's room, but choosing the right place to hide the note was another matter. It was disturbing to find so many of the king's personal belongings scattered about. He was spending as much time in her chambers as his own—which could be problematic. It wouldn't do for him to stumble upon the note.

The intruder circled the room. Twice. Then finally found the perfect spot and tucked the note where it was certain only she would find it. This might finally send her back to the mortal world. If not, there were other ways.

With the note in place, the intruder took another minute to remove every trace of the intrusion with a cleansing spell. White smoke circled the room, removing scent, footprints on carpet, even the intruder's aura, which was exceptionally strong.

Mae was the one who had made the contact, knowing the intruder was in a certain trow's debt. It was a silence that had to be paid for over and over again.

CHAPTER 92

By the time they returned to the palace, Tyghan was exhausted. Three days of parties and surprises had left little time for rest, even by his standards. He handed August's reins to Master Woodhouse and headed straight to Lir Rotunda to work with his officers on strategies for rescuing Cael.

"We have a lot to decide," he told Bristol before he kissed her goodbye.

She grabbed his arm. "Maybe I should come, too—"

"No. Just the officers. Go rest. You deserve it." He had given all the recruits the rest of the day off, and they had rejoiced, eager for long naps, but Bristol had probably thought Tyghan would be joining her in bed.

"And stay in your room," he added.

She balked. "My room? But I—" Her expression turned to stone. "Why? Do you have concerns?"

"We just don't need any more surprises."

"*We?*" Her weight shifted like she was ready to block his path. "Does this have anything to do with Kasta? I saw her whispering and grumbling. Is she angry with me?"

"Knights follow orders. They don't act unilaterally. She—"

"They were all grumbling about that, weren't they? I saw way too much huddling between all of you on the way to the farm. They were as subtle as an earthquake."

Tyghan was surprised she had noticed, since she was riding ahead of them.

She waited for an answer, her lips pulled in a familiar hard line.

"They're only concerned that—"

"What? That I closed the portal? That I found your brother? I thought those were *good* things."

"You danced with Kormick after being told explicitly to avoid him," Tyghan snapped back. "Kasta feels you put everyone at risk."

"Is that so? And what do *you* think?"

His ire rose, heat flushing his neck. "Yes, you did put everyone at risk, including yourself. You don't know everything about this world, including what Kormick is capable of, and yet you walked right into his arms."

"I had a plan."

"That we knew nothing about."

"*There—wasn't—time*," she spat out. "And what about you? You punched him in the face! Was that part of the plan?"

"I'm allowed to make changes to plans. I'm king, in case you haven't heard."

"Oh, *the king*," she said, her eyes growing wide. "La. Di. Da."

La-di-da? He wasn't sure what that meant, but it probably wasn't a compliment. "Bri, please," he said, trying to reel back the strain escalating between them. "We're both tired. I'm not saying I'm not pleased with the end result of what you did. Of course I am. But there are only a few weeks until the Choosing Ceremony. Nerves are wound tight. At this point, we have to be sure we're all working together. Knights expect surprises from the enemy, but not from their own team. I need you to trust me with this. Please. Go to your room and rest."

He reached out and took her hand, rubbing her knuckles with

his thumb, and the fire faded from her eyes. "I'll join you as soon as I can."

As Bristol walked back to her room, she wondered if she and Tyghan had just had their first fight. Though their voices had never exactly been raised. And it had ended with their tongues in each other's mouths. *No, that wasn't a fight*, she thought, *more of a brisk disagreement with a pleasant ending.*

When she opened the door to her room, she was greeted by a tray of refreshments—apples, cheeses, a tall flask of golden wine—complete with a crystal vase of the deepest purple hyacinth she had ever seen. Her bed was already turned down like a tantalizing invitation. *I'm being seduced by bedsheets*, she thought, and she was perfectly okay with it. She would concede that much. She was tired and testy. When Tyghan reached out and took her hand, brushing his thumb over her knuckles, the fight in her had drained away. Even Sashka, who had the energy of a lightning bolt, announced she planned to sleep the entire afternoon.

She gave the tray a cursory glance. It seemed like all she had done these past few days was eat. Even this morning at the farmhouse, Tyghan and Cully had made everyone a huge breakfast, and except for an egg that rolled off the table *almost* to the floor, before Tyghan flicked his fingers and made it return safely to his hand, they did it without using any magic. Perfect frittatas, fresh berry compotes, seared herbed salmon. It drew a round of applause from them all. She had eyed him with new curiosity. Maybe he wouldn't fumble with pizza toppings after all.

She downed a handful of shelled hazelnuts from a dish on the tray, and suddenly resting seemed like a perfectly logical thing to do. She pulled off her boots and went to the bathing chamber to run a hot bath. As the tub filled, she went to the dressing table to deal with her horrible mass of tangles. She regretted not braiding her hair for the ride home. August had torn over sky and road, prodded by Tyghan to get home quickly. As she lifted her brush to her scalp, something bright caught her eye. Tucked between the black bristles was a tiny piece of paper. She smiled. A love note from Tyghan? He had left other little gifts for her around her room—a perfectly round citrine crystal, an enchanted harp that played itself, a rose on her pillow. She pulled the folded piece of paper from the bristles and unfolded it.

It wasn't a love note.

CHAPTER 93

Guilt lapped at Tyghan's conscience as he headed for Lir Rotunda. The wrongness of what he had done stuck in his throat like a fishbone. *I didn't control her mind*, he reasoned with himself. The horrors of dark magic were too deeply ingrained in him to do such a thing. It wasn't even a spell he had used when he grabbed her hand. Only a calming maneuver. Madame Chastain used it on patients. He had used it on Bristol at the farm, so she could sleep. Pulling tense energies from muscles, that's all it was. But today, Bristol hadn't wanted to relax. She was wearing those tensions for battle. He should have let them be—except that he was tired. He didn't want to battle with her. He just wanted to get his meeting over with and have a plan set, because he knew Kormick was strategizing every minute of every day. Tyghan had a bigger fight ahead of him, and he wanted to end the one at hand.

"There you are!" Quin hooted, as if Tyghan was hours late instead of just a few minutes. Did you take care of—"

"The topic is off the table!" he snapped. "Do you understand? I won't control her mind unless you want me to control your minds, too."

"*Slow down.*" Kasta's reply was sharp, the admonishment of a friend, not a subject. "We weren't talking about dark magic. We were talking about the kind of control you exert over all your knights. Like *following orders?*"

The fire in Tyghan drained, and he backed down. Of course they weren't asking him to use dark magic. Why had his mind even gone there? Maybe three full days without any sleep had stretched even his limits.

"These maps are useless," Quin grumbled, trying to pull their attention back to the business of rescuing Cael.

Tyghan circled the table, pulling one map from the pile.

It was true. Maps of Fomoria were old and unreliable. They only provided basic geological landmarks—rivers, mountains, gorges, and forests—but they didn't show where new fortresses, bridges, or traps might be.

Except for dangerous sprints into the interior, the landscape hadn't been traversed by outsiders in a generation, and with thick forests, there was only so much you could see from the air. Tyghan was on one of those quick sprints in the last botched search attempt that ended in an ambush. They had passed a warded citadel that defied their detection until it was too late. Fomorian warriors had swarmed out like wasps from a nest, outnumbering them ten to one.

"We stick to the air, then," Cully said. "Invisible."

Kasta shook her head. "That can only get us so far." Magics and weapons had diminished power under the veil of invisibility. Eventually they had to navigate the forest that circled the high cliffs like a dark leafy moat—and they needed swift weapons and magic to do it. And they couldn't land two dozen horses on the narrow cliff ledge, open and exposed like Kormick had done, unmindful of the noise they made. They might as well blare a horn alerting the guards.

"Down here," Dalagorn said, his thick finger pointing to a plateau just below the tree line of the forest. "We land here and climb up the backside to the lookout."

Tyghan nodded. It might work. "But we're going to need a glamoured proxy to leave in Cael's place. A missing prisoner would alert Kormick that we're up to something."

Dalagorn eyed the map, shaking his head. "Why not just gut the guards and ditch the bodies? It would be easy enough."

"Unless someone comes to check on the prisoner," Kasta said. "Like Kormick, or one of his wizards."

And now they were back to a proxy.

"What should we leave in his place?" Quin wondered aloud.

Several possibilities were offered up but dismissed for one reason or another, mostly because of their vocalizations. Voices were harder to glamour. "A hare," Cully said. "They're mostly silent, and they kick like hell."

"And they have big ears," Dalagorn added.

Chuckles rolled around the table. Cael was known for hearing every rumor that rolled through the palace. It was settled. A glamoured hare would be left in Cael's place.

Next, they moved on to the Abyss portal, narrowing its location down to a smaller area, based on recent sightings of the restless dead.

"If we can pinpoint that," Quin said, "Kormick's ass is ours."

The note trembled between Bristol's fingers.

> *My Brije,*
> *This note is for your eyes only. Do not share it with anyone. I need you to come to a secret location immediately. Follow the city road past the end of Tatha Bridge. After twelve miles, take the northern fork for another forty miles until you reach the forest. Someone will be waiting there and will lead you to where I'm hiding. Come alone, and make sure you're not followed. I know you can do this. My life depends on your silence. Trust no one. I need you, Brije. Hurry.*

She paced her bath chamber, then stopped to read the note on her dressing table again. She'd already read it several times now, as if each new time would reveal something she had missed. How did the note get there? Surely it wasn't her father who brought it, or he would just have stayed until she returned. Who had placed it there? Her skin prickled with suspicion, and she searched her room in case an intruder still lurked. In the time she was away, any number of fae could have sneaked into her room. She couldn't leave based on a note. Could she? She washed her face. Furiously brushed at the horrible tangles still in her hair. Leaned against the wall and closed her eyes. Then paced again. It was impossible not to share this note with anyone. *Impossible.* And yet.

She sat at the table to study the note one more time. *Brije.* It was her father's pet name for her. No one else knew it besides Cat and Harper. And the note was in her father's neat script. *He was alive.* But her relief was tempered by wariness. Go alone? Tell no one? That part felt like a trap. And yet.

All her reasoning ended this way. And yet.

My life depends on your silence.

It was her father pleading for help. Somehow, he had received news that she was there. Her forays into the city and countryside hadn't been for nothing after all. This wasn't a note she could afford to ignore—or apparently share, either. *Why?* He was afraid.

She remembered Eris making them all swear an oath of silence, keeping news of Cael a secret, even from the council. News could spread quickly there.

The words from the note glared up at her. *Do not share it with anyone.*

How would she even get to this faraway place where he was hiding? It was almost sixty miles away. A carriage would take hours and—

But there might be a way. If she was willing to take a chance.

And she was.

She put her boots back on, then rummaged through Tyghan's things in the wardrobe. He had several small knives in a drawer. She took one of them, and also his short sword hanging from a hook. What else did she need? *Magic.* She had to be prepared to use what little magic she had mastered, and other than closing the portal, she hadn't practiced any in days. Levitation? Glamour? Summoning objects?

Fire, she thought. Fire was a good deterrent. She eyed the unused bath she had drawn, dried petals and foamy swirls of oil floating on the top. "*Ante feru la—*" She hadn't even finished her spell for fire, or drawn her hands together to direct the chant, when the water erupted into a blazing inferno. A blast of heat hit her face, and flames licked upward to the coffered ceiling, singeing it black. "*Treima! Treima!*" she shouted. *Die.* The flames immediately vanished, but not without leaving their smoky print above the tub. Her heart raced. That had never happened before. Previously she had only created small, tame flames on candles. This fire was anything but tame. What had she done wrong? She wished she knew a command for erase or repair, but there wasn't time to worry about the ceiling.

She headed for the door, and as she passed her tray, she grabbed an apple, because it was possible, likely even, that she was going to need it.

CHAPTER 94

Tyghan couldn't remember the last time he had dozed off in the middle of the day. He had seen Kasta slumped over on the table using her crossed arms as a pillow and Quin leaning back in his chair, his eyes closed and mouth open, all the knights in their own form of repose, resting for just a few minutes after their midday meal. Tyghan had only slouched back in his chair for a moment to mull over their discussions when he felt someone shaking his shoulder. He startled awake, his boots dropping from the table to the floor with a loud thud. It was Dalagorn.

"What?" Tyghan asked trying to get oriented. "What is it?"

"Master Woodhouse is at the door. Something he needs to tell you."

Now? But Tyghan rubbed his eyes and nodded. "Bring him in."

Master Woodhouse shuffled in because the old spriggan never rushed, but the bright color of his flora showed that he was distressed. By then, all the officers had lifted their heads, alert and curious.

"What's wrong?" Tyghan asked.

"It's August. He's gone. His saddle is gone, too. I was at the other end of the stable grooming Fenella, and when I finished and walked past his stall, it was empty."

"Someone *stole* his horse?" Cully blurted out.

Tyghan was confused. No one took the king's horse. Not if they wanted to live. Besides, August would never leave with anyone else, anyway—but he might go visit a mare in another meadow. It was spring, after all. Maybe the old spriggan just overlooked the saddle? "I'm sure he hasn't gone far. Probably just—"

"He's gone," Master Woodhouse reiterated firmly. "I think your friend took him."

Tyghan leaned forward. "*My friend?*"

"The recruit. Miss Keats. She strolled in while I was on my way to groom Fenella. I thought she was just stopping by to chat a bit with August. She had an apple in her hand. He's become fond of her, I think. He might go with her, especially since she just returned on his back today. I saw her scratching his ears. He seemed to like it."

Bristol? Left with August? Tyghan stood there for a moment, still thinking there had to be a mistake. He told her not to go anywhere. To stay in her room. And she had agreed. Where would she go, anyway? Why would she . . . *Something was wrong.*

His first thought jumped to Kormick. He should have walked her all the way back to her room. He shot to his feet and ordered Dalagorn to check the palace gates. "See if anyone saw her leave." He headed for the door. "I'll check her room." Instead of walking, Tyghan night-jumped to the palace wing that held her chamber and ran the rest of the way, leaving his knights to catch up to him. He stumbled into her room and immediately noted the silence. Her bed was empty, the bath chamber quiet. No running water. No footsteps. But a smell. Smoke and ash. A fist tightened between his ribs.

His gaze circled the room, searching for any clue of where she had gone—or who might have forced her to leave. Her food tray appeared untouched. When he went into the bath chamber, his attention immediately landed on the black ash floating on a full tub of water, and then darted to the scorched ceiling. His worst fears stabbed his throat. Something had happened. He scanned the rest of the chamber, not even admitting to himself that he was looking for blood. It didn't matter that Master Woodhouse had seen her stroll into the barn, *something* had forced her to leave, and the ash and smoke confirmed it began in this room. The entire room looked untouched, except for splashed water around the basin and—

Her brush. He spotted it on her dressing table, askew. She'd had time to use it, and by its appearance, she had vigorously attacked her hair. Broken strands were woven through the bristles. *Fresh hair.*

He grabbed the brush but heard the echo of Eris's voice lecturing him when he tried to take Bristol's lock at Timbercrest Castle. *Don't do it. It's too risky. Somehow, you've managed to close your mind to the remaining demons. You can't open new doors at this point and make it easy for them to find their way back in.*

But Bristol was missing, and the fresh hair was there, waiting to be used. He had no choice. A flame had already risen from his palm, and by the time his officers rushed into Bristol's room, he had already breathed in the first plumes of smoke. *Aramascue odemas.*

He heard Quin groan when he saw what Tyghan was doing, but Tyghan remained focused on what he was seeing. "She's going over a bridge," he told them. "It's—" He tried to identify which one it was, but she was only looking down at August's mane. Finally, she glanced to the side and he saw a pub he recognized. "Tatha Bridge. She's at the end of Tatha. Call for horses," he ordered.

"Already done," Kasta answered. "They're waiting at the sea cliff. Melizan and Cosette will join us there."

"Is she with anyone?" Quin asked.

And that's what confused him. He couldn't see anyone forcing her along. "I don't think so. Unless they're riding behind her."

"Maybe someone found out she's bloodmarked," Cully speculated aloud. "Kormick? Do you think he's behind this?"

Tyghan wasn't sure. He had already backtracked to the day she closed the portal, who was present, who might have talked, who might have been spying on them. Or perhaps Kormick changed his mind about her being useless. His mind ran wild. *She's a passionate creature, isn't she?* He forced himself to focus on the images behind his eyes.

"She's leaving the bridge," Tyghan said, but then he saw her fingers take hold of August's thick mane, her perspective changing slightly to a higher position. "No," he whispered. "Don't do it. No—"

"What's happening?" Kasta demanded.

The landscape became a rush of color. "She's given August free rein. I can't see anything. It's all a blur."

Quin voiced what they were all thinking. "*Fuck*." It took years of training to master a Tuatha destrier at top speed. It was dangerous for a novice like her to even try.

"We'll never overtake her," Kasta said.

Now Tyghan had no choice but to stay and carefully trace her path so they could find her when she stopped.

Long seconds passed, Tyghan still breathing in the smoke, though there was little to see.

"Wait," he said. "She's at the fork. She's going north."

Cully groaned. "Only thing at the end of that road is the Wilds."

Once Bristol and August passed over the bridge, she dug her feet into the stirrups, putting her weight in her heels, and leaned forward. She let go of the reins and wrapped her hands in August's thick mane instead. His pace quickened to a canter as if he knew her intention. She had never ridden him at top speed before without Tyghan at her back, and she hoped she knew the right way to do it. If she fell off, she was doomed. She swallowed, hesitating for only a second, then whispered the command for speed to him. "Mind the road, but ride the wind."

In seconds the countryside became a smudged haze, the road barely distinguishable from the rolling hills around her. Wind roared past her ears in a deafening hum. In only a few spare seconds she saw the fork approaching. "North!" she said, giving August's mane a gentle tug with her left hand, hoping he understood. She was relieved when he followed her command. The landscape raced past in all shades of green, and in a short minute, the blur of road ahead disappeared into the huge black mouth of a forest.

"Slow!" she ordered. This was where she was to meet the mysterious someone who would take her to her father.

"She's stopping," Tyghan said, relieved that she hadn't fallen off. He described her cautious approach to the dark woods, her eyes scanning the shadows. *Good*, he thought. *Be afraid. Turn back.* But she wasn't moving.

And then he saw it. A figure emerged from the shadows. "No. Run, Bristol. *Now.*"

The others inched forward. "What is it?"

"There's someone on a horse," he told them. "I'm certain the rider is glamoured. The color of the robe, the glimmer, something is off. She's talking to him."

"*Brae taspian machor*," Tyghan whispered. *Show your true nature.* But the spell to uncloak glamour was useless. He couldn't force Bristol to see through it, and right now he could only see what she saw.

"She's going into the forest with him."

CHAPTER 95

Bristol's mind jumped between fire and blades. Which should she use? She thought about the unexpected explosion of fire in her bathtub and found the idea of burning someone to a crisp—even a potential enemy—repulsive, so her hand eased toward the knife on her belt. As he came closer, she still couldn't see the horseman's face. A cloak and hood shrouded most of his body.

"I wouldn't," the horseman said, seeing Bristol reach for her knife. "Trust me, my magic is swifter than your blade—and far more lethal. But it's all a waste of energy anyway. I've been hired to lead you, not harm you. Unless necessary. Will it be necessary, Miss Keats?"

She shivered at the mention of her name. "No," she answered. "It won't be necessary."

"This way," he said, turning his horse back toward the woods.

She followed hesitantly, her gaze jumping to the deep shadows on either side of her, the trees looming closer. These were the Wilds, the kind of place whole companies of knights avoided if they could. She listened for noises, things hiding in the murk. "Who hired you?" she asked.

"I was hired to lead and deliver. Not answer questions. That will cost you more."

"I have no money."

"Then I suggest you follow quietly."

Reckless, Bristol thought. The word thumped in her chest.

But this is what she came for. Her father. Every risky step was worth it.

A warning rumble vibrated from August's chest. He didn't approve of this dark path, but eventually the gloom began to lift, and the forest thinned. Their path opened onto a sunny valley, a pastoral setting as inviting as any Durand landscape. Deer grazed in the distance, and tucked up against the trees on the other side of the valley was a worn wooden barn, its paint a hazy memory.

"This is as far as I take you. It's time for me to go," the horseman said, and pointed. "Over there."

Bristol looked from the barn to the horseman. "And how do I get back?"

"You'll find your way, Miss Keats. Assuming you go back at all."

Why did he keep calling her *Miss Keats*? Her father kept her name a secret in the note. It didn't seem like he would he reveal it to this dubious escort. "How do you know my name?"

He rubbed his fingers together, indicating it would cost her coin.

A ruthless mercenary, but he seemed to have a decided opinion on her prospects. Bristol looked behind her at the eerie forest she had just traversed, then ahead again. "Yes, I will find my way, and I will be going back. *With* my father."

The horseman shook his head, doubtful. "I wouldn't—" But before he could dissuade her, she pressed her knees to August's flanks and said, "*Ride!*"

August flew across the valley, eager to leave their escort behind too. "Slow, boy. Slow," Bristol said softly as they neared the barn. She looked back. The horseman was already gone.

A trap. The thought occurred to her again. She scanned the surrounding forest, but it was as still as a painting. She checked the knives at her side and reviewed the evasive maneuvers Melizan and Cosette had drilled into her, then pulled in a grounding breath. She slid from the saddle. If it was a trap, she was as ready as she would ever be.

"Wait here," she whispered to August. She had only taken one step when she heard the screech of a rusty hinge and someone pushed open the barn door.

CHAPTER 96

T here's a clearing in the forest." Tyghan described the valley,
the grazing deer, all the things that Bristol saw, including the
horseman pointing across the valley—and then her sudden departure, leaving the horseman behind.

"What's she up to now?" Quin asked.

Tyghan didn't know, except that she was doing something behind
their backs—again. He felt the tension in the room rise.

"She's outside the barn, scanning the perimeters," he told them.
"She's getting down. This is it. This is the destination." Tyghan knew
the valley, and the old abandoned barn. Sticking to the skies, they could
be there in minutes. "Let's go—"

But as he stood, the smoke was still in his nostrils, his mind, the
images still coming, and he saw the barn door opening. Tyghan froze
midstep.

"What's wrong?" Kasta asked. "Do you see something else?"

A vise clamped down on Tyghan's chest. His hands curled to fists.
He saw a figure standing in the doorway. His face was masked in
shadows, but Tyghan knew the stance. The height. The way he filled
doorways. The way his arms hung at his sides, never far from his
weapons. The attention he commanded without saying a word.

"It's Kierus," he answered. "She's meeting with her father."

CHAPTER 97

Bristol stared at the figure in the doorway, afraid to believe.

Her throat shriveled, tight and useless.

Months ago, the impossible had happened. Her father had died. She had always believed him to be invincible. Instead, he had been brutally ripped from their lives. There was no notice. No goodbyes. It was a sudden, horrible death that she was reminded of every day as she rode into town, an ever-present roadside memorial haunting her with morbid thoughts. The guilt was always there, that she couldn't make him happy in his last days. Guilt that she should have done something differently. Guilt that he had suffered a violent death. He had deserved more than a casual slaughter at the side of the road.

But there in the doorway stood a man. Alive. As robust as he had always been. *Logan Keats.* But dressed differently. Not like her father. He was dressed for this world. A long cloak swept back over his shoulders. Weapons hung at his side. A sword rested on his back like he actually knew what to do with it. Instead of loafers or flips-flops, he wore high boots. The man stared back at her like she was a bizarre sight, a second sun rising in the sky, stunning and frightening all at once.

She had traveled over oceans, mountains, and entire worlds to reach him. Risked everything for this moment, but inexplicably, now she couldn't move. Was this just another illusion? There had been so many.

And then he put his arms out for her, the way he always had, whether she was four, twelve, or twenty. That was all it took. She ran into her father's arms.

"*Brije*," he whispered into her hair, his voice catching, holding her tightly.

"Daddy," she choked, clutching him in the same desperate way, her face buried in his chest.

"It's all right," he whispered. "I'm here."

When she was in his arms, she was a child again, safe. His voice soothed her, made her believe that everything would be all right.

But then he pulled away and grabbed her arm. He glanced across the valley, a sharp eye scanning for threats, before drawing her inside the barn. A dusty beam of light poured through a hole in the thatch roof, lighting the space between them.

"What are you doing here?" There was an unexpected edge in his voice.

"You sent me a note?" she answered hesitantly.

"No, I mean in *this* world. Elphame."

"Willow told me you weren't dead. That she saw trows take you. I made a bargain with the Danu Nation so I could come here to find you and help you out of whatever trouble you're in. I'm here to bring you back home."

"*What?*"

She didn't see the relief she had expected. Or the happiness. What was wrong with him? "We always knew you and Mother were running from something," she explained. "After Willow told me what she saw, I thought it was the trows that finally caught up to you. Willow said—"

He whirled, raking his fingers through his hair, hissing. "Bristol! No!"

"What's wrong?"

He turned back to her. "I wasn't running from trows. I needed their help to come here. They helped me fake my death and got me here through a portal."

Bristol's head swam, like she had just walked into a wall and was knocked senseless, like the pressure in the entire universe had just changed. Her ears rang. *Faked death?* The words couldn't quite find purchase. They were sand spilling from a steep cliff. She felt herself slipping, right along with words that were impossible.

He faked his own death?

She only saw the real one, the death she had lived with all this time. She saw the sheriff standing on their porch, his hat in hand, his voice shaking. She saw the funeral home, the full pews, his urn of ashes center stage, the urn she had to carry home and put on a shelf out in his workshop. She saw the roadside memorial with faded silk flowers, and the bills they struggled to pay. She and Cat trying to be not just sisters but parents to Harper. Blood pooled in her limbs, her fingers cold, her voice a whisper. "You mean . . . you deliberately led us to believe you were dead?"

"*Brije*—"

Heat flooded back in, her voice alive again, his words finally reaching her like a hard slap across her face. Every inch of her stung. "Stop! I am not your *Brije*! I am your daughter who has been grieving all these past months! How could you do this to us? Do you have any idea what our lives have been like? How could—"

"*Bristol!*" he shouted. "Let me explain!"

But she wasn't done. "Explain what? The misery you've put us through? The heartache? We've been through hell! Is there anything truthful about you at all? Jasmine told me she had raised you and you left without even saying goodbye! Is that what you do to all your families? Abandon them?"

His dark brown eyes that could cast spells glistened, and a smudge of fatigue settled beneath them. "*Please*," he said, his voice so low and broken it made her muscles ache. "Let me explain," he pleaded again.

Her voice quieted, but it only made it sound more bitter. "You've lied to me my entire life. Foster care. Your reasons for running. You hid it all from us. Why should I believe you now?"

Something inside him caved, like his bones had cracked and shrunk. He stumbled to an overturned cart and sat, too weak to stand.

He looked like he did after her mother died, waves of grief stealing his strength.

His chest rose in controlled breaths, as he wrestled with some demon in his head. He finally looked up. "I don't blame you, *Brije*. I understand why you're angry, but everything I did, I did to protect my family, and I would do it again. I love you all more than life itself. You need to know that. I didn't want to lose any of you. If you'll give me a chance, I promise I'll tell you the whole truth. All of it this time."

But could he? Bristol's insides were raw, still trying to comprehend a faked death, the cruelty of it. *I love you all more than life itself.*

And yet she knew that much was true. She had always known it, always heard it in his voice, seen in in his eyes and in his actions. He *loved* his family. But was love enough? Was it a good enough excuse for what he had done?

Did she even want his answers? He abandoned them, but he loved them? None of it made sense. *He faked his death.* She was trapped in a mathematical conundrum, a place where two and two no longer equaled four, an Escher drawing where stairways led you in circles. There was no way out. No logic.

He stared at her. Hurting. Desperate. That much was not fake.

She reluctantly nodded and righted a toppled milking stool and sat down to listen.

He leaned forward, his elbows resting on his thighs, his hands weaving together in front of him. "I didn't want to leave you all that way," he explained. "It tore me apart, I swear, but my death had to be believable. It was the only way to keep you safe. Your grief had to be believable, or it would put you all in danger. And honestly, I wasn't sure I would ever make it back. I was going after your mother. I had to—"

Bristol dug her fingers into her scalp, despair and frustration gripping her again. "*Mother is dead,*" she moaned. "Why can't you accept that? She deserted us, and she's dead. How many times do I have to say it? You identified the body yourself."

An unexpected laugh jumped from his throat, and Bristol wondered if he had truly gone mad. That would explain the shadows beneath his eyes and his belief that he'd had to chase after his dead wife. Was he still stuck in some grief-twisted world? But then just as quickly, his mirth turned sharp, her cunning father returned, a different kind of amusement in his eyes.

"He didn't tell you about us. Who she was, or who I was, did he?"

"He?"

"The prince of Danu. Tyghan."

"You mean the king."

"Now he is. He wasn't then."

Her skin prickled. "You know him?"

He nodded. "Better than most."

"But he's only twenty-six, and you've been—"

Jasmine's voice slammed into her. *Time in Faerie can pass quite differently in the mortal world.* The words hit her with new clarity, making twisted stairways suddenly make sense.

"I left six, maybe seven months ago," he said, "when I was twenty-five. At least here, it's only been that long. In our world, I've been gone a lifetime. I wasn't running from trows all those years. I was running from Tyghan. He sent an army of hunters to track me down."

Bristol's mouth went dry. She knew what he was going to say next, *how* he knew Tyghan, but she didn't want to hear it. Her mind was already trying to back away from his next words, but it was too late. He spoke her worst nightmare.

"At one time, we were like brothers," he said. "Tyghan was my best friend."

CHAPTER 98

K asta and the other officers gave Tyghan a long second glance. He was as cold and methodical as a timepiece, his movements precise and unforgiving.

He had changed these past months, like he was trying to find a new version of himself. Kasta thought this version suited him. Sharp. Sure. Vengeful. A Knight Commander.

"Now?" Kasta mouthed.

He only replied with a single nod and pressed a finger to his lips. *Quiet.* He went invisible then, and they all followed his lead, leaving the cover of the forest and spreading out around the barn to their assigned places until it was surrounded.

Tyghan had already set the orders. Wait for someone to emerge. No one said it, but it was understood—none of them were certain which side Bristol was playing on anymore. A secret rendezvous with her traitorous father planted doubt in all of them. All contingencies were covered. Tyghan left nothing to chance. He said if Bristol emerged with her father they were to grab her before her father could.

You really think he would harm his own daughter? Cully had asked.

Tyghan only answered with a cold, dead stare. Cully understood the message. Look what Kierus had done to his best friend. He was capable of anything.

If Bristol should come out alone, they were to stay put and invisible until she left and was out of sight—then move in. He didn't want Bristol to know they had followed her to the valley or laid a trap for her father. Cully would follow her to make sure she went straight back to the palace. Once the others moved in on Kierus, they were to kill anyone with him, but under no circumstance were they to kill Kierus. He wouldn't get off that easy.

Kasta was glad for it. Like Tyghan, she had loved Kierus, too. She had believed him, *in him*, but she paid a hefty price for that belief. She wanted Kierus to pay a price now, too. A price that would never let him rest.

Before he took his position, Tyghan walked over to August, who was nibbling on the low branch of a hawthorn tree. August startled, sensing Tyghan's approach even if he couldn't see him. "You useless bag of dog bones," Tyghan whispered close to his silky muzzle. "You betray me for an apple?" August replied with a guilty snort. "You will take her straight back to the palace, no matter what she tells you. Do you understand?"

August's back shivered, and his tail whipped the air.

He understood.

Tyghan took his position near the corner of the barn, the seconds lasting hours. Sweat trickled down his back. *What if she resists?* He still didn't know what he would do.

CHAPTER 99

Bristol leaned forward, her head in her hands, sickened, a sour taste swelling on her tongue. She stared at her boots. Swirling in the dirt beneath them she saw the horror of Tyghan's study. The scrawled hash marks on walls. The shattered glass. Melted candles. Madness.

We were like brothers.

It was her father who had stabbed Tyghan with the demon blade. He was the traitorous best friend. Her father, *the knight*. The one who had lived in this world just a short time ago. Now she knew why he left Elphame without saying goodbye to Jasmine and his aunts. The aunts had known all along who he was and his reason for leaving.

And so had Tyghan.

Her shoulders shivered with ice, her fingers numb. She was in Dante's ninth circle of hell. And her father had led her there.

Scream.

Cry.

Do something.

But she couldn't. There was nothing left in her. She'd been chasing trows when she should have been chasing something else. Or not chasing anything at all. When she should have stayed home with her sisters. Stayed home where a tick on her back would have remained an innocent ladybug birthmark.

"You're the one who stabbed him," she said, her realization spoken aloud.

"He told you."

She shook her head. "He didn't name you. He only said it was his best friend."

"I didn't want to, but he gave me no choice. I couldn't change his mind. He was going to kill your mother."

His accusations were getting crazier by the moment. "Why would Tyghan want to kill her?"

"Because—" He grimaced like he didn't want to say it.

"You promised me the whole truth."

He looked at her, his eyes a dark, bottomless well. "Your mother . . . By some, she's known as the Darkland monster."

Bristol's next question pooled somewhere inside her, lost, the barn, the floor, everything becoming a murky mist. Blood swelled in her veins, the deep leaden throb of it filling her ears. The ground at her feet ebbed and flowed, a blurred tide circling her ankles, her knees. She was drowning. Water rising, past her chin, her mouth, her nose. It was never going to stop. She was in over her head. She looked up, watching her father's lips move, sounds coming from them. It echoed in waves, surreal, distant, like nothing she heard was real.

He told her the plan that he and Tyghan had concocted together. They heard the Darkland monster favored mortal lovers, and it was her father's job to seduce and kill her, but their plan had gone awry. "I fell in love with her instead. It wasn't planned. I never intended to betray Danu. But she wasn't what any of us thought. She was trapped in her world as much as I was trapped in mine. It was only in those days and weeks with her that I realized, I wanted out. We both wanted out." He told her they both wanted to live different lives. He had gone to the king two years earlier and asked for a leave so he could study art again, and the king had laughed him out of the throne room. He'd been ashamed that he ever entertained such a wild idea. "And your mother, she never had a chance to choose any life at all. One horror rolled into another. She was only sixteen when Kormick found her in the forest chained to a post."

"Kormick?" The name was a gust of wind, and Bristol's fog vanished.

"The king of Fomoria," he clarified. "Her uncles explained to him that she kept running away, creating portals to escape. That's why they chained her. They saw her portals as defiance and an evil kind of magic because it was so rare. Kormick saw it as opportunity. He gave them a purse full of gold and said he would take her off their hands. But he had other plans for her."

He explained that Kormick treated her well—at least compared to her uncles and cousins who terrorized her, and that she thought of him as her savior. For a time. Kormick educated her in the arts, languages, literature, and schooled her in magic. He gave her the finest gowns to wear, servants to wait on her, tutors, her own personal guards, and he never beat her, as her uncles had done. "Most important, he gave her power—in measured doses. He seduced her with her own frailties and fears. He kept her scars fresh. Her first victims were her uncles. What better way to help her control her nightmares than to let her become one?"

He said with each passing day together in the cottage, Kormick's hold over her waned and their love grew. "We were planning to leave when Kasta found us."

"Kasta found you first?"

"Yes. I begged her to walk away, to give your mother and me a chance to leave together, and she did. But only minutes later, as we prepared to set out, Tyghan found us too. I asked the same thing of him. Walk away. Let us go. I told him we were in love. But he wouldn't listen. I stepped in front of him, tried to block his way, but he drew his sword, claiming she had enchanted me, and started toward the cottage. I had already sold my weapons, and the only one I had was her knife, and I used it, but not to kill. Just to slow him down.

At that point, she and I ran, and we've been running ever since. Until now."

"Mother is the Darkland monster."

"That's what they call her, but she's not—"

"She's alive. You're certain. *She* is the Darkland monster."

He nodded and told Bristol how she came by the name, about her life in the Darkland Forest. Her parents were weavers of repute and sold their blankets and shawls in local hamlets. They were killed in a goblin raid when she was eleven. Her ne'er-do-well uncles moved in on the spoils, claiming her parents' house—and her.

"But she left us to come here," Bristol said, almost as a question.

"She had no choice. Kormick caught up with us in Bowskeep, and there was no getting away. His warriors infiltrated the town. They knew every step our family took. He knew where you were, too, a hundred miles away." He explained that Kormick wanted her back and he was determined. She had broken her pledge to serve him, and there was a steep debt to pay. Kormick promised her if she returned with him willingly, he wouldn't *involve her family*. "She wasn't sure what that meant, but it was more than she could bear. She refused to take a chance and fight back. She had vowed her daughters' lives would be different from hers, so she struck a bargain with him—and I had to agree not to follow. Your mother . . . she sacrificed everything to keep us safe."

"That was your fight the day she left."

He nodded. "I wanted to find another way, but her mind was made up."

Bristol remembered what Cat told her about kissing them goodbye. Her mother knew she would never be back. She had left to save them.

"And just how do you think you're going to bring her home? Knock on Kormick's door and ask to speak to her? You weren't supposed to follow."

"I have a plan." He explained that when they first met, she told him about an abandoned cottage on the banks of the Runic River, not far from her original home. She went there to be alone, usually on market days, like that would bring her sojourn some extra kind of magic. Kormick kept a loom for her there, the only remnant of her past life, a souvenir from her home after she killed her uncles. She practiced weaving, struggling to remember the blankets her parents used to make and recreate them.

After she killed her uncles. A casual mention, like people killed their relatives every day. This was the rotten family she refused to speak about.

Bristol remembered the *click, clack, clacking* of the shuttle flying back and forth through her loom, the snap of the picking stick, the creaking of pedals, like a musical instrument—that was what Bristol saw on her mother's face as she worked, a song she was trying to remember, her head sometimes turning slightly like she had found a note, and then the feverish clacking, like she was trying to find another.

"She told me she would try to find a way back to us, but after months passed, I knew Kormick had made her forget."

"Is she under a spell?"

He shook his head uncertainly. "Not exactly, but she might as well be. Kormick's influence is consuming. He's a powerful demigod. His words become the air she breathes, twisting and prodding her thoughts. He reminds her of where she came from and where she could return. He amplifies her fear and her rage, then soothes her when she bends to his will. He portrays everyone as a potential enemy, but reminds her of the power at her fingertips to make the fear and pain go away. That power is a numbing drug for her. She can control legions of demons instead of the other way around."

Bristol remembered how Mick soothed her own fears in those days just after her father's supposed death, the magnetism he had possessed. The timbre of his voice was almost hypnotic, and the torn things inside her seemed to mend during those encounters. She had lost perspective, and couldn't see how he was using her, until he was gone.

"Everything's my fault," her father continued. "I grew complacent. Weak. Too full of myself in the mortal world, thinking I could reason with anyone. That I could charm the damn birds out of the trees. When

Harper begged to stay in Bowskeep, I thought I could make that happen too. That we could stay and be safe. But it came at a cost I refused to see coming. Your mother warned me."

He leaned forward, burying his face in his hands. "She has given me every true and beautiful thing in my life. I can't turn my back on her now. She doesn't deserve this." His last words were choked, and he struggled to regain his composure. It was like watching him sob on the stairs after her mother left. Bristol's stomach sank, those grieving days flooding back to her. She wished she had at least cried for her mother.

"Daddy." She rose from the milking stool. "I'll find her. I'll bring her—"

His head snapped up. "No! You can't—"

"I'm not afraid of Kormick. I'll go to her—"

"It's your mother you need to be afraid of. I told you, Kormick uses his power to make her forget. She may not even know you. That's why I need to go. I got through to her the first time. I can do it again. You need to go home. Today. That's what this—"

"I'm not going anywhere," she said firmly. "I made a promise to Danu."

His voice turned low, bitter. "You don't owe them anything."

"I'm staying," she repeated. "My decision."

He stood, eyeing her guardedly. His lips pulled into that hard Keats line. "You mean you made a promise to Tyghan? It's him, isn't it? Has he taken you to his bed?"

Her stomach caved like she'd been punched. "That has nothing to do with this."

He cursed and looked away. "Can't you see? He did it as revenge. He's using you to make me pay, and it's only going to get worse."

"No." She shook her head. "It's not like that between us. He cares about me, but of course, he's hurting. He was stabbed by his best friend. Do you have any idea what that did to him?"

"*To him?* Do you have any idea what it did to me? In a split second I had to choose between two people I loved. I chose your mother. And I will never regret it."

Her heart went still.

Her mother. Tyghan tried to kill her mother.

But the world her mother had unleashed had nearly killed Bristol. And it had killed countless others. She remembered the lord breaking down in the throne room, his son taken by the restless dead. Bristol's head pounded. Who was the most deeply wronged? Tyghan? Her father? Her mother? She couldn't sort it out. Not now. Maybe not ever.

"I'm leaving now, to somehow fix this mess. However you got here, find the same way home. Go back, Father. Cat and Harper need you."

She tried to walk past him toward the door, but he grabbed her by the shoulders. "*Brije*, I know this world! It's dangerous and unforgiving. I navigated it for years as a powerful knight. You haven't. I don't want to have to worry about you, too. I need you to go home—"

She pulled free and backed away, staring at him. *A powerful knight.* She'd been hit with so much so fast, it was all sinking in out of order.

"*You* were going to kill Mother."

Now he looked like he was the one who had been punched. "It was my intention," he admitted, "but I told you already, I changed my mind."

"Have you killed other people?"

"It's not who I am anymore. You know that."

"Answer my question. Have you?"

His handsome face clouded with an answer he didn't want to give. He nodded. "Yes, I've killed many. I was a knight in the king's service. I did as I was told."

Many. She didn't ask how many. She didn't want to know.

A huge part of the father she loved was a stranger to her.

Every inch of her felt battered, limp, like she was rag doll pulled in different directions, torn beyond repair. Some of her pain was for her father, caught up in something beyond his control, but he wasn't an innocent in this either. He had made his choices, including placing a tick on the back of a baby. She shook her head. "I'm not leaving this to you. Not this time. I'll make my own choices and do what I need to do. Go home."

But she knew he wouldn't go. How could you save someone who didn't want to be saved? Someone who faked his own death to be there? But as she walked out, he said her name one more time, a plea, and she heard the desperate love woven through each syllable. It plundered what was left of her strength, and she could barely see as she stumbled out the door.

CHAPTER 100

T he door of the barn swung open, and she stepped out—alone. Tyghan exhaled a relieved breath. But now he wondered, *What is she thinking?* He studied her face, searching for clues, but her expression was blank, like she was in a trance. Even her steps were listless.

What had Kierus done to her? She went straight to August and reached up, grabbing hold of the saddle, but instead of getting into it, she slumped against its skirt, her face buried in her arms. Still. Quiet.

Tyghan's stomach went hollow. He had never seen her like this. Breaking down. Not even in training when she was injured. Instead, she always pushed forward, staying ahead of whatever pain she masked. She turned a phrase. She talked fast. She talked back. She got angry. She was a smart-ass. Sheer stubbornness twisted something inside her into iron. But she wasn't doing any of those things now.

He knew the others were watching too. Wondering.

What did Kierus tell her?

Everything? At least his version of it.

She finally pushed away, wiping her cheeks, and gently tugged August's mane so he would bow, and she climbed onto his enormous back. Once she was settled in the saddle, she faced the barn door a moment longer, like she was wrestling with one last thought—or waiting for someone—but when she turned August around to head out of the valley, Tyghan saw her eyes, no longer dazed but hot and bright. She nudged August, and they tore across the valley.

As soon as she was out of sight, his focus went back to the barn, cold and sharp, and with every step he took toward the door, he shed the veil that hid him. When he met with Kierus, it would be face-to-face. He didn't bother to be mindful of his footsteps or the sticks that snapped beneath his boots. He didn't care if Kierus heard him coming. There was nowhere for him to go.

When Tyghan pushed open the door, Kierus was alone, waiting and ready. He'd heard Tyghan coming and had already drawn his sword.

Tyghan didn't draw his in return. He could lift a hand and send Kierus flying backward through the barn wall. Maybe. He noted the wide embossed wrist cuffs on Kierus's arms, no doubt inscribed with wards to deflect magic. He also had three combat belts circling his hips and shoulder, all embedded with metal discs, all finely wrought, and expensive—the sort of amulets and wards formidable sorcerers might create. Kierus had rich and powerful allies, but even if it came down to sword against sword, he had little chance. Though Tyghan didn't want him dead. He didn't even want him unconscious. This time there would be words.

Their eyes met, and that part was hard, that momentary recognition of things past, the history between them, followed by the swift painful stab of the present and the immeasurable things that had been lost. It was a jarring equilibrium that shook them both, even if they wouldn't show it, their gazes locked as they both stared quietly.

"Hello, Kierus," Tyghan finally said. He noted the fine lines around Kierus's eyes, the hint of gray sprinkled in his thick black hair, the furrow between his brows. *Twenty-three years.* Of course he had aged, but it still took Tyghan by surprise. In his mind, except for a handful of months, they were both still the same age and no time had passed. But it wasn't just Kierus's appearance that had changed. There was a different manner about him too. *A husband. A father.* Things Tyghan hadn't yet experienced. It was hard to pinpoint how it showed, but he saw it, a different kind of weight in Kierus's shoulders, his eyes. But the intensity, the confidence, the magnetism that had always surrounded Kierus, that was all still there. In some ways, he hadn't changed at all.

"Tyghan," he answered. "I see you're well."

Tyghan smiled. "Is that what I am? Well? No thanks to you."

"Come on. It was only a little stab. I could have killed you easily. You know that. I wasn't called the Butcher of Celwyth for nothing. I know my way around a blade—and a body. I only wanted to slow you down."

"While you got on with your life."

"That's right. And I don't regret it."

You will, Tyghan thought. *A thousand years from now, you will regret it.*

"What about you, Tyghan? You must not regret it either. You're fucking my daughter, after all." Kierus was the master of delivery, pairing a smile with a blow meant to knock you off your feet.

Tyghan didn't blink, returning with scathing insinuation, "Yes, I am fucking her. And I don't regret that, either."

Kierus's weight shifted, his sword rising. Tyghan had found the sliver beneath his skin. He pressed a little harder. "I'm doing other things to her too. Shall I describe—"

"Leave her be, Tyghan! Do you hear me? She has nothing to do with this."

"Too late to start acting like the protective father now, Kierus. I know what you did to her. I saw the tick. It's grown to the size of a monster now. She's so repulsed by it she can't look at her own back. That's what *you* did to her, to save your own ass."

"It was to protect my whole family. To keep you from hunting us down."

"Sure, keep telling yourself that, thwart her magic at any cost. Luckily, we found her before Kormick did. She's bloodmarked, you know? Just like her mother."

Kierus paled.

Just like her mother. The trait was rare, usually skipping several generations, which made it impossible to track or predict.

"Don't use her, Tyghan. Don't do to her what Kormick did to my wife. I'm warning you—"

"Or what, Kierus? What will you do?"

His grip adjusted on his sword. His stance inched wider, but then, one by one, the other officers made their presence known, shedding their invisibility. They surrounded him from all sides, eager to use their poised weapons, cold rage sewn across their faces.

"So this is how it is?" Kierus asked. "Six powerful fae against one mortal? Do I make you that afraid, Tygh?"

"That's right, Kierus. This is how it is. Do you know how many lost their lives searching for you, others risking their lives to save you, when you didn't need saving at all? While all along, you were conspiring with the enemy?"

"She's not the enemy. She's my wife. The mother of my daughter you're now doing *things* to. I knew you were capable of a lot, but I never thought you would stoop this low. I'm here to take my wife back home. That's all. This time, for all of Elphame's sake, walk away. I can right this. Please, I never wanted to hurt you. I'm asking you as a friend."

Tyghan felt the force of the word like a sharp blow in his side. "*A friend?* That knife just accidentally slipped into my gut? *A friend?*"

"I told you—"

"It was a demon blade, Kierus! A fucking demon blade!"

Kierus's brow furrowed, not comprehending—or refusing to. Tyghan raged with something so broken and empty he could barely see.

"We've got it from here, Your Majesty," Kasta said. "You can go."

And Tyghan did. There were so many things he still wanted to say, planned to say, but all he could do was turn and walk away. "Have your fun with him," he told his knights as he left, "and then bring him to the palace."

"Don't do this, Tyghan!" Kierus yelled after him. "Don't walk away from me! I'm warning you! Don't do this—"

The screams continued, but Tyghan kept walking. He walked away, and he didn't look back.

CHAPTER 101

The gallery was as quiet as a morgue in the middle of the night. It didn't feel like a place to buy art, and Cat and Harper shuffled in, sticking close together.

"Don't be nervous," Sonja whispered as she turned the sign on the door to Closed. "They only want to ask you a few questions."

The art had checked out, confirmed by two sets of experts. The sketches were real, drawn by Leonardo da Vinci. Sonja led them to her small office in the back, where two men sat in chairs against the wall. Two empty chairs sat across from them. The men were FBI agents, and they looked the part. Neat, short haircuts, crisp dark suits, ties knotted perfectly at their necks, one red, one blue.

They introduced themselves with firm handshakes and names that sped past Cat and Harper, then began with small talk, commenting on the quaintness of Bowskeep and the good pie at Starky's down the street, but then got right down to it. "Bowskeep is an out-of-the-way place for art to turn up. Such a small town. Where did you say your sister got the art?"

"I didn't say," Cat answered.

"A swap meet," Harper said at almost the same time. "They were stuffed in an old book she bought."

"Which swap meet?"

"We're not sure. She didn't say."

"May we see that book?"

"No, she took it with her."

"Where did she go?"

"She said she went to see a friend."

"She's been gone quite some time now, I understand. Are you worried about her?"

"No."

"We'd like to ask her a few questions. Do you have an address?"

"No."

"Are you trying to hide—"

"She's gone to Faerieland to find our dead father!" Cat snapped. "There is no address unless you have wings! Get over it."

A hint of a smile sprouted on Sonja's lips, and she offered Cat a sly nod. "Gentlemen, I think these ladies have told you all they know. And since there is no record of the sketches in the first place, they can hardly be considered stolen. If you have any further questions, I'm sure their attorney can help you—his office is right above Starky's. The place with the great pie? You should have no trouble finding it."

They took a few more notes, one raising his brow as he wrote and whispered, "Sister is in Faerieland. No address."

As soon as they left, Harper asked, "Is Bri in trouble?"

"*No*," Sonja said emphatically, "at least not here. But she has been gone for a long time. Do you know where she is, really?"

"Faerieland," Cat repeated.

"She's fine," Harper added.

Sonja grinned and put her arms around their shoulders, still wondering about Bristol's disappearance, but if neither of her sisters was worried, she would try not to worry either. "Good enough. Come on. It's been a day. I'll buy us all some molten ganache at Starky's."

CHAPTER 102

Bristol didn't know what to do with herself. She had never felt so many emotions at once. Rage, heartache, shame, misery. By the time she got back to the palace and left August in his stall, her scattered thoughts had whirled out of control.

They helped me fake my death. Your grief had to be believable.

It was! she screamed in her head. *Our grief was real!* She fought disbelief that their own father would do this to them, but then his justification clawed through her chest. *It was the only way to keep you safe. I had to agree not to follow.*

They made a bargain. A bargain with Kormick.

Mick came to Bowskeep to check on the news himself. He used Bristol to confirm her father's death, probing, asking questions—and then, as long as he was there, he used her in other ways too. *God, how he had used her.*

Her skull squeezed painfully tighter with each new thought, and she stumbled along, not paying attention to her path.

I didn't want to stab him.

He was going to kill your mother.

Tyghan knew who her mother was. Who her father was.

They all did. It was a vast conspiracy that began all the way back at the Willoughby Inn. Her eyes stung with fury.

She reached out, using a pillar to steady herself. *Her mother.* Bristol had felt so betrayed that her mother left their family without explanation. Bristol was the one who had to put the shattered pieces of their lives back together and she'd been so concerned about her father's broken heart, she couldn't address her own. There wasn't time for her to grieve. *Do you love her?* When Tyghan asked her that she couldn't even bring herself to say yes. A sob tore from her throat and she pressed her cheek against the cool marble. *My mother.* Her chest twisted with misery and she pushed away from the pillar, wiping the sting from her eyes.

Only a second later she turned a corner and ran into Cully. He moved to the center of the path, blocking her. "Get out of my way," she ordered.

He widened his stance instead. "I'm charged with escorting you—"

"I don't need an escort—"

"You were missing. Where were you?" he asked, like she was late showing up to the training grounds. Bristol was not a recruit anymore.

"Where I go is no one's fucking business."

His shoulders pulled back, like he was trying to salvage some scrap of his authority. "You stole the king's horse. That makes it his business."

"As you can see, the king's horse is back, so get out of my sight!" she hissed.

"But—"

She drew her knife because he was as complicit as the rest. *He knew.* "Now!" she ordered. "Leave. Me. Alone." Her voice broke on the last word, which only made her rage burn hotter.

He put his hands up in surrender and backed away.

She continued down the path, not certain where she would go. Not certain that it mattered. But she was certain Cully still tailed her from a distance, ever true to his duty.

Her mind jumped to home. She had all but promised Harper her happy ending. Guilt gripped her, and she bent over, hugging her stomach. She wanted so badly to hold Cat and Harper, she couldn't breathe.

What was she even doing here? It had been so clear once. But now she was in a Boschian nightmare, painted onto a canvas of monsters and demons, and her mother was one of them.

She forced air into her lungs and slowly straightened, finding herself at the top of the grand staircase overlooking Sun Court. It was empty, most fae still resting before another night of carousing. It was a lonely sight when deserted, a lethargic behemoth waiting for a spark of magic to bring it to life.

She looked past the palace grounds, to the city and distant mountains, this world she had thought she was beginning to understand. She came to Elphame only wishing to find her father and answers. She had found both—and more things than she ever wanted to know.

"Hey there!" Sashka surprised her from behind, looping her arm through Bristol's and tugging her down the steps. "How'd you sleep? We're meeting at the buffet tables. The others are already there. We're starved!" Bristol stumbled on a step, but Sashka was quick and caught her. "Are you all right?"

Bristol looked at her, not sure how to answer. "I didn't sleep," she answered.

"No wonder you look so dazed. We'll get you coffee. Ivy makes sure there's always a fresh pot there just for us. She has a lot of sway around here. At least Cully thinks so. *Ivy this, Ivy that.* You would think she was queen. Well, I guess in his eyes, she is. But . . ."

Sashka continued to chatter, but Bristol's mind was still mired in the last two hours, trapped in a hideous maze created by Tyghan and her father, worse than any maze at the training grounds. *In a split second I had to choose between two people I loved.*

An impossible choice. But if he hadn't made the choice he did—

"There they are! Looks like we have the whole court to ourselves." Rose, Hollis, and Avery were tucked into an alcove near the buffet tables. As they arrived, Julia walked up from the other direction to join them. Her normally well-coiffed hair hung in a tangled mess around her shoulders.

Sashka winced. "What happened to you? Were you out riding one of those mad-ass horses again?"

Julia startled. "No, just out for a walk." She quickly tried to comb back the tangles with her fingers. "I ran into a cloud of sprites. You know how they love hair. What's all this?" she asked, pointing at the table.

It was already loaded with berries, sweet pies, and teapots. "Sit!" Hollis ordered, still in her silky pink pajamas.

Rose licked powdered sugar from her upper lip. "We knew you'd come, so we brought over everyone's favorites."

For Bristol, the delicacies were only a colorful blur.

"She didn't get any sleep," Sashka explained. "She needs coffee first!"

"Got it!" Hollis said, lifting a flowered pot, then poured a cup, adding cream because she knew how Bristol liked it.

She settled into a chair, and Rose pushed a plate of raspberry cream tarts in front of her. "Maybe these will perk you up too."

When Bristol made no move to eat them, Rose frowned. "I thought those were your favorite? I can get something else if—"

"The tarts are fine." Bristol lifted one to her lips and took a small bite to appease Rose.

Sashka continued a story she was telling about a letter she got from her older brother, how happy he was that she had already made such loyal friends. "It wasn't always easy to make friends in Frankfurt. There aren't many fae there, and all I wanted to do when I got home was get rid of my glamour. Not that glamour was hard, but it's kind of like wearing a bra. After a whole day of wearing one, you can't wait to hang that sucker on a doorknob."

They all laughed, and Rose talked about her family, too. They couldn't wait to join her in Elphame and settle in. "They worry about me, but I told them I have all of you. That we look out for each other."

Avery said her boyfriend complained in all his letters, wondering when she was coming home. "I hate to tell him that I might not."

This news spawned a flurry of surprised questions. "I like it here," Avery explained. "And Wynn and I were already iffy."

"What about your studies?" Julia asked.

"They have a university here, too. And the farms here are amazing."

Bristol listened to all their plans, their hopes, but they all hinged on the outcome of the Choosing Ceremony and who ultimately ruled Elphame. All their plans that, in a mere blink, could go so wrong.

"I found him," she blurted out. "I found my father."

They stared at her, confused. It should have been happy news. It was what she came here for, and yet it was obvious to them she was troubled.

"That's great news—isn't it?" Hollis said uncertainly. "Where is he now?"

"Gone again. He went to find my mother. He thinks he'll find her in an abandoned cottage on the banks of the Runic River."

Avery choked on her sip of nectar, spilling some onto the table. "I thought you said your mother was dead?"

"According to him, she's alive."

"Is he not quite well?" Sashka asked, tapping her temple.

Bristol's gaze circled the table like she was seeing them all for the first time. "Did you know all along who my parents really were?"

"What do you mean by *really*?" Rose asked.

Bristol's voice trembled as she told them, like she was unzipping a dark secret she was never meant to know and certainly never meant to tell, like she was confessing a sin that she didn't commit. She was tangled in something ugly that she didn't create, and all sides had made her an unwitting fool in the process. By the time she finished, she had shed her foggy daze and her anger burned bright again.

They all sat quietly, as disturbed by the news as she was.

"No, we didn't know," Hollis whispered.

"I knew," Julia said, stunning them all to silence. "I only found out a short time ago, and wasn't sure how much you knew—or wanted anyone else to know. I'm sorry I didn't tell you."

Bristol shook her head. "I guess we were all caught up in a web of lies."

Sashka blew out a long breath. "It's all so fucked up."

"Yes, it is," Bristol agreed.

Sashka reached out and held her hand. "But it doesn't change anything between us. We're still a team." The others mumbled agreement.

"Do the officers and king know that you know?" Avery asked.

Bristol shook her head. "Not yet. But they're about to."

CHAPTER 103

E ris sat at the council table with Dahlia and Tyghan, afternoon
light filtering through the high cupola windows. He eyed the
king, slouched in his seat, too silent for his liking. Tyghan had
stopped asking, *Where are they?* lost in his thoughts again, his thumb
absently stroking the arm of his chair. He had already told them what
had happened, sharing details that he normally never would, like the
sound of Kierus's screams as he left the barn. The emotion Eris had
seen twisting Tyghan's face just minutes earlier had retreated, leaving
only a hard mask. It tore Eris in two, seeing him this way, wanting
to give him more than the guidance of a royal counselor. He wanted
to hold Tyghan, comfort him, but their relationship had never been
like that.

Tyghan's thumb continued to stroke the wood of the chair like he
was trying to erase something—a regret, a memory, a demon? He had
never walked away from a prisoner before, but then, no prisoner had
ever been a Danu knight. And never his best friend. Never a prisoner
who had betrayed him so deeply. He had gone into that barn expecting finality, closure—maybe vengeance. Instead, he'd been gutted all
over again.

It was only a little stab.

Perhaps those words had cut him the deepest. *Only.* Tyghan would have given his life to save Kierus. He nearly had many times. His voice was almost a whisper when he had repeated the words to Eris and Dahlia. They beaded on his lips like fresh blood.

The light inside the rotunda grew dimmer, the enormous expanse of the council table transforming to a black hole that swallowed their thoughts. Dahlia lifted her hand toward the torches on the wall, her long fingers flicking her whispered words to bring them to life. It didn't lighten the somberness of the room. There was no satisfaction in this completed goal. No victory. It couldn't erase the damage already done.

Just as Eris was about to ask, *Where are they?* heavy boots echoed in the portico and the door latch rattled.

Tyghan's eyes froze on the door as it swung open and the knights filed in, first Dalagorn, then Melizan and Cosette, and finally Quin and Kasta.

There was no sign of Kierus.

Tyghan rose to his feet. "Where is he?"

Kasta glanced at Quin, then back to Tyghan, a scowl creasing her brow. She shook her head and stated simply, "He got away."

Tyghan was silent for a moment, his lips parted with disbelief, but then he roared to life. "What do you mean, *got away?* He escaped? Is that what you're telling me? How could he get past *five* knights?"

"There was a shadow," Quin said. "It came out of nowhere. And then he was gone."

"I think it was a nightjump," Cosette said.

"He's a fucking mortal!" Tyghan yelled. "Even you can't night-jump!"

"It happened!" Melizan snapped. "Don't blame the messenger. We had him surrounded, and there was a dark flash of *something*, like a cloak, and he was gone. Just like that."

Kasta's eyes glowed with fire. "We think someone took him the way Kormick took Bristol that night. Someone who wanted to help him."

Tyghan paced, trying to comprehend how such a thing could happen. Arguments erupted over who it could have been. Trows were Kierus's obvious allies, but they weren't able to nightjump, and Kormick definitely would not help him. Tyghan raked his fingers through his hair, still pacing the rotunda. "I should have brought him back myself."

"You can't stop a nightjump any more than the rest of us can," Dalagorn barked, heaving his hulk into a chair. It groaned under his weight. The others grabbed chairs from the outer walls of the rotunda and dragged them to the table.

Their frustration unleashed as they explained what happened, their accounts and curses overlapping.

"The barn."

"The meadow."

"Son of a bitch!"

"The nearby woods, too."

"He had help."

"We looked everywhere."

"That traitorous motherfucker."

Quin said they had spread out, searching everywhere within a hundred yards—the outside limits of a nightjump. Then they had taken to the air on their horses, searching even farther.

Kasta leaned back, huffing out a frustrated breath. "There wasn't a sign of him anywhere."

"Whoever helped him must have been lying in wait inside the barn all along," Dalagorn said.

But who would help him? There were only a handful of fae in Danu who could nightjump at all, and no one had known where they were going, not even Master Woodhouse.

"What about Keats?" Quin asked. "Maybe she told someone where she was going."

That was a possibility. And there was the unknown rider who had met her in the woods—the glamoured one who didn't want to be recognized.

Eris drew a piece of parchment from his ledger and began making a list of those they knew who could nightjump. "Besides you two," he said, nodding to Madame Chastain and Tyghan, "there's also Lord Csorba, Olivia, Reuben . . ."

"The Lumessa," Tyghan said.

Madame Chastain shook her head. "No, not anymore. She's too weak. But the Sisters Izzy and Camille are still capable."

Capable. Tyghan thought about his unexpected encounter with Julia. *I won't be opening or closing any doors for you—but I am still quite powerful.*

"Write down Julia, too," Tyghan added.

"The recruit? But she—"

"We don't know everything she can or can't do. Question her." He pushed the list across the table to Quin. "And then find out where each of them was this afternoon."

The latch rattled again, and everyone's attention darted to the door. Cully walked in, oblivious to the turmoil inside, and reported that Bristol was back on the palace grounds. "No other attempted stops. She came straight here. She's at the pavilion now." He pulled on his earlobe uncomfortably. "But there was an incident."

"Meaning?" Kasta said.

"She's not happy. She drew a knife on me and ordered me to leave her alone."

Tyghan blinked slowly, absorbing the answer. It was settled now. Kierus had told her everything.

"But she came back of her own accord," Eris spoke up, trying to dispel assumptions, "and she didn't disappear with Kierus. That is telling. She is still committed."

"Threatening an officer with a knife?" Madame Chastain countered. "That is more telling. I wouldn't count on her commitment."

"Of course she's torn, Dahlia. Kierus is her father."

Quin sighed. "We have big trouble now."

Tyghan pushed up from the table. "I'll go speak to her—"

Pounding shook the rotunda door before it swung wide, banging into the stone wall.

Melizan clucked her tongue. "Looks like the trouble has come to you."

CHAPTER 104

Tyghan didn't expect to see a smile on Bristol's face. Or her slow, comfortable swagger into the room. Worse, he didn't expect her eyes to be so unreadable. They were nothing like the night he met her at the Willoughby Inn when she struggled to hide her feelings. Now there was no struggle in her expression at all. There was nothing but a smile that didn't reach past the corner of her lips. Her eyes were as dead as deep winter. She looked more like Maire than she ever had.

The knives he had left in her room were sheathed on her belt. All three of them.

"Good afternoon," she said. "Or is it evening? I suppose we're on the cusp, which is always an interesting place to be. Twilight, maybe? Is that what you would call it, Counselor? You're so precise about words."

Eris rose to his feet. "I try to be," he said uncertainly.

"But not always successful, I suppose."

"It's twilight," Madame Chastain said. "Now that that important piece of news is settled, what else can we do for you, Miss Keats?"

The smile again, the one that was not her. "I'm glad you asked."

Tyghan started to walk around the table to usher her out. "Bristol, I think you and I should speak alone."

"No, Your Majesty," she said sharply. Her eyes rested on his for the first time. "This concerns the bargain I made with all of you. Everyone should hear what I have to say."

Your Majesty? Her formality hit him in the pit of his stomach. *Oh, the king, la-di-da.* This wasn't going to go well, but he couldn't delay the inevitable. He folded his arms in front of him and nodded in acquiescence.

Her gaze circled the room, and Tyghan saw the first break in her well-collected demeanor, the bite of her lower lip, but then her face hardened like she was redoubling her efforts to maintain her cool facade. "It's come to my attention there were hidden clauses in the bargain I made with you."

Madame Chastain shrugged. "We don't know what you're talking about."

The corner of Bristol's mouth pulled in mock disappointment. "*Really?* I'll refresh your memory—that you had plans to eliminate the Darkland monster?"

Tyghan gritted his teeth but vowed to keep his mouth shut—at least as long as he could. She might as well get it all out.

"That was not a clause, nor was it hidden," Madame Chastain replied. "Simply kingdom business that does not concern you."

Bristol clasped her hands in front of her. "But that's the crux of it. I'm afraid it does concern me, considering the Darkland monster is my mother. And *that* you did keep hidden. My *mother.*" She swallowed like the word was a stone in her mouth. "And she has a name. Leanna Keats."

As she continued, her voice changed. Word by word, her composure fell away like scales from armor. Her glare chilled the room. "And you have a thousand arrows ready to pierce her heart as soon as I shut that portal. Elven—like Cully—are busy whittling their little instruments of death just for her. But no worries. I have a hidden clause too that will remedy the situation—oh—we'll call it kingdom business, if you prefer."

The High Witch rose to her feet, standing beside Eris. "Your sarcasm is tiresome and inappropriate. You're in the presence of High Fae and the king of Danu. You will show due respect."

Bristol laughed. "And here I thought I was. At least as much as you deserve." Her focus shifted to Eris before Madame Chastain could respond. "Back to my clause. I will keep my end of the bargain, closing the Abyss portal, but there will be no more arrows aimed at my mother. And you will stop hunting my father. I plan to take them both home with me when this is over."

"Impossible," Eris replied. "Your father's sentence has already been passed by the full council. It would take another vote to rescind it."

"Then I suggest you vote."

"There isn't time—"

"*Make* time."

"Why should they?" Quin said. "You can barely shut a portal without a long-protracted visit with a knife. You aren't exactly a sure bet."

"But I'm the best bet you have, aren't I?"

Tyghan stepped forward. "All right, you're angry. We get that. But we needed your help, Bristol," he said. "If we had told you the truth from the start, would you have helped us?"

"I was never given the choice to decide. It was decided for me."

"You're avoiding the question. Would you have helped us?"

"I would have done just what you did—used you the way you used me. I would have turned the game board around so I was playing with different game pieces. I would have been smarter about the defenses I let down and the trust I gave too freely. But yes, I would have helped you, because in the end, I find Kormick marginally more despicable than all of you, and there are a few people here that I actually still care about. Now it's my turn to ask. If you had it to do over again, would you tell me the truth? See if you can be honest."

Tyghan shook his head. "No. It wasn't a chance I could take. Elphame is desperate for your help."

"Desperate? Then you better start groveling a bit more, Your Majesty, and convince your council to meet my demands."

"You arrogant little—" Kasta lunged at Bristol, but Quin held her back.

"That's enough," Tyghan said. "We'll talk later, Bristol. The things you're asking aren't that simple—"

"Yes, they are! *That simple.* Take or leave my proposal."

"You heard the king, Miss Keats," Madame Chastain snapped. "The Butcher of Celwyth will not be pardoned, and the arrows will not be stopped. You're dismissed."

Bristol's anger ripped loose. "I am not done!" she yelled, and her hand swept up in a quick stopping motion, like it would block her dismissal. Instead, a fireball erupted from her palm and barreled across the room toward Tyghan. He dove aside and swiped his hand upward as he fell to the floor, sending the fiery ball roaring up to the cupola. Sparks rained down and the knights drew their swords, but Madame Chastain stepped forward first, throwing her hands up. A stream of blinding light shot from her palms, slamming Bristol against the wall, twisting around her limbs like rope and across her mouth like a gag.

"Yes, you *are* done!" Madame Chastain declared. "And you'll stay up there until we decide what to do with you!"

Tyghan got back to his feet, brushing sparks from his shirt singed with holes. Bristol struggled to twist free from the force pinning her high on the wall, but the more she struggled, the stronger Madame Chastain's force became. Bristol's eyes landed on Tyghan, furious, betrayed, but he had seen the momentary shock in them, too, her chest sucking in a fast breath as the ball of fire flew from her hand. Was she as taken by surprise as the rest of them? He thought about the fire in her room. Was that an accident? Had she come into more power she didn't know she had? He remembered the faint line of golden scales on her shoulder blade . . .

"Let her down," he ordered.

"She just made an attempt on your life! She's trying to finish what her father started!"

Tyghan's fingers dug across his scalp. He couldn't deny that was how it appeared, but he shook his head. "Let her down," he repeated. "Now."

Madame Chastain's hands dropped in disgust, and Bristol fell to the floor on her hands and knees.

Tyghan stepped forward to help her up, but she cut him off. "Get away from me."

He reached down and grabbed her arm anyway, bringing her to her feet.

She jerked free, taking a few steps back before addressing the room again. "As you've probably gathered by now, I've found and spoken with my father. We had a long and interesting talk."

"We're aware," Tyghan said. "We saw you both. We used hair in your brush to find you—"

"But by the time we got there, you were both gone," Kasta said, twisting the narrative so Bristol wouldn't know they had captured Kierus—at least temporarily.

"How did you find him?" Tyghan asked.

"With no help from you. He sent a note for me to meet him. Someone left it in my room."

Tyghan's jaw clenched. It was getting worse by the minute. Kierus had access to someone in the palace. "Who was it?"

"I didn't see who delivered the note, nor would I tell you if I did."

The veins in Quin's neck rose, and Dalagorn's hand curled into a meaty fist.

"Easy," Melizan warned. "If one of these knights snapped right now, no one would blame them."

Tyghan pulled out a chair and sat down. "So, you snuck out behind my back after promising you wouldn't, took my horse without permission, and, no doubt, your father has now told you his version of events."

"That pretty much sums it up," she answered unapologetically.

Kasta huffed out an angry breath. "There are not two versions to this story."

Bristol laughed. "Is that so?" She tapped her lips. "All right, what about a third version? Mine. I can definitely vouch for that one. All these past weeks, I thought I was hunting down trows. *Fucking trows.*" Her chin dimpled briefly. "What a laugh you all must have had, feeding me leads that went nowhere. Well done." Her eyes glistened, and she blinked several times. "It was you all along. You were the ones who hunted my family like we were animals. That's the version I grew up with, because it wasn't only my parents you made run for over two decades. My sisters and I had to run, too. Do you have any idea what it's like to run from something your entire life and not know what it is? To live out of a duffle bag in one dingy motel after another? To have to flee in the middle of the night and not even know why? To never have any place you could call home?"

She paused, looking down, her lips twisted, then looked directly at Tyghan. "I was named after a shithole flea market in some obscure town my parents couldn't even remember because of you. They didn't understand their world any better than I did. Thank god they didn't give me a middle name, because it probably would have been Avenue."

"The way your parents raised you reflects on them, not us. It was their choice," Tyghan replied.

"What choice did they have? When they finally stopped running, two kingdoms tracked them down!"

"Get to your point, Miss Keats," Madame Chastain said.

"*My point?*" Her palms met like she was trying to hold back from barreling another fireball across the room. "You lied to me!" she finally answered. "Do fae have any kind of conscience at all? You weren't helping me find my father. Just the opposite, you were hunting him down."

Eris cleared his throat. "Yes," he admitted, his tone grave. "We were. But your father committed a serious crime. We had no grievance against you."

"He wanted out. That's it. A different life. That was his crime."

A different life? Tyghan jumped to his feet, the chair screeching behind him. He'd heard enough of this version. "What about my life? He stabbed me! And damn near killed me!"

"You were going to kill my mother!"

"She wasn't your mother yet! She was a monster terrorizing Elphame!"

"Because she had no choice! Can't a person ever start over? That's all they wanted. To be something else than what you all made them be. A second chance."

"There are no second chances! Not for what he did! You're defending a stranger. A man you don't even know. Don't lecture us about conscience. He was going to kill your mother first! Did he tell you that? And look what he did to his own daughter! Did you tell him you nearly died trying to remove that tick?"

"He had to put it there because of *you*!"

"Don't you dare put his actions on me!"

With each accusation they had inched closer, until they were toe to toe.

"They were in love, Tyghan," Bristol said more softly. "They were young, scared, and in love."

"You're going to buy everything he's said after the lifetime of lies he fed you?"

"I know what I saw! He loved my mother, and he loved her deeply!"

Tyghan shook, fury blinding him. "You're telling me he threw away a lifetime of duty for a toss in a bed? He knew her for what? Three weeks? It wasn't love! No one falls in love that fast! She was a good fuck! That's all!"

Bristol stared at him, her mouth open, breathless.

The harshness of his words reverberated through the room. *No one falls in love that fast.*

She nodded. "Of course," she answered. A numb glaze coated her voice. "Of course. I'm glad you made that clear. Your Majesty. Good to know."

She turned to leave, but he caught her arm. "Bristol, wait. You know that's not what I meant."

She looked back at him, her pupils overwhelming her irises like she was in a deep, dark cave. "I think you spoke truthfully. Maybe it's the first honest thing you've ever said to me."

She pulled free of his grip and walked toward the door but turned one last time, returning to a picture of reserve, the chilling smile back on her face. "Assuming you meet my demands, I'll see you all at drills tomorrow. Don't be late."

And then she was gone. The echo of her footsteps in the portico faded until the room was silent. Stifling.

"That's it?" Kasta finally said. "You're just going to let her walk away after she—"

"Let it be, Kasta," Tyghan replied, still reeling from his incredibly bad choice of words.

"But she's—"

"I said, let it be! I know what I'm doing!" he yelled. But he didn't. This had all become too complicated, too impossible, just as Kasta had warned. He walked to the far side of the rotunda, trying to think of orders to yell, something to take the focus off his last words with Bristol. Instead, he stopped and leaned against the wall, pressing his palm to the stone, staring at the floor, trying to piece together one coherent thought. "Follow her," he said to Cully. "Make sure she doesn't leave the grounds."

More awkward silence followed, and Eris stepped up to fill it. "Let's not overreact. She's still on our side. She just needs time."

Madame Chastain slammed her hands down on the table. "Our side? Were you paying attention at all? Time is not going to cure this mess. Everything doesn't always have a happy ending, Eris."

"And everything doesn't always end in doom and gloom either, Dahlia! I wish just once you would trust my judgment!"

"Your judgment is what got us here in the first place. I warned you she could be a problem and now it's the eleventh hour—"

Eris threw his hands in the air. "I'm done for the day." He headed for the door, his robe billowing behind him. "I suggest we all do as Miss Keats said, and not be late for drills in the morning."

CHAPTER 105

Bristol's plan had unraveled so quickly, she may as well have not had one at all. Her emotions had slipped out of seams she thought she had carefully sewn shut.

She managed to summon one last bit of calm before she left them all gaping in the rotunda, her last desperate grab at control, but it vanished as soon as she stepped into her room, like a cork popped free from a bottle.

No one falls in love that fast.

She grabbed the vase of hyacinths on her breakfast table and sent it flying across the room. The glass shattered against the wall, and the crushed purple flowers dropped in a wet bruise to the floor. But it wasn't enough. It didn't stop the lightning crackling beneath her skin. She yanked the cloth from the table, and dishes crashed to the floor, untouched pastries rolling like dead soldiers across the carpet. It still wasn't enough.

It wasn't rage that consumed her, but something deeper and more painful. A devouring despair was eating her alive.

She searched for something else to throw, destroy, something to block out the voices in her head, and spotted the wardrobe. Her chest heaved, and she lunged at it as if it was a living beast, and threw open its doors.

Dusk closed in around Tyghan, the palace grounds blinking alive, but he saw and heard none of it. The rest of the world was a blur as he beat a straight path to Bristol's room. Their discussion was not over.

Quin and Melizan both warned him not to go, to give Bristol time, but Madame Chastain was right in this instance. Time would not fix this problem. It would only allow it to fester like a dirty wound. He had to clear the air with Bristol. Give her context to events that had happened. She had heard Kierus's version first, but she would hear his version last. He turned the corner to the hallway that led to her room, and his steps slowed, then stopped altogether. The hallway—

Its full length was littered with items he recognized, like a raiding troop of wild things had passed through, scattering them helter-skelter. His shirts. Boots. Trousers. Halfway down the hall, his knives—all three—were stabbed into a mirror frame. Jackets, combs, belts, every personal item of his that had made its way into Bristol's room these past weeks was flung out like things so foul, they had to be disposed of immediately.

Amid the bedlam, something else caught his eye. Something small, sparkling, and green. He walked closer and knelt. It was one of the emerald earrings he had given her. He remembered kissing each of her earlobes before he gave them to her. He picked up the earring, cupping it in his palm, remembering her saying, *Your love is more precious to me than any jewel.*

Apparently not anymore.

He looked around for the other earring, but it was lost somewhere under the mounds of mayhem. He shoved the lone jewel in his pocket and walked toward her door.

This wasn't over yet.

Bristol's thumb throbbed. There was no question that she had broken it after slamming the wardrobe door shut during her rampage. She could go to Olivia or Esmee to have it healed, but then she might run into someone, and there were at least a dozen people she wanted to avoid.

And maybe the throbbing was a good thing, something else to occupy her because she was tired of thinking. It hurt too much, far more than a broken thumb.

She stretched out, perched at the end of her bed, wishing she could fall asleep, wishing she hadn't broken the flask of wine on her table. Wishing she had two more just like it. Every time she closed her eyes, a new voice would creep in, making her question everything she had ever believed about her life.

Come away, child.

Her mother pleading with a four-year-old girl. What was so dangerous about that tree? What did her mother fear? That it was a portal that would take Bristol away? A goblin that might eat Bristol whole? A king's hunter who might whisk the unsuspecting child back to Elphame? Or was it simply all the secrets that Bristol might unlock?

That long-ago afternoon was a collage of blurred memories, her mother's lips pressed to her temple, the strange words she whispered against her skin, the frayed edges of secrets they held, her mother's desperation making her careless. *Spells. She was casting spells.* If only Bristol had been old enough to make sense of it all.

She felt her mother's grip around her again, tight and full of dread. *She sacrificed everything for you.* Leanna Keats had never been good at expressing her feelings, not like her father, who had a tongue of honey and optimism. But with her mother, there was always the watchful eye, somehow grabbing her three daughters' hands at once, like a hen's broad wing around chicks, and pulling them closer. She always feared dangers they couldn't see, the dangers her mother couldn't forget. Bristol remembered the many times she and Cat tried to wriggle free from her clutch. Even when they camped in a meadow, her mother always walked the perimeter first before any supplies were pulled from the van or fires were lit. She'd claim she was gathering stones for the firepit or checking for snakes, but until she signaled Bristol's father, the girls weren't allowed more than an arm's length from the van. What had she really been searching for? Lurking fae?

Her parents were killed in a goblin raid. And then on the heels of that, her uncles had abused her and chained her to a post. Were those the nightmares her father had to wake her from? He sang to her, repeating the same few stanzas from a poem as he stroked her head until she fell back asleep. Those were the fears that Kormick bound her with.

Bristol was just getting used to the idea of her mother being fae, the secret settling into her bones, but now she had to grasp that her mother was regarded as a monster, too—Kormick's monster. And yet . . . her father was called the Butcher of Celwyth, a title that, at one time at least, had commanded respect and awe. Some even called him the wonder of Danu. *I killed many. I did as I was told.* Her father served one king, her mother another, one regarded as an esteemed knight, the other reviled as a monster. The fae world was a poisonous pot of contradictions.

Two sudden raps on the door broke the silence of her room. She sat up, her heart beating faster. Two more quick raps. Impatience. The rap of a king.

"I'm busy," she called.

The door flew open, and Tyghan stepped in.

Bristol swung her feet to the floor, ready to take up a weapon. "Get out of my room!"

Tyghan surveyed the damage, his expression growing darker as he viewed the shattered glass and the overturned table. His nostrils flared. He looked as formidable and dangerous as he had the first time Bristol laid eyes on him. "Until yesterday, this was *our* room."

"That was yesterday."

His hand swept angrily out toward the hallway. "And that? What does that mean? Everything is over between us just like that?"

She rose from the bed. "Just what was between us, Your Majesty? From the moment we met at the Willoughby Inn, it was all a charade. More like a cheap carnival con. Sleight of hand. Reel the mortal in. Make her take the prize."

"You're not mortal."

"Half. Or do you want to pretend my father's half doesn't exist? Wouldn't that be convenient? Oh, but then there's my mother's half. I guess you lose all the way around, since you hate them both. Now

I know why you were always so angry at me when we first met. You hated me too, didn't you? You hated me because I reminded you of them."

"I didn't hate you. I was wary. A lot has happened since that first day at the inn."

Her brows rose. "*A lot*. Such a lovely euphemism. You mean all the times we fucked? I guess we can chalk that up to Beltane, can't we? A season of mistakes."

"That's what you think? That we were a mistake? Dammit, Bristol! Yes, a lot of mistakes were made, but they weren't all mine. When I made the deal with you to search for your father, I didn't know he was still alive. I was duped as much as you were."

"But you wanted him dead."

A tic pulsed near his temple. "Not that way."

"Because you wanted to kill him yourself."

"Yes," he answered without remorse.

"Why couldn't you just let it go, Tyghan? It was a mistake! He didn't know it was a demon blade or what it would do to you."

His lips parted. "A mistake?" he finally said. His face flushed with color. But it was his eyes that Bristol noticed, the wince around his lids, the smallest movement that showed the greatest pain. When he spoke again, each word was chiseled stone. "He was my friend, and he knew it was a *blade*. A blade that could kill me. I bleed and can die just like anyone else—and he knew that. *He knew.*"

He headed for the door, but when he opened it and saw all the chaos in the hallway again, he stopped and looked back at her, his lips rolling over his teeth like he was struggling to hold back more words. He failed. "Just this morning I told you I loved you. I meant it."

She saw the hurt in his face, his shoulders squaring, bracing himself against the pain. She didn't care. She wanted to hurt him more. She wanted things to be even, fair. She wanted the pain in her own head to stop. "Don't try to pretend you ever loved me. You're a disgusting liar, and you don't even know what love is."

A final punch. She saw that too, in the deadening of his gaze.

He nodded. "Maybe not," he answered. "Maybe neither of us do. See you at drills in the morning, Keats. And just so you know, Eris is working on your demands, even if it means more knights might die because of them."

He left, slamming the door behind him.

CHAPTER 106

Cosette's silken lips traveled down Melizan's back. She whispered soft, gentle things, her voice as seductive as a balmy breeze, but Melizan studied her palm like she could read something in its creases. Cosette flipped onto her back and sighed a frustrated breath. "Where the hell are you?"

Melizan turned to Cosette, only a little contrite for her lack of attention. "I'm still in that fucking barn, trying to figure out how a mere mortal slipped right through our fingers. Tyghan has every right to be furious. I never would have believed it myself. Whose loose lips—"

"You think this is all my fault, don't you? You still blame me."

"What?"

Cosette rose from the bed, snatching up her robe. "For Cael."

Melizan sighed. "Not that again. Let it go, Cosette. I never blamed you."

"Tyghan did, or at least he suspected me."

"I never told him anything. Cael was a fool to travel without an escort."

"But my slip—"

"Elphame is nothing if not a writhing pit of wagging tongues. Especially when royal affairs are on the menu. Even solemn oaths can't keep them from wagging. A dozen people saw Cael leave that day. It could have been anyone."

But Cosette was the last one to see him. The last one to speak to him. And then she went down to the shore to see her family. Tyghan had noted that.

"I've done everything I can to make up for it. You know my family, they just want news of anything. Life in the river can be so dull—"

Melizan's head cocked to the side as if struck by a thought. "Have you told your family that Kierus is back?"

"No! I told you, I don't tell them anything anymore."

"Hmm," Melizan mused, tapping her finger to her chin. "Maybe you should?" She held her hand out to Cosette. "Come back to bed. Maybe there's a way your family can help us. But first, let me make up for my inattention."

"Have you grown tired of me?" Cosette asked, her lower lip halfway between a pout and a deadly threat.

Nothing could have been farther from the truth. Cosette was Melizan's match in every way, the only one—but the idea of marriage, which Cosette brought up frequently—frightened Melizan, the idea of caring too much, because it seemed that was a certain way of losing someone. And she never wanted to lose Cosette.

"Come back to bed, my love, and you'll find out."

CHAPTER 107

Ivy peeked into Eris's office. He was surrounded by ledgers and books piled on his desk and a dozen messages already sealed with wax, waiting to be delivered. "Sorry to interrupt you, Counselor. There's a recruit outside. She says she needs to see you?"

"Now is not a good time. Can't she—"

"She says it's important. It concerns the Butcher of Celwyth."

Eris set his quill down. Recruits came to him often, usually wanting news of their family or wanting to send a message, but this time it was news of a different kind—news that piqued his interest. "I have a few minutes."

Ivy ushered her in and left, and Eris listened silently, trying to show no surprise as she shared what she had learned—the possible whereabouts of Kierus.

"I thought I should come to you. After what he did to Bristol with the tick and then abandoning her. She's so upset. I hate seeing her this way. And then of course, what he did to the king is unthinkable. . . ." She paused, hugging her arms to her chest. "I was afraid he might do something else, something worse, and I don't want either of them to be hurt again. And with the Choosing Ceremony so close, he might jeopardize everything." A shaky breath rattled her chest. "Was it right for me to tell you?"

No doubt Bristol had told her this information in confidence, but Eris nodded, because it was information he wanted—and needed. If their friendship was shattered because of this breach, so be it. Maybe this would finally bring Tyghan the resolution he needed. "You did the right thing. But we'll keep this information just between us, all right?"

Rose nodded, the worry fading from her face, and Eris walked her to the door.

CHAPTER 108

The rampage in her room hadn't brought Bristol the relief she sought. Neither had hurling cruel words at Tyghan. She felt as desolate and lost now as when she turned her back on her father in the barn.

She hesitated outside Julia's door. It was late, but she tapped lightly anyway.

Julia was still shrugging a long floral robe over her gown when the door opened. "Bri, what are you doing here?"

"Do you know anything about healing?" And then she fell into Julia's arms. She didn't cry. She just held on to Julia like she was all the people in her life she couldn't be near, people who were too far away, too lost, too angry. Too impossible to be with.

When she ushered Bristol inside and closed the door, the tears came. A gentle shuddering at first, and then sobs like she was mourning a death, like a part of her was dying. And Julia held her.

When the tears were spent, Julia tucked Bristol into an overstuffed chair in the corner of the room and examined her hand.

"Rest here while I prepare a few things."

The first of those things was to pour them each a glass of wine. "It is the French way," she explained with a heavier accent than usual. "The mood must be set."

"For healing a thumb?"

Julia smiled as she gathered balm and bandages. "Even for that. How did you know about me? Did you see me heal my own wounds?"

"No," Bristol answered, sipping her Bordeaux, wondering how Julia came by French wine in Elphame. "But I never saw Esmee or Olivia treat you, and your cuts and bruises still magically disappeared. Why would you keep it a secret?"

"Every woman should have a few secrets." She shrugged. "An arsenal as needed."

Bristol winced as Julia pressed on the fleshy part of her thumb. "Cracked, but luckily not shattered. How'd this come about? I hope the council didn't—"

"No, I did this fully and stupidly on my own. I declared war against a heavy wardrobe door, and the door won."

"Your meeting went that badly?"

"Worse. I unraveled. All my calm and cool went out the window. Ugly things were said to me. I said them back. I made demands. I wanted to hurt them. I wanted—" Bristol shook her head. "I really don't know what I want anymore. It was a mistake to ever come here."

"Because you learned the truth? Isn't that what you came for? Was the doubt better?"

"Maybe," Bristol answered, and felt the lie of it instantly. She shook her head. "No. The doubt was suffocating me. The unseen threat hovering over our heads for all those years—I couldn't take it anymore. Not for me or my family. I couldn't move forward."

"And just what does moving forward mean for you now?"

Bristol saw the concern in Julia's eyes. So far Bristol was the only known bloodmarked in Danu—and if she left, she could destroy all their dreams. But she couldn't lie. "I'm not sure what it means now. A lot of trust has been destroyed. Bridges burned. I screamed at them all—my father, Tyghan, the council. I've done more shouting in the last day than I've done in a lifetime. And they all have different defenses, excuses. I don't know who's right and who's wrong anymore. What my father did to Tyghan, what he did to me as a baby, what Tyghan and the council did to my family, all the lies, I can't stop thinking about it."

"Sometimes desperate people do desperate things."

"I expected the truth to be easier."

"I suppose we all do, but the dark side of truth is usually riddled with regret." She turned Bristol's hand and lightly skimmed the base of her thumb as she whispered words, then began bandaging it.

"What about you, Julia? Do you have things you regret?"

She huffed out a breath. "Too many to count."

"Deeply regret," Bristol clarified.

Julia nodded, almost reluctantly. "Early on, there were things I did as a lioness that I would never do as a human. And some things I did as a human that I would never do as a lioness. Maybe even things I wouldn't do as either."

"Unforgivable things?"

Creases deepened around her eyes. "Unforgivable is a tricky word. Only you can decide what that means. Not kings or councils. Forgiveness is a thing of the heart, and every heart is wounded and mended in its own way."

Bristol couldn't imagine her heart ever mending after this. "Sometimes forgiveness never comes."

Julia sighed. "That too." She placed Bristol's bandaged hand back in her lap. "Unlike bones, there is no magic for healing a damaged heart."

CHAPTER 109

In the morning, Bristol dragged herself to drills, her own quiet room too stifling to endure any longer. The day began in Ceridwen Hall with Olivia, Esmee, and Reuben bombarding them with magics to deflect and perform on demand. The chairs, tables, and lectern were gone, the hall empty except for the upper floors still filled with books. The recruits stood in a circle, the witches and wizard hitting hard with rapid commands. A moment's hesitation brought a stinging shock that represented a kill. Within the first ten minutes, they were all "dead."

"Again," Reuben grumbled, reminding them their amulets weren't there to complement their eye color. "Use them, dammit!" But many amulets required a simple word to bring their power to life, and even a word required a second to recall—not to mention there were a dozen words for "deflect" alone—depending on the object.

Olivia and Esmee were just as harsh, taunting and jeering in ways they never had before. They took turns, pointing to a random recruit with an order. Some required simple spells, like levitating objects, but then others required more complicated spells for actually throwing those objects as distraction and defense.

Their commands alone were like weapons, echoing through the cavernous hall.

"Invisible!"

"Shape-shift!"

"Summon!"

"Glamour!"

"Levitate!"

"Mist!"

"Fauna!"

"Deflect!"

The one thing they didn't ask for was fire. At least not from Bristol, and she was grateful, because she still didn't understand how the ability she had controlled perfectly just a few days ago had become so unstable inside her.

But by the fourth round, with their aggravation growing, the re- cruits began working in unison without even speaking, their weeks of practice together blooming into its own kind of magic, an instinctive language and trust allowing them to deflect, throw, and summon for one another, stepping in when another hesitated, working with their strengths, even throwing glamour on one another, a more advanced skill, until soon Olivia, Esmee, and Reuben couldn't keep up with com- mands or identify who was who, and Esmee finally raised her hands in mock surrender. "Well done! That was cheating a bit, but working as a team is a cheat I approve of. Olivia?"

"If it keeps them alive, that's all that matters. Reuben?"

He frowned. "Go on to your field drills. And don't come back dead."

As they filed out of the room, Hollis whispered, "Doesn't he have a way with words? Be still my heart."

Bristol thought about all the demands and painful words that had passed yesterday—hers, Tyghan's, and her father's. They made Reu- ben's words seem like a veritable love letter. It was chilling how one day and a little perspective could change everything.

Kasta paced in front of them, an angry beat in her footsteps. She was an enigma to Bristol. Kind but vengeful, disciplined but—softhearted?

Was that why she had walked away when her father pleaded with her to ignore her discovery? She seemed like the last knight who would do such a thing. Clearly, Tyghan didn't know what she had done. Bristol guessed Kasta regretted her decision now and the secrecy of it ate at her. This morning she was all business, but business with a sharp edge. Was she still seething about Bristol's demands? She refused to back down from those. Cully, Sloan, and a commander from the Badbe Garrison lined up behind Kasta, all of them standing with their hands behind their backs, like they were in some kind of grim procession.

"We leave tomorrow at dawn," Kasta said. "It's likely our last opportunity to rescue Cael before the ceremony. The rescue party will be small for the best chance of remaining undetected. Only Rose and Hollis will join the officers on the mission, while the rest of you will stay behind and aid Commander Sloan in protecting the palace. Olivia will also join us in case Cael requires special care. We don't know how weak or injured he might be."

Bristol eased forward. "I thought I was supposed to go along too, to pinpoint the precise location of the portal for the—"

"The plan has changed."

"But—"

Kasta stepped forward briskly, almost pouncing on Bristol. "There are no buts, Keats. Do you understand? None! You will keep your fucking mouth shut. Unless someone has elevated you to the position of officer? Has that happened?"

Kasta's reaction was beyond the pale. Bristol stepped back and shook her head, not wishing to get into another confrontation—but something wasn't right. This wasn't just about Bristol's demands. She saw the confusion in Julia's eyes, too. First Madame Chastain was absent that morning from what appeared to be a crucial test by the team of sorcerers, and now Tyghan was absent from this final briefing before the rescue? He always led briefings. His last words to her were that he would see her in the morning.

"Rose and Hollis, come with me. The rest of you can go with Commander Sloan."

The recruits stepped forward, slightly dazed at the speed of events. Bristol paused. "And Tyghan? Where is he today? Why isn't he here?"

"King Trénallis is tending to other important matters."

"What's more important than this?" Bristol asked.

"The king's affairs are none of your business. Now follow orders."

"Keats, this way," Sloan called.

Important matters. Like meeting her demands? Bristol reluctantly followed Sloan.

The day passed dismally slowly. With the clock ticking, it seemed imperative that they be doing something more vital than reviewing key defense stations around the palace that any knight from the garrison could handle. Tyghan's absence became more noticeable as the day wore on. Was he mired in a contentious council meeting? *Eris is working on your demands, even if it means more knights might die. Which knights?* she wondered. She glanced at Avery and Sashka walking beside her. Last night she didn't care if there were costs. Tyghan and the others had created this nightmare, not her, and she wanted them to suffer for it. She'd backed them into a corner and counted it as a victory. But now she kept wondering, *Which knights?* And how would they die?

It was late afternoon when Sloan finally dismissed the recruits for the day. Bristol went straight to Lir Rotunda to speak directly with Tyghan about going along on the mission to rescue Cael—but the rotunda was deserted. She circled the table, and her stomach fluttered. Ashes from the day before still littered its surface. She hadn't meant to throw the fireball, but remembered the strange release she felt and then the horror of what she had done. Chairs were still in the same disarray as when she left yesterday, as if no one had been in there since.

But if Tyghan hadn't been at the rotunda all day, where was he? Why hadn't the council met? No one had been there to address her demands? They were lying to her again. She didn't think she had any more adrenaline left inside her to get angry, but she felt needles pulse through her skin at the thought of more lies. She headed for Tyghan's room. He had to be somewhere.

As she walked down the hall toward his suite, two servants emerged from his room. They carried trays piled high with dishes of half-eaten food. The hob and a pixie recognized her from her many late-night rendezvous with Tyghan.

"The king is not taking visitors," the hob said as she passed him.

But it appeared he definitely was. All that food wasn't for him. Something pinched inside her. Who was he entertaining?

She continued toward his door, but then hesitated, afraid to knock, afraid of who might answer, when she shouldn't care at all. She didn't care. *Important matters?* Like hell. She knocked, loud and hard. Muffled voices hummed inside—a female voice.

The door opened a crack. It was a beautiful spriggan, her tawny leaves glimmering in the candlelight. "Go away. The king is occupied," she said, then closed the door before Bristol could respond.

Occupied? With *what*? She knocked again. There was no answer, and the door wouldn't give. A blaze lit inside her, but instead of pounding again, she stepped aside and waited. She didn't have to wait long. The door opened, and another servant stepped out, this time with a basket of laundry. Bristol caught the door before it could close and motioned for the surprised hob to move on.

When she stepped into the foyer, low conversations rumbled from the next room. *Madame Chastain.* She was asking a servant to bring supplies. What was going on? It didn't sound like a council meeting. She heard Quin and Melizan talking softly, but still no Tyghan. As she listened for other voices, she glanced up at the elaborate mirror that was the focal point of the foyer—but there was an oddness about it. The snake was in a different position than she remembered, his head now at the top of the frame, and there was a large bulge sagging in the middle of his belly she was certain hadn't been there before, as if the carved wooden animal had eaten something. She reached out to touch it, but then heard a loud slam and Eris shouting.

"I told him! I warned him what could happen! I warned him a hundred times!"

Who? Bristol wondered, and why were they all gathered here?

She stepped out of the foyer, revealing her presence. Quin and Melizan were sprawled on one of the long sofas, and Cully slouched in a chair, his eyes half-closed. Eris paced the room, and the High Witch glowered as she rummaged through her bag. They all looked tired. The spriggan who had answered the door spotted Bristol and rushed out of the suite, clutching an amulet hanging from her neck.

"Where's Tyghan?" Bristol asked.

Madame Chastain snapped her bag shut. "This is not your—"

Tyghan stumbled around the corner, shirtless, his eyes bloodshot. Damp strands of hair fell over his brow. He clutched the doorway, then walked to the sofa, bracing one hand on the back of it like it was the only thing holding him up. Loose trousers hung low on his hips. A thick bandage circled his left wrist. "Now is not a good time, Bristol," he said, his voice weak.

"What happened?"

"He—"

Tyghan's hand shot up, and he shot a warning glare at Eris. "She doesn't need to know." His gaze turned back to Bristol, as he struggled to stand. "Get out."

Something was wrong. How did he hurt his wrist? And why did he look so tired? This wasn't what she expected to find. "I think this concerns me."

"No," he said. "It doesn't. Leave."

Quin stood, his eyes almost as red as Tyghan's. "I'll walk you out."

He gripped Bristol's upper arm and led her out to the hallway. After he closed the door behind them, he explained what had happened— Tyghan had been up all night wrestling with a legion of demons. "He was the one who used the hair from your brush. He breathed the smoke."

"*What?* Why would he do that? He knew what it could do—"

"He was afraid, and I was too late getting to your room to stop him. When he saw the ashes and scorched ceiling over your tub, he assumed something terrible had happened to you. For him, every second counted. He took the risk."

For you. Quin didn't say it. Maybe he didn't even think it. But Bristol felt it. "Don't try to blame this on me."

"I'm only telling you the facts." The words were hard on his lips.

Queasiness churned in her gut. "It was a stupid thing for him to do."

"No argument there. Stupid. Compounded by incredibly bad timing." He sighed, rubbing his forehead with his palm. "Like Tygh said, you need to go. The rest of us have another long night ahead." He went back inside, shutting the door, and Bristol leaned against the opposite wall, closing her eyes. *Demons?* The scrawled hash marks marring his study walls swam in her head, the broken glass, the frenzied piles of books, the room that made him dizzy just by walking inside. Breathing the smoke was a foolish thing for him to do. But it wasn't her fault—

Desperate people do desperate things.

Desperate to find her. "It's not my fault," she whispered to herself.

She pushed off the wall, marching down the hallway, refusing to let guilt or worry creep in, but when she reached the end of the hall, she stopped. Instead of her next step, she saw Tyghan's hooded eyes, his face glistening with sweat, his weakness as he leaned against the sofa for support. *Some nights, I didn't want to survive at all. I wanted to give up.*

Something cold spread through her chest, and she spun, heading back down the hallway. She knew she wasn't welcome, but with every step, she steadied her breathing, and put on her best sales persona. And then she flung open Tyghan's door.

CHAPTER 110

She sold it hard, focusing on the easiest target in the room—Eris—who for some reason had always believed in her. "We need him for this mission, and I can get him through the night. I promised you I would help. I'm true to my word."

Eris tried to respond, but Tyghan was yelling. "Get her out! Now! She doesn't belong in here! Out!"

She focused on the High Witch as Quin began dragging her toward the door. "Are you going to listen to a half-mad king or someone who knows him? What are you afraid of, Madame Chastain? That I'm right?" It wasn't exactly a typical sales pitch, but she had to gear her words for the particular customer, and the High Witch was more particular than most. She took up the gauntlet, and it bought Bristol at least a temporary reprieve. She stopped Quin from throwing Bristol out, but then went off on a tirade, revealing more of her own fears than she probably intended. *Annihilation. A dead king. Failure.*

"Failure?" Bristol said. "Aren't we there already? The leader and most powerful fae of your nation is delirious and can barely stand. Look at him! He needs sleep. Real sleep!"

Even as she said the words, Tyghan was already collapsing in Eris's and Cully's arms and they were helping him back to his chamber.

Once he was out of the room, Bristol asked, "How much more do you really have to lose by trusting me?"

The High Witch hesitated, as if considering, but her fingers still twitched like she was ready to slam Bristol against another wall.

Bristol turned to Melizan, who was curled up on the sofa, and shot her a pleading glance. Genuine. No sales pitch. *Please. Help me.*

Melizan's chin lifted as she coolly eyed Bristol. "So . . . what's in this for you?"

Her cynicism made Bristol's stomach clench. "I told you yesterday, I still care about Elphame and want it to survive. And I don't want the mortal world to be next on Kormick's annihilation list. That hasn't changed, and the king is part of that survival."

"Elphame and the mortal world?" A small snicker escaped Melizan's lips. "That's the only reason you're here? That's all you care about?"

Bristol's eyes stung. *Don't*, she thought. *Don't make me say it.* She hadn't resolved in her own conflicted head what she was feeling. She was still juggling lies and loyalties, and it was tearing her in two. She blinked, her vision blurring. "No, that's not all I care about," she answered quietly.

"Good," Melizan answered, and gestured toward Tyghan's chamber. "Go."

And astonishingly, neither Quin nor the High Witch tried to stop her.

The counselor was walking out of Tyghan's bedchamber as Bristol walked in. "I heard what you said out there," he whispered. "If you can somehow give him six or seven hours, that's all he needs. A few hours of real rest to get his strength back. To fortify his resistance and close the doors that were opened. He already went three days without sleep during Beltane and then last night—" He winced, like the events of the previous night were too unspeakable. "Be careful. When the demons take hold, he's not himself. They may not physically be in the room, but when they enter his mind, the torture is real. Their control is real."

Bristol nodded and closed the chamber doors behind her.

Eris settled onto the sofa beside Dahlia. She leaned into him, resting her head on his shoulder, forgetting her revered protocols.

"Do you think it's safe for her to be in there?" Cully asked.

"Safe for him or for her?" Quin asked.

Cully thought for a moment. "Either one."

"Neither," Dahlia murmured, her eyes closed. "But as our shining recruit noted, what more do we have to lose?"

"What do you think she's doing in there?" Quin asked. "It's too quiet. I don't hear him screaming."

Melizan stretched and headed for the door. "Thank the gods. I'm going back to my suite to sleep. If one of them murders the other, don't call me."

Eris rose from the sofa and intercepted her at the door. The unexpected snag of Tyghan's health had pushed Rose's confession to the back of his mind. "I didn't want the others distracted by some news I received," he explained, "but since you aren't going on the mission tomorrow, I thought you might be able to follow up on something else for me—discreetly. It was told to me in confidence."

Melizan smiled as he conveyed the details of Rose's news. "The Runic River? That's a thousand miles of riverbanks to search, but we'll look into it. I may have resources to help me narrow it down."

Eris nodded. He knew exactly who she meant. Cosette's relatives ranged far and wide. When Melizan left, he returned to the sofa and the stifling silence. After a few minutes, Cully got up and went to listen by the bedchamber door.

"Hear anything?" Eris asked.

Cully shook his head. "Nothing."

And none of them were sure if that was a good or a bad thing. Eris put his arm around Dahlia and pulled her closer. She didn't resist, and that, at least, was a good thing. Unless it meant she had given up entirely.

The room was dark, the drapes drawn, but the walls flickered with warm light from a single candle in the corner. Tyghan lay in his bed, his sheets and blankets twisted in piles on the floor. His body sunk into the mattress like he was dead. He was so still it made Bristol pause.

She inched a few steps closer. His bare chest glistened with sweat, and she watched to see if he was breathing at all. His eyes were open, but they only stared blankly at the ceiling and he didn't seem to know she was there.

Most disturbing, an iron shackle embedded with unknown stones was secured around his wrist and attached to a long chain anchored to the wall. That's what the thick bandage on his wrist was for—in case he strained against it. But he wasn't straining. He was like a trapped animal that had given up. Her throat knotted. This was what the demons had done to him in one night?

She didn't move. She barely breathed herself. Now what?

She had no plan. She had rushed into his suite the same way she had rushed into Elphame—recklessly. But she had to act while she could and figure out the finer points later.

Bristol stared, wishing he would move or even flutter a finger— and then his chest rose in a shallow breath. He hadn't given up yet. She'd make sure he never did. Though she didn't have a plan for that either.

She stepped forward, and as she approached, his head turned. He tried to brace himself up on one arm but fell back. "I already told you, I don't want you here."

"Lovely welcome. Hello to you, too."

"Get out."

"Or what?" she taunted. "What are you going to do? Chase me until your leash runs out?"

"I still have some magic." But he only lifted his free hand a few inches off the bed before it fell limply back at his side. His lids shut momentarily, like he was shamed by his weakened state. "Please. Go away."

Instead, she stepped up to his bedside and looked down at him. "That was a stupid thing you did."

He groaned. "You too? I've already been told several times. Thanks for reminding me."

"Hindsight's a boastful shithead, isn't it?"

The bitterness of their words from the day before still lurked in his eyes. "At the time it seemed like a good idea. I had to make a quick decision. I guess it was the wrong one."

"I suppose anyone could make a stupid, desperate decision in the heat of the moment."

Even in his miserable state, her innuendo was not lost on him. He sighed. "Why are you here, Keats?"

"Don't make me choose, Tyghan."

Only a sliver of blue showed beneath his heavy lids, but it was icy and sharp, still fighting for control. "Choose what?"

"Don't make me choose between you and my father. You've both made some desperate and bad decisions . . . but I still love you both."

He grimaced and looked away, like her confession gutted him. In the dim light, she saw the wetness rimming his eyes. She sat on the bed beside him and reached out, wiping his lashes with her thumb. "Yes, I love you. I'm hurt, Tyghan. I'm angry. But I haven't stopped loving you."

His hand slid across his chest and grabbed hers, his grip weak. He tugged, and she laid her head on his chest, and felt it tremble beneath her cheek.

"Still want me to leave?" she asked.

"Never."

They lay there a long while, her head resting on his chest, and he somehow gathered the strength to stroke her cheek.

"You have to promise me, if I fall asleep, you'll leave. Immediately."

"I will," she answered, but she had broken so many promises at that point, what was one more?

It was almost midnight—seven hours since she went in. Cully put his ear to the door again. "She's still singing," he whispered.

"Can you hear the words?" Eris asked.

"No, but it seems to be the same short tune over and over again."

"Maybe it's some kind of spell she's casting," Quin said.

Madame Chastain shook her head, still nestled in the crook of Eris's arm. "No spell that she learned from me, and there's no spell in the grimoires that takes seven hours to cast."

"Maybe it's another kind of spell," Eris said. "He has one open door in his mind, and she's making sure it only leads to her."

"But—"

"It could be a different kind of magic, Dahlia. A mortal one, perhaps? It's working. That's all that matters."

The attack came out of nowhere. Bristol thought Tyghan was peacefully sleeping, but after a few restless mumbles, he leapt on top of her, pinning her down, the chain on his wrist rattling, his mouth twisted into something brutal and cold. The hatred in his eyes iced her veins. He uttered nonsense in a low, frightening rasp while his fingers tightened around her throat. "You won't win! Go back to your hellhole. You'll never—"

"Tyghan! Tyg—" She desperately pulled at his hands, pleading with him, trying to bring him back before he choked the life from her. "It's me, Bri—let go—" She pried at his fingers, searching for air, and managed a few more desperate words. "I love you, Tyghan. Remember. *Please*—"

His crazed expression was replaced with one of terror, and then recognition, finally seeing her and not the demon in his mind. He let go, his fingers spreading wide like they were on fire, and collapsed back on the bed.

He gasped for air.

"It's all right," she murmured. "You're with me. Shh."

"No," he moaned. "You have to leave."

"And you need rest. Just listen to my voice. Only my voice. Don't stop listening. I'm here with you. Only me. No one else." She began singing a short snip of a John Keats poem over his weak protests, the one her father used to sing to her mother when she woke from nightmares, repeating the same stanzas, over and over again.

Oh come, dearest love, the rose is full blown
And the riches of Flora are lavishly strown;
We will hasten, my fair, to the opening glades,
The quaintly carv'd seats, and the freshening shades;
And when thou art weary, I'll find thee a bed,
Of mosses, and flowers to pillow thy head.

She stroked his head and in seconds he was asleep again, but she continued to sing. An hour passed. Three. Five. She took quick sips of water from his bedside table, but she didn't stop. As long as he slept, she wouldn't stop. A dull throb behind her sternum helped keep her awake, a deeper understanding of what he had suffered because of her father, and what he had risked again to save her.

Her throat grew weak, her tongue dry. She wasn't sure how much time had passed. It was surely near midnight. How much longer could she keep singing? But his face was serene, and she couldn't bear to see the agony twisting across it again. She would be the one invading the halls of his mind now, and no other. She took a sip of the sweet, honeyed wine on his bedstand and sang another verse.

Tyghan opened his eyes. The candle in the corner had long burned out, but silver splinters of moonlight crept through gaps in the drapes. His head no longer pounded and—

He sucked in a startled breath. Bristol was curled up against him, her breaths light against his shoulder. Sleeping. He blinked, trying to get his bearings. The singing. Yes, he remembered now. It wasn't a dream. Had he really gone from being trapped in a demon nightmare to having her back in his arms? His throat swelled, and he studied her in the darkness. Moonlight dusted her lashes, her lips. Her expression was peaceful, the opposite of who she was two days ago. Or was it three? Her singing during the night had been a distant beacon for him to follow, a straight path that led only to her. How long had she sung before she finally succumbed to exhaustion herself? It was a stupid thing for her to do, a risk—

Her fingers stirred against his skin and he looked down. Her hand rested low on his belly, a finger tangled in the loose tie of his trousers. He pulled her snugly against him, his hand sliding beneath her shirt, his fingers gliding up her back, just holding her—but he wanted to do more.

"None of that," she whispered, and her lashes fluttered open. "You need to save your strength. Just lie there."

"I'm strong enough," Tyghan answered. "Want to see?"

She sat up. "You heard me, Mr. High and Mighty," she said, and pushed on his shoulder. "Lie back." She hovered over him, her eyes a dark sea meeting his own. A hundred messages passed in them, and he was certain he could spend the rest of his life wordlessly drowning in her gaze. There were so many things he wanted to say, things he wanted to take back, but he didn't want to move or do anything that might make her look away, that might make the magic vanish. And then gently, like he might break, her head dipped lower and her lips grazed his, feather-light.

"Bri," he whispered against them. "I have to—"

She pressed a finger to his lips. "No words either." She pulled the string on his trousers loose. "There have been enough words between us in the last day. I can't bear any more. I don't think you can either. Besides, you need to save your strength for other things." And then piece by piece she began shedding her clothing until her naked body glimmered in the moonlight.

His breath shuddered in his chest. "I—"

"Shhh," she reminded him. He didn't move as she guided his trousers lower, past his hips, past his knees. Then she slid her thigh across until she was sitting on him, looking down.

Tyghan swallowed. If she wanted to be in complete control, he was fine with that, but his energy was already surging in ways he couldn't control, and saving his strength was the last concern on his mind. She lifted, then slowly slid down on him, and rocked gently, teasing, her eyes still locked onto his, until he was deep inside her. "Now," she whispered, "if you must utter a sound, I only want to hear your gasps and groans." She looked at his left wrist, still chained to the wall, and smiled. "And since I have you chained, I suppose you may beg me for mercy. I've begged you often enough."

But Tyghan didn't want mercy. He wanted every part of him inside every part of her, her skin against his, her scent, her warmth. He wanted her breaths on his shoulder when she slept, and her fingers strumming his abdomen when she woke. He wanted her beside him, waking, sleeping, walking, laughing, touching with a crushing need he couldn't explain. She pushed down hard, and he came up to meet her, his hands gripped on her hips, thrusting deeper inside her, and then his fingers slid upward along her ribs, her breasts, her nipples erect and firm beneath his touch. Her moans sent lightning through him and he reached up, his fingers tangling through her hair, pulling her down until her mouth was on his, her lips tasting of honey and wine, sorrow and second chances, their breaths ragged across each other's lips.

He knew more words would come between them. Later. Hard words, painful words, but for now he only wanted what she wanted, to mend what was left between them, and to see if it could be saved.

Cully startled awake and jumped to his feet when he heard the screaming.

"No," Madame Chastain said. "Stay put. That is not a scream of pain. The king does not need rescuing."

ACKNOWLEDGMENTS

I can't believe it's been eight years since I wrote the first few wisps of this story, dabbling with a shadowy tale that had been calling my name for some time. But alas, I had other books to finish first. In 2019, I was finally able to jump back in with both feet, but talk about plot twist, and portals! I ventured into a whole new world and writing style . . . and fell in love.

But that journey into the unknown was not without its bumps and turns, and many stepped up along the way to help and encourage me.

First, thank you to my husband, who knew I was embarking on a different writing journey and encouraged me all the way to write *whatever* I wanted to write, and to take as long as I needed, even if it was years. His encouragement and belief in me gave me the freedom and courage to take chances—much like Bristol did.

All manner of advice, thoughtful insights, quick feedback, and encouragement also came from Jessica Butler, Karen Beiswenger, Melissa Wyatt, Marlene Perez, Adalyn Grace, Tricia Levenseller, Brigid Kemmerer, Jay Kristoff, and Alyson Noël, and I am so thankful to these very smart and generous friends.

Deepest thanks to Stephanie Garber for all the impromptu phone chats, and willingness to read the full, very rough draft and offer invaluable feedback. You went above and beyond and were a lifesaver.

And thank you too, for the last-minute inspiration from our scary walk through a dark Scottish forest. I want you to know "*the rustlings*" made it into the book and will always make me smile when I read it.

Jodi Meadows, you are a multitalented human being—from amazing writer to amazing weaver—and I knew just who to go to when I had questions about yarn. Thank you for sharing your expertise—and also for the infinite ferret antics over the years. They inspired me when I needed a sly and magical pet. Katniss and Angus would have been fast friends.

Alicia Calhoun, you are smart, inspiring, fun, and ever so kind and I treasure your friendship. Thank you for sharing coffee and your thoughtful insights with me. You are the best.

I'm indebted to Dr. Allyson B. Williams, SDSU art history professor, for graciously answering my many questions about art, sketches, Leonardo da Vinci, and the pursuit of art degrees. You spurred on my imagination—and Bristol's.

Enormous thanks to my two whip-smart agents, Rosemary Stimola and Allison Remcheck, who are actually shape-shifters in disguise, going from fierce lionesses to gentle counselors to brilliant caped advisors in quick magical turns. They believed in this new book and then found the perfect home for it. I am grateful to them and the whole Stimola Literary Studio team for all the incredible work they do to help books like mine become realities.

Huge thanks also to Stimola team wonder Allison Hellegers and to my foreign agents for finding yet more perfect homes with more publishers. It fills me with wonder to know my book will be read in other languages all over the world and travel to places I can only dream of.

I'm in awe of all the readers who have made this possible. You have spread the word in infinite ways and your excitement is contagious. You are not only book people but also book angels. Thank you.

I will be forever grateful to my editor Sarah Barley, who, from day one, told me she couldn't stop thinking about this book. Her joy and excitement never lagged, and she helped me bring it to the next level with questions and insights that sharpened every aspect of the story, and then, as if I wasn't already lucky enough with one amazing editor, I got another one! Caroline Bleeke took up the torch with such enthusiasm and offered still more fantastic ideas and insights to launch this book into the world. Her energy astounds me as she brings this story to the finish line. There are magical queens in Bristol's world, and I clearly have two in mine as well. Thank you, Sarah and Caroline. I owe you both a crown.

I am incredibly grateful to Flatiron Books and the dedicated team there, as valiant as any army of knights, who have embraced *The Courting of Bristol Keats* with such vigor and creativity. A mountain of thanks to Bob Miller, Megan Lynch, Malati Chavali, Sydney Jeon, Louis Grilli, Nancy Trypuc, Maris Tasaka, Brittany Leddy, Emily Walters, Molly Bloom, Ana Deboo, Emma Paige West, Steve Wagner, Drew Kilman, Eva Diaz, Bria Strothers, Claire McLaughlin, and the countless others working behind the scenes. I hope I can meet and thank each of you in person one day.

The physical book is drop-dead gorgeous, and I have the deepest awe for the art and design team who made this magic happen. Tremendous thanks to Keith Hayes, Jim Tierney, Donna S. Noetzel, and Kelly Gatesman. When I learned that Virginia Allyn would be creating the map, I gave out a loud whoop and holler! Her work is stunning and fun and I'm so grateful she brought this world to life so we can all navigate the secrets of Elphame.

Finally, I want to thank my family, Jessica, Dan, Karen, Ben, and the little mischievous sprites, Ava, Emily, Leah, and Riley, who make me smile, laugh, and feel like the luckiest mother and ama in the world. They make me believe in miracles, and wonder, and all the good things of this world.

And last, because all roads circle back to him, thank you to my husband, Dennis, a man of heart and integrity, who makes me feel fearless and has made every day of our lives an adventure.

ABOUT THE AUTHOR

Mary E. Pearson is the international and *New York Times* bestselling author of the Dance of Thieves duology, the Remnant Chronicles trilogy, the Jenna Fox Chronicles, and more books for young readers. *The Courting of Bristol Keats* is her first novel for adults. She writes from her home in California.